"Pamela Sargent deals with big themes—genetic engineering, immortality, the ultimate fate of humanity—but she deals with them in the context of individual human lives. *The Golden Space* reminds me of Olaf Stapledon in the breadth of its vision, and of Kate Wilhelm in its ability to make characters, even humans in the strangest of forms, seem like real people."

—James Gunn, author of *The Listeners*

"Brilliantly handled . . . all of us have got to hand an accolade to the author."

—A.E. van Vogt

"a writer of almost frightening insight and potential . . . Sargent has become a strikingly able and unusual storyteller."

—Michael Bishop, author of *No Enemy But Time*

"Sargent writes well, the many ideas are fresh, and their handling is intelligent in the extreme."

—Baird Searles, *Isaac Asimov's Science Fiction Magazine*

PAMELA SARGENT

THE GOLDEN SPACE

A TIMESCAPE BOOK
PUBLISHED BY POCKET BOOKS NEW YORK

Another *Original* publication of TIMESCAPE BOOKS

The section entitled "The Renewal" was originally published in slightly different form in the anthology *Immortal* (Harper & Row). Copyright © 1978 by Jack Dann.

The section entitled "The Summer's Dust" was originally published in slightly different form in *The Magazine of Fantasy & Science Fiction*, July 1981. Copyright © 1981 by Mercury Press, Inc.

The lines from "The Treasure" are reprinted by permission of Dodd, Mead and Company, Inc. from *The Collected Poems of Rupert Brooke*. Copyright 1915 by Dodd, Mead and Company. Copyright renewed 1943 by Edward Marsh. Permission also granted by the Canadian publishers, McClelland and Stewart, Limited, Toronto.

A Timescape Book published by
POCKET BOOKS, a Simon & Schuster division of
GULF & WESTERN CORPORATION
1230 Avenue of the Americas, New York, N.Y. 10020

To the memory of John McHale

Still may Time hold some golden space
    Where I'll unpack that scented store
Of song and flower and sky and face,
    And count, and touch, and turn them o'er . . .

—RUPERT BROOKE

Contents

The Renewal

JOSEPHA LOOKED AT THE MAPLE TREE. IT DOMINATED THE clearing in front of her small home, marking the boundary between the trimmed lawn and the overgrown field. The tree was probably as old as she was; it had been there when she had cleared the land and moved into the house.

The other trees, the hundreds along the creek in back of the house and the thousands on the slopes of the nearby hills, had to struggle. She and the gardeners had cleared away the deadwood and cut down dying trees many times. Gradually, she had become aware of changes. The pine trees across the creek flourished; the young oaks that had once grown near the circle of flat stones were gone.

A young apple tree grew thirty paces from the maple. She had planted it a year ago—or was it two years? Two gardeners, directed by her computer, had planted the tree, holding it carefully in their pincerlike metal limbs. She did not know if it would survive. A low wire fence circled the tree to protect it from the small animals that would gnaw at its bark. The fence had been knocked over a few times.

Josepha looked past the clearing to the dirt road which wound through the wooded hills. A white hovercraft hugged

the road, moving silently toward the field. The vehicle was a
large insect with a clear bubble over its top. Small clouds of
dust billowed around it as it moved. The craft stopped near the
tangled bushes along the road, the bubble disappeared, and a
man leaped gracefully out onto the road.

Merripen Allen had arrived a day late.

Josepha waved as he jogged toward her. He looked up and
raised an arm. She wondered again why she had asked him to
come. They had said everything and she had made her decision.

But she wanted to see him anyway. There was a difference
between seeing someone in the flesh and using the holo; even if
an image appeared as substantial as a body, that impression
was dispelled when one reached out to it and clutched air.

He looked, as she expected, exactly like his image. His wavy
black hair curled around his collar, framing his olive-skinned
face. A thick mustache drooped around his mouth. But he
seemed smaller than the amplified image, less imposing.

She was still holding her cigarette as he came up to her. She
had been living alone too long and had forgotten how some
felt about such habits. She concealed it in her palm, hoping
Merripen had not seen it, then dropped it, grinding it into the
ground with her foot. She entered the house, motioning for
him to follow.

Josepha disliked thinking about her life before the Transition. But her mind had become a network of involuntary
associations, a mire of memories. She had been living in her
isolated house for almost thirty years and would not have
realized it without checking the dates.

It was time to pack up and leave, go somewhere else, do
something she had not tried. Her mind resonated here. The
sight of an object would evoke a memory; an odor would be
followed by the image of a past experience; an event, even
viewed at a distance, would touch off a recollection until it
seemed she could barely get through the day without suc-
cumbing to reveries.

Josepha was more than three hundred years old but she
could still feel startled by the fact. She looked twenty-two—except that when she had actually been twenty-two she had been
overweight, myopic, and had dyed her hair auburn. She had
become a slim woman with black hair and good vision. She

was no longer plagued by asthma and migraine headaches and could not remember how they felt.

But she remembered other things. The events of her youth sprang into her mind, often in greater detail than more recent happenings. She had thought of clearing out the memories; RNA doses, some rest, and the reverberations would be gone, the world would be fresh and new. But that was too much like dying. Her memories made her life, uneventful and pacific as it was, more meaningful.

But now Merripen was here and the peace would soon end.

Merripen Allen slouched in the dark blue chair near the window. His dark brown eyes surveyed the room restlessly. He seemed weary, yet alert and decisive. All the biologists were like that, Josepha thought. They were the ones who had made the world, who kept it alive, who had banished death. They held the power no one else wanted.

Merripen was the descendant of English gypsies. His clipped speech was punctuated by his expressive arm gestures. Josepha suspected that he deliberately cultivated the contrast.

They had spent several minutes engaging in courtesies; exchanging compliments, describing the weather to each other, asking after people they both knew, making an elaborate ceremony of dialing for refreshments. Now they sat across the room from each other silently sipping their white wine.

Josepha wanted to speak but knew that would be rude; Merripen was still savoring the Chablis. He might want another glass and after that there would be more ceremonial banter, perhaps a flirtation. He would pay her compliments, embellishing them with quotations from Catullus, his trademark, and she would fence with him. She had gone through all this in abbreviated form with his image. A seduction, at least in theory, could last forever. Sex, however inventive, and however long it went on in all its permutations, grew duller. It was too much a reminder that other things still lived and died.

Merripen finished the wine, then gazed out her window at the clearing, twirling the glass in his fingers. At last he turned back to her.

"Delicious," he said. "Perhaps I'll have another." He rose to his feet. She motioned to him to sit, got up, and walked slowly to the oak cabinet in the corner where the opened bottle stood. She brought it to him and poured the wine carefully, placed the bottle on the table under the window, then sat down again.

Merripen sipped. His visage blurred as she focused on the red rose in the slender silver vase on the low table in front of her. As she leaned back, the rose obscured Merripen's body. The redness dominated her vision; she saw a red bedspread over a double bed in the center of a yellow room. She was back in her old room, in the house of her parents, long ago.

She was fourteen and it was time to die. She locked her door.

She gazed at the small bottle, fumbling with the cap, suspended in time past, vividly conscious of the red capsules, the red bedspread, the cheerful flowered curtains over her window. The pain these sights usually brought receded for a moment. A voice called to her, the same soft voice that had called to her before, the disembodied voice she had never located.

She had been dying all along. The black void inside her had grown while the pain at its edges quivered. It would end now. As she swallowed the capsules, she was being captured by eternity, where she would live at last. . . .

She had emerged from a coma bewildered, uncomprehending, connected to tubes and catheters, realizing dimly that she still breathed. She tried to cry out and heard only a sighing whistle. She reached with her left hand for her throat, touched the hollow at the base of her neck, and felt an open hole. They had cut her open and forced her to live as they lived.

At night, as she lay in the hospital bed trying not to disturb the needle in her right wrist, she remembered a kind voice and its promise. Someone had spoken to her while she lay dying, while she hovered over her drugged body watching a tube being forced into her failing lungs. The voice had not frightened her as had the voice she had been hearing for months. It had been gentle, promising her that she would live on, that she would one day join it, and then had forced her to return. She was again trapped in her body.

Perhaps her illness or the barbiturates had induced the vision. Yet it had seemed too real for that. She knew dimly that she could not discuss it, could not make anyone understand it, could not even be sure it was real. She felt she had lost something without even being sure of what it was. But the promise remained: *not now, but another time.*

Josepha touched the rose and a petal fell. Her death was still denied her. She had lived, coming to believe she should not seek death actively, that three hundred, or a thousand, or a million years did not matter if the promise had been real.

Merripen spoke. She looked away from the rose.

The evening light bathed the room in a rosy glow. Merripen's skin was coppery and his tight white shirt was pinkish. "You are still with us," he said.

"Yes."

"You still want to be a parent to these children."

"Certainly." Josepha had decided to become a parent two years earlier and had registered her wish. Her request had been granted—few people were raising children now. Her genes would be analyzed and an ectogenetic chamber would be licensed for the fetus. She had been surprised when Merripen Allen contacted her, saying that before she went ahead with her plans he had a proposal to make.

He and a few other biologists wanted to create a new variant of humanity. They had been consulting for years, using computer minds to help them decide what sort of redesigned person might be viable. Painstakingly, they had constructed a model of such a being and its capacities, not wanting to alter the human form too radically for fear of the unknown consequences, yet seeking more than minor changes.

Merripen sighed, looking relieved. "I expected you wouldn't back out now. Almost no one has, but two people changed their minds last week. When you asked me here I thought you had also."

She smiled and shook her head. It was Merripen's motives she wished to consider. She had worried that she might change her mind after seeing the child, but that was unlikely. There were no guarantees even with a normal child, since the biologists, afraid of too much tampering with human versatility, simply ensured that flawed genes were not passed on rather than actively creating a certain type of child.

Even so, she had wondered when Merripen first made his offer. They had argued, he saying that human society was becoming stagnant while she countered by mentioning the diversity of human communities both on Earth and in space.

"We need new blood," he said now, apparently thinking along similar lines. "Oh, we have diversity, but it's all on the surface. I've seen a hundred different cultures and at bottom they're the same, a way of passing time. Even the death cults . . ."

She recoiled from the obscenity. "In Japan," he went on, "it's *seppuku* over any insult or failure, in India it's slow starvation and extreme asceticism, in England it's trial by combat, and here you play with guns. For every person we bring back from death, another dies, and the people we bring back try again or become murderers so that we're forced to allow them to die for the benefit of others." He glanced apologetically at her, apparently aware he was repeating old arguments.

Josepha did not want to think about death cults and the sudden flare-ups of violence that had reminded her of the Transition and had made her retreat to this house. She looked down at the small blue stone set into a gold bracelet on her wrist, the Bond which linked everyone through a central system. The microcomputer link lit up and rang softly when someone called her; she could respond over her holo or touch her finger to the stone, indicating that she was unavailable and that a message should be left. More important, the Bond protected her and could summon aid. But even the blue stone could not guard her from everything; many knew how to circumvent the mechanism.

"But matters must be different in space," she replied, thinking of the huge, cylindrical dwellings that hovered in space at the Trojan points equidistant from Earth and moon.

Merripen shrugged. "Not as much as you might think. The space dwellers were more innovative when they first left Earth, but now . . . you know, they pride themselves on being safe from the vicissitudes of life here, the storms, the quakes, the natural disasters. They make endless plans for space exploration and carry out none of them. Their cult is a cult of life with no risks."

"But there are the people on Mars, the ones out near Saturn, or the scientists who left our solar system a century ago. Surely they're not stagnating."

"They are so few, Josepha. And as for the ones who left, we have heard nothing. They may be dead or they may have found something, but in any event, it'll have no effect on us."

"I think you're too pessimistic," she argued, wanting to believe her own words. "How long have we had our extended lives? A little more than two hundred years. That's hardly long enough for a fair test. People change, they need time."

"I'm afraid the only thing time does for some people is to confirm them in their habits. Oh, some change, those who have cultivated flexibility. But they are so few. The others are a heavy weight holding us back. In the past, it took great deprivation and a strong leader to make such people change. There is no deprivation now and no leader. Perhaps these new children will open our eyes."

She found this turn in the conversation distasteful, but she had to expect such views from Merripen. He was too young to remember the surge of creativity, the high hopes that had existed for a short time after the difficulties of the Transition, but he knew of them and must sometimes have longed for them. She tried not to think of her own placid life and how hard it had been to force herself to consider being a parent. Stability, serenity, the eternal present—she would forsake them for something less sure. She thought of the ones who had left the solar system and wondered how they had brought themselves to do it.

"The children," she murmured. "I'd rather discuss them for a bit, settle some of my questions, I still don't understand completely." She was trying to draw Merripen away from his disturbing speculations.

"You've heard it all before."

"I didn't really listen, though. I didn't want to confront the details, I guess."

Merripen frowned. "If you're still ambivalent, you'd better back out now."

"But I'm not ambivalent. I agree with your general goal at least. And maybe part of it is that I'm afraid if I don't try something different now, I may never be able to . . . that's not the best motive, but . . ." She was silent.

"I understand."

"You said the children won't have our hormones. Won't that limit them?"

"That's not accurate," he replied. "Certain hormonal or glandular secretions are needed to insure their growth. But they won't be subject to something like the sudden rush of adrenaline we feel when disturbed or under stress."

"That could be dangerous. They might not react quickly enough."

"We've allowed for that. Refinements in the nervous system, quicker reflexes, will allow them to respond as quickly as we do, perhaps even a bit more quickly. The difference is that they won't act inappropriately. Our behavior is often the result of feelings, which are in turn rooted in our instincts and our survival biology. Their behavior will be based on rational decisions as much as on that."

"Our instincts have served us well enough in the past."

"They may not serve us well any longer. We don't have inevitable physical death any more, yet our instincts probably go on preparing us for it. The rationality of these children will take the place of instinct and complement the instincts that remain."

Merripen paused as Josepha considered what he had told her before. The children would look human, but would have stronger muscles, and bones less vulnerable to injury. They would have the ability to synthesize certain amino acids and vitamins, such as C and B_{12}; they would be able to live on a limited vegetable diet.

But the most extreme change, she knew, involved their gender. Merripen had explained that thoroughly, although she was aware that she had only a general understanding of it. They would have no gender—or maybe it was more appropriate to say they would have two genders. They would bear both male and female reproductive organs. They could reproduce naturally, each one able to be either father or mother, or by using the same techniques human beings now used. But they would lack sexuality. Their desires and ability to reproduce would become actualized only when they decided to have offspring; they would have conscious control of the process. Merripen had outlined this, too, in detail, but she recalled it only vaguely.

Josepha imagined that this radical alteration had probably alienated prospective parents who might otherwise have participated in the project. They must have thought it too much; sex had been separated from reproduction for ages and androgynous behavior was commonplace for men and women. Physically androgynous beings seemed unnecessary; the lack of sexuality, such a major part of human life, repellent.

Josepha was not bothered by it because sex, she thought sadly, thinking of the few men she had loved, had never been very important to her. But Merripen was reputed to be a compulsive sexual adventurer. She wondered if that was why he asserted that the children would be more rational without such an intense drive. He might be fooling himself; the children might develop sexual desires of their own once they started to reproduce.

"We don't really know what they'll be like in the end," she said.

"We've done the projections," he answered. "We have a pretty good idea. But it *is* an experiment. Nothing is guaranteed." He picked up the empty wine bottle and turned it in his hands. "This entire society is an experiment. The results are not yet in. All of us crossed that line a long time ago."

The room had grown dark. Josepha reached over and touched the globular lamp on the table near her. It glowed, bathing the room in a soft blue light. "It's late," she said. "You're probably hungry."

He nodded.

"Let's have some supper."

Later, alone in her room, Josepha mused. She could not hear Merripen, who was in the bedroom at the end of the hall, but she sensed his presence. She had been alone in the house for so long that the presence of anyone impinged on her; her mind could no longer expand to fill up the house's empty space. She drew up her coverlet.

Merripen had once discussed what he called the "natural selection" of immortality, his belief that certain mechanisms still operated, that those unsuited to extended life would fall by the wayside. He believed this even as he tried to prevent death. The Transition had weeded out many. The passing centuries would dispose of many more.

Ironically, she had survived. Nothing in her previous life had prepared her for this, yet here she was. She had been a student, a file clerk, a wife, a divorcée, a saleswoman, a sales manager, a wife again, a widow. She had been a passive graduate student who thought knowledge would give her a direction; she had succeeded only in gaining some small expertise on the pottery of Periclean Athens and in avoiding the real world. She has always worked because her first husband had been a student and her second an attorney paying child support and alimony to his first wife. Her purse had been snatched once, her home had been burglarized once, she had undergone two abortions. In this ordinary fashion, while the world lurched toward the greatest historical discontinuity it had ever experienced, Josepha had survived to witness the

Transition. Only now did she feel, after so long, that she was even approaching an understanding of the world and her place in it.

She had been in her fifties when the techniques for extended life became available. The treatment had seemed simple enough; it consisted of shots which would remove the collagen formed by the cross-linkage of proteins and thus halt or retard the physical manifestations of aging. Even this technique, which could make one no younger but only keep one from aging as rapidly, had created controversy, raising the specter of millions of old citizens lingering past their time. Many chose to die anyway. Others had themselves frozen cryonically after death, hoping they would be revived when medical science could heal them and make them live forever. Cryonics became big business. Some concerns were legitimate. Many were fraudulent, consigning their customers to an expensive, cold, permanent death.

Josepha, retired but in need of extra money, became a maintenance worker for a cryonic interment service. She walked among the stacks of frozen dead, peering at dials. By chance, she found that several of her fellow workers dealt illegally in anticollagen shots, selling them to people under sixty-five, the mandatory age for recipients. Knowing that penalties for selling the shots were severe, she was too frightened to become a pusher. But she bought a few shots.

Soon after, work on the mechanisms which caused cancers to multiply, along with genetic research, had yielded a way of restoring youth. Research papers had been presented tentatively; most people had waited cautiously, until at last impatience outran caution and the world entered the Transition in bits and pieces, one country after another.

There were failures, although few wanted to remember them now; people who were victims of virulent cancers, those who could not be made younger, a few who grew younger and then died suddenly. Some theorized that the mechanisms of death could not be held in check forever; that in the future, death might come rapidly and wipe out millions. Testing the new technique thoroughly would have taken hundreds of years, and people would not go on living and dying while potential immortals were being sustained in their midst.

Everyone knew about the Transition—the upheavals, the collapsing governments, the deaths, the demands. There were some facts not fully known, that were still strangely absent from computer banks and information centers; exact figures on suicides, records of how many were killed by the treatments themselves, who the first subjects had been and what had happened to them. Josepha had searched and found only unpleasant hints; one small town with a thirty percent mortality rate after treatment, prisoner-subjects who had mysteriously disappeared, an increase in "accidental" deaths. She had lived through it, surviving a bullet wound as a bystander at a demonstration of older citizens, hiding out in a small out-of-the-way village, and yet any present-day historian knew more than she could remember. She suspected that the only people who knew almost everything were a few old biologists and any political leaders who were still alive.

In her nineties, half-blinded by cataracts, hands distorted into claws by arthritis, Josepha had at last been treated and begun her extended life. She had survived Peter Beaulieu, her first husband, and Gene Kolodny, her second. She had outlived her brother and her parents and her few close friends. And until now, she often thought, she had done little to justify that survival.

She could not accept that so many had died for the world as it was now. The vigor and liveliness had gone out of human life, or so it seemed. Perhaps those who would have provided it were gone and the meek had inherited the earth after all.

But she could change. She was changing. Either the death cultists were right and their lives were meaningless or their extended lives were an opportunity which must be seized. She recalled her own near-death and the promise of another life; even that possibility did not change things. She had to earn that life, if there was such a thing, with a meaningful life here, and if there was no other life, then this one was all she had.

More than three hundred years to discover that—it was absurd. There were no more excuses for failure, which explained the suicides and death cults at least in part. Merripen's project would force the issue. She remembered how his enthusiasm for his dream had been conveyed to her during their first discussion, in spite of her doubts. She thought: Maybe most of us are slow learners, that's all; well, we'll learn or be supplanted.

She refused to think of another possibility: that the world might not accept the children, that any future beyond the present was unthinkable.

* * *

A month after her visit with Merripen, Josepha arrived at the village where the parents and children were to live. Three houses, resembling chalets, stood on one side of a clearing. Four others, with enclosed front porches, sat almost two hundred meters away on the other side of the clearing. Behind them, on a hill, she saw a red brick building that was large enough for several people.

A bulldozer, a heavy, lumbering, metallic beast, excavated land doggedly while two men watched. She assumed that the two were involved in the project, although they might have been only curious bystanders.

Josepha walked through the clearing, which would be transformed into a park. A tall black man stood on the porch of one house, his back to her. She saw no one else. She came to a stone path and followed it, passing the unoccupied houses. Each was surrounded by a plot of ground which would become a garden. The park would eventually contain two large buildings: a hall where everyone could gather for meals, recreation, or meetings, and a hostel for the children. One part of the recreation hall would be used as a school.

The path ended at a low stone wall. Josepha stood in front of an open metal gate and looked past a small courtyard at a two-story stone house. She approached the gray structure and peered through a window. She saw sturdy walls instead of movable panels, a stairway instead of a ramp, and decided this was where she would live. The house was too large for only one parent and child, but she could find someone to share it with her.

She heard footsteps and turned. The tall black man stood at the gate. He adjusted his gold-trimmed blue robe and bowed slightly. She returned the bow and moved toward him, stopping about half a meter away. His black hair was short and his beard closely trimmed. "Chane Maggio," he said in a deep voice as he extended his right hand.

She was puzzled, startled by the lack of ceremony. She suddenly realized that he was telling her his name. He continued to hold out his hand and at last she took it, shook hands, and released it. "I'm Josepha Ryba."

"You are startled by my informality." He folded his slender arms over his chest. "Perhaps I am being rude, but we have little time to become acquainted, only a few months before gestation begins and then only nine months to the birth of the children. I am afraid we cannot stand on ceremony in our salutations."

She smiled. "How long have you been here?"

"I arrived this morning. I believe we are the only prospective parents here." He offered his arm and she took it. They began to amble along the stone path.

She sensed that Chane Maggio remembered the Transition. She was not sure how she knew; perhaps it was the informality of his greeting, the sense of contingency in his voice, or his silence now as they strolled. Younger people always wanted to fill the silences with words or games or actions of some kind. The Transition was only history to them. To Josepha, and those like her, it would forever be the most important time of their lives, however long they lived. It had made them survivors with the guilt of survivors. The simplest sensation meant both more and less to them than to those born later. Josepha, acutely conscious of Chane's arm, the clatter of their sandals on the stones, the warm breeze which brushed her hair, remembered that she was alive and that others were not and that she was somehow coarsened by this. A younger person, caught in the timeless present, would accept the sensations for themselves.

"This venture promises to be most interesting," Chane said softly in his deep voice. "I have raised children before—I had a son and daughter long ago—a rewarding task, watching a child grow, trying to—." He paused.

Josepha waited, not wanting to be rude by interrupting. "There are problems, of course," he continued, and she caught an undercurrent of bitterness and disappointment. "There is always the unexpected." His voice changed again, becoming lighter and more casual. "They live on Asgard now; at least they did fifty years ago. They claim it's too dangerous to live here."

"I once wanted to visit a space community," Josepha said. "For years I kept intending to go, but I never did."

"More people live in space than on Earth, but of course you know that."

"I didn't know."

Chane raised an eyebrow. "I was a statistician until recently. There are approximately two billion people on Earth and almost twice as many in space."

"That many," Josepha murmured, inwardly chastising herself for not knowing. She could have asked her Bond.

"Of course, there has been a small but noticeable decline in the population." The man paused again, having strayed too near an unpleasant topic. "Tell me," he went on, "did you ever make pottery? I believe I own a vase you made—it was a gift from a friend.''

"That was a long time ago. I had a shop with a friend, Hisa Onoda. Hisa made jewelry and I did pottery. That was a little while after the Transition, when we all still had to credit purchases to our accounts.''

"This was later, after accounts.''

"Well, we stayed in business after that just for our amusement. We'd trade our items for things we liked—paintings, sculptures—but the materializer finally ruined it for us. We refused to duplicate anything we made, but others duped the items anyway.''

"Even so,'' he said, "what is important about a thing is its beauty or utility, not its scarcity.''

"I know that,'' she replied. "I don't think Hisa understood it, though. She'd always made jewelry, things like that. It was important to her that each item be unique, she used to tell me that everything she made was only for a certain individual, was right for that person and wrong for anyone else. Sometimes she would refuse to sell a particular object to a customer; she would insist that he look at something else. What's strange is that the customer would always prefer the item she would pick out.'' An image of Hisa's small body crossed her mind: Hisa in her sunken tub, wrists slashed, lips pale, red blood in swirls on the water, her Bond detached and resting helplessly on the floor. Josepha quickly buried the image. "I'd been a salesperson before the Transition, but Hisa made it an art.''

"I was once a politician,'' Chane said. He stopped walking and released her arm. "Does that startle you?''

She thought: What must you have done? She did not reply; she could not judge him.

"I was fortunate. I survived because I saw clearly where things were going and knew when to relinquish my power and wait. I saw that those in power could not hold the tide back indefinitely, and that those who tried to hang on to it would suffer—as they did.''

She listened, only too conscious of her own past sins of omission. She had heard the stories of powerful people who had gained access to the treatments, then given up their positions to go into hiding. Not all had survived. Others had kept their power, many hoping to restrict the gift of extended life to themselves. Both groups bore responsibility for the collapse of civil order at the beginning of the Transition.

"I have changed," he was saying. "I have little interest in such things now." She nodded, almost hearing his unspoken challenge: Would it be better if I had died?

The mood of their meeting had been destroyed. Chane bowed, murmured a few courteous phrases, and departed.

The other parents had been arriving, one at a time, for several months. Construction was finished; the machines had moved to a nearby lake, where three lodges would be built.

Josepha, unused to groups, had grown more reticent. She was quiet at the frequent parties for the thirty prospective parents and at the meetings with the biologists and psychologists who lived nearby. The parties were usually formal; word games were played, objects and sensations were exhaustively described or put into short poems in various languages by the literarily gifted. Direct questions were never asked.

Most of the villagers had remained only names to her. She saw Chane Maggio fairly often, although even he seemed more reserved. Wanting to know more about her companions, she had resorted to the public records in her computer.

She had discovered what she had suspected; most of them were veterans of the Transition. Had Merripen wanted older people, or were older people the only ones willing to volunteer for the project?

Her other discoveries were more intimidating. She reviewed them now as she sat in her living room knitting a sleeve for a sweater. The villagers included Amarisa Drew, who had been both an agronomist and a well-known athlete; Dawud al-Ahmad, former poet and chief engineer of the Asgard life support systems; and Chen Li Hua, a clothing designer and geologist.

She looked up from the blue wool and saw Merripen Allen entering her courtyard. She called to him, telling him to enter. Her door slid open; Merripen stamped his feet in the small foyer, then entered the living room.

He settled in a high-backed gray chair in the corner across from her. "What can I do for you?" she asked.

"I've been visiting each person here individually, I want to be sure there aren't any problems and that everybody's settling in. I hope you'll all start loosening up soon, get to know each other better."

"That takes time," she said, "especially if you're used to solitude. And I have to . . ."

"Yes?"

"I don't quite know how to put it. Everyone else seems so accomplished."

"It's difficult to live a long time without that being the case."

"No, it's not," she replied. "I haven't done much."

Merripen chuckled. "Almost everyone I've seen has told me that. So I'll have to tell you what I told them. First of all, I wouldn't have asked any of you to become involved unless I had a good opinion of you. Second, although I've always admired modesty, I don't like meekness, especially in prospective parents who need strength for any problems they may face. You should all be more at ease when you become better acquainted."

"I guess," she responded, as if accepting his exhortation. He was not deceiving her. Almost no one wanted to be a parent now; of the few who did, most had probably rejected Merripen's offer. He had probably taken those he could get, rejecting only those obviously unsuitable.

Merripen seemed worried. He was pulling at his mustache. Josepha resumed her knitting. "I hope," she said, "that you're not having doubts." She said it lightly.

"Of course I am," he replied, startling her with his harsh tone.

"But then why—"

"Not about you people, not about whether we should go ahead—that's settled." She sat up stiffly, clutching her needles, shocked at the way he had interrupted her in mid-sentence.

"I'm terribly sorry, please forgive me," he said more quietly. "At any rate, I didn't come here to discuss my worries. I wanted to talk about your child. Have you decided on who the second parent will be, or do you intend to form a liaison with one of the people here?" Each child, she knew, was to have two biological parents, as that would provide each with more links to other human beings and avoid possible emotional problems for a parent whose child was his or hers alone. It was hoped that the children, whomever they grew up with, would regard all of the people in the village as members of a family. "We need time to make tests, as you know," he went on. "We have to check for possible incompatibilities or flaws that need correcting."

"I've decided. I made up my mind a while ago and just

didn't realize it until now.'' She put the knitting aside. "Nicholas Krol."

"Excuse me?"

"Nicholas Krol," she repeated. "The other parent. He was a composer, maybe you've heard the name."

"Did you know him?"

"Yes, I knew him. I knew him well. I was in love with him." As she spoke, Josepha saw Nicholas Krol's steady gray eyes and his ash-brown hair, but she could not remember his face clearly. Something inside her seemed to break at the realization. "I met him after my divorce and we lived together for a couple of years. He was ambitious—he wanted me to be ambitious too, accomplish something, but I was afraid to try, too afraid of failing. We broke up, finally. He didn't want to, but I—" For a moment, she recalled his face. She tried desperately to hold it in her mind, and lost it.

"Why?" Merripen asked. "Why Krol?"

"I don't know if I can explain it. He challenged me, he encouraged me. Everyone else just accepted me the way I was. I shouldn't have left him."

"Then why did you leave?"

"Because it was easier to give up."

Merripen seemed puzzled. "It seems a strange motive for picking him, your having regrets."

"It isn't only regrets. He was the most important person in my life, although it took me much too long to see that." She realized she sounded shrill. "I was self-destructive when I was in my twenties, always acting against my own self-interest. That's why I left Nick. Later I changed and acquired a sort of stubborn passivity." She closed her eyes for a moment, waiting for her sorrow and bitterness to pass.

"May I be frank?" the biologist asked. She nodded. "You want the child of a man you loved long ago, so perhaps you're trying to recapture that love. Is Krol still alive?"

She shook her head.

"So guilt enters the picture as well. You're alive and he isn't. Do you even know whether we can acquire his genetic material?"

"He would have had his sperm frozen, I know it. You don't know what he was like. He would have made sure of it. He had a bit of vanity. I used to tease him about it."

"I'm sorry, Josepha. I think you're making a mistake."

"If you have another suggestion, please offer it. I'm

willing to listen. But I don't think I'll change my mind."

"I would like your child to be mine as well."

She stiffened in surprise. She was sure that the man had no romantic interest in her. "Why?"

"I'm in charge of this project, it was really my idea in the beginning. I'll be living here most of the time, and it seems only suitable that I should also be a parent and share this role with you people. If you wish, I can become your lover, if you feel that would strengthen our bond as parents."

The proposal repelled her. She picked up her knitting. Her needles clicked. She heard a few Chinese phrases as two people passed the gate outside. At last she put down the needles and looked at Merripen.

"I must say no." She could not leave it at that. "I think it would be a mistake for you to have your own child here. If you're going to be in charge, you shouldn't be in a position where you might favor one child over the others. And you should try to preserve some objectivity."

"You think it's possible for anyone to be completely objective?"

"Of course not. I do think you can get so personally involved that you don't notice certain things, that emotional considerations become more important. And anyway, I think you want this child out of some misplaced desire to be like all of us here—you can feel noble, not asking us to do something you wouldn't do yourself, and . . ." She paused. "There's only one reason for having a child, Merripen."

"And what is that?"

"Because you want to help another human being learn and grow. You should regard all the children here as yours. Isn't that enough for you? You don't have to prove anything to the parents here, and you might ruin what you're working for by trying."

"You won't reconsider?"

"No. I suppose, if you wanted to, you could prevent me from having a child at all as well as barring me from the project."

"What do you think I am?" Merripen replied in injured tones. "We don't force our desires on others. Our work is for everyone's benefit. You should know that by now."

"You have power whether you want it or not and whether you want to recognize it or not. Everyone knows it. It's just nicer not to mention it."

"Are my wishes more irrational than yours?" He smiled lopsidedly. "You want a dead lover as the father."

"I knew him. Krol's child will have intelligence and strength. And if we really do value life as much as we profess to, then what is so irrational about wanting some part of a dead man to live again?"

He slouched in his chair. For a moment, Josepha thought she saw conflicting emotions in his dark eyes, disappointment warring with relief. He had made his noble gesture without having to follow it up.

"You have to remember," the biologist said softly, "that these children will not be quite like us. You may be disappointed if you're trying to recapture something you've lost."

Josepha sighed. "I suppose you'll ask someone else to be a parent with you."

"No. The others have already made their choices."

She felt relieved by the answer, but remained disturbed. She worried again about Merripen's reasons for beginning the project.

Josepha had gradually become better acquainted with the other village residents. She felt most at ease with the three now sitting at her round mahogany table sipping brandy; Vladislav Pascal, a small, wiry man who had been a painter; Warner Chavez, a tall, slender woman with large black eyes who was once an architect; and Chane Maggio.

Warner and Vladislav were going to raise a child together. Many of the villagers had already paired off or formed groups, but Josepha was still alone.

She had gone that afternoon to the nearby laboratory where the embryos were gestating. She had peered at the glassy womb enclosing her child, Krol's child—it had looked like all the others. Feeling vaguely uneasy, she had left quickly.

Looking around the table at her guests, Josepha saw Warner gaze sleepily at Vladislav. Chane had said little all evening as the three reminisced about their second youth during the Transition, everyone's favorite topic lately; even the hardships of the period had acquired a benign glow in retrospect. The shabbiness of the towns and decay of the cities had not mattered to any of them. With their newly youthful bodies and restored health, anything had seemed possible.

Josepha had migrated to the nearest large city after her treatments, with hordes of others. She had lived in a decrepit hotel, sharing a bathroom with ten people, and had not minded. Surrounded by people constantly meeting to plan new cities, new machines, new arts, new ventures and experiments, she had known that the hardships would be temporary. They were all high on dreams, sure the worst was over, too busy to remember the dead. Now she sat, like the others, amid what they had built and looked backward to the building and dreaming while awaiting a new beginning.

Warner smoothed back her thick red hair and rose. Vladislav got up also. "No, don't show us out," he said to Josepha before she could stand. "Lovely meal, lovely. Don't forget tomorrow, we're expecting you both. Most of the village will probably be there and we'll all try to forget that it's a party for the psychologists." He bowed to Chane and the couple left.

Chane seemed abstracted. He toyed with his snifter. She said nothing, sensing that he wanted silence.

She did not know Chane that well in spite of his frequent visits. The public record of his life had told her little. He had been his African nation's ambassador to China, then its foreign minister during the years before the Transition. His grandfather had been an Italian. His life during the Transition was a mystery. But somehow she was at ease with him. She could sit there pursuing her thoughts while he was lost in his own. Occasionally they looked at each other and smiled; they did not have to fill the silences with words.

Tonight he seemed more apprehensive than usual. She lit a cigarette and pushed the ivory cigarette box across the table to him; Chane, too, was a secret smoker. He shook his head. "I must ask you something, Josepha. I've been putting it off. May I be open with you?" His deep voice was subdued.

"Of course."

He put his hands in front of him, palms down on the dark wood. "I must tell you something first. As you know, I was married in my previous life and had a family. You have undoubtedly guessed that my relations with them left something to be desired."

She nodded, not knowing what to say.

"My wife was an intelligent, educated woman and I thought enough of her to make her one of my advisors. We married late in life, in our thirties. We agreed on everything, almost never fighting. After our children were born, I began to feel that she became more demanding, that instead of helping me, she was distracting me. I began to blame her for everything that went wrong, and took to spending more time away from her. It probably seems a familiar story. Eventually, we separated. I was very bitter about it."

"Chane, why are you telling me this? You don't have to justify yourself to me."

"But I want you to understand this before I make my request. It took a long time for me to see that much of this was my fault. I was telling myself how important my ministry was; my country was in a very difficult period then and I couldn't take the time for personal problems."

"Wasn't it true?"

"Of course it was," he replied. "It's no excuse. Work is a wonderful thing, especially demanding work. It means you have a good excuse for not trying to solve your personal problems, for avoiding them, for taking and not giving because the work is more important than anything."

"Well, sometimes it is, isn't it?" She stubbed out her cigarette, spilling some ashes on the table.

"Oh, sometimes. Very rarely. The world is moved by historical forces, by certain developments, by things we don't control."

"The Transition changed things, and that was the result of scientific research by a few people."

Chane finished his brandy and lit a cigarette. "A transition of some sort was bound to happen anyway, events were moving toward one. It was a more complex situation than you imply. The world was already changing and the biologists only hastened it. Look at them now. What can they really do?"

Josepha shook her head. "You're wrong, Chane. Here we are with this project. You're saying it won't make any difference at all, but you're here just the same. You're contradicting—"

"No, you don't hear what I'm saying." His voice was firm. "There is only one way people can influence the future and that is by the quality of their relationships with others, the ways in which they treat people, caring about them and showing it constructively. Sharing what you might learn with someone, loving someone, raising a child to be both inquisitive and compassionate. There is no one more powerless than a person who has the power to intervene—you either become driven by it and by forces you don't understand, holding it at whatever cost, or you realize that all you can do is be a moral and rational example, a symbol, perhaps, of something better. Or you run away in the end, as I did."

Chane paused. A pale blue wisp of smoke circled his head.

"Merripen believes," he continued, "that the children here will change the world, in other words, that he himself will. It's a deception. Yes, they may make a difference, but not because of a peculiar physiological makeup. It will be our relationships with them as parents, our personal attention, how we act toward them, that will make them what they might be. If we raised a group of children like ourselves and tried to give them a creative and open view, the results might very well be similar. Except that it may be easier for these children."

"Yet you agreed."

He smiled. "Oh, yes. I wanted to be part of it, I don't want to run away as I did before."

Josepha considered Chane's arguments. She was not sure that she agreed; it seemed that the combination of heredity and environment was needed. But she did not feel like arguing about it now. "Who is to be your child's other parent?" she asked.

"My wife, of course. You're surprised. She's still alive and she's agreed. I've been lucky, able to patch things up instead of living with guilt and ghosts." The statement seemed forced. Josepha looked down as he spoke. "She's a stranger now," he went on. "I suppose I am, too."

"What did you want to ask me before, Chane?"

"I . . . it's hard to know how to phrase it. I'd like you to consider sharing your life here with me, raising our children together."

She looked up, startled. He lowered his eyes and put out his cigarette. She knew that she found Chane attractive, although neither of them had nourished the attraction with the usual romantic games and ploys. She liked him. It seemed a rather weak foundation for a relationship.

"Why?" she asked gently.

"I feel at ease with you, that's the main reason. Let's try it, at least. If it doesn't work out I can move again after the children are born." Something in the tone of his voice reminded her of Merripen Allen. Again she worried about the reasons for the project. She thought: It's a mistake, it may hurt the children in the end, it will change all of us here forever.

But that was false. If it failed, it would change nothing and would be forgotten by the parents as everything was when one had enough time. She shook her head.

"You're refusing me, then," Chane said.

"Oh, no, I was thinking of something else. I'd like you to

stay. This house is really too big for one parent and child."
That sounded too cold, too pragmatic. "I think we'll get
along," she added.

She wished that she could feel happier about the decision.

Josepha adjusted easily to Chane's presence. Their life together was marred only by an occasional gentle argument. But
Chane remained impenetrable. Josepha imagined that she
must appear the same way to him. Even their lovemaking did
not bridge the gap.

It was probably just as well, she thought. This way, at least,
she could preserve some sense of privacy. Both could keep an
emotional equilibrium that would conserve the strength they
would need when the children were born.

She knew, however, that they could not remain on that
peaceful plateau forever. Their shared lives would force them
into confrontations sooner or later. But it was hard to break
old habits, difficult to believe that there might not be time
enough to let events happen and allow differences to be re-
solved. Better, she knew, to settle each issue as it came up,
instead of trying to sort everything out now.

When she finally realized that there had been no time, only a
few months, and that she and Chane were still far from understanding very much about each other, all the children were
ready to leave their wombs and enter her world.

II

Teno, her child, Krol's child, was with her at last. She had
been surprised at how ordinary, how normal, the infant appeared. Teno had her dark hair, a face like a small bulldog's,
and olive skin. She could see nothing of Nicholas Krol in the
child; perhaps that resemblance would come with maturity.

Josepha often felt tired. She leaned against the courtyard
gate, inhaling the mild spring air, grateful for a few moments
to herself. The flow of time had fragmented into a million discrete segments which seemed to jostle against one another. The
children had to be fed, washed, taken outside for a few
minutes of air, played with, hugged, dressed, undressed, and
put to bed. The village had shaken off its lassitude; the
children were now the center of everything. It would have been
easier to let the psychologists, with the aid of a few robots,

assume many of the parental duties, but almost no one took
much advantage of that. It was as if they all wanted to be sure
nothing went wrong, that the children would not be damaged
by neglect.

"Hey!" a woman's voice shouted. Warner Chavez was approaching her along the stone path. Josepha put a finger to her
lips as she opened the gate.

"Everyone's asleep," she exclaimed as her friend entered
the courtyard. "Even Chane, he's exhausted. He was up at
dawn with Teno and Ramli." Ramli was Chane's child.

Warner smiled. "So's Vlad. He and Nenum are probably
both stacking deltas by now." Josepha found herself thinking:
Men don't have as much stamina.

Warner sat down on the grass, folding her trousered legs in a
half lotus. There were pale blue shadows under her black eyes.
Josepha sat down with her back against the stone wall, wrapping her arms around her legs. She, too, was tired, not
fatigued enough to sleep, but too weary to concentrate. A part
of her always seemed removed, watchful, listening in case the
children should need her. Chane was like that, too. Neither of
them could sit for more than a few minutes lately without listening for sounds or getting up now and then to check things.

Warner was gazing at the red tulips blooming in a row next
to the house. She looked away quickly, probably wondering
why Josepha planted such short-lived flowers. "Tell me, Jo,
have you talked to Chane much about the children?"

Josepha shrugged. "We haven't had that many conversa-
tions lately. It's hard to keep talking when you're tired all the
time. I can't even watch the holo without feeling sleepy. I guess I
didn't think looking after them would take so much out of me."

"What I meant was, has Chane said anything to you about
the kids? He was a parent once, wasn't he?"

"What do you expect him to say about them?"

"What they're like compared to normal . . . compared to
other kids. Maybe I'm being silly, but there's something un-
nerving about them."

"Is there?" Josepha rested her chin on her knees. "Teno's
really not much of a problem, all things considered. I was
expecting all kinds of little crises."

"Think about the way they cry, for instance. Doesn't it
seem strange to you?"

"Is it strange?" Josepha asked. "I wouldn't know, I suppose. I was never around children that much. My brother

Charlie was older than I was, and I didn't have a younger brother or sister."

"Well," Warner replied, "it's not that awful squalling I remember, the kind of crying that sounds like a cat in heat and you know the poor kid is colicky or damp or maybe hungry. With these kids, it's more of a steady cry. I don't know how to describe it. It's . . . calm, steady and calm. Sometimes I'll hear a real howl, but it's as if they're only exercising their lungs. That's what my Nenum does anyway, and others, too. Aren't Teno and Ramli like that?"

Josepha nodded. "That isn't normal?"

"No." A breeze ruffled Warner's long red hair. "All right, they're not quite like us, with their immunities and their modified neurons and reflexes, they weren't meant to be, but they look so much like ordinary kids that . . . I picked up Nenum yesterday, after a nap, just to hug my child—you know the feeling. You just want to let them know you're there and you care. Nenum just sort of put up with it, that's all. It's always like that. There's just no response at all."

"Maybe you're making too much of it, Warner. You said it yourself, they weren't meant to be like us. Anyway, things don't look right when you're tired most of the time. You make more of them or think something's the matter when it isn't."

"I know that."

"They're still our children."

"Of course. They made sure of that—genetic bonds as well as emotional ones." Warner's fine-featured face contorted. "I don't know what they'll be. I don't know what they are or what they'll become. I don't even know whether Nenum is my son or daughter. Am I supposed to call my child 'it'?" Her slender body drooped.

"Does that really matter? It wouldn't change how you act toward Nenum. And you didn't know what your other children would be like, or what kinds of adults they would become."

"I knew they were human," her friend said harshly. "I can't even look at Nenum without remembering that, I keep seeing . . . maybe I wasn't ready for this, Jo."

Josepha felt at a loss. She tried to look reassuringly at Warner. "Yes, you were," she said as firmly as possible. She got up and sat near her friend, putting an arm over the red-haired woman's shoulders. "Look, Merripen wouldn't have had you come here if he thought otherwise." She tried to sound convincing, recalling her doubts about how Merripen had selected the parents. "It's normal to have doubts. Maybe when you feel this way you should just go and hold Nenum and put those thoughts out of your mind. It doesn't matter. You and Vladislav have to take care of your child, that's all. Think of things that way."

Warner smoothed back her hair with the chubby hands that seemed unmatched to her slim arms. "You're right. Maybe I'm just disoriented. I'm not used to anything different after all this time."

Josepha, hearing a cry, suddenly sat up. The cry was steady, punctuated by short stops, a smooth cry without any variation in pitch. A second cry, slightly lower, joined the first. Teno and Ramli were awake.

Teno and Ramli were toddlers, trying to walk.

Only a short time ago, it seemed, the children had been unable to sit up. Now Josepha and Chane watched as the two struggled across the floor.

She and Chane had preserved their quiet and reserved relationship. Much of their conversation concerned the children. Their lovemaking was partly a formality, partly a friendly and often humorous way of reassuring each other during moments of loneliness. Most of the time it was easier for each of them to wire up and live out a fantasy encounter.

Chane sat at one end of the sofa, Josepha at another. Ramli toddled unsteadily toward Chane and stretched out small brown hands to him. Teno moved to Josepha, grabbing for her arms almost before she held them out.

"Very good!" she said brightly. Teno, solemn-faced, held her hands for a moment, then sat on the floor. Chane picked up Ramli, seating the baby on his lap. He held up a hand, holding out one finger, and Ramli began to pull at the other fingers Chane had concealed. The child studied them intently for a moment, then quietly looked away, as if losing interest.

The children were always like that. If she or Chane wanted to play a game, they would respond in a serious, quiet way. If she wanted to show them some affection, they put up with it, with expressions that almost seemed to say: I can do without this, but obviously you need it.

What did they need? She watched as Chane placed Ramli on the floor. The two children crawled over the rug, peering intently at its gold and blue pattern. Did they require something they were not receiving from the adults around them? An observant person could tell if an ordinary child might be having a serious problem. Even given the wide variations in normal behavior, abnormal responses became obvious in time. But they did not know what normal behavior would be for these children.

She sighed, thinking of old stories; children raised by wolves who could never learn to speak, could never really be human. She watched as Teno and Ramli poked at the bright spot where a beam of sunlight struck the rug.

Teno looked like her, with black hair, olive skin, high cheek-bones—but the eyes were not her brown ones. One could look at dark eyes and read expressions too easily. Knowing this, Josepha had always had difficulty gazing directly at people, wondering if they could read her thoughts. Teno's eyes were Krol's gray ones, impossible to read, always distant. She saw the quiet, mildly curious expression on her child's face and was suddenly frightened.

She realized that Chane was staring at her. Her worries must be showing on her face. She smiled reassuringly. His sad eyes met hers; he did not smile back. Then he turned his head toward the window.

She felt like reaching out to him, holding him, and the force of her desire surprised her. But she restrained herself, and the moment passed.

When the children were two and a half years old, it became customary to take them to the recreation hall and let them play together under the supervision of a few parents and psychologists. Kelii Morgan, who had once been a teacher and was now a parent, was often with them.

The children responded to him in their restrained fashion. They were patient when the affectionate Kelii laughed or hugged them impulsively, but they enjoyed the folk stories and myths he had learned from his Welsh and Hawaiian forebears. They responded most to tales of a quest for some great piece of knowledge. They heard the humorous stories, too, but never laughed.

Josepha came often to see them at play. The children were already used to one another, having visited each other's homes frequently. They liked new places and had never clung to a parent in fear. But their play seemed to her a solemn affair. She had expected rivalries, fussing over toys, laughter, teasing, a few tears.

Instead, she saw red-headed Nenum taking apart a toy space

city, peering at the different levels and at the tiny painted lake and trees at its center while Ramli looked on. When Ramli grabbed one level, Josepha expected Nenum to become possessive. But the two began to reassemble it together, whispering all the while.

She saw Teno play with a set of Russian dolls, removing each wooden doll from a larger one until the smallest doll was discovered. When Dawli, the frail-looking child of Teofilo Schmidt, came to Teno's side, Teno willingly yielded the dolls and crawled off in search of another toy.

It was all strange to her. If one played alone, it was because the child wanted to be alone, not because the others left the child out. Josepha searched for tears or the formation of childish cliques, and saw only inquisitiveness and cooperation. Even the muscular, big-boned Kelii, who seemed to be their favorite adult, got no special affection. If he held a picture book on his spacious lap, a child might climb up and sit there, but only to see the illustrations more clearly.

They never misbehaved, at least not in the normal way. If a child wandered off, pursued shortly by a worried parent or psychologist, the young one was usually found investigating a plant or a toy or how a toilet worked. If they were told not to play with the computers until they were shown how to push the buttons, they listened, asked questions, and tried to understand the machines.

On one occasion, Ramli had punched Teno in the stomach. Teno had retaliated with a blow to the arm. Each cried out in pain as Josepha, worried and at the same time almost relieved by the show of normality, rose to her feet to stop it. But the battle was over. The two had learned that violence caused pain.

Although she tried to ignore it, she often felt frustrated. Chane had become more withdrawn, making frequent calls to old friends late at night behind the closed doors of his study. The children could not reward her love with spontaneous displays of affection. She wondered how long it would be before a parent, bewildered by the lack of any real emotional contact with a child, might lash out at one of them.

Josepha and Chane sat in the park with their children. The spring day was unseasonably warm, the blue sky cloudless. A week ago, a third birthday celebration had been held for all the children. The adults had been sociable and gregarious, the young ones solemn and bemused.

Teno and Ramli knelt on the grass, playing an elaborate game with marbles and pebbles; only they knew its rules. Ten meters away, under an elm, Edwin Joreme lay on a brown blanket with his head on Gurit Stern's lap. Edwin's child, Linsay, poked at the grass with a stick. Gurit had apparently left Aleph, her child, at home.

Edwin was a thin man with ash blond hair who looked almost adolescent. Gurit, auburn-haired, green-eyed, and stocky, was one of the few people in the village who still intimidated Josepha. Gurit had been a soldier before the Transition. Although she seemed a friendly, hearty sort, there was something hard in her, a toughness, a competence that made Josepha ill at ease. Watching Gurit, she thought of what the woman must have seen and imagined that she was one who probably savored her extended life instead of simply accepting it.

Edwin sat up and moved closer to Linsay. He spoke to the child; Linsay listened, then returned to probing the ground. Josepha thought that Gurit might have passed as the mother of both. Lines creased her face at the eyes and mouth, and in the bright afternoon sunlight one clearly saw the threads of gray hair framing her face. Chane had once asked Gurit why she had not wanted a more youthful appearance. She had laughed, saying she got tired of seeing young faces all the time.

Edwin was still trying to distract Linsay, murmuring to the child intently. Josepha turned to Chane. He had brought some notes with him, but he was ignoring them, gazing absently in the children's direction.

"Is something wrong?" she asked.

He shook his head.

"What are the notes for?" They were written in Italian and Swahili, two languages she did not know.

He was silent for a few moments before replying. "Just some reminiscences, personal things, incidents I might otherwise forget."

"Can't you just consult the computer records?"

"Those are public records, Josepha. They tell nothing of subjective attitudes or personal reactions. And several incidents aren't recorded." His lowered eyelids hid his dark eyes from her.

Impulsively, she touched his arm. Then she heard a cry, a thin, piercing wail.

Edwin was shaking Linsay, muttering under his breath at

the child. Linsay wailed. Josepha froze, not understanding what was happening. Chane jumped to his feet, his red caftan swirling around his ankles.

Gurit quickly grabbed Edwin's arms. "Stop it," she said firmly. "What's the matter with you?" He pushed her away violently. Trembling, he stared at his child and then, shockingly, slapped Linsay.

Josepha tensed at the sound. "Why can't you respond?" Edwin was shouting. "I'm sick to death of it, you're as bad as a robot, not the slightest human feeling—"

Gurit again seized Edwin, holding him tightly, and this time he was unable to break away from her strong arms. He crumpled against her. Linsay sat calmly, blond head tilted to one side.

Josepha got up. "I think we should go," she murmured to Chane. Teno and Ramli had stopped playing and were staring at Edwin, fascinated. Josepha thought wearily of all the questions she and Chane would have to answer later.

"We're going home," she said to the children.

III

A small death had entered their lives. Josepha and the children were burying the cat.

They had walked to the woods north of the village and stopped at a weedy clearing. Josepha wore a silvery lifesuit under her gray tunic; she always wore the protective garment when in the forest. She stood under a maple tree, shaded from the summer heat, while Teno and Ramli placed the small furry body in the grave they had dug. The children were dressed only in sleeveless yellow shirts and green shorts. Their stronger bones and muscles did not need lifesuit protection.

The children were seven now. Their rapid growth and the cat's death made Josepha feel she was aging. Her child had been a toddler so recently. Now Teno was a student, learning to read and calculate or going off with Kelii and a few parents to the lake for a day or two to learn about the outdoors.

Teno was more of a companion to her as well. The child would ask questions about the desk computer, a sandwich, the lilac tree outside, about Ramli and Chane, about what parents were, and after Josepha had explained about Krol, questions about death. The child never smiled, never frowned. Josepha would see only expressions of thoughtfulness, concentration, curiosity, puzzlement.

Ramli and Teno began to cover the cat with dirt and leaves. They had kept the animal for three years; Chane felt that having pets was good for children. They had named the orange and white cat Pericles. Josepha loved animals but had never kept a dog or cat before, knowing that eventually the creature would die. It had been easier, when she lived alone, to watch the robins return to the trees, or the geese fly back to her pond after their migration. She could imagine that the same birds were returning.

The children had got along with Pericles in their solemn way. They had learned that tweaking his tail caused him pain and that he would repay any affront to his feline dignity with a baleful stare and the swipe of a paw. They had cleaned out his box, scratched him behind the ears so he would purr, and protected him from the forays of Kaveri Dananda's cocker spaniel, Kali, although Josepha had always felt that Kali, despite the ferocity of her name, was frightened of the cat.

But they had also learned that Pericles would kill. Josepha had not always been able to hide the dead birds from the children. It had been hard for her to explain the cruelties of nature and the instincts of animals that even humankind still retained. The children had listened and absorbed the information, but she did not know if they were reconciled to it.

Now Pericles was dead. He had disappeared for a few days, to be discovered by Chane near the woods outside the village that morning. The small furry body he had carried home had been unmarked. Josepha, seeing it, had wanted to cry. The children did not cry. Heartlessly, it seemed, they had the computer link sensor scan the body to determine the cause of death, which had been, oddly enough, kidney failure. Then Ramli had kindly suggested that they bury the creature in the woods he had loved.

The children had finished. Josepha went to them and they stood by the grave silently for a few minutes, then began to walk slowly back toward the village.

"Do cats always die?" Teno asked.

"All animals do sooner or later."

"From accidents?"

"Sometimes. Other times it's disease, or getting old."

"Some people die from accidents, too," Teno said emphatically.

"They don't have to," she replied quickly. "If the medical robots and rescue teams get to them in time they don't, and usually they reach them in time because of the Bond; that's why we all wear them."

"Some people want to die," Ramli said loftily. Josepha was too startled to reply. "I saw about it. They kill themselves or sometimes they kill somebody else or ask somebody to do it and they fix their Bonds so they don't find them in time."

"I know that," Teno replied. "I saw a dead guy on the holo. He shot himself and there was blood all over; he put a bullet right in his head and they couldn't bring him back."

Josepha felt sick. She wanted to tell them not to use words like kill, but that would only turn it into a potent obscenity for them. She wished Chance were here instead of home getting dinner ready. "Where did you see such a thing?" she said, trying to keep her voice steady. "You couldn't have seen it at home or at school."

"Over at Nenum's," Teno said.

"Don't lie to me," she answered harshly, stopping along the narrow path and turning to confront them. "Warner and Vladislav wouldn't allow it. They lock their holo."

"Nenum knows how to override."

She could read no expression in Teno's gray eyes or Ramli's black ones. She wanted to get angry, be firm, forbid them to look at such things again, but knew it would do no good. It would only make them more curious.

"Why do they want to die?" Ramli asked.

Josepha shook her head. "It's hard to explain. Sometimes they're unhappy or just tired of everything or . . . people like us used to die, you know that. Many of us still don't know how to handle long lives."

"That's dumb," Ramli said tonelessly. "I want to find out everything and it'll take forever. I don't want to die."

She smiled at them. "Of course you don't." She motioned to them and they resumed walking.

"Is Pericles a ghost?" Teno inquired.

"Where did you hear about ghosts?"

"Kelii told us stories about them. They're dead people except they're ghosts, and you can't see them except sometimes."

She recalled the voice that had spoken to her years ago and was silent. "Are there ghosts, Josepha?" her child said.

"What do you think?"

"I don't think there are any."

"Kelii says it's made-up stuff," Ramli said. "He says people made it up because they didn't know anything. I said if I didn't know I'd find out. I wouldn't make it up."

"Did you ever see a ghost, Josepha?" Teno asked.

"How can she see one if there aren't any?" Ramli muttered.

"She can think she did."

"No," she responded, feeling that she was being honest only technically. She could not explain her own experience and conviction until they were older, though she doubted they would understand her even then.

She thought of all the deaths she had seen and suddenly felt very old, too old to be raising children. The responsibility weighed heavily on her. The decisions were too difficult, the mistakes too frequent. She remembered her own father and mother and the problems they had encountered with her and her brother Charles. Her parents had died in an auto accident a few years after she had married Gene Kolodny. But she had been estranged from them long before, deeply resenting them for reasons never fully understood, knowing she had failed them in some undefined manner but afraid to find out how. After their deaths, filled with guilt and regrets about things left unsaid and undone, she had been forced to put them out of her mind.

They reached the edge of the forest and looked out at the village. The paths were filled with strollers; others sat on front porches sipping cool drinks. Josepha looked down at Teno and realized that now she could think about her mother and father without the old feelings. It was as if she had a bond with them through the child, as if she were no longer cut off from them even by death.

"It's fair," Teno said suddenly, interrupting her reverie.

"What's fair?"

"Pericles' dying. He killed things and now he's dead."

More visitors now came to the village. They had been arriving ever since the children's birth.

There had once been talk of raising the young ones with other, "normal" children, but nothing had come of it. The visiting children, however curious they might be at first, soon learned that the children here were uninterested in their games, pranks, emotional displays, and rivalries. The visits ended with each group of children keeping to itself.

A few biologists and psychologists came, but most of the visitors were simply curious. Now that the children were older and the differences between them and the rest of humankind were more obvious, more outsiders arrived. They peered into the recreation hall at Kelii and the children. They went down to the lake where the young ones were being taught to swim. The children bore up well under this inquisitiveness, being even more courteous and well behaved while under observation. Josepha sensed, however, that the visitors might have preferred seeing the children scream or yell or laugh or cry or gang up on someone.

She saw Chane standing with Edwin Joreme and a group of visitors, ten tall Tartars who had congregated in front of Merripen's small cottage. They had just arrived; Chane had accompanied them to the village.

He had been visiting old friends. She had urged him to get away for a few weeks, remembering how refreshed she had felt after a solitary sojourn at her old home. But he looked weary to her. She waved at him and bowed to the Tartars, who bowed back.

Chane seemed surprised to see her. He made his farewells to the visitors and came toward her, greeting her with a light kiss on her forehead. "I didn't expect you to meet me," he said.

"We missed you." She took his arm and they began to walk through the park toward their house. The dark gray sky seemed to hang over them and the brown grass, scattered with red and yellow leaves, was desolate. Chane shivered slightly in his long gray coat. Edwin had taken charge of the visitors, leading them over toward the recreation hall. Josepha recalled the day he had struck Linsay; since then, he had become one of the gentlest and most patient parents here. She could only wonder at what it cost him. His hazel eyes were often doubt-filled and distant.

"Were there many visitors here while I was away?" Chane asked.

"Indeed there were. Didn't I mention it to you when you called? Maybe I didn't."

"I don't think you did."

"Well, don't worry about them, Chane. Everyone pretty much ignores them now."

"I have good reason for worrying. I'm even more concerned after being outside. Before, when I called my friends, I was sure they were exaggerating the suspicion and hostility of others toward this community. Now I know they weren't."

She felt a slight prickle of fear. "What are they upset about? What can possibly happen here?"

"They're afraid of the children, of what they might become."

"But that's so silly. What could they do? If anything, the kids should be afraid of us. That is, if they could feel fear. I don't know if they can."

"Granted, it's foolish," Chane replied. "But you've seen the visitors here. They all act a bit apprehensive. The group I came back here with did. I don't understand Russian or Tartar, but I saw that much. And that's nothing compared to what I've seen elsewhere. Those who come here at least give us the benefit of a doubt." He sighed. "People don't want things to change," he murmured, as if speaking to himself.

She was silent. They approached the house and stopped at the gate. "Are Teno and Ramli home?" Chane asked apprehensively.

"They're over at the hall."

They entered the house, hanging their coats in the hallway. Chane went to the living room and sat on the sofa; he sprawled, head forward, feet out. "I heard one rather interesting proposal," he said as she came into the room and sat next to him. "Some believe that the children should be taken away from here."

"Taken away!" She clasped his hand tightly.

"There was talk of exile, putting them on a colony out by Saturn or some such place."

Josepha was stunned. Recently various groups had started to send murderers and other very disturbed people out to small space colonies under robotic guards. Eventually, it was hoped, they would be aided by new biological or psychological techniques. In reality, they were usually forgotten. Josepha doubted that anything much would ever be done for them. It was small wonder so many murderers attempted suicide rather than risking such an exile.

"But the children aren't criminals," she said. "They've done nothing. Sending them away would only guarantee their bitterness. How are they going to feel about people who would do that to them? They might, in their reasonable way, decide that they have to defend themselves."

"I said that. If they're exiled now, though, so the idea goes, there's not much they can do; they're only children. And once they're gone, there's nothing they can do anyway if they're guarded. I argued with a lot of people, Josepha. I didn't get far." He withdrew his hand and looked away.

She suddenly wanted to hurry to the hall and make sure Teno and Ramli were safe. Instead, she leaned back and closed her eyes. The village had become a fortress, a settlement surrounded by danger, uncertainty, hostility. The visitors were members of reconnaissance missions, spies, enemies.

Teno sat on the floor, placing furniture inside a small dollhouse. Josepha sprawled on Teno's bed, watching the solemn eight-year-old arrange the tiny sofa and chairs Chane had carved. Little figurines lay next to the child—a small mahogany Chane in a red robe, a tiny Josepha with waist-length black hair, and two smaller dolls.

"Two kids from outside were at the hall today," Teno said. "I don't think they liked me." The child's tones were quiet and measured.

"Why do you say that?"

"I could tell when I talked to them."

Josepha peered at Teno. The child's eyes were hidden by long dark lashes. "Did you like them?"

Teno shrugged. "I don't know. Kelii told me I could show them the garden so we went outside, but then the boy said to go around the side of the hall, so I did, and then the girl said for me to take down my pants."

"She said what?"

"Take down my pants. She said they wanted to see me there and I said I would if they would, so they showed me theirs and I showed them mine and they said I was a freak."

She wanted to reach over and hug the child, but Teno seemed calm and undisturbed. "What happened then, dear?" she managed to ask.

"I said I wasn't and I liked having a penis and vagina and they only had half of what I had and I don't think they liked that. Then the boy said a lot of people didn't like us because we were different from them and I said that was stupid because everybody's a little different from everybody else. I think he was going to hit me but he didn't and we went back inside."

Josepha sat up on the bed, folding her legs under her. "Do things like that bother you, Teno?"

"No, it's just dumb." The child picked up the Chane doll and put it inside the house.

"Listen," she said quickly, "maybe all of us can go down to

the lake this weekend and take out the sailboat. Would you like that?''

"You forgot, we have a camping test then." The children were going to be set loose in the forests beneath the nearby mountains for three days, with only a knife, compass, and poncho each. The young ones were well prepared; they were all skilled campers, and robots in the area would be alert to any danger. But Josepha found herself worrying anyway.

"Tell me," she murmured, "why are you so interested in campcraft?"

"We all are."

"I know that." It was one of their peculiarities. Although the children varied in their interests and aptitudes—Teno enjoyed mathematics while Ramli preferred botany—they always remained interested in what all the others were doing. It was as if they thought that if one was interested in something, it might be worthwhile for all of them. "I didn't ask that," Josepha went on. "I asked why *you* are interested."

"It's fun. I like to go and watch the deer, but you have to sneak up on them or they run away. I like to watch the campfire when we sit around. Anyway, we need to know that stuff."

"Why?"

"I might have to live in the woods. Luckily we don't need as much food as you, so we wouldn't have to hunt anything. We could stay a long time."

"Why would you have to live in the woods that way?"

"Maybe they won't let us live anywhere else and we'll have to hide."

"Who won't?"

"The people that don't like us." Teno picked up the Josepha doll and held it.

"Teno," Josepha said quietly, "do you mind it, being different?"

The gray eyes gazed steadily at her. "No. I'm the way I am. I'm me."

Josepha saw the woman before Alf Heldstrom did.

She and Alf were designing a history course for the children. Even with the computer's aid, the project was more difficult than they had expected. They were arguing over how to present the history of the Transition when Josepha noticed that a woman, an outsider, was watching them.

The visitor was standing under a nearby weeping willow.

She was thin, almost emaciated. Her pale platinum hair was clipped short.

"Have you seen that woman before?" Josepha whispered to Alf.

"Never." Alf brushed a wavy lock of long golden hair off his delicate face. "She seems to be alone. Usually visitors come in groups."

"I don't like the way she's looking at us."

The woman walked toward them. Josepha nodded and the blond woman nodded back. She stood in front of them, nervously pulling at the sleeve of her blue jacket.

"Hello," the woman said softly. "Are you parents?"

Josepha was startled by the directness of the question. She glanced at Alf. He raised an eyebrow and stared back blankly with his blue eyes. She turned back to the visitor. "Yes," she replied.

Alf uncrossed his legs and sat up. He and the woman stared silently at each other while Josepha tried to keep from fidgeting. At last the woman looked away. "I'm Nola Reann," she said to the air, speaking so softly that Josepha had to lean forward to catch the name. "Where are the children?" She looked at Josepha.

"Camping."

"Camping. I can't imagine why."

"I'm Josepha Ryba. This is Alf Heldstrom. Won't you sit down?"

"Thank you. I'll stand." Nola Reann put her hands inside the pockets of the blue jacket she wore over her silver lifesuit.

"Most of the people who come here are biologists or psychologists," Alf said. "We do, of course, get a cross-section of other types, too."

"I'm a meteorologist. I'm in space most of the time."

"What did you do before that?"

"I didn't do anything before that. I'm only twenty."

Josepha glanced at Alf, who seemed as surprised as she was. It was easy to forget that there were young people in the world. She tried to recall what it felt like to be twenty.

"Are you here to study the weather?" Alf asked, as Josepha attempted to decide if he was being courteous or sarcastic.

"No." Nola swayed on her feet as she surveyed the village. Her dark eyes betrayed her uneasiness. She seemed oddly impatient. She had not lived long enough, Josepha supposed, to be anything else. "What are you trying to do here?" the young woman said suddenly.

"I beg your pardon?" Alf murmured.

"What are you trying to do here?"

"We're trying," Josepha answered calmly, "to raise our children."

"Why these children? They're not even normal. They're alien and disgusting."

"I *beg* your *pardon*," Alf said harshly. "You have no right to say that. Do you know them? Have you seen them or talked to them?"

"I've seen them on the holo. That's all I need to see. You don't know what you're doing."

"You have no right to say that," Josepha replied. "You have no right to come here and discuss our children in such a hostile way."

Nola Reann stepped back. "Hostile! I'm not hostile. Your biologists are hostile, enemies of the human body and what it represents. They want to change it and mold it—it's only dead matter to them. They want to change it because they hate it, which means they must hate themselves on some level."

Josepha thought of Merripen. "Tell me," Alf said, smiling slightly, "since you're a meteorologist, how do you rationalize the implants I know you have, the ones that provide you with a direct link to the machines you need to do your work?"

Nola glared. "That's not the same thing at all. Such devices merely amplify the potential of the human form and mind." She waved her right hand in a gesture of dismissal.

"And your human form could not even be standing here in front of us without the aid of an exoskeleton," Alf went on. Josepha squinted, noticing for the first time the slender silver wires on Nola's hand and the metal support around her neck, partly concealed by her high-collared blue jacket. The woman, she realized, had spent her life either on the moon or a low-gravity colony.

"Do you have any idea," Alf was saying, "what people three hundred years ago might have thought of you?"

Nola smiled, once again hiding her hands in her pockets. "I'm still a human being. I think like you, I feel like you. Everything I use simply aids me in achieving my full potential. I don't lack emotions or sexuality as your children do." She turned her head and looked at Josepha with conviction. "Extended life has at last made it possible for us to become fully human. We can be everything a human being can be. There is no other point to life. These children insult us by saying that we cannot succeed as we are."

"How strange," Josepha said. "If I reasoned the way you do, I might conclude that extended life denied us our humanity by denying us death." She forced out the words with difficulty. "Some people obviously do feel that way."

"You mean murderers and suicides," Nola said blatantly. "I quarrel only with the means they use. They anticipate death, that is all, reach for it prematurely instead of awaiting its eventual arrival. Of course, murder and suicide are at least human talents."

"So is rationality," Alf said.

"What is reason without the fuel of the emotions, the tension between the two that makes all achievement possible? A dead, soulless thing." Nola lowered her voice. "Your biologists are trying to cloak their despair by creating these new beings. They're not giving us a chance to succeed as we are."

"Are you a meteorologist or a missionary?" Alf asked, raising an eyebrow. "Do you think the human body is sacrosanct? It's only nature's set of compromises. People have been trying to alter it in small ways, either for aesthetic or practical reasons, for centuries."

"Not this drastically." Nola paused, as if at a loss. "It's a mistake."

Josepha thought: There's nothing more to say. We won't even know if we were right or wrong for a long time.

Nola Reann turned and strode away quickly, without a farewell. Josepha moved closer to Alf. "She's unusual, isn't she?" she said softly. "Others aren't like that."

"Do you talk with many people elsewhere?"

She shook her head.

"She may be extreme, but she's not all that unusual."

"What will they do?"

He sighed. "I don't know. There's not really much they can do."

Josepha looked up and gazed past the park. Behind the houses ahead, robot guards patrolled the grounds. There were more guards lately.

Teno and Ramli were playing with four other children in the living room. Josepha could hear them from her study: Teno's inflections, Ramli's slight drawl, Nenum's murmur, Aleph's rasp, Yoshi's singsong, Linsay's guttural throat noises. They had already passed their wilderness survival test, although it would hardly have mattered if they had not. Unobtrusive robots had been near them at all times. The village had held a celebration for the children when they returned, but the ceremony had meant more to the parents than to the young ones, who seemed content with success alone.

She did not mind the noise, although there was more of it than usual. She paid it little attention as she sat at her desk, watching the history syllabus roll by on her reader screen. If neither she nor Alf had anything further to add, they would put it into its final form, show it to a teacher, then program the computer.

She tried to concentrate, not wanting to think of Chane. He and Warner had gone to one of the lodges for the day. She felt a pang at the thought. Vladislav, still living with Warner, had taken up with Chen Li Hua some time ago. Warner had begun seeing Chane a while later.

Chane had not tried to deceive her and she had made no objections. Yet even after two months of this, Josepha still felt twinges. At least Warner and Vladislav knew how they felt about each other. Josepha knew only that she would be hurt if she lost Chane and that she missed him when he was not with her. But she did not know what he felt. Oddly enough, their lovemaking had improved. Jealousy was always a good aphrodisiac, but the price was too high.

She sighed. She and Chane had lived in isolation from each other since the very beginning. Except for the children and their upbringing, they shared very little of real substance. Their other obligations and pursuits had been carefully divided into equal portions, everything from rooms to housework to time alone to time with friends. There had been nothing strange about that; it seemed reasonable and practical.

But, looking back, she felt as if she had deceived herself. People grew closer, or changed, or grew apart; they were not capable of maintaining the same static arrangements day after day, year after year. Josepha, afraid to admit it to herself before, now knew that she was coming to love Chane.

She put her hands, palms down, on the reader's flat surface. She did not want to be alone any more, surrounded by walls of sensible arrangements which protected only a solitary mind reflecting endlessly on itself and its own uniqueness. She had deluded herself by thinking that she could preserve those barriers in this village. The children had already penetrated them, binding her to the future and the past.

She recalled her pre-Transition life. It had not been that

unusual in its isolation from family, demanding relationships, and any sense of continuity. The techniques guaranteeing personal immortality had preserved the individualistic society in which she had lived. Without that development, her fragmenting culture might well have been overrun by those who were unified and bound together in a common purpose. Only the attainment of the ancient dream of eternal life had been enough to save her culture and conquer the others as well. Small wonder, she thought, that Nola Reann and those like her felt threatened by the children, whose existence once more questioned everything.

The sound of a laugh startled her. She sat up and pushed the reader to one side. The laugh was hollow, devoid of merriment. She got up and walked softly out of the study, peering around the stairway into the living room.

The children were talking, lounging in various uncharacteristic attitudes around the room. Nenum stood slouching, hands on hips, looking quite pretty. A peculiar but familiar-sounding whine had crept in the child's voice.

"I don't *know* why," Nenum was saying, tucking a short lock of reddish hair behind an ear. "I just feel depressed, you know, everything seems . . ." Josepha recognized the voice of Warner and the words of one of her common complaints.

Teno ambled over to Nenum. Her child's face was contorted in an odd expression, eyes wide, mouth pulled down. "Don't worry," Teno said, putting a hand on Nenum's shoulder. "Ah, you need to take a mood and you'll feel better. Uh, sometimes I feel that way myself. It'll go away."

"Why don't we have a party?" Aleph said, mimicking Gurit's tones. "I haven't tied one on in a while."

"I have a headache," Linsay growled, stomping fiercely around the room. Josepha recognized the tense but controlled voice of Edwin Joreme. "They get to me sometimes, they get to me."

"Oh, Edwin," Teno replied, "you don't mean that, ah, I know you. You *dote* on Linsay." Josepha heard herself, the pauses, the hesitation, the rising inflection at the end of sentences, and shrank back near the wall. Was that how she sounded, that silly mixture of melioration and insecurity? Was that how they all sounded? She wanted to tiptoe back to the study, but puzzlement and curiosity held her as she listened:

RAMLI *(firmly):* Don't worry, I just have to make two calls. I won't be on long. Then we'll go. Why get there early?

TENO: I know I shouldn't, but, uh, I always feel so silly there. Li Hua's so intelligent she always makes me feel ignorant.

ALEPH: You know what I think? We could do with some tough times again. Builds character. Everyone's getting soft. If we had some hardships, a lot of people wouldn't make it.

NENUM *(whining):* I get depressed when I hear that. You're a hard person.

YOSHI *(gruffly):* The last time I was on Asgard, I noticed an interesting refinement in their holo transmissions.

LINSAY: Not *again*. Do we have to listen to that *again?*

TENO: Now, don't be so rude.

Josepha peered around the staircase once more, still hidden in the shadows. She felt like a spy. Ramli was sitting on the sofa slouched over, feet extended. Teno fluttered around the room nervously, looking very pretty and very insecure. Nenum lounged in the corner, gazing seductively at Ramli. Pained by the too-familiar scene, Josepha closed her eyes for a moment.

When she opened them, the children were themselves, seated on the floor, arms folded, murmuring softly. "I don't understand it," Teno said clearly.

"It's the way they are," Aleph replied. "You know that. They're confused."

"That's not what I meant. They wanted us to be different from them, right?" Teno paused. "That means they wanted us to be better. So if they think we're better, then why don't they act more like us?"

"You know why," Linsay said. "They can't help it. Their bodies are different. They like feelings but they lie about them, too. They lie about sex the most."

"Well, I don't know why people like to think things that aren't true. When I touch myself or Ramli does, it feels nice and that's all, but they act as if it's the most important thing in the world."

"It must feel different to them," Nenum muttered.

"But they made us so we're different," Teno said. "I don't think they like themselves the way they are. And if they liked

us, they'd try to be like us. They have minds, they can think.
So if they aren't like us, it has to be because they can't help it
and their feelings are stronger, or it's because they don't like
the way we are either.''

"But they made us this way," Ramli responded.

"We're an experiment. Experiments don't always work."

Josepha crept back to her study, knowing she had eaves-
dropped too long. She paused at her desk, remembering the
calmness in the young voices as well as the eerie precision with
which they had imitated the adults. The voices had lacked both
humor and contempt. They had only been trying to make
sense of their parents' behavior.

She wondered what else the children might be concluding
about them.

Josepha shivered slightly in her light jumpsuit and jacket.
Gurit Stern stood with her. The weather was cooler; before
them, the lake rippled. The water was calmer near the shore;
farther out, the wind was whipping up whitecaps.

Aleph, Teno, and Ramli were on the dock, tying up the
canoe they had taken out that morning. The young ones had
wisely decided not to stay out on the lake. There was still time
to have a meal inside one of the lodges before going back to
the village.

Gurit, dressed only in a beige short-sleeved shirt and brown
slacks, did not seem to feel cold. She smiled sympathetically at
Josepha, then walked out onto the dock to make certain the
canoe had been tied up properly. There was really no need to
check. The children usually made only one mistake before
learning a skill.

She was wondering idly whether they should turn the canoe
over on the dock instead when she heard a voice. "Josepha?"
She turned and saw Warner and Nenum scurrying down the
hill toward the lake. She waved at them.

"I didn't think anyone would be out here today," Warner
called as she came nearer.

Josepha smiled. "No one else is. Believe me, we wouldn't be
either if we'd known it was going to be this cold."

Warner, dressed warmly in a red coat, smiled nervously.
Nenum hurried down to the dock to greet the others. "We
thought that as long as we've walked this far, we might as well
eat before going home."

"We were just about to have lunch ourselves." Warner's

eyes did not meet hers. "You must join us," Josepha continued. "I miss you. I don't see you as much lately."

"I wasn't sure if you wanted to."

"Oh, Warner. You're my friend." Josepha took Warner's arm as they began to climb the stone steps which led to the lodge, a large log cabin surrounded by evergreens.

"He loves you, Jo." Josepha, startled, let go.

"What do you mean?"

"I can tell. He hasn't said so, but it's obvious. I think he's afraid to tell you. I don't know why. Maybe he's not sure how you'll take it."

She was about to reply when she saw something move in the woods above. A man stepped from behind the trees. He was looking down toward the lake. He was dressed entirely in white; there were dirt and grass stains on his knees. He held his hands behind him, as if concealing something. Thick, dark, shoulder-length hair hung around his face.

He stood fifteen meters above them without moving. Josepha stopped and glanced quickly at Warner.

"Visitor?" Warner murmured.

"Alone? Out here?" Josepha looked back at the man. Farther up the hill behind him, a small robot moved swiftly toward the stranger on its treads. And then the man quickly raised his arm and she saw the weapon, a small silver cylinder.

He aimed. She heard Gurit scream, "Get down!" A beam of light flashed from the weapon.

Josepha turned numbly. Gurit had thrown herself over one child's body, two others lay near her, the fourth . . . something was wrong with the fourth. There was another flash of light, shocking her out of her paralysis. She looked back.

The man's headless torso toppled over into the foliage. For a moment she thought the robot had fired on him; then she realized the man had turned his weapon on himself. The robot reached his side and stood there helplessly, too late.

She turned to Warner. Her friend's head shook from side to side soundlessly. She held out her hands to Josepha, then spun around and began to run down to the children. Josepha followed her.

Gurit stood up, her hands on Ramli's shoulders. Teno, still lying on the ground, looked up. Josepha thought: They're safe, they're all right.

Gurit reached out to Aleph and pulled her child near her. But another small body did not move. Josepha suddenly realized that she could not see Nenum's red hair. Warner was running to the small, still body.

Josepha rushed to her friend, throwing her arms around Warner. "Don't," she managed to say. Warner pulled away and finally stood over her child.

Nenum, too, was beyond revival, head burned off by the visitor's weapon. Nenum's mother was silent, clenching and unclenching her fists, shaking her head, staring at Josepha with black, frightened eyes. Josepha opened her mouth and found she had no voice. Her knees buckled and she sat down hard on the ground, hugging her legs with her arms. Dimly, she saw Gurit go to Warner.

Warner began to wail. Gurit held her. Aleph observed them with pale green eyes. Josepha drew her legs closer to her chest.

Teno and Ramli were standing over her. She thought: We should go, I can't keep them here with this, what do I say, how can I explain it? Fear swept over her and she found herself shaking. Teno reached out and held her hands until she stopped.

Others, she knew, would be there soon. The robot had probably already signaled to them. The machine intelligence, having failed to protect them, waited on the hill, its head slowly spinning as it continued to survey the woods. It held the weapon in its metal fist. The children were silent, watching her with calm, questioning eyes.

Josepha wound her way past the cots and mats, trying not to disturb the children who lay on them. The young ones had been living here in the recreation hall for a week, always watched, never left alone or allowed to wander. Two robots stood in the back of the room; another was posted near a doorway.

Kelii Morgan sat in a straight-backed chair near the mat where his child Alani was sleeping. He was unarmed; the robots would stun anyone entering the room with a weapon. She motioned to him. He did not move. The children slept, breathing rhythmically. They had not rebelled against the restrictions placed on them.

She moved closer to Kelii. "Should we go downstairs now?" she whispered. Alani stirred slightly. Kelii leaned over and adjusted the child's blanket.

"I'll stay here," he replied softly. "Go on, Josepha, you can tell me what happened later on."

"Sure you don't want company?"

"Go on, it's all right. I want to be here in case one of them wakes up."

She left the room and hurried down the ramp. Below, in the room where the children usually played and studied, parents sat among the desks, computer consoles, tables, and chairs. Most of them sat on the floor. A few were on benches near the walls. Here three robots also stood guard, and she knew that there were others outside.

Chen Li Hua, who had taken it upon herself to call the parents together, stood under the screen in the front of the room. "Where's Kelii?" she asked in her flat, hoarse voice.

"He wants to stay upstairs."

"Then we might as well start, and I'll say what I have to say."

Josepha saw Chane near the doorway and made her way to him, sitting down next to him on the floor. "Where's Merripen?" a man asked, and she recognized the voice of Edwin Joreme.

"I didn't ask him," Li Hua replied. "I didn't ask anyone except parents to come here tonight. If any of the others arrive, as I suppose they might, that's fine, but I think any decisions we make should be ours." She cleared her throat and squinted; her eyes became slits. "Some of us have been asking for better security here all along, for restrictions on visitors, for supervision of any stranger who came here. We allowed ourselves to be talked out of it, supposedly for the good of the children. You see where that got us. It's time we insisted on whatever we think is right." The small woman brushed a hand over her short cap of straight dark hair.

Chane, looking sad and pensive, reached for Josepha's hand and held it. "They're gone," he murmured to her. "I went over to their home and Li Hua told me. They left this morning, before anyone was up."

"Where did they go?"

"I don't know. Vladislav went with two psychologists. Warner left with a friend who came for her."

She was silent, thinking of what she could have done, what she could have said to Warner and Vladislav, what she had been unable to do. It had not been enough, holding Vladislav while he sobbed, calming Warner, trying to figure out how to bury poor Nenum after skin scrapings had been stored for possible cloning.

Josepha had aided Warner in arranging a small ceremony in the foothills beyond the nearby woods. She, Chane, and Gurit had accompanied Warner and Vladislav. As they stood, watching two robots place the small body in the ground, Josepha realized that the ceremony had been a terrible mistake. They were marking an irrational act, an insane act completely outside the fabric of their society. They could gain nothing from Nenum's death. The death of any child would have been horrifying enough in former times; even during ages when such deaths were commonplace and expected, there had at least been the hope of a life beyond or the harsher view that the deaths of the weak might make future generations stronger. Their discovery that the murderer had been a man with two suicide attempts to his credit only made the whole thing more absurd.

Josepha, standing with her friends, had found herself praying, clinging to the hope that the visions she had glimpsed so long ago were real. She wanted to speak of them to Warner and Vladislav, offer them something that would ease their pain. But she kept silent, thinking they would not understand or, worse yet, think she was mocking them with false hopes.

Warner had rejected the idea of raising Nenum's clone and had talked Vladislav out of it, too. Instead, she had gone to Merripen, asking him to have the experience removed from her memory. He had called in a psychologist; at last they had agreed. It was a delicate business, this erasing of one's memory, and Josepha knew it would help Warner only in the short run. Her friend would lose the past nine years, but eventually she would become aware of discontinuities of blank spots, and would attempt to fill them in; the memories, little by little, would return and have to be faced. And in the meantime, a black emptiness would exist in the back of her mind to bother her without her ever being quite sure of what it was until the recollections returned, perhaps wrenchingly, in dreams and disassociated fragments. Better to let him handle it, better to absorb it, face it, and let it fade. Merripen, she was sure, had agreed to the procedure only to assuage his own guilt and sense of failure in his responsibilities. The psychologist should have treated him.

But no psychologist could treat a biologist without the biologist's request. The biologists had created the society and sustained it with their techniques; to question the motivations of one would be to question the society. Eventually, of course, the children, these children of Merripen's mind, might question it and seek to change it, and then Merripen would be held to account, but not yet.

Li Hua was still speaking, apparently answering another question. She paused, and Josepha saw Gurit rise to her feet.

"Listen," the former soldier said firmly, "you have something to tell us and you've been beating around the bush. Make your point, Li Hua."

"Very well. You all know about those who want to exile the children. Now, some think we should have raised them with other children from the beginning, but most of us thought that would be a hardship, that there might be animosity, or a lack of understanding between the two groups. In any event, we thought it wiser to wait until the children were older, and we did encourage visitors, which was probably a mistake as I see it. The children are better off developing in their own way."

Gurit coughed. "The point, Li Hua, the point."

"I propose that we agree with the proponents of exile and move to a space colony of our own as soon as possible."

Gurit sat down. Everyone absorbed the statement. A few shook their heads. Amarisa Drew, a tall Eurasian who was one of Yoshi's parents, waved an arm. "How is that going to solve anything?" she asked in her musical voice.

"It will ease the fears of those who distrust the children," Li Hua replied. "Security precautions will be simpler. The children won't have to face hostility. Any latent talents they have can develop more openly. Later, when they're older, they can return or lead out their lives wherever they choose."

"One moment, please," Dawud al-Ahmad called out. "Why should such a measure help? Why wouldn't those who fear the children grow more afraid in their absence? Ignorance is usually a greater spur to fear than knowledge." He tugged at his short beard. "Wisdom cannot grow in isolation."

"There's a practical problem," Kaveri Dananda said, "that you haven't mentioned either."

"And what is that?" Li Hua asked.

Kaveri stood, adjusting her green sari. "What is to prevent a group of the insane from attacking our little colony in space?"

The Chinese woman shook her head. "Such an action requires planning and teamwork, something I hardly think fanatics would be able to do successfully."

"Nonsense," Kaveri replied.

"An isolated attack like the one Josepha and Gurit witnessed is one thing, a concerted attack quite another. Most people now have lost a good deal of the ability to work with others smoothly—we have been cultivating our individuality for too long. Disturbed people have this tendency to an even greater degree.''

"But we would be vulnerable," Kaveri said. "And I think you underestimate the driving force of a mad idea deeply held."

"We would have ample warning. We could defend ourselves, and could station ourselves at such a distance from others that we would constitute no threat."

"But we could still be attacked," Dawud said. "Here, at worst, a few of us could survive. In space, we might all . . ." He held out his hands.

Josepha found herself rising to her feet. Nervously, she surveyed the room. Li Hua turned toward her.

"Josepha?"

She cleared her throat. "We're down here talking," Josepha began, "while the children are upstairs under guard. I don't know whether any of them actually feels fear or not, but they'll certainly acquire a good imitation of it if we go on this way. They'll learn to distrust and fear almost everyone if they haven't already. And if they turn into alienated adults, as some fear they will, we'll have ourselves to blame, not the madman who shot poor Nenum. This exile will only make it worse for them. The only way we can help them is by returning to some semblance of normal life, here in our homes, as soon as possible."

"A pretty set of sentiments," Li Hua muttered. "But how do we keep the same thing from happening again?"

"Don't you see?" Josepha focused first on Kaveri, then turned toward Amarisa, hoping for support. "Don't you realize how many people will feel sympathy for us now? Distrust is one thing, murder quite another. If we communicate openly with others, we can win their trust."

"We tried that," Edwin said from across the room, "and you see what happened. My advice is to have the biologists tell everyone to leave us alone and let them know what might happen if they don't. They're the ones with power."

"You're wrong," Josepha answered. "They don't believe they have much power. Ask Merripen if you don't believe me. And even if they did, that would be no solution; it would only create more hostility." She glanced around. Amarisa, Kaveri, and Dawud were nodding their heads in agreement.

"Li Hua has suggested a specific course of action," Edwin went on. "You have offered only vague possibilities. Give us a course of action. What exactly would you have us do?"

It was a fair question. She did not know how to reply.

Then Chane spoke. "It's obvious," he said in his deep voice. "First, we must invite people to live here if they wish. I'm talking about welcoming them, not the sort of halfhearted tolerance of outsiders we have now. Second, some of us must leave the village for short periods to communicate with others, propagandize them, if you will. I have spoken to many people over the holo, but such a measure does not have the impact of personal, face-to-face communication."

"And who will go?" Lulee Bernard called out, looking like a small, auburn-haired, serious child herself. "Isn't it more important that we stay with our children?"

"Perhaps it is," Chane replied, "although I don't know how much good that'll do them if they have no place in our world."

Several parents nodded their heads, murmuring, "It might be dangerous for the ones who leave," Edwin objected. "Have you thought of that? You can't be protected as well, if at all."

"It's a risk we'll have to take," Chane responded. Josepha saw fear in his eyes. "We have little time to spare, for once," he continued. "If we hadn't all grown so slow to act, we would have seen the wisdom of this course a long time ago. Since I brought this up, I'll volunteer my own services, if it's all right with the rest of you."

Josepha felt her muscles tighten. She could not look at Chane. He should have spoken with her before making such an offer. She could not object here in front of everyone and she could not stop him if he wanted to leave.

She thought: Warner was wrong. She was mistaken about Chane loving me, and now I can't even ask her about it. Numbly she listened to the discussion go on, not really hearing any of it.

Josepha gave in; she had no choice. Chane had persuaded the villagers. He would be accompanied by Amarisa Drew and Timmi Akakse, a handsome Jamaican woman with a forceful voice and presence.

She wanted to argue with Chane, but she did not. Instead, she tried to act calmly, explaining to the children why he was leaving them for a bit. They did not seem disturbed, asking only why they could not go as well. She had replied lamely that their studies were more important. But later she heard Teno tell Ramli that the parents were afraid they might be harmed by someone.

Whenever Chane glanced at her, she smiled, perhaps too brightly and reassuringly. The night before he left, he held her in bed and looked directly into her eyes and she knew she had not fooled him at all. She waited for him to ask her how she really felt, hoping she could stem the flow of angry and resentful words that would pour from her, but he did not speak, possibly afraid of what she might say.

She waited until he was ready to leave the next morning, off to join Timmi and Amarisa for a final session with Merripen before departure. Hating herself for speaking at such an awkward time, she heard her words: "You're leaving because of me."

Chane pulled back as if he had been struck. "No," he said finally, placing his hands on her shoulders. She wanted to twist away.

"Yes. First it was Warner and now this. You want to get away."

"You're wrong, Josepha, it has nothing to do with you. There's more to it than you think."

"It might be dangerous," she said, wishing she could stop the pointless argument. He took his hands away and she waited for him to walk out the door.

"I won't be gone that long. I wanted to bring you and the children along, but I know how hard it is for you to meet a lot of strangers. Anyway, you know we decided it just wasn't fair to ask young children, however rational, to defend their existence before people they don't even know."

She was beaten. She forced herself to smile again, to exercise the patience she should have learned during her long life. "I guess I'm being unfair," she murmured. "I'll miss you, but . . ."

"I'll be back before you know it."

He was gone.

She went to the window and watched him stride across the courtyard, closing the gate behind him.

IV

Teno was as tall as Josepha, Ramli somewhat taller. They had grown rapidly during the past years. They had retained their sexual ambiguity; slender bodies, slightly broad shoulders, a range of gestures that flowed from the delicate to the clumsy to the athletic. They were strangers.

They had not always been strangers. After Chane had left, Josepha had grown closer to them. She had taught them how to make pottery and how to sketch. She had been delighted when she found that they in turn were teaching these skills to the other children, though she was a bit disappointed with what they produced: accurate, photographically realistic drawings and simple, utilitarian plates and vases. She had found at first that as she spent more time with Teno and Ramli, she missed Chane less.

Chane's first trip should have lasted two months. It had stretched into almost half a year. Had he been returning to her alone, it would not have mattered. But the children grew, the life of the village went on. She had consulted him during his calls and the children had bantered pleasantly with his image, but Josepha had made the day-to-day decisions. Chane had returned to people who got along perfectly well without him.

He, Amarisa, and Timmi stayed away from the village for longer and longer periods of time. Estranged from their families while apparently having some success on the outside, Josepha knew they found their absences easier to rationalize as time passed. Perhaps they were also telling themselves that there would be time enough to renew their relationships with their children and their lovers after they had succeeded in their outside tasks.

Josepha sat in her favorite chair knitting while Teno and Ramli sprawled on the living room rug, poring over printouts and diagrams. She thought of Chane. She missed him more now, alone in this house with two increasingly impenetrable strangers. The hours she kept filled with new projects, friends, even a new intellectual challenge—she had decided to learn something about microbiology, equipping herself with a microscope and slides—only seemed to make her loneliness worse when she was alone with her thoughts.

She knitted and ruminated, remembering two encounters, realizing again how poorly she had handled both.

One had been with Chane during his first visit home. They had gone sailing on the lake with the children, then enjoyed a quiet dinner by themselves. She had filled him in on the events during his absence. He had told her about some of the understanding people with whom he had spoken.

"Have you become involved with anyone else yet?" he asked her as they sipped their after-dinner brandy.

"Why should I?"

"I don't expect you to deprive yourself simply because I'm away."

"Oh, Chane." She chuckled softly. "I'm used to being by myself, I used to like living that way, you know. You needn't worry about me. I don't need to be involved with another man."

She looked down at the pale green yarn, remembering that comment. She had fancied that she was reassuring Chane. But she had made the remark because of a dimly felt resentment, sure he had not missed the children or her that much; knowing also, since he had not tried to hide it, that he had enjoyed a few casual sexual adventures while away. She had spoken and told herself self-righteously that she would ease him. She had succeeded only in telling him bluntly that she could live alone and be happy about it while at the same time making him feel guilty about his own perfectly natural sexual involvements. She had hurt him, as she had unconsciously intended.

The second encounter had been with Merripen. The biologist had taken to visiting her and the children while Chane was away. She had been sympathetic, knowing that Merripen had grown depressed about the project. He had come to feel that it had escaped his control and that he no longer had anything to say about future events. He was an obsolete functionary wandering about the village, not needed by the children, unnecessary to the parents who had taken matters into their own hands. She knew the visits cheered him up and had been glad of it. But then she had hurt Merripen, too.

He had come to her one night. The children were sleeping and she was alone. She offered him some wine but he refused it. Instead, he took her arm and led her to the sofa.

"Let me stay with you tonight, Josepha."

She drew back, surprised. "I can't, Merripen."

"Why not?"

"Well . . . there is . . ."

"Don't be silly. Chane's not denying himself—why should you?"

"I can't explain. It's different for me."

She had been foolish. Her needles clicked; the children chattered. It would have taken so little effort to give Merripen the human contact he had probably needed as much as the sex. And it would have been no sacrifice either; she had felt a sudden desire for the handsome biologist even as she refused him. Why did I do it? she asked herself silently, but she knew the answer. She did not want emotional risks. Merripen might have wanted a commitment of some kind; for sex alone he could easily have turned elsewhere.

She did not want things this way. She no longer wanted her self-imposed exile from life. She could not do anything about Merripen; she had turned him away for the last time. She wondered if it were too late to do anything about Chane.

Merripen, at least, had now found his way back into village life. All of the children sought him out. He was the only adult they did seek out. The rest of them, even Kelii, were ignored or tolerated.

It had started when the children were eleven. They were not overtly hostile or rebellious, simply more indifferent. Lulee spoke of not knowing where her child was much of the time; Edwin, even grumpier than usual, muttered about being told he didn't know much; Gurit complained about being asked embarrassing questions and having her answers rejected out of hand.

The children were thirteen now. She watched them as they sat on the rug surveying their diagrams and charts. They were adolescents. She should have expected it. They kept to themselves, cultivating a flat, inexpressive manner of speech, wearing short, clipped hair and simple clothing. All of these new young people were austere in appearance, as if criticizing the more flamboyant and varied garb of their parents.

"What are you looking at so intently?" she asked the children. Neither replied. "What is it?" she said again.

Finally Teno looked up. The child's short hair was curled at the ends, making the face seem almost pretty. "Ectogenesis chamber," the young one remarked.

"More biology? Is that all you think about?" They were silent. Josepha imagined that Merripen must be gratified by this recent obsession. "Whatever for?"

"See how it works."

"We have to use it someday," Ramli added.

"I know, but you don't seem to pay any attention to anything else," she responded, trying to sound lighthearted. "You spend so little time on your art now, or history, and you used to enjoy those things."

"This is more important," Ramli said tersely.

"I didn't say it wasn't, I just said there are other things."
They remained silent.

"You could at least reply."

"Aren't you supposed to see Gurit this afternoon?" Teno said blandly before turning back to the diagrams.

Josepha felt unaccountably depressed. Of course they were obsessed with biology; for all she knew, it was their substitute for the pair-bonding of normal adolescents. She did not know why they had not paired off; it might have little to do with their physiology. Having been raised together almost as siblings or relatives, the young people were following the pattern normal to such groups by not forming couples. Whether they would form such bonds outside the group remained to be seen.

There were, at any rate, good reasons for this interest in biological techniques. The young ones did not want to run the risk of natural childbirth even though, theoretically, they were capable of it. If they were to control their own reproduction, they would have to learn what the biologists knew. Perhaps they were also protecting themselves in case at some future time the biologists decided that this "experiment" was a failure.

She watched them, wondering what they might do if they began to think of themselves as an evolutionary dead end. In their rational way, they might simply design another kind of being, one better suited to life than either they or the human beings who had raised them.

Josepha thought: We're the dead end. Merripen believed that and he was the person they saw most often now. *We're the dead end.*

Josepha, standing near the gate, noticed the young visitors. There were four, two boys and two girls. They were dressed in shiny, copper-colored suits with high collars. One boy slouched; the other stood straight, hands on hips. One of the girls, tall and muscular, was speaking; she gestured with her arms, flinging them out from the shoulders. The other girl stood on one leg, flexing the other, pointing one foot toward the ground. Teno and Aleph stood listening; they were still as statues. Teno was in a worn brown corduroy jacket and pants and Aleph wore gray overalls.

"What are you staring at?" Li Hua said in her hoarse voice. She sat with her back to the stone wall.

"Nothing. Some visitors, that's all." Josepha swung the gate gently. The hinges no longer squeaked, but the latch was still not working properly.

"As I was saying, Timmi was kind of discouraged about her trip to Madrid. There's a character there who's opposed to almost all biological modifications. Timmi couldn't understand his arguments. She suspects he may have doubts about extended life as well, but he has a following. Well, it just proves that if you use shit for fertilizer something always grows."

Josepha peered at the latch. "Why don't you have a robot fix it?" Li Hua asked.

"I guess I'll have to. This place needs work. One of the solar panels on the roof needs checking and one of my faucets keeps dripping."

"Your homeostat must need fixing, too. This house always seemed poorly designed to me."

"Maybe, but I never liked the newer designs, they always seemed—" A movement caught her eye. She looked up and saw the tall, muscular girl draw her arm back. Suddenly she struck Teno. Teno staggered back.

Aleph leaped at the girl. The other copper-clothed outsiders moved in and Josepha could no longer see Aleph's stocky form. "They're fighting," she said uncertainly.

Li Hua got up and came to the gate. Josepha said, "We'd better stop it."

"Don't bother, I think they can take care of themselves. Look." Ramli and three others were running toward the battle. They reached the outsiders and pushed them away, dodging their punches. Teno and Aleph got to their feet. The tall girl and one of the boys moved back in, flailing wildly with their fists. Josepha saw that the village children were fighting defensively, blocking the blows, then pushing the others away.

The outcome, she realized, was not in doubt. There were six villagers to four visitors. Teno and the others also had quicker reflexes and sturdier muscles. They chopped and kicked efficiently. The visitors quickly retreated a few meters and stood together grumbling, nursing their injuries.

The violence sickened Josepha. She pushed the gate open

and walked across the park with Li Hua close behind. She passed the outsiders, who seemed curiously unmarked by the fight in spite of their groaning. She reached Teno. One of her child's eyes was discolored. Aleph, Ramli, and the others were scratched and beaten; their clothes were torn. Yet they had won, or so it seemed.

"What was that all about?" she asked harshly. Teno stared back calmly.

"We had to defend ourselves." The child's voice sounded regretful. "They wouldn't have stopped trying to hurt us unless we did." Josepha spotted the scratches on Aleph's face and an ugly bruise on Ramli's arm. The visitors had tried their best to hurt them, yet the village children had responded only with defensive gestures.

"But how did it start?" she said.

"They don't like us and they're afraid."

Li Hua sighed. "What now?"

"We'd better talk to them," Ramli murmured. "We shouldn't just leave them there."

"It was hardly a fair fight anyway," Li Hua said. "Six against four."

The young people seemed mystified. "What's fair about a fight?" Aleph asked. "The point is to stop it."

"Let's go," Teno said. They moved past Li Hua and Josepha toward the outsiders.

But the visitors were already leaving the park. Teno called to them; they did not answer. Josepha watched them get into a blue hovercraft parked near Warner's empty house and drive away.

The children had gone camping in the foothills.

Josepha had seen Teno and Ramli off, helping them pack their gear, seeing them meet their friends outside the courtyard. As she watched them stride away in groups of two or three, hands clasped, packs on their slender backs, she had felt tired and old.

There had been no reason to worry. The young people wore Bonds and needed little food and water. But now a week and a half had passed and the children had not returned, nor had they transmitted a message. Josepha, somewhat uneasy, consulted her computer, which indicated that they were still in the foothills.

She called Alf. His image, seated behind a compositor, appeared. "Josepha! Haven't seen you since Lulee's party. Why don't you come over for lunch?"

"I'm worried about the children. Teno and Ramli haven't called in at all. Have you heard anything?"

"You shouldn't worry. They're in the foothills, I know the region. They can take care of themselves."

"I know where they are: I just found out."

"Look, if anything were wrong an emergency signal would have come in by now."

"Does Merripen know what they're doing?"

Alf shook his head.

She noticed a light flashing on the console. "Alf, someone else is calling. Can I get back to you?"

"Sure. Come on over if you like." Alf disappeared and was replaced by the image of Chane.

They exchanged their ritualized greetings. Josepha wanted to reach out to him, mend the rift, but she did not know how to do it. He asked about Ramli and Teno.

"They're not here now. The children all decided to go camping more than a week ago."

"I guess they're all right, then."

"I'm sure they are, but they haven't called in . . . Well, I have to admit I'm a little worried."

"Did they say why they were going?"

"No, but . . ."

"Didn't anyone ask?"

"It's hard to ask them anything now, they seem to resent it, if they can resent anything. You'd know that if you—" Josepha caught herself in time. "They're older now; they aren't docile little children."

"So everyone just let them go off."

"Oh, Chane, it isn't as if they aren't prepared or hadn't gone before. If something were wrong, we would have had a signal."

He looked exasperated. "As if nothing could go wrong with their Bonds or they couldn't make a mistake or someone couldn't harm them."

"Who the hell are you to be so concerned?" she burst out at last. "You aren't even here most of the time." She stopped. This was no time to pick a fight with him. "Very well," she continued, "we'll go look for them. I imagine they'll be annoyed with us, or at least puzzled." They might have made an error, she thought. It was too easy to assume that because the young people were rational, they were infallible. "Chane, do you have any appointments today?"

"Late this afternoon."

"Break them. Please come home."

"What for?"

"I thought you were concerned about the kids." She paused. "That isn't the only reason. I miss you."

"I was just there."

"Almost five months ago."

"That's not so long."

"It is. It seems longer here. I miss you."

"You get along pretty well by yourself."

"Yes, I get along by myself, but I don't like it. I get along because, like you and everyone else, I think there'll be plenty of time to take care of things later on. It's a bad habit all of us have. And you see what happens. Later never gets here. I love you, Chane." Her face perspired. Her hands shook. She drew them under her desk where Chane could not see them. "Please come home." She waited, expecting him to smooth it all over while refusing.

"I'll be home tomorrow."

Startled, she gazed at his image silently, then held out a hand to it. "I'll go look for the children," she managed to say. "I'll let you know what's happened."

Josepha, accompanied by Alf and Gurit, glided swiftly over the treetops, surveying the ground below. The belt around her waist was constricting, the jet on her back heavy. But this way they had maneuverability; a vehicle would have restricted their movements. She steered herself carefully as they passed over a small clearing and saw the remains of a campfire, a blackened area surrounded by stones and covered with dirt.

Josepha was frightened now, trying desperately not to give in to panic, not wanting to suspect the worst. Immediately after the call from Chane, she had contacted a robot in the foothills and sent it to where the children should have been. Looking through the robot's eyes, her screen had shown only a deserted clearing while the computer told her that the young people were there.

The signal she and the others were following, a low hum, grew louder. They were in the foothills. Josepha saw a glint of metal through the trees up ahead.

They came to another clearing and circled it, focusing on the signal. The robot Josepha had sent out waited there. The signal hummed in short bursts, telling her that the children were there. But they saw no one; only the signs, once again, of a campfire.

They dropped quickly to the ground. Josepha landed clumsily, stumbling onto her hands and knees. Alf helped her to her feet.

"I don't understand it," Gurit said as she strode around the clearing, peering at the trees, searching the ground for signs. Her middle-aged face was tense with worry; the lines near her lips were deep. Josepha waited unsteadily, still feeling unbalanced by the jet. Gurit stopped, bent over, then stood up. She held something in her hand.

She came back to Josepha and Alf, holding out the object. "Look, a Bond bracelet."

"I don't understand," Alf murmured.

"Very clever," Gurit said.

"But we should be getting signals from the other Bonds, shouldn't we?"

"This is a tricky business," Gurit replied. "Someone has relayed the signals through this one device and has managed to do it without triggering any emergency alert systems. I wouldn't know how to begin doing that."

"Then how," Alf said, his trembling voice betraying his fear, "are we going to find them?"

"The computer can track them if we turn off this Bond," Gurit said, "assuming, of course, that no one's fooled with the other Bonds."

"You think the children could have done this?"

Gurit looked from Alf to Josepha. "Possibly. I don't know why they would."

Josepha felt cold and uncomfortable, as if the weather had suddenly changed. "What should we do, Gurit?"

"We can go back home, put the computer to work, send robots out to search, and request a satellite scan of the entire area, but that might take days." She paused. "Or we can keep searching."

"But we don't know where—" Josepha began.

"I have an idea," Gurit interrupted. "Don't get scared when I tell you this. There was a landslide near here four days ago after that severe storm we had. My computer mentioned it after the storm was over, but I didn't think about it. I was sure the children had found shelter or else . . ." Gurit gazed

guiltily down at her feet. Josepha knew what she was thinking:
all of them had relied too much on the machines to guard the
children. "They may be trapped," Gurit finished. She did not
mention the other possibilities.

"That settles it, then," Alf said. "We must look for them
near the landslide." His voice quavered.

A hill of dirt and rocks stood before them.

"There was a cave here, I think," Gurit murmured. "They
might have gone inside during the storm." She removed her jet
as she spoke, dropping it on the ground with a soft thud. She
hurried to the mound and began to climb carefully.

Josepha reached for Alf's hand. She was numb, imagining
Teno entombed inside, without food, without air. They could
live without the food, but air . . . She thought: Nature has
killed them because they're mutants, travesties—and it wants
to let us know that we can still die here, that nothing can
protect us forever. She recalled the frequent trips of the young
people from the village, their attempts to understand the
natural world that was part of them and yet outside them.

Alf gripped her hand tightly, and she realized she would be
hysterical if she gave in to her thoughts. Alf's hand was
sweaty, his delicate face frozen. His blue eyes were filled with
fear. He leaned against her heavily; she put her arms around
him and his jet.

She watched quietly as Gurit scrambled over the rocks near
the top of the mound. Gurit fell to her knees and did not
move. Josepha waited, wondering what the woman had seen.

Then Gurit stood. "There's an opening here," she shouted
down. Josepha sighed; the young people could not have suffo-
cated. Gurit was bending over again.

"Do you hear something?" Josepha asked Alf, sure she was
imagining the sound of another voice. Alf shook his head.

"They're inside," Gurit cried. She sat down suddenly at the
top of the hill. "Call for help—they're inside."

Josepha had expected Chane to be angry, to reproach her
and the other parents for their lack of supervision or to turn
his wrath on the children. Instead, he had silently thrown his
arms around Ramli, then Teno.

She had wanted to question the children about the reasons
for their actions. But Teno and Ramli had been too tired to do
more than bathe and eat a few raw vegetables before going to

sleep. Chane's journey home had wearied him as well. The accounting would have to take place the next day.

She entered the living room. Chane was sitting on the sofa smoking a cigarette. She sat down next to him and touched his hand gently. He did not speak.

Most of the village had gathered near the cave that afternoon, waiting as the robots dug, sighing and crying when the young people finally emerged. Merripen, standing near Josepha, had unexpectedly hugged her when he saw the children.

The children had been tired and dirty but seemed to have few injuries. Three medical robots had treated the cuts and bruises while protein tablets and water were distributed and adults hurried to the young people. Josepha had waited with Teno and Ramli for the hovercrafts that would take them all home.

Both children had been remarkably calm, describing some of their ordeal in steady voices. They had been trapped after taking shelter from the storm. After discovering that air could still reach them, they had parceled out the few provisions they had. Aided by the glow of their portable lanterns, they had tried to repair a Bond in order to signal for help.

"We shorted out four Bonds," Teno said quietly. "It's not that easy to repair them after fooling with them. By then a few lanterns had given out and we had to conserve the rest. I was making some progress with my Bond when Gurit came."

It was impossible for her to tell if they had been frightened at all. She gazed at them, trying to discern some difference, then saw one; neither child would look at her directly. "We made a mistake, rigging the Bonds," Ramli said.

"Why did you do it then?"

"We were sure you wouldn't worry about us, and we didn't want others to find us. You know some don't wish us well."

"You could have died." Instantly Josepha wished that she had not spoken so harshly.

"I know. We all thought we might. We didn't want to."

They had said little more on the way home.

"Don't be sad," Josepha said now to Chane. He tried to smile, but his dark eyes remained morose. "They're safe, and maybe they've learned something from all of this, something we couldn't have taught. I'll admit it's learning things the hard way, but—"

"They've learned they can die," he responded. "And

before that, when Nenum was killed, they learned they might have to hide. Do you think those are useful lessons, Josepha?" She did not reply. "They have learned fear."

"I don't know if they have or not. I couldn't tell."

"And they may react the way many of us have, by retreating."

"Is something else bothering you, Chane?"

He put out his cigarette and lit another, passing the box to her. "I will tell you something you won't find in any public record of my life," he said suddenly. "Do you want to hear it? It's not pleasant."

She lit her cigarette. "If you want to tell it, I'll listen."

"You know that during the Transition I was in hiding. I trusted only two people with information about where I was. I wanted to live until it was over and like many in public life I had enemies. A friend contacted me, one of those I trusted. He pleaded with me to return to the capital. Another government had fallen and he wanted me to help form a new one; they needed my foreign contacts and experience. As you may know, some countries managed to restore civil order before many African countries could. As an additional incentive, he told me that my wife and one of my children were imprisoned, prisoners of a tribe sometimes hostile to my own. He was trying to get them and others released but needed my aid."

Josepha waited for him to continue, tapping her ashes into a pewter tray. Chane was hunched over, elbows on knees, staring down at his feet. "I didn't go," he said at last, so softly she could barely hear him. "It was too risky, I thought, telling myself I couldn't have done much anyway. I didn't go. I hid. In fact, I moved so that no one could contact me again."

She had to say something. She reached toward him, then pulled her arm back. "But," she began. She swallowed. "You said," she went on, "that your wife and children were still alive."

"They are. Does that make me any less culpable? Do you want to know what she went through during her imprisonment? Her body was repaired and her mind was wiped of the experience afterward, but I am still a witness to it. I was told everything. I will never have it wiped from my memory. That is part of my punishment."

She stubbed out her cigarette. He moved away from her and slouched at the other end of the sofa. "I have wanted to redeem myself since then. That's why I came here and it is also why I left after Nenum's death. At least that's what I thought at the time—I wanted to stay here, but I thought speaking to others was more important. Maybe it was just an excuse to retreat from you."

"Why didn't you tell me this before?"

"Don't you see? At first I didn't think I knew you well enough, and later . . . I couldn't tell how you felt toward me. You never even argued with me very much."

She sat up. "Why should I have argued with you?"

"It would have shown you cared."

"I thought trying to be rational and pleasant was a better way of showing care. There isn't very much worth arguing about when you know sooner or later it'll be forgotten."

He sighed. "That sounds like selfishness, not concern."

"Why?"

He rose and paced to the window, then turned to face her. "It keeps you from getting involved, from committing yourself. I know, I'm guilty of the same thing. Why didn't you get angry over Warner?"

Josepha opened her mouth to speak, but Chane continued. "Because you would have had to admit your pain and maybe that it was partly your fault as well. Why did I do it? Maybe in some way I was testing you, Josepha. Why didn't you do the same thing? Because you could make me feel guilty by not retaliating, yet avoid any real confrontation where we might have had to make a decision one way or another."

"But I love you," she said, feeling the words were almost useless. "I have for a while. What you did long ago doesn't matter to me now. All of us did things like that or we wouldn't be alive today." She paused, then forced herself to continue. "I worked for a shady cryonic service, even though I suspected many of their clients would never be revived. I bought longevity shots illegally. I didn't do much to make anyone's life better. And before that, out of fear, I ran away from the only man I ever really loved, and when I was an adolescent, I tried to run away through suicide."

"I guess," Chane replied, "that we have at last laid our cards on the table. We humans are peculiar, aren't we? I can see why Merripen wanted a change."

She stood up. "What do we do now, Chane?"

He crossed the room and put an arm around her. "We settle things with Teno and Ramli, between ourselves, and then . . ." He paused. "Right now, I think we need rest."

The children, Josepha noticed, looked almost guilty. They poked at their bananas and milk, gazing obliquely at her and Chane across the table.

"You caused us a lot of pain and worry," Chane began. "I want to know the reasons."

"Chane," Josepha said hesitantly, "can't we wait until we've finished breakfast first?"

"No."

"We made a mistake," Teno said softly. "We needed to be alone for a while, we had some things to work out and decisions to make."

"Couldn't you have made your decisions here?" Chane asked.

"We had to be by ourselves. We didn't think you would worry and we wanted to make sure no one hostile to us knew where we were."

"But you could have gone to the lodges," Josepha said. "You could have had robots protect you there."

Teno stared directly at her. "That didn't help Nenum."

"We're sorry," Ramli said. "Maybe we should have told you. We thought you'd have more trust in us. We forgot that you don't see things quite the way we do. And we didn't count on an accident, though we should have. We were too busy protecting ourselves from other people."

They're trying to twist it around, Josepha thought, trying to make it our fault. It should not have surprised her; quite naturally, the young people thought themselves more rational than their parents. "Have you decided anything?" she asked.

"We had to decide," Teno said calmly, "whether to stay here, voluntarily exile ourselves, or pursue a third course."

"Wait a minute," Chane interrupted. "Don't you think your parents have anything to say about what you're going to do?"

"Please let me finish," Teno replied tonelessly. "You were right when you decided to speak to people outside the village and to have more visitors here. The problem is that you didn't go far enough. We need to live with other people now. Maybe we should have been brought up with other children from the beginning. We want to move away from here. It will be hard— I don't know how well we'll get along, but we have to start."

"You want us to build another village somewhere else?" Chane said.

"No," Teno responded. "That would be the same thing we

have now. We want to live with others. Some of us may live off-planet, the others in different societies here. It won't be easy, having to leave each other, but it's the only way. People won't see us as a group then, but as individuals. And we'll be forced to learn, to get along, to find out what to do, each of us, because we won't have the others to lean on. Instead of isolating ourselves, we'll learn how we can help."

"But you're so young," Josepha said, looking to Chane for support. "You're children, you don't know what you're doing. You can't decide something like that yet."

"We're not like you, Josepha," her child said. "We don't have much experience, but that doesn't make us children. Physically, we're grown. We don't have the hormonal changes and emotional problems others do at our age."

"It's time for us to lead our own lives," Ramli added.

"And what are we to do?" Chane said, sounding weary. "Go with you? Stay where? Do what we want? Did you think of us at all?"

"Do what you think is best," Ramli said. It sounded cold to Josepha; the child seemed to realize that. "We're not abandoning you," Ramli went on. "You'll see us often; you can advise us. You'll have to tell us if we're doing something wrong."

Josepha, looking at the two serious young faces, knew that they and the others would have their way, whatever the parents or Merripen or anyone else thought. The children would take their leave; she and Chane would have their own decisions to make. They would leave the village; there would be no point in remaining. It all reminded her of death, the end of one thing, the beginning of another.

V

The autumn leaves, bright spots of orange, red, and yellow, covered the ground near the creek. They rustled under the feet of Josepha and Teno, muffling the cracks of dead twigs. Overhead, sunlight shrouded by gray clouds penetrated the webbing of bare tree limbs.

Teno, clothed in sweat pants and a heavy red jacket, walked with hands shoved into pockets. The child's gray eyes matched the cloudy sky and seemed to hide as much. "I'll call you from

Asgard," Teno was saying. "I may go to the moon afterward."

"I've never been off Earth," Josepha murmured. "It seems silly now, sort of unenterprising."

"Maybe you'll visit me," her child said. "Isn't it about time you went?"

"Probably. I hope I can bring myself to set foot in a shuttle."

"The future may be there. We talked about it, all of us. We want to find out more. We're curious. I think we'll go on a long journey someday, or our descendants will. They probably won't be anything like you or us."

"Probably not."

"Even we might not be the same. We've talked about somatic changes, readjustments in our bodies, but I think we'll need more experience before deciding what to do."

They turned from the creek and walked back toward the house. The old maple tree still remained; the apple tree Josepha had planted still lived, although its fruit was small and bitter. The house itself looked the same but felt old, unused, musty. She had left the village hoping to gain some strength from her old home and had felt only displaced. She could no longer live here.

"Will you go live with Chane, Josepha?"

"Yes, at least for a while. He wants me to travel with him, meet some of his friends. He feels he has to continue speaking for you. He's probably right."

"He is right. Our plans may not work out. Some call us infiltrators—as if we're subversive." Teno sniffed loudly. "It's good that you'll be with Chane. Without Ramli and me to worry about all the time, you'll be able to work things out between you."

Josepha stopped and turned to her child, gazing into Nicholas Krol's gray eyes. "Teno," she said hesitantly, "there's one thing I have to ask. It may seem strange or silly to you, but humor me for a bit." She paused. "I don't know how to put it exactly. Do you have any feelings for me at all, as a parent? Do you really, deep down, feel any sort of an attachment, any concern? I just want to know."

The gray, quiet eyes watched her calmly. "It would be strange," the child answered, "if we could have lived among you without coming to some understanding of your feelings. Of course I'm concerned. I care about you and I'd feel a loss if

I no longer saw you or couldn't speak to you. If one loses a friend or companion, one loses another perspective, another viewpoint, a different set of ideas and the personality that has formed them."

"That isn't quite what I meant." Josepha struggled with the words. "Do you feel any love?" She waited, wondering what Teno thought.

Teno was silent for a few moments. Josepha thought: I shouldn't have asked. A person could profess love, but actions were what counted. Teno and the others had tried to show all the love they were capable of feeling, if they could feel it at all. One could not ask, should not ask.

"Do you believe," Teno said softly, "that only your physiology, your glands, your hormones can produce love? It isn't true. Love is part of a relationship—it can't be reduced to physical characteristics or body chemistry. I love you, Josepha. I'll care about you as long as I know you or remember you."

She should not have asked. The words could tell her nothing. She could still doubt, still wonder if the child was telling her what would be most comforting.

But Teno's face was changing. As she watched, she saw the child's lips form a crescent, and realized with a shock that Teno was smiling. It was a slow smile, a gentle smile, compassionate but impenetrable. A softness seemed to flicker behind the gray eyes. It was Teno's parting gift.

The smile, too, might be a comforting mask. But as she entered the house with her child, Josepha decided she would accept it.

Unguided Days

I

EARTH WAS A FARAWAY PEARL IN THE BLACKNESS.

It grew into a mottled marble as the ship drew nearer. Pinpoints of light glittered on the nightside. The globe waned into a silver crescent, offering a setting for the jewel of the rising sun.

The seat held her. She tensed, eyes closed, waiting for the gravitic shield to shut down.

Her legs jerked, and Nola opened her eyes. She was in a floater; the gravitic generator, a small golden square resting on the floor, shimmered. Nola lifted her head, gazing through the transparent shields of the floater at the empty room's pale yellow walls. She saw the green outside the window on her left, and remembered.

The dream had faded. She signaled to her implant, and the generator shut down; Earth's gravity bound her again. The slender silvery wires which held her body began to stimulate her muscles and nerves. The shield slid open. Arms at her sides, she crossed the room with tiny steps, catching a glimpse of her hand as she opened the door. Her hand was a pale claw; the silver threads on it glistened.

Nola left the room and passed through the hall. Her long pants were weights pulling at her hips; her blouse seemed to bind her, pulling at her shoulders. As she descended the spiral staircase, she smelled onions and garlic and heard someone singing. The song was a wail. Yasmin, her hostess, was cooking.

The first floor of Yasmin's house was a large room with sofas and chairs in one corner, a table and chairs in another. The rest of the room was cluttered with piles of books, tapestries, manuscripts, vases of flowers, and a few dust balls. The dust made her nose twitch. She threaded her way carefully among piles of books and stood by a window, studying the settlement. It seemed primitive and dull. One man in a nearby house tended a garden; a man and a woman strolled by along the road.

In the late-afternoon light, the grass outside was a deeper green; the hills in the distance were blue. She squinted at the unfamiliar, disorienting landscape and thought of Luna's long afternoon, the black shadows and tall pale mountains.

Nola turned away from the window and walked toward the kitchen, which was separated from the large room by a partition. She peered in at Yasmin. The short, dark-haired woman stood before a butcher's block, chopping onions.

"May I help?" Nola asked.

"Oh, no, I like to cook. It relaxes me." Yasmin reached toward the dispenser, pulled some carrots from it, and went back to chopping, wielding her blade forcefully. Yasmin wore no Bond; she had said that no one in the settlement did. Nola, eyes stinging from the onions, looked away from Yasmin's chubby Bondless wrist.

"I'm sorry," Yasmin said suddenly. Her cleaver clattered against the block. "You came here to see Mischa." Before Nola could protest, the other woman had taken her arm gently and drawn her back through the large room to the front door. The door opened. "See that house over there?" Yasmin pointed. "That one, the one that looks like a yurt. That's his house. He's probably there now. Go ahead, I won't have anything ready for a while."

Nola hesitated, then walked outside. The scent of Yasmin's lilac trees was thick; Earth was a place of strong odors. She had followed Mikhail Vilny to this lush, disturbing place, and she was no longer sure that she wanted to see him. She turned her head. The village was surrounded by a low stone wall; its rusty iron gate was unlocked, as if the people here had nothing to fear. A turret of stone stood near the center of the settlement.

Nola lingered at the edge of the dirt road, then began to walk toward Mikhail's house. It stood away from the curving road, about one hundred meters from Yasmin's home. It's curved sides were made of wood; the thatched roof perched on the house like a pointed hat. A path through the weedy lawn led past a rose garden to the door. She gazed at the budding bushes and remembered the roses he had grown on Luna, white and fat, with stems almost as tall as trees, blooms open to the artificial light. There had been no thorns in those rosebushes. She reached out for a pink bud, then withdrew her hand.

She climbed the two front steps, knocked, and waited. The door opened and she saw him.

Mikhail was the same. His reddish-brown hair was longer, his face a little rounder. His blue eyes stared straight at her; he was one of the few men from Earth whom she knew who was as tall as she.

"Nola." He smiled when he said it. He was happy to see her. Her relief made her unable to speak for a moment.

"Mikhail." She did not know what else to say. She kept her hands behind her back, pressed against the bottom of her spine.

"Did you come here just to see me?"

"Yes. You don't think—" She paused, and looked down at her feet. "I went to see your friend Lise Trang first. She told me you were here. I asked her to come with me, but she wouldn't."

"She was angry. People tell a lot of lies."

Nola looked up. "She was also frightened. She never leaves her house. She wouldn't let me stay there. She had a creature watching me while I was with her, an android that looked like an elf. She called it a kobold."

Mikhail's smile faded. "I've seen them. Implants tell them what to do. They're one of the new toys the biologists are making for us. You won't find them here."

"Lise told me this was a death cult." Nola spoke rapidly. "She said a man named Giancarlo Lawrence was the leader. She must be mistaken. You can't have joined such a thing."

Mikhail stepped back. "Please come in."

Nola entered the house, looking around nervously at the large, darkened room. It was bare except for mats thrown on the floor, as if Mikhail were a nomad camping here. She settled herself on a mat while Mikhail pressed a button on the wall. The curtains opened; sunlight brightened the room. A bed near the wall hung from the ceiling, attached by ropes. Near it, surrounded by flat stones, a pool shimmered. Mikhail settled on a mat near her. He looked as though he was at peace; she had not expected that.

"Did you come here just to see me?" he asked again. "Or were you coming here anyway?"

"To see you, of course."

"Perhaps that's what you tell yourself. You once thought your life seemed empty."

She shook her head. "That was a bad moment, a mood. Maybe your earthly ideas contaminated me." She tried to smile.

"Are you still angry with me, Nola?"

"No." She gazed into his eyes as she spoke. "I wanted to tell you face-to-face that I wasn't."

"I couldn't have stayed. Luna isn't for me; this is my home. I kept thinking of how hard it would be to return if I stayed away too long."

"I understand." The wire web supporting her body reminded her of his argument. "And I can't stay here. It isn't just the gravity, it's everything else."

"You didn't come here just to see me."

"But I did."

"I don't think so. You didn't have to come to Earth for that. You're looking for something else."

"But I'm not."

"I think you are."

If she listened long enough, she would believe him. "Lise said this was a death cult."

Mikhail chuckled. "She doesn't understand. There's no death here, only life. We have no weapons, not even many tranquilizing rods. You saw the gate—it's not even locked, and the wall is just a boundary, not a barrier. We don't seek death, but we don't fear it either."

Nola watched his face. This settlement, she thought, was only another of those groups so common here now. There were many of these cults, and not all were dangerous; most were simply foolish, at least to her way of thinking. People here seemed unable to take the world as it was. They sought to construct edifices of ideas, as if that would somehow yield a truth, and, in so doing, they lost what was already present in the world. They could look at a storm and impart some meaning to it, a purpose. Nola, riding above Earth, would see only a pattern of clouds, the product of meeting masses of air, a calm and steady eye at the center of whirling wisps.

Then why was it that Mikhail, with his new ideas, smiled, and she, with her empiricism, frowned and knew despair? When it was time to sleep, she slept, and quickly, because she knew that if she lay awake, the terrors would come, the feelings of pointlessness about a series of endless, meaningless actions, the growing conviction that life was indeed too short and that she would die after all. Mikhail was her excuse; something else had brought her here.

She tried to shake the feeling. She had come to see Mikhail. He was all right. She had nothing else to do and might as well stay here for a while.

"Are you going to stay?" he asked, echoing her thoughts.

"For a while. I was told I needed a rest. It's difficult to argue the matter with an antagonist attached to your brain." She gestured at her forehead, at the implant under her scalp. "Yasmin Hallal met me at the gate when I arrived. She told me I could stay with her. She has a floater in one bedroom, so I should be comfortable."

She waited for Mikhail to invite her to stay with him, but he did not. As he rose to show her to the door, she knew at last that she had lost him.

Yasmin had invited a friend for supper. They ate at the table. Behind Yasmin, unhung abstract paintings leaned against one of the large windows.

Yasmin's friend was a yellow-haired woman named Hilde. Hilde, like Yasmin, smiled a lot and looked pretty when she did. Without the smile, her round, plain, coarse-featured face with its large brown eyes was placid and bovine until reanimated by another smile.

"We don't get many visitors from up there, as a rule," Hilde said as she poured some wine.

"Actually, I'm from Luna, but I spend much of my time in upper Earthspace. I doubt I'll be here long."

"Well, you might want to stay." Hilde picked at her food while Yasmin devoured hers. "Some visitors do. It's very peaceful here."

Nola concentrated on her food. Yasmin had served her too much. Hilde was eating very slowly, as if trying to make the dinner last as long as possible; Yasmin was already helping herself to seconds.

Hilde said, "Sometimes I think I'm ready to depart." Her low nasal voice rose a bit. "And then I lose the feeling, and I'm caught again."

Yasmin nodded. "I'm not ready. When it comes, it comes." She ran a hand through her short black hair. "Suicide wouldn't be right." Nola lifted her head, startled. "I'm just grateful the fear is no longer with me."

"The fear?" Nola said.

Yasmin turned toward her. "You've seen it, haven't you?" She hooked her stubby fingers around her wineglass. "Maybe it isn't the same for you, you're probably used to danger."

Nola shrugged. "It depends. People on the moon accept some danger, and so do those on Mars, but the ones on Asgard and the Floating Bridge of Heaven and the Egg think it's more dangerous here. They have jokes about it. They talk of earthquakes and storms and floods and wonder why all of us don't live in space, in controlled environments with plenty of shielding."

"I had the fear," Yasmin said, staring past Nola. "With me, it started earlier than with most. At first, I simply made sure that I always wore a lifesuit and never went to isolated places. But soon I didn't travel at all." She paused to sip some wine. "Oh, I still saw some friends and went to parties, but that meant there were always a few strangers around. I began to wonder about them. Perhaps one of them was a fanatic, just waiting for a moment to strike."

Nola turned a bit. Hilde, who must have heard the story before, was staring at her, as if waiting to see how Nola would react.

"I was living in Jeddah then," Yasmin went on. "Once in a while, a rumor would start about unchanged people who lived in the desert, who had resumed the life of the Bedu. The story was that these people believed that by accepting immortality, we had upset the pattern of Allah. Instead of accepting God's judgment on our lives, we had created Paradise here. The Prophet said, 'Do not weep for your dead.' These people went further, so it was told; they rejoiced in death. It was rumored that they sent assassins who would conceal themselves in our cities, mingling with us, choosing the people they would dispatch to the Throne of God."

Nola kept her face still. "Often, at a party," Yasmin continued, "someone would tell a gruesome story of bloodied bodies and severed heads, of a man with a scimitar murdering unprotected people." Nola choked and pushed her plate away.

"This kind of thing always seemed to be happening far away, or in a city by the Gulf, and whenever anyone tried to check on it, the story would fade, vanishing like a tent in a sandstorm. There were no computer records of such things, no reports, but the rumors, after a while, would circulate once more."

Yasmin smiled. "I now think that the stories were simply a way for some to deal with our long lives. We could accept our endless existence while still believing that our judgment would come eventually. The stories weren't lies. Those who told them believed them because they filled a purpose. Do you understand?"

"I think so," Nola replied, wishing that she did not.

"I believed them. I stopped going to the homes of my friends. I would speak to them only over the holo, and invited only those I knew well to my home. Then I began to worry. What if a friend were really a disguised assassin only waiting for the right moment? What if someone I knew had changed? Soon I was not seeing my friends. I grew afraid even to speak to them on the holo, as if they could step from the screen and crush me. It was as though some ancestral trait had been re-awakened, as if I had become one of those veiled women whose worlds were bounded by the walls of their homes, but, unlike those women, I did not even have the consolations of gossip with friends, a family, or an occasional trip to the *souk* to buy a bauble."

Nola lifted her wine slowly and sipped. Yasmin lowered her eyelids. "Perhaps I would still be in Meddah if a friend had not left me a message. 'Follow me,' she said, 'speak to Giancarlo Lawrence.' I listened to Giancarlo over the holo, but it took all the courage I had to leave my home and come here. By then I was almost ready for death, just to be rid of the fear. It was such a paradox, wanting to die so the fear would leave me, while having that overwhelming fear of death itself. Giancarlo gave me back my life." She stretched out her arms. "I went through the little death, and my fear was gone."

Nola leaned forward. "The little death?"

"It's only a name. You should talk to Giancarlo, Nola. I'm not good at explaining it, I'm afraid."

Hilde began to speak of her vegetable garden, losing Nola's attention. She knew all she had to know about this settlement. Giancarlo Lawrence was obviously some crank who had cooked up a theory and talked others into believing it. There were many such theorists; even Luna had a few, though their notions usually did not survive in that barren place and they often left for more fertile soil.

Lawrence was probably one of the harmless ones. Those who wanted a sense of community would sometimes cluster around a charismatic figure. There was lots of time to try on new ideas and see which ones fit. The fact of long life and the possibility of learning as much as one could did not seem to hold the emotional power of a closed system that seemed certain and final.

The world had wanted immortality, and that had been bestowed. What greater gift could there be? Now the biologists made only toys; she thought of Lise Trang's android elf.

Nola gazed at the darkened window, thinking of Luna's night and the unchanging rocky landscape of a dead world. She rarely thought of it as dead; it was eternal, a fitting home for people who were deathless. On Earth, nature's cycle still continued; death still called.

II

The tower drew Nola. She stood at the fork in the road, then turned right. Maple trees lined the road. A breeze stirred the limbs and she felt droplets of water on her face and arms. The road was muddy; dirt clung to her boots.

She reached the tower's shadow and looked up. At the top of the turret, under the roof, she saw openings, and she thought of archers. It was a watchtower, a place for sentries and guards.

She approached the heavy wooden door, leaned against it, then pushed it with her hands.

"It isn't locked."

Nola turned. A slim figure covered by a cape was coming around the side of the turret; a solemn face, framed by a blue hood, watched her. The stranger seemed very young; only a young person would seem so serious, since frivolity was a characteristic of the old.

"I wasn't going to go inside," Nola said.

"You can if you like."

She stepped back. "Maybe I'd better not."

"I haven't been inside either." The stranger's voice was a high-pitched tenor. "I haven't been here very long. My name's Teno."

"I'm Nola Reann."

"We don't see many people from space."

She felt herself slouching, as if to minimize her height. "You can imagine why. Even with the wire web, it's difficult. Your body feels heavy and fragile at the same time. The weather is disorienting. And walking around like this on the surface—well, I can never shake the feeling that it's dangerous, that I'm unprotected."

"I think I know what you mean," Teno said. "I lived on Asgard for a while. When I came back to Earth, it seemed inside out, because I was used to looking up and seeing the clouds and, beyond them, the other side of the world. It took a while to get over that."

Nola turned back toward the door, and when she looked around, Teno was gone. She saw a flash of blue among the trees. She backed away from the turret; the air seemed chillier in its shadow.

She went back down the road, retracing her steps until she stood before a square gray house faced with flat stones. A man in a robe of red silk sat on the patio sipping tea. He waved, motioning for her to join him. She went up to the patio, sat down in a wicker chair, and he handed her a cup.

"I am Jiro Ikiru," he said.

"Nola Reann."

He gazed at her sticklike arms. "I'd guess you're from the moon. You're too lean for Mars."

She nodded.

"I thought I saw another hovercraft near Yasmin Hallal's," he went on, being courteously indirect.

"It's mine." Nola sipped her tea. "I just met her yesterday, but she asked me to be her guest."

"Now that it's summer, more people will return. Many don't care to brave the rigors of winter. I'm sure you'll enjoy meeting them."

"I knew Mikhail Vilny before," she said. "I met a woman named Hilde last night, and someone called Teno a few minutes ago, by the turret."

Jiro was silent as he passed her a plate of tiny pastries. Then he leaned back in his chair. "Some people feel a little uncomfortable around Teno."

"Why?"

"There was a project a few decades back. A biologist produced people who were physically stronger and presumably more rational than we. These beings don't have certain hormonal reactions, don't feel our emotions. They're hermaphroditic as well. Teno is one of them."

"Now I remember," Nola said. "I went to the place where their parents were bringing them up. I had an argument with two people there. I told them that they were trying to change human nature before they fully understood what we were. We're adaptable, we have minds, we have all the time we need to learn."

"You thought the project was premature?"

"I thought it was wrong." The emotional force of her objections surprised her once again. The creatures looked like human beings; that seemed the worst travesty of all.

"When Teno came here," Jiro said, "it upset some people. Even Giancarlo was worried." He paused. "You see, what we have here is based on faith—our lives are the result of certain convictions which are perhaps hard for anyone to accept who hasn't spoken to Giancarlo or heard of the higher state. I don't know if Teno can feel this faith or grasp it. But Giancarlo realized it's not his place to decide these matters or to bar anyone from the truth. So Teno remains."

Nola stirred restlessly. "I don't know what you're talking about."

Jiro smiled, obviously anxious to explain. "You really should talk to Giancarlo, but I can tell you a bit. The higher state is simply the life after this one. All of us here have seen it —we've stepped outside these bodies and experienced it."

Nola stared at him. His light brown face glowed; he seemed convinced of what he had said. "And how have you seen this higher state?"

"By dying." She started, and gripped the arms of her chair. "Oh, it's not what you think. We're monitored the whole time. We're put under, suspended, and gradually our life functions are stopped. This lasts only a few moments, but in those moments, we see the next life; we are held by eternity. Then we're revived. It takes only a few seconds or so—of our time here, of course—and I haven't yet seen anyone who hasn't come away changed."

Nola watched him cautiously. "Forgive me for saying this, but it sounds mad, and dangerous as well."

"It isn't, believe me. We use the same equipment rescue teams use. Giancarlo knows medicine and was part of a rescue team. That was how he made his discovery. He spends some time teaching us rescue techniques." Jiro peered at her with his small dark eyes. "It may seem strange to you. But look around. Has it harmed us? Have you met anyone who isn't at peace?"

"I've met almost no one here," she said drily. "And it isn't that simple. There are people who get along; they aren't all unhappy."

"Of course. But many pursue enjoyment for its own sake. That can't remain satisfying. Many only seek sensations, with no concern for others."

"Are you that different?" she asked. "You're here, hiding away from the world."

"We're preparing ourselves," he replied. "We leave when we're ready. Most of us will probably join rescue teams. We don't plan to stay here forever. Nothing is forever in this world." He smiled at his little joke.

Nola did not smile back. Metaphysical discussions made her uncomfortable and irritable. Assumptions were advanced which could neither be proven false nor demonstrated in the world, and those who had swallowed them wore looks of complacency and pitied those who failed to understand or agree. She thought of her own beliefs, her feeling that the biologists were wrong to tamper with the human form and mind. It isn't the same, she told herself. Their experiments would fail and they would find out they had been wrong not to allow humankind to evolve in its own way. Tampering with biology could narrow the range of possibilities; granting immortality had not been tampering, only opening each life to more possibilities.

Nola's chain of reasoning stopped there. Did she believe that in fact there was some purpose, some end toward which all life moved? Was there a metaphysical assumption buried somewhere in her thinking? She shook off the feeling. That was the trouble with this sort of pondering; it led one to doubt common sense.

"You seem unconvinced," Jiro said softly. "But argument won't convince you of what Giancarlo teaches, and it's not the evidence by itself that matters. It won't convince anyone trapped in doubt."

"I don't think of doubt as a trap. I think of it as a useful procedure."

"I suppose it is, up to a point. We've all doubted. It's necessary at first."

Nola rose. "Thank you for the tea. I must go."

Jiro stood up and bowed. "We must talk again."

Nola had still not met Giancarlo Lawrence, but she had seen his house, a large log cabin down the left side of the forked road. At first she had been surprised by the simple structure, then annoyed; it seemed so blatant, this simple home for the simple man of faith.

She had thought of searching the computer for information on the man, or for his visual image. Her implant could have helped her in the search, but she did not rely on it as much here. Somehow, in this setting, during the long, unscheduled days, the device seemed intrusive, something that interfered with her senses instead of aiding them. She would try to approach this Giancarlo Lawrence without preconceptions and see him as he was.

She thought about all this as she and Jiro climbed a hill just outside the stone wall. The hill had been cleared of most of its trees, and Jiro had suggested a picnic. He carried a basket while Nola trudged behind him. The warm air was thick with odors; the scents of pine cones, grass, wildflowers, and her own sweat threatened to choke her. A bee buzzed past her and she froze for a moment until it flew away.

Jiro stopped and rummaged in the basket while Nola sat down carefully, looking around apprehensively at the ground. Jiro spread a white cloth. She looked out over the settlement. Three people were walking toward the turret; she recognized Hilde's yellow hair. Two others were with her.

"There's Giancarlo," Jiro said as he struggled with a corkscrew. Nola leaned forward, but the trio was inside the tower before she could get a good look. "The one in the long white tunic." He handed her a glass of wine and she sipped it while he laid out their lunch. She nibbled at pâté and an egg while Jiro sat on his heels and gnawed at a piece of chicken. His long black hair swayed around his face as he moved his head and looked up the hill. "I think we're going to have guests."

She followed his glance. Mikhail and Teno were walking down the hill toward them. As they came nearer, Mikhail nodded at Jiro, then turned to Nola. "We don't want to disturb you," he said.

"Don't be silly," Jiro replied. "There's plenty of food." Mikhail sat down. Teno sat between him and Nola. Jiro produced two more glasses and plates; he had come equipped.

"No wine for me," Teno said. Mikhail accepted a glass and helped himself to a little of everything. Teno took only a few carrot sticks and strawberries.

Nola drained her glass and accepted more wine. The careless mood of the outing had been shattered. She glanced from Mikhail to Teno. Mikhail grinned nervously; he looked away from her eyes. He was obviously surprised to see her here. She thought: He wanted me to leave. He wanted me to say I wasn't angry and then go.

"You must be adjusting," he said to her. "You climbed up this hill."

"I have been feeling better," she said coldly. "The web helps, of course. Sometimes it overcompensates, and then I'm even stronger." She heard an arch tone in her voice which she did not like.

Mikhail was silent. She noticed that Teno was wearing a Bond, the only one beside her own that she had seen here.

"I saw Hilde going to the tower again, with Giancarlo and Ramon," Jiro murmured.

"Again?" Mikhail shook his head. "Whatever for?" His voice was higher and his blue eyes were wide. He seemed relieved at having his attention drawn away from Nola. "Does she need to relive it so often?"

Jiro bit into an egg. "I think Hilde hopes that Giancarlo won't be able to bring her back."

Mikhail shook his head. "No, that can't be it. There are other ways. Besides, Giancarlo has told us that suicide is wrong. As Socrates said, we must not desert our post without a sign from our Keeper."

He nodded and smiled, while Jiro smiled back. Nola was exasperated with their smug, happy faces; Mikhail had put down his plate and was hugging himself with his arms, as if nurturing a secret truth.

"What about you?" she asked the solemn Teno. "Have you been through this whatever-it-is?"

"No," Teno replied.

"Do you plan to?"

"I haven't decided. I came here out of curiosity, not out of need. I think Giancarlo would like to see me experience the little death as a test of some sort. He seems to feel it would support his philosophy if my experience is the same as that of the others. I find that attitude paradoxical. If he has faith, which by its very nature cannot be verified or disproven, then why would he seek such verification?"

"He's not looking for verification," Jiro responded. "He only wants you to understand." .

"I do understand. Giancarlo wants belief." Teno reached for another carrot stick.

Nola let her glass drop to the cloth. The wine had gone to her head; she felt dazed. "Listen, Jiro." Her voice was a little too loud. "You go through something that convinces you there's another life. But you don't die. If someone can be revived, it means he wasn't really dead in the first place—just in suspension. So how do you know that what you experience is anything more than biochemical brain activity, and how do you know that it doesn't stop as soon as you're dead?"

"I have," said Teno softly, "asked that myself. There is a contradiction involved in asking what happens to you when you're dead—in other words, when you don't exist. It's like asking where you were before you were born."

Jiro shook his head. "If you've experienced it yourself, the question has no meaning. You know."

"How do you know?" Nola leaned forward, unwilling to let go of the argument. "You just think you know. You have no proof. All that you have is the activity of a dying brain, and you supply the interpretation yourself. Maybe your faith is caused by brain damage. Have you ever thought of that?"

Jiro laughed. Nola drew back, resting on one elbow. It was useless. She had supposed that she could introduce a doubt into Jiro's mind, or Mikhail's, but they had probably heard all the arguments before.

"What can I say?" Jiro answered. "It isn't a matter in which you can argue your way to truth."

Teno was watching her. She lifted a brow. For a moment she thought Teno was trying to form a silent bond with her: We're in this together—at least we understand that they're deluding themselves. But the gray eyes were empty. Teno either did not feel like an outsider or was used to being one.

Giancarlo Lawrence was clever, concealing himself from the newcomer while she lived among them, knowing that they were content while she was not. By the time he showed himself, she would be more than willing to accept his ideas. Well, he didn't know her. She would not be so easy to convince.

Mikhail got to his knees. "We must be going." He stood up. The shadow of his arm on the cloth embraced Nola's silhouette. He smiled at her and turned away.

She watched them go down the hill. An ant was crawling over the cloth; she brushed at it idly with her hand while Jiro searched his basket. "Apple pie," he said, tempting her.

"You must be joking." She was stuffed; she realized that she had been nibbling nervously while Mikhail and Teno had been with them.

"Well, I'm going to have some." Jiro held a wedge of pie in his hand and gobbled it, taking swipes at his lips with a napkin. Teno and Mikhail, now approaching the stone wall, seemed deep in conversation. Mikhail hopped over the wall easily, then extended a hand to Teno.

Nola stretched out on the grass and stared at the sky. It was blue and cloudless; the clear weather would hold for at least one more day. "Doesn't Teno make you uncomfortable?" she asked.

"No," Jiro answered, his mouth full of pie. "At least I know I'm not going to get some sort of emotional outburst or a signal of boredom, or any of that."

"I wouldn't have thought you'd have such problems here, where you all possess the truth." She tried to soften the sarcasm with a smile.

"We have our difficulties. Hilde, for instance. Everything is settled for her. Her curiosity is at an end, though I don't imagine she had much to begin with. I think that's an error. Even the higher state—the life beyond—isn't a permanent, unchanging one—learning still continues."

"How can you possibly know that?"

"I could tell you that it was revealed to me when I underwent the little death. But you'd say it's a delusion."

"I suppose I would."

"Teno is willing to consider the possibility. A rational being, one designed for reasoned and dispassionate action, without our capacity to make errors by heeding only our feelings, lives here and is willing to listen to what Giancarlo has to say."

"Teno still seems doubtful."

Jiro shrugged. "We'll see."

The setting sun bathed Nola in pink light. She stood at the window, watching Yasmin and Jiro walk toward the fork in the road. Two other people joined them; the group turned toward Giancarlo Lawrence's log cabin. She saw Mikhail leave his house, and turned away.

She threaded her way past stacks of books and settled herself on the sofa after clearing away a pile of papers. The voice inside her spoke: *Did you come here only to be alone?*

Nola sighed. Clarify, her mind murmured back to the voice.

You spend a great deal of time alone at your work, and you needed to be among people. Yet here you are in a group where you are an outsider.

She assented silently.

My recommendation is that you leave and visit a space settlement. There would be less physical strain on a low-gravity world, and you would be among others like yourself.

She felt irritated. I can get along fine, she replied.

But you are not getting along fine. You are lonely. You feel sad.

The soft, gentle voice lulled her and prodded her at the same time. She thought of the cybernetic mind that spoke to her through the implanted link, and wondered again if it was her servant or her master. She was its eyes and ears; she, and others like her, carried it to places it would not otherwise see. It knew the thoughts and feelings she did not share with others. It was learning a lot about human beings; it would draw its own conclusions. Eventually, all the cyberminds would grow silent, and people, searching for malfunctions and trying to make repairs, would not realize that at last they had been abandoned. The links would no longer speak.

Sing to me, she said. There was a short silence, and a chamber orchestra played; she heard the tinkle of a harpsichord. Mikhail had resented the implant; he had never understood it, feeling that it was a third party in their relationship and not part of her at all. She remembered the last days before he left, when she had told him she would have it removed, knowing as she said it that she could not have done so.

The music soothed her. The melody was simple, the rhythm repetitive. She closed her eyes.

She came to herself abruptly. A violin was singing in her ears. She opened her eyes. The room was dark. She shut off the music and heard voices.

A light went on overhead. Yasmin was waving her arms and laughing while Teno followed her into the room. She glanced at Nola before she sat down. "Did you fall asleep in here?"

Nola sat up. A muscle in her shoulder ached. "I guess so. I ate too much today. All that food makes me tired."

"It's the meat and wine that do it," Teno said, sitting down in a chair.

"I don't suppose they affect you," Nola said.

"They would if I consumed them. I can live on vegetables and fruit; my metabolism is quite efficient. I remember my first experience with drinking. At first, it seemed to help my reasoning. Illumination seemed to come more quickly. I drank more and began to lose track of my thoughts. Then I became sick. I saw no reason to cloud my mind in that way, so I'll only take a sip of wine now if it will put others at ease."

"How reasonable of you," Nola said, wondering if Teno was trying to be funny. "Doesn't it ever bother you? Do you ever resent what was done to you?" She was being rude; she wondered if Teno understood rudeness.

"What, exactly, was done to me, Nola?"

"You were an experiment, weren't you? You're not like us, you're another kind of being. They didn't have to do that to you."

"Why should I resent that? Do you resent the fact that you were born and raised on the moon and can't come here without an exoskeleton?"

Nola shook her head. "Of course not. But that isn't the same. I'm still human."

"I am the way that I am." Teno's gray eyes gazed steadily at her. "If I resented it, that would mean that I wanted to be somebody else. And if I were someone else, which is clearly impossible, then I wouldn't be me. It's irrational and pointless to hope for such a thing."

"I suppose you have a reasonable answer to everything."

"No, not everything. Sometimes I have to say that I don't know the answer."

Nola frowned, wondering for a moment if that was a joke, and if Teno knew how to be sarcastic.

"You're tired," Yasmin said.

"Yes, I know." Nola stood up. "Good night." She went to the spiral staircase and trudged up it wearily. As she moved toward her room, she heard footsteps behind her. She stopped at the door of her room and turned. Teno and Yasmin passed her. "Good night," Teno said. The pair lingered in front of Yasmin's door, then went inside together, closing the door behind them.

Nola stared into the darkness, feeling dizzy. She clung to the door, then managed to close it. She shuddered. How could Yasmin look at that body without being disgusted? How could Teno have any feelings of love or affection? She tried to imagine the scene; the childlike face, the build too broad in the shoulders and a bit too wide in the hips, the groin, the double set of organs. Did Yasmin make love to the woman or to the man?

Nola crossed the room, shedding her robe and letting the garment drop to the floor. She gazed toward her window; no moonlight shone tonight. She thought of Yasmin and Teno, able to see them all too vividly in her mind, Yasmin reclining on the bed, Teno bending over her—had Yasmin dimmed the lights? Or had she left them on, attracted by the visible mound and pestle and the possibilities they represented? Teno's reason apparently did not entail asexuality; she wondered if that had surprised Teno's creators.

She was still a Lunar provincial after all. If she wanted variety, there was enough in weightlessness at a space habitat after work, or on the moon with an earthborn partner, or with a surrogate image presented by the implant. She had not yet lived long enough to grow jaded, and often grew impatient with the lengthy, calculated flirtations designed to postpone consummation, and the inevitable boredom that followed it, for as long as possible. She thought of Mikhail. He had been able to lift her as if she were a child, bending her body in new positions.

She froze, her hand on a transparent shield. Teno had been with Mikhail that afternoon. Perhaps there was something between them. She shook, feeling the jealousy and helpless rage she had thought she could not feel any more. She remembered Mikhail's farewell. All her arguments came back, the same ones every rejected lover must have made at such a moment: Why can't you wait until it's over for me, too? What is another year, or decade, when you have so many ahead of you? It costs you nothing to stay until then; don't you care enough to give me the extra time? You won't suffer if you stay, but I'll suffer if you go now, and all it will cost you is a little extra time. We waste time, we throw it away. For a moment, she was back on Luna, hearing the whine in her voice as her mind repeated the words. None of it had mattered. He had left anyway.

She looked down at her feet, barely visible in the glow of the gravitic generator. They were long and thin, covered with a network of blue veins and the silver threads of her web. She was suddenly conscious of how she must appear to people here; pale-skinned, arms and legs little more than bones and epidermis, a hollow belly, tiny breasts, every one of her ribs so clearly outlined that each could be counted. She would seem repellent to many, perhaps intriguing or birdlike to some. Maybe that had been her attraction for Mikhail; she must have seemed a freak. Now he wanted another freak.

She walked into the chamber, signaled her implant, lifted herself from the floor and floated; in a moment she was calm again, picturing Luna's clean, barren landscape.

III

As Nola descended the staircase, Yasmin bustled below; her pink robe billowed around her, making her dark head appear to be at the center of a flower. The other woman waved a hand at the table near the window as she passed Nola.

Nola sat down at the table; there were only two cups next to the porcelain coffee pot and plate of rolls. Yasmin returned and put a bowl of oranges next to the rolls, then sat down with her back to the window. The morning fog was a misty curtain beyond the glass.

"Where's Teno?" Nola asked carefully.

"Home." Yasmin peeled an orange. "By the way, I have important news. That's why I'm up so early. Giancarlo wants to see you. He called this morning." She handed part of the orange to Nola.

"How nice," Nola replied. "So I'm to be summoned into the great man's presence at last. Do I attend him at his house? Is there a special title by which I address him?"

"Of course not. He'll come here tonight. He's busy; that's why he hasn't come before."

"I should think he would be busy. Promoting gullibility is very time-consuming." She chewed on an orange section while Yasmin poured coffee.

"I once felt that way. I wouldn't have come here if I hadn't been desperate. Giancarlo's used to doubts; you won't have to be polite."

"I'm always polite, in my own way."

"Giancarlo has a lot to do. There's his rescue work."

Nola looked up from her coffee. "He's still on a team?"

"Of course."

"That must be convenient. People who've had a close call must make good recruits."

"Giancarlo doesn't force anything on people. If someone's interested, that's fine."

Nola sipped coffee, finished her orange, and reached for a roll. She already knew what Giancarlo Lawrence wanted; she had seen it in the reverential faces of Yasmin and Jiro and Hilde as they spoke of him. It gratified him to see that look, the adoring eyes, the respectful voices. He had everything else, as did everyone; time and any material possessions he desired, along with youth and health. The only thing left to seek was power. He could not gain it by promising anything in this world, so he promised more in the next, and was rewarded with adoration.

Nola had never thought much about the people who worked on rescue teams. She had assumed that they were selfless sorts who willingly gave much of their time watching for the distress signals sent by Bonds when people were in trouble, and were ready to travel into areas that could be remote and dangerous. Now she wondered. She saw them rushing to aid a person while filled with a sense of their own virtue and power, presenting themselves as saviors, dispensing life. Giancarlo was a rescuer. He savored the grateful glances. He must have decided that he wanted even more.

Nola got up. "Excuse me. I'd better get a walk in now. I'll need to rest this afternoon."

"The fog—" Yasmin started to say, but Nola was already hurrying to the door. She stepped into the mist, feeling the moisture on her face and hands. She was lost, without signposts. Yasmin's house had disappeared when she looked back; the road ahead led into the unknown. She followed the road until the iron gate floated before her, then left it and crossed the grass to the stone wall, seating herself on the damp surface.

She had heard Yasmin's tale; she knew that the woman's present life was better than the closed-off, fearful one she had once led. But it made her angry that Yasmin had lost her fear by allowing herself to be deceived. The fog was lifting slightly; she could now see more of the road.

An image came to her mind. Part of it was vague; something had happened, and the people here had lost faith in Giancarlo. They gathered in front of the turret, doubt and fear on their faces. They seized Giancarlo and dragged him to the gate, thrusting him through it, expelling him from their midst. She tried to summon up an image of the man, but he remained only a pair of arms and an indistinct voice, pleading. Nola stood at the gate, smiling.

And then the doubt-filled faces turned to her. Mikhail came forward and took her hand and she smiled still more as she clasped his. She had revealed the deception. They would now have to live as she did.

Yasmin had brought out hashish, setting the pipes on the glass-topped table next to a bowl of candies. Nola sat in a large, overstuffed chair, her feet on an ottoman. She had hidden her skinniness under a blue velvet caftan. Yasmin fidgeted, plucking at her yellow robe. She had cleaned the area around the table, making it an oasis of order and banishing the dust balls to other parts of the room, but she had forgotten to polish the glass; the top of the table was streaked.

Nola heard footsteps outside the front door. She stiffened, but did not rise. A shadow stepped through the doorway and into the light.

She was not sure what she had expected to see in the man; perhaps a large build, a domineering manner, or a magnetic, vivid presence with a loud voice and expansive gestures. This man was thin and small. His dark hair was short; his face was that of a boy. He said, "I'm Giancarlo Lawrence." He said it as if he were apologizing for it.

"Nola Reann," she said. He came to her and she touched his extended hand carefully; too often, people here would grip her hand too tightly, forgetting her fragility, and she would return the clasp with firmness, unmindful of the added strength the web gave her. The greeting would end with sore hands and embarrassment. But Giancarlo touched her hand lightly, then withdrew.

He bowed to Yasmin; his hands hung awkwardly at his sides. Then he seated himself at one end of the sofa, bumping a leg against the table, and stared at his hands, as if he did not know what to do with them. He did not seem at home in his body. He wore an old blue shirt and wrinkled white cotton slacks; his feet were sandaled. The more she looked at him, the more calculated his appearance seemed; the simple clothes, the boyishness. And a little child shall lead them. Her mouth twisted. He would not only dominate them with odd notions, but would also call on their protective instincts. It had to be deliberate; with regeneration, they were all able to choose how to look. Giancarlo had the unfinished features and the awkwardness of a person near the end of adolescence. She lowered her eyes slightly, and noticed something else.

She almost laughed. Giancarlo raised an eyebrow as she spoke. "You're wearing a Bond."

He nodded.

"That doesn't show much faith in your ideas."

"What do you know of my ideas?"

"Enough. There's another life. The others don't wear Bonds, meaning that they don't worry too much about saying their final farewells. But you do."

He smiled. His face was open and ingenuous, and his smile twisted his thin lips. "I don't wear it for myself," he replied. "I'm a rescuer—I can be called at any time. Without my Bond, precious moments could be lost."

Yasmin lit a pipe. She glanced from Giancarlo to Nola and then back, smiling all the time. Nola refused to smile, frowning as she accepted the pipe from Yasmin.

"Why have you come here, Nola?" Giancarlo asked.

"To see my friend Mikhail Vilny."

"You've seen Mischa, but you're still here."

"I'm curious. And maybe I'm waiting to see if Mikhail comes to his senses. I can always hope that he will."

"Then you feel no need for guidance or help."

"No. I don't think much of cults. Some of them are harmless enough, but some are filled with dangerous, suicidal sorts who've decided they'll take others with them. I don't particularly care what they do to themselves; I can even admire it at times, since it shows that they have the courage of their convictions, but not when they take someone else along. Maybe we need them to give our lives a little excitement." She gestured with her pipe. "You seem harmless, but deluded."

"I don't think I'm deluded," he said calmly. "But I can understand why you might think so. Here we are, with eternal life and youth, able to do whatever we like. If there is something beyond our capabilities now, we have time enough to develop a means for achieving it. We no longer have to tell ourselves metaphysical fairy tales about a greater purpose or a god who loves us or an afterlife where justice is meted out as a consolation for our brief existence and the unfairness of life here. We have our lives, we create our own purpose. What happens to us now is only the result of our own carelessness or ignorance or failure of malevolence. We are free, if we want to be." He tilted his head. "Have I got it right?"

Nola felt annoyed. She drew in smoke from her pipe and did not answer.

"We're free," he said softly. "How could we wish for more? We might live a thousand years, two thousand, a million. Theoretically, there's no limit. If our brains get too cluttered, we can clear them and start over—we've even achieved a form of reincarnation. If our sun becomes unstable, we can leave this system and go elsewhere. Perhaps we might even transform the material of our bodies and outlive the death of the universe. Isn't that so?"

She had to strain to hear his voice. She wondered if the man always spoke this way, so quietly that one had to concentrate to catch every word. The hashish was burning her throat; she put her pipe down.

Giancarlo sucked on his pipe, then set it on the table. "Once, human beings looked beyond this life. It was only the prelude to another. But at the same time, they struggled to transform this one. And why not? Why suffer needlessly? Why not make this life better? And what if there were nothing else? Then the suffering and pain would be useless." His dark eyes glistened; he blinked, as if suppressing tears. "Notions of immateriality are fragile. The material world will always drag one back. The argument *ad lapidam* is always powerful; you will keep stubbing your toe on the stone. Change the stone— don't pretend it isn't there or isn't important. Move it out of your path, or shatter it, or make a sculpture out of it. Control the world, don't be a victim of it. We've freed ourselves. Haven't we?"

"Yes, we have," Nola said firmly.

"Then why is there still unhappiness? Why do so many hide, prisoners of their long lives?"

She shook her head. "It's obvious. A lot of people just don't have sense. They're stupid, or easily bored. They don't have enough curiosity to learn new things and they begin to see danger where there isn't any. It's their own fault. It's a kind of natural selection, in a way. Some will adapt to long life, and others won't."

Giancarlo leaned forward. "Don't you wonder if they aren't being logical, given what most of them believe? These lives are all they have, the material world is all there is. A bit of inconvenience is enough to throw many people into a rage—as if the world is deliberately affronting them." He smiled. "Here we've overcome some of those attitudes. We live simply, so that we don't have too much of an attachment to material things. We are preparing ourselves for another life."

Nola laughed softly, trying to shake off the spell of his voice. "I see. In its own way, it sounds as self-indulgent as anything else. Ever since I arrived, I've seen self-satisfaction and smug smiles and people nurturing their so-called truth."

"I can understand your feelings," he said calmly. "But this is only a temporary abode for those who need a place to recover their sense of purpose and to lose their fears. Eventually, they become rescuers and leave, though some feel that they can serve best in other ways. People aren't truly happy unless they look outside themselves to some greater purpose, and being on a rescue team is important work. Not enough people want to do it."

Nola frowned. "How commendable of you. And it doesn't hurt that such work is useful to you. You have a captive audience. I'll bet you don't miss a chance to get your ideas across."

Giancarlo did not seem disturbed by her comment. "If someone is interested, I share what I know."

"I'm sure you do. But don't call it knowledge."

"How can I help you understand?" He held out his hands, palms up. "I know that there is another life, and that a part of us lives on after death. I have seen God's promise to us. A part of us survives."

"And is this part of us material?" Nola asked. "And if it isn't, how is it connected to the material world? And if it is itself material, how do you know it survives? How do you know it doesn't die eventually?"

"I know. I have been near death myself."

"You don't know anything. You've seen hallucinations; you have no proof. You've only come up with a new version of a very old idea. Maybe people needed it once, but we don't need it now. I'm not even sure you believe all that nonsense."

Giancarlo lifted his chin. "Would I be here if I didn't believe it?"

"Oh, come now. Surely you're gratified that other people turn to you and honor you, maybe even worship you." She glanced at Yasmin, who was sliding the bowl of candies toward Giancarlo.

"Why are you still here, Nola? You say you're curious, yet you dismiss what I tell you." He spoke slowly. He was not smiling.

"Are you going to ask me to leave?" She stared straight at him, searching his face for signs of the charlatan. He stared back. "Why don't you throw me out? You wouldn't want to have too many doubts raised. It might get uncomfortable for you."

He looked down. "Why should I ask you to leave?" He rested his arms on his legs. "I don't mind questions. Talk to others. If you want to question what I teach, you're free to do so. My ideas can withstand doubt, and I'm sure my companions here can, too. Ideas should be tested, after all." His patient, gentle voice pronounced each word carefully, but quickly, as if he had said the phrases many times before. He rose. "I must go. If you'd like to speak to me again, please feel free to come to my home. I'd enjoy the discussion, I'm sure."

She thought: No, you wouldn't. As he moved toward the door, he halted and looked back at her. "You might find that I have something to offer you, Nola."

"I'm content the way I am."

"Perhaps." He left.

Nola, depressed, began to think of arguments she should have made. "Was I polite enough?" she asked Yasmin.

"I'm sure he's heard worse."

"Maybe I should have been more severe, then."

Yasmin refilled her pipe, lit it, and drew up her feet. "Want some more?"

"No." Nola suddenly wanted to get out of the room. Her limbs seemed paralyzed; she was unable to move. Help me, her mind whispered to itself. Giancarlo had hypnotized her; she was sure of it. She stared silently at Yasmin, envying the woman's complacence.

"He can help you," Yasmin said. "You're unhappy—I can see it. You have a sickness of the soul. Giancarlo can help you."

Nola sighed.

The blond stranger was coming up the road in a red electric cart piled high with knapsacks. He was slouched over the front panel, peering through the windshield. His wavy hair fluttered. He drove up to the fork in the road and stopped, then turned back, halting in front of Jiro's lawn.

"Jiro," Nola said. Jiro turned off his weeder and looked up. The man was getting out of the cart. "Do you know him?"

Jiro shook his head. The visitor's long white shirt flapped around his hips as he walked. His perfect face was deeply tanned; his pants, cut off above the knees, revealed muscular brown legs covered with blond down. He raised a hand.

"Hello," Jiro said, holding his weeder as if it were a spear.

"I'm looking for Giancarlo Lawrence," the man called out.

"Take the road to the left. You'll see a log cabin with a weeping willow in the front."

"Thanks." The stranger turned away.

"Wait," Nola said impulsively, following the man to the road. "I'll show you the way."

"That's very kind of you. Let's walk. I need to stretch my legs."

He left his cart at the side of the road and they walked together silently to the fork. Nola kept to the shade under the nearby trees, worrying about sunburn and regretting her short blue shift. The man strode quickly, his arms swinging at his sides. She glanced at his face. He seemed calm; he did not have the look of desperation or doubt. She wondered why he was here.

"Does Giancarlo know you?" she asked as they turned left.

"No."

"Does he know you're coming?"

"No."

"Maybe he won't be able to see you, then."

"Why shouldn't he?"

"He might be busy. I was here for quite a while before he deigned to pay me a visit."

The man looked at her from the sides of his eyes. "You sound as though you're a little disappointed in Giancarlo Lawrence."

"Oh, not really. I didn't expect much to begin with, so I can hardly say I'm disappointed. I guess I should warn you. I'm the resident skeptic at the moment."

The blond man smiled. It seemed a curious reaction. Perhaps the visitor was here for the same reason she had come; he might be looking for a deluded friend or lover. Unlike her, he was going to take direct action instead of wasting his time.

They approached Giancarlo's house. The man raised an eyebrow when he saw it. "How nice," he said. She thought she heard a chuckle. "How very Leo Tolstoy. The humble, spiritual man." He began to walk up the flagstone path. She hesitated, then followed him. He stopped for a moment.

"Do you want me to go?" she asked.

His lip curled. "Please stay, by all means. I'd rather have you here."

"He might not be home."

His blue eyes narrowed. Nola felt uneasy. He continued up the path.

As they reached the front door, it opened. Teno came outside, followed by Giancarlo, who raised his eyebrows when he saw the stranger and Nola.

"Is one of you Giancarlo Lawrence?" the man asked.

"Yes," Giancarlo answered. "I am."

"I thought so. I just wanted to be sure." The stranger bent forward a bit, fumbling with his shirt. Then he was holding a weapon, aiming it at Giancarlo.

Nola froze. She thought: He's from another cult. Giancarlo was raising his slender hands. She saw his eyes. He was terrified. He backed away.

"No." Giancarlo's voice was high. Teno moved slowly to one side, crouching a bit, as if preparing to leap at the visitor. Nola held her breath. Teno's gray eyes were cold, as if the mind behind them were calculating the chances of thwarting the attack. Giancarlo's hands were shaking. He pressed them together, as if praying. "No."

"No?" The blond man suddenly dropped his wand. "Don't worry," he said harshly. "It isn't even charged. So you're afraid, too, in spite of what you say. Oh, I wanted to see that. I'm not about to make you a martyr." The visitor turned and hurried down the path.

Nola was too stunned to go after him. Giancarlo stared at the wand in the grass. Teno leaned over and picked it up.

"He was right," Teno said. "It isn't charged."

"You were afraid," Nola said, "weren't you."

Giancarlo raised his head. Two red spots had appeared on his cheeks. "It wasn't time. I have too much to do. You shouldn't have brought him here." His voice croaked the words.

"I didn't know what he was going to do. I thought he was looking for your guidance." She tried to summon up some sympathy for Giancarlo, but failed. "Strange, you being afraid. I thought you didn't fear death. Maybe the next one will bring a loaded weapon. Then at least you'll be able to give your theory a real test."

Giancarlo was watching her. The red spots were larger, and the pale skin of his face was drawn tight against his skull. He was angry. She wondered if he was angrier at the visitor or at her. He clasped his hands together and looked down at the ground. When he raised his head again, he seemed calmer.

"It isn't death that frightens me," he murmured. "It's being injured, or feeling pain. We can repair so much damage to the body, and yet it still seems so fragile."

Nola did not believe him. It was death that had frightened him; even his faith had not dispelled all his fears.

"Would you like me to stay?" Teno asked in a toneless voice.

"No. I think I'd rather be alone." Giancarlo went back up the path to his door.

Nola turned away and walked toward the road. Teno was following her; she slowed her pace. "What do you think?" she asked. "Was he afraid, or wasn't he?"

"I'm sure he was. Anyone would be. Certain reactions take place in the body, and reason is slow to override them."

"But that isn't true of you, is it. You weren't afraid."

"I don't have the same physiology. I don't react that way. Of course, my reflexes must be quicker than yours in order to make up for that, or my reason would be too slow to take action when necessary."

"You could have made a mistake. The man might have had a charged weapon."

"Of course I could have made a mistake. But I wouldn't have acted unless I was sure my chances were good."

They walked to the fork in the road without speaking. A breeze fluttered Teno's dark curls. Nola looked down the road. The red cart was rolling toward the gate.

Teno said, "I went to see Giancarlo to tell him that I wish to undergo the little death."

Nola turned. She searched the olive-skinned face, trying to imagine that solemn visage with one of the self-satisfied smiles everyone else here wore. "You surprise me, Teno."

"I don't see why I should."

"I thought you didn't have our little quirks."

"I'm curious. I want to see what happens to me. Giancarlo is pleased. But the faith he feels is not possible for me."

They moved toward Jiro's lawn. Jiro had put down his weeder and was wiping his brow with one bare arm. "Why isn't it possible?" Nola asked.

"Faith involves an emotional conviction. Sometimes reason can aid or support it, sometimes faith goes against reason. But reason alone cannot lead one to a faith such as Giancarlo's. There is that leap that is required, and I can't make the leap."

"Then why bother?" she said. "Why go through all that, if you know you can't accept it?"

"Because I would like to see if I experience what others here have. And though I can't have the sort of faith Giancarlo de-

mands, I can at least assign some sort of probability to his
notions, based on my own reason."

She stepped into the shade under an oak. She was beginning
to wonder if her companion was being honest with her. Did
Teno secretly feel a stirring of emotion, a need for something
more than reason? "You see," Teno went on, "it might be
possible to support what he says rationally, once one has gone
to the other side. Here one needs faith; one can't have anything else. It's like a baby trying to think of being outside the
womb."

Teno walked on. She hurried out of the shade and stubbed
her toe. She stared at the rock, then strode after Teno. "It's
nonsense," she said as she caught up.

"Is it? Giancarlo has some sort of notion that the next
world, or the higher state, as he calls it, represents the next
evolutionary step, and that, in a sense, we become another sort
of being. Now, I present a problem here. Do I exist on this
evolutionary ladder, or am I outside of it? I may have origi-
nated in human genetic material, but I was altered at concep-
tion."

Nola shrugged. "Any child born now is altered in some
way." She was trying to be generous. Teno still remained alien
and disorienting.

"But most are unchanged. They are completely human. Except for having certain genes tailored to avoid genetic defects,
they're no different from people born before the Transition.
Even you aren't different, because what's happened to you is
an adaptation to another environment. But I am different. In a
sense, I'm a member of a new species." Teno paused. "Giancarlo doesn't know how to react to what the biologists might
do, what they're already starting to do. He wants to know
whether the creation of new beings is in keeping with this pattern of his. If it is, then he can accept what the biologists do. If
not, then he must condemn it and take a stand against such
manipulations."

She frowned. "Surely you're not going to believe that your
existence was a mistake."

"Don't you already believe that?"

Nola refused to answer.

"Look." Teno gestured at the gate. Just beyond the stone
wall, the blond man who had threatened Giancarlo was pitch-
ing a tent. She smiled. "I must go," Teno continued. "I did
want to ask you something. I would like to have you there

when I go through my little death. Giancarlo tells me it's customary to invite anyone you wish to have present."

"Are you sure you want me there?" She looked away. "You must know that you make me uneasy."

"I'm used to that. I make many people uneasy. This is one of the few places I've been where most of the people feel comfortable with me." Nola thought she caught a trace of wistfulness in the steady voice; she was probably imagining it. "Perhaps I simply need another doubter with me when I endure Giancarlo's ministrations."

Teno raised a hand, then walked off, cutting across a grassy hill to another path, striding in the direction of Mikhail's home.

She made fists of her hands. She strode quickly to the gate. The tent was up now, and the blond man had disappeared inside it. She leaned against the gate. The stranger peeked out as he lifted a tent flap, and caught sight of her.

He waved and came out. She opened the gate and went toward him. "My name's Leif Arnesson." He showed his even white teeth. "And who might you be?"

"Nola Reann." She glanced at the faded green tent. "I didn't expect to see you again. Are you going to stay?"

"Why shouldn't I? Why give a man a scare and run away? It hardly seems sporting. I have everything I need, though I hope I can prevail on someone to feed me a good dinner once in a while. That is, if Lawrence doesn't run me off. I suppose he's a bit peeved."

"He won't make you leave. He believes he has the truth, so he can't very well bar someone from it."

Leif sat down on the ground, folding his legs. "He was scared. These death cult people are all the same."

"I don't think this is a death cult."

Leif snorted. "Anyone who says death is all right is a death cultist, wouldn't you say?" He brushed back a lock of hair. "He isn't the first one of those I've seen." He had lowered his voice, adopting a conspiratorial tone. "I visited another bunch a while back. The leader was scared of me. She talked a lot about suicide and risks, but I didn't see her rushing to have her name programmed into Mr. Death's banks." He laughed.

Nola stepped back. "What did you do?"

"I barely got out of there. They burned my leg off, and the rescue team just reached me in time. The attack on me gave some psychologists an excuse to go in. While I was in the hospital regenerating, I found out that some of the cultists had killed themselves, but the others, including the leader, had been sent to an asteroid. It's where they belong, don't you think?'' He grinned. "No way out if their reconditioning doesn't take.'' He rose and flexed his legs; he was almost as tall as she. "Bet you can't tell which one I lost.''

"Isn't it dangerous to go looking for trouble?''

Leif sat down again. "Oh, the danger doesn't bother me. I don't take real chances, anyway. I just don't like seeing what idiotic ideas do to people.''

"The people here seem content.''

"I thought you were a skeptic.''

"I am. I'm just stating a fact.''

He narrowed his eyes. "You don't seem to know what you think. Why did you come here, anyway?''

She looked down. "A man I knew came here. I followed him.''

Leif was staring at her slender legs. "A man. Well, that can be remedied. Do you have to wear those wires all the time?''

"All the time I'm here.''

"You were born out there, then.''

"Yes.''

"Do they get in the way?''

"Not at all.''

"Maybe you can give me a chance to find out whether they do or not. You could ask me to dinner some evening.'' He reached up and touched her fingertips. "You remind me of a birch tree.'' He took her hand. "But there are spiders' webs on your limbs.'' She had heard that particular comparison before. "I do hope we'll meet again soon.''

She released her hand, turned, and walked back to the gate, thinking of Mikhail.

Yasmin's loom clattered and hummed. She had designed a new tapestry and was waiting for the loom to weave it. "It's bad enough that he's here,'' she said to Nola. "But you needn't have asked him to my house.'' She was talking about Leif.

"He's only been here for a couple of days,'' Nola responded. "When he sees how jolly you all are, maybe he'll change his mind about Giancarlo. After all, he didn't hurt him. He has a strange sense of humor, that's all.'' She watched the loom, almost hypnotized by the clicking and the geometric

pattern of the tapestry. Her attention was caught by one blue
line in the middle trapped between mirror images of a hexagon
surrounding six-pointed stars. Something was drawing her to
Leif; he seemed dangerous, and instead of repelling her it
attracted her. He was reckless; he claimed that he avoided real
danger, yet he had almost died. She wasn't used to reckless
people; on Luna or in orbit, they were too likely to have accidents.

"At least we won't be alone with him tonight," Yasmin
murmured. "I asked some guests of my own to supper."

"Hilde and Jiro?" Nola asked absently.

"Teno and Mischa."

Nola looked up. "Tell me something," she said carefully.
"Do Teno and Mikhail spend a lot of time together?"

"Why, I don't know. I guess they have been together a lot
recently. Teno's very calming, in a way."

"Teno can't accept what the rest of you believe. Doesn't
that disturb you?"

"I don't know if that's true. Teno has to approach it from a
different direction, of course."

"And if Teno stays, it helps Giancarlo. By letting Teno stay,
Giancarlo seems to approve of what the biologists do, and in
return Teno can say his teachings are reasonable."

The loom clattered to a stop. Yasmin rose and lifted the
tapestry from it, glanced at the pattern, then threw it over the
back of the sofa. Now that she had finished the design and
seen it woven, she seemed to have lost interest in the tapestry
itself.

The door chimed. Yasmin went to answer it. Nola stared
over the sofa at the window beyond. The sky was darkening
early; it would rain.

Leif entered the room. He wore only his shorts; pale hairs
curled over his tan chest. Nola masked her unease with a smile.

The others did not join them until Yasmin had finished
cooking. Teno and Mikhail sat across from Nola and Leif.
Yasmin was at the head of the table.

After a flurry of greetings, they fell silent. Only the tinkling
of wineglasses and the clatter of cutlery on the plates could be
heard. Outside the open window, the clouds still threatened.

Nola felt disoriented. She had drunk too much with Leif
earlier while he skewered the world with verbal knives. She saw
the settlement, and those beyond it, crumbling and vanishing

from the earth. It all seemed impermanent and transitory; it was as though their long lives only emphasized the far longer life of the universe. Even a life of a million years was less than a second of cosmic time; they would flutter through their lives and disappear from the world, and the universe would be as it was. In the end, the remains of their decomposed bodies would mingle with the dust of those who had lived only a few years.

Nola realized that she had been staring; Yasmin was looking at her questioningly. Leif and Mikhail were eating heartily; Teno had taken only vegetables and sipped water instead of wine.

Leif was watching Teno. At last he said, "You're a strange one."

"I was part of an experiment of sorts," Teno said calmly.

"Oh, I suspected as much. I think I know where you're from. Allen's project. Wasn't that it?"

Teno nodded. "Does my being what I am bother you?"

"Not at all," Leif replied. "We should have done more biological modification, maybe tried something radical. What difference does it make? We're all immortal, and that's the most unnatural thing there is. Anything else is a minor modification."

Nola turned toward him. "Are you a biologist, Leif?"

"I was, once." He frowned. "Why be one now? There's nothing for us to do; truly original work ended some time ago. All we have to do now is make sure everyone stays alive and happy. Everything's perfect the way it is, isn't it? Don't you think so?" He slumped in his chair and said more softly, "How mistaken we were. Death was our spur; we once knew we would die, but at least our knowledge and our achievements would go on. Now we have what we want. There's no need to know anything except how to keep what we have."

Nola leaned toward him. "I thought you didn't approve of people thinking death might be good."

"I don't. But we lack motivation, which death once provided."

"That's not true away from Earth."

"Just wait." Leif poured himself more wine. "Most of you, on the average, are still younger than people here. You'll reach the impasse—you're getting there already. A short time after the Transition, a ship left the solar system. It was the first. I think it was also the last. We've never sent another."

"No one knows what happened to it," Yasmin murmured.

"Why should that stop us? All the more reason to follow up, wouldn't you say? But we don't."

"There are others who feel as you do," Teno said. "The biologists who gave me life wanted change. I and those like me were made for the world as it is now. You still have instincts for a different kind of life."

"Then why are you here?" Leif asked, waving an arm and almost knocking over his wineglass.

"We're young. We're still learning. We have to understand. That is why I'm going to experience the little death soon. I shall see what happens to me. You're welcome to attend."

Mikhail reached over and took Teno's hand for a moment, then released it. Nola gripped the arms of her chair, pressing her nails against the smooth wood.

"I'll want to see that," Leif replied. "Giancarlo will be surprised to see me there."

Yasmin looked around at everyone, and then began to speak of some poetry she had read recently. Her voice sang as it recited the Arabic. Nola did not know Arabic, but apparently the others did. Yasmin sighed as she reached the end of a verse. "There's no other language for poetry," she said.

"Perhaps," Teno said. "There's so much behind every word. Perfect for metaphors; you can hardly avoid them, but it's difficult to make a straightforward, unambiguous assertion in such a language."

Yasmin smiled. "You would say that."

It was very dark outside now. The air was still. The dim light in the room left faces in shadow. Teno seemed to be smiling, but that had to be an illusion. Leif lolled in his chair. Mikhail's mouth curved; his eyes gazed longingly at Teno. Once, Nola thought, he had looked at her that way. His eyes met hers. For a moment, she thought he would speak.

She felt as though she were smothering. The air was humid; the silence pressed against her ears. She stood up slowly.

"Nola?" Yasmin said softly.

"I'm tired. I think I'll excuse myself." Nola continued to look at Mikhail.

"If you like," Yasmin said, "come back down later."

Nola turned to go, then let one hand rest on Leif's shoulder. "If you like, come upstairs later."

"Oh, I'll come now." He followed her to the staircase without saying a word to the others. Nola glanced at Mikhail. He didn't care. She was surprised that she had thought he would.

She led him up to her room, opened her door, and put her hand on the wall panel. The ceiling flowed with light. She took off her robe.

Leif said, "You're direct. No flirtation for you."

She shrugged.

"That fellow down there is the one you followed, isn't he."

"How do you know?"

"I can tell."

"It makes me sick."

"It shouldn't." He shed his shorts. He was a dark shape with a golden nimbus around his head. He came to her and traced the wires on her body. "You're right." His fingers touched the metal threads over her hips. "They don't get in the way."

She turned to the floater and led him inside, then signaled the generator. She drifted up and he reached for her, pressing his lips against one small breast. He seemed more awkward in the floater; his head bumped hers. She circled his waist with her legs and held him as her fingers caressed his chest.

His fingers dug into her skin, clawing between the wires on her back, then grabbing at her ribs; his hands seemed hard. She thought of Mikhail, remembering how he had twisted under her as she had hovered over him. She nudged Leif with her legs, then released him, brushing his belly lightly with one hand.

Leif spun and twisted. His feet met a shield, and he launched himself toward her. She held his shoulders with her hands. His blue eyes were wide; his mouth was a straight, narrow line. He gripped her again, firmly; his hands held her buttocks. The walls outside the floater swirled past her until she was floating upside down, with Leif behind her, their feet pointed at the lighted ceiling. She gasped as his fingers danced over her; he let her drift away, then touched her again, and she moaned as he floated under her.

She was about to speak but something in his eyes, a flicker, stopped her. They circled each other, touching only with lips and fingers until he suddenly reached for her. Her shoulders bounced against a shield. He was holding on to her very tightly, gripping her waist while thrusting against her. Before she could pull away, he was inside her, hanging on to her hips, his body arching away from her; she could not see his face. She heard him cry out. She shuddered and moaned, drawing up her knees until her feet were against his ribs. As she came, she cried out, and part of her mind seemed to leave her body with the cry.

He let go. She drifted toward the floor. She did not look at him. She felt his breath on her ear. His arms circled her, more gently this time. She closed her eyes, still feeling the roughness of his hands.

Nola was awake early; she saw gray sky outside her window. The room was dark. Leif was gone.

She left the floater and went into the bathroom. As she washed, she noticed small bruises, the size of fingertips, on her hips and legs. Mikhail had never left a bruise.

She put on her robe and went downstairs. She heard footsteps; the front door clicked shut. She hurried to the window and looked outside.

The morning mist deepened the green of the grass. There were puddles in the hollows of Yasmin's lawn. Mikhail and Teno were walking toward the road. Teno held out a hand to Mikhail, and the two joined arms as they strolled toward Mikhail's house, becoming shadows in the mist.

She stared at Teno's back. I hope you die. I hope something goes wrong, and that Giancarlo can't stop it, and that you die. Her hands were shaking. The others would turn on Giancarlo then; Leif would be there to urge them on. The image was so vivid that she had to catch herself, afraid she had cried out loud. She pressed her forehead against the cool glass.

IV

Nola approached the turret, slowing her pace so that Yasmin could keep up with her. Teno had invited almost everyone to the tower today. "That's unusual," Yasmin had said to Nola. "Usually, you ask only a couple of friends. I went in alone, except for Giancarlo."

The tall wooden door was open. Yasmin, dressed in a long rose-colored robe, waited for Nola to step through, then followed. Nola shivered; it was cooler inside, and she had worn only a loose cotton shirt and gray pants.

A stone stairway between stone walls led into darkness. Nola's heels clattered against the floor; Yasmin's sandals slapped the surface. They climbed the stairs. Nola moved toward the wall to her left, feeling her way along it. The wall was damp. The stairway curved, bending around the tower. She followed the shuffling sound of Yasmin's feet, and then saw a distant light.

The light came from a door in the wall on the left. Nola climbed more quickly, moving toward the light, and followed Yasmin inside.

The room was large and bright. Overhead, Nola saw openings near the top of the turret. The sun's rays flooded the room; other lights, resembling torches, were set in the walls. The center of the room held a blue platform covered with wires, which were attached to a console resting on a heavy mahogany table.

Nola lingered in the doorway, surveying the room. Large red and blue pillows covered the floor. Jiro sat with a tall dark man; he waved at her. Then Nola saw Leif. He was sitting near a wall, his back against a pillow.

Yasmin walked toward Jiro. "Excuse me," a voice said behind Nola. She stepped back and let Hilde enter. "I didn't expect to see you here. Maybe you'll be convinced, but perhaps you won't until something terrible happens to you."

"Something terrible?" Nola said, annoyed.

"Someone you love could die. It happened to me. I lost my husband, before the Transition. He died suddenly. Afterward, I thought of all the things I'd never said to him. Often my own words would run through my mind—I kept repeating everything I wanted to say to him and could never say. Later, I forgot. There were decades when I never thought of him at all. Then I underwent the little death. He spoke to me. He's part of the higher state now, and I know I'll be with him again."

Nola could not speak. Even when most unhappy, she had never thought of staying with Mikhail forever; she had known that they would separate in time. Her feelings suddenly seemed shallow compared to Hilde's.

Hilde left her and walked toward the others. Nola went to Leif. His legs were stretched out in front of him; his bare feet were dirty. He smiled as she sat down near him. His cheeks and chin bristled with pale hairs; his blue eyes seemed darker, the pupils enlarged even in the light. His skin was yellowish. He said, "We skeptics ought to stick together."

Two men and a woman wandered in and sat near the platform. "I hope he puts on a good show, at least," Leif continued, leaning toward her. His breath smelled sour, and he slurred the words.

"Are you all right?"

"I'm fine. I'm mighty fine." Two more women had come in. "It doesn't look as though Teno's going to get much of a crowd. Too bad. Maybe old Giancarlo's losing his touch."

Nola was looking at the console. "What is that?"

"Just a suspender. Standard medical stuff. It keeps the body suspended, so to speak, until a rescue team can get it to a medical center for treatment. They hooked me up to one after my leg got burned."

"Did you see visions?"

"Oh, come now. Of course not."

"Maybe Giancarlo made some adjustments or alterations."

"I thought of that. I checked it already; I was here before anyone else. It's not changed. Besides, he doesn't have to do anything to it—he's dealing with people who want to believe. All he has to do is suggest something, and their minds will do the rest. It won't prove a thing."

Nola sighed. She heard Leif chuckle. "What's so funny?"

"You're disappointed, Nola. You want to believe it, don't you. You want it to prove something. That's why you're here. That's why you stayed."

"You're wrong."

"Oh, no, I'm not."

"Then why are you here?"

"For amusement. Maybe to see the look on Giancarlo's face when he finds me sitting here." Leif scratched his bare thigh. "But that's not why you're here. You'd better be careful, Nola. You're ripe. You could start here and end up in a death cult that means business."

"You're wrong. You don't know me at all."

"I know enough. You think that you accept the world as it is—that's what you tell yourself. But you don't. You hate it. It's too bleak for you; you struggle against it. That's why you don't like being around Teno. A person like that is a reminder of something you'd rather forget."

"And what is that?" she asked softly.

"That human beings will eventually create their own successors. That people like us aren't the crown of creation. I've seen your type before. How you struggle against the idea that perhaps the only thing we have left to do is die out. The cults are just the first sign of that. We cling to the notion that there's something else beyond this world, and we still want to die, but we also want to live on."

She said, "You're making no sense."

Leif's eyes were slits. "Giancarlo may be cleverer than some
—I'll grant him that—because he's tried to make his beliefs
compatible with the world we have. He accepts immortality
and biological change. It's a path religions often took before
the Transition—they'd modify certain tenets or try to show
that new discoveries or attitudes didn't contradict their
truths." His lip curled. "But it won't work, because his beliefs
are based on a dogma that can't be proven or falsified and
must be taken on faith. Eventually, something will happen
that he'll have to reject, and his followers will have to choose
—accommodation won't be possible."

Nola turned away from him, wrapping her arms around her
legs. "Our successors will be great," Leif muttered. "I'm sure
of it. They'll reach for things we can't even envision."

Teno and Mikhail had entered the room, with Giancarlo just
behind them. Nola followed them with her eyes as they moved
toward the platform. When they reached it, Mikhail looked
around and saw her. He stared at Leif for a long moment. Leif
stared back and showed his teeth; the muscles of his arms
tightened. Then he leaned back, as if bored once more.

Teno stretched out on the platform. Giancarlo began to
attach the wires and circlets. Mikhail sat on a cushion and
bowed his head.

Nola had always known that her real work was learning, not
meteorology. She orbited the earth, not to do the tasks that
cybernetic minds could have done as well, but to conserve the
knowledge and experience in a human mind. Weather was
still sometimes indeterminate, unpredictable—storms could
change course, a stream of air could shift.

Now she felt as though she had been watching the unpredictable patterns of this community as they swirled around Giancarlo, the eye of the storm. She frowned at that comparison;
the settlement was placid and dull. Yet her nerves hummed, as
if sensing that the weather was about to change. She was doing
the same work she had always done, except that here she could
not observe from a distance. She was part of the pattern, and
her own mental weather was being affected.

Giancarlo stood behind the console. He wore a white shirt
and white pants; a beam of light shone down on him, making his
pale face luminous. Nola frowned at the obvious theatricality. He
pressed a panel on the console. Teno seemed to be asleep.

"Most of you have heard what I have to say," Giancarlo began. "But I speak for the benefit of our visitors, who are unfamiliar with my message." His voice was low, but Nola heard him clearly.

"There is a higher state," he went on, "and another life. I know this to be true, because those who have been near death have returned to this life to speak of it. They tell the same story. They step outside their bodies, they travel down the tunnel, they witness the events of their lives, speak with those beyond, and meet the Light of God."

Leif cleared his throat.

"Now, some will say that there are those who have been through such an experience and have no such tales to tell. Some, of course, may only have forgotten." Giancarlo stood very still, arms at his sides. "But I have found that certain injuries or medications can interfere with a person's ability to perceive the higher state. That is why I use this suspender." He waved a hand at the console. "It shuts down the body gradually. For a few seconds, the body will not function—it will be dead, in a manner of speaking. The soul will be outside that body, and then, before any physical harm can take place, the body will be revived, and the mind and soul will speak of what they have seen."

Teno's chest still rose and fell. The head was circled by a wide metal band; the face was very pale. Nola wanted to hear what Teno would say; the strength of that desire surprised her. She glanced at Leif. He leaned forward, eyes on the console.

"This is how we must approach the higher state," Giancarlo continued. "This way, or through a death which is often violent or painful and which hurls the soul from this world. But it will not always be so. We have extended life now, but each of us continues to evolve. As we live, our souls grow stronger, seeking that other existence. In time, many ages from now, the soul will detach itself from the body, shedding it as the body sheds a coat—or perhaps the body will simply wear away. There will be no death as we know it. All humankind will live on in that higher state. I know this to be true. That will be the Final Transition."

He believes it, Nola thought. Somehow, that frightened her more than thinking that he was only a man wanting control of others. Teno was still. Giancarlo bent over the platform. He's right, he knows. She was convinced of it now, even before hearing Teno bear witness. She sat up, lifting her head, want-

ing to speak her newfound convictions aloud. The sunlight on
Giancarlo glowed; the souls of those beyond sang to her. The
others in the room were only shadows in a cave.

The machine began to hum. Giancarlo hovered over it, his
slender hands fluttering. Teno's brain was no longer functioning; it would start to die. Leif was suddenly on his feet. Nola
lifted her hand to her mouth; the moment had passed, the
world had pulled her back. Then the console was silent. Leif
sighed and sat down.

Teno's chest was moving again. Leif moved closer to Nola.
He muttered something but she did not catch the words.

"Teno will speak to us soon," Giancarlo said. "Our vision
will be shared by another soul, and another soul will be at
peace."

Leif scowled. The others in the room were still. Teno's arm
moved. Giancarlo bent down, touching the metal band with
one hand. Teno's eyes opened. Giancarlo's lips moved and
Teno managed to nod. Then Giancarlo began to remove the
wires and bands. Nola fidgeted, waiting. Teno's words would
restore her conviction; she would hear that steady voice
describe the vision, and she would know.

Giancarlo helped Teno sit up. Yasmin's mouth was slightly
open; Mikhail's back was very straight. Hilde and a man near
her smiled complacently. "What have you seen?" Giancarlo
asked.

There was no reply. Teno surveyed the room; Nola thought
she saw a frown.

"What have you seen?"
Nola held her breath. Teno looked down at the floor.
"What have you seen?" Giancarlo's voice was higher.
"I was in a tunnel," Teno began in a weak voice. "I was
falling through it, or past it; I couldn't be sure. Ahead, I saw a
dark point. It began to grow larger as I fell. At first, I thought
it was black." Someone in the room gasped. "I could not see it
when I looked at it. I had left my body far behind, and it had
captured me. Dimly, I recalled standing over my body in this
room; images of my life unfolded before me, and I watched
them as if they were another's life. I fell toward the dark spot,
and it grew larger as I approached. It was not black. It was
nothing, and it was going to swallow me. I was moving toward
oblivion. I struggled against it, but I was lost. Then I was
pulled back. That is what I saw."

Giancarlo held out his hands, as though pleading. "That

can't be. Everyone who has endured the little death has had the vision. It's never failed."

"That was my vision." Teno's voice was stronger.

"It can't be." Giancarlo's voice shook. He peered at the console, tracing the panels with his fingers. "Something must be wrong."

Hilde stood up. She looked around the room; her eyes were narrowed. "You know what it means," she said. Her voice was loud; it filled the room. "You all know what it means. It means that Teno has no soul. The way to the higher state is closed to such beings."

Giancarlo was shaking his head, as if denying the words. Mikhail got up and went toward Teno, then stopped, as though afraid to be too near his friend.

"You know I'm right," Hilde went on. "This is the sign. The biologists have created beings who cannot reach the higher state, and we must now oppose them. What greater crime can there be?"

Nola gazed at the others. Even Yasmin, eyes wide, was nodding her head. Teno rose slowly, then walked past Mikhail and toward the door. Nola looked up as Teno passed her; the blank gray eyes met hers for a moment. She looked down.

Teno was gone.

She heard a snort. Leif was laughing, covering his mouth and nose with one hand. "You know I'm right, Giancarlo," Hilde was saying. "If we don't stand against them, they'll continue their evil work. Can we enter the higher state with that on our conscience?"

Nola could not bear it. She leaped up and ran from the room, stumbling down the stairs in the darkness. She imagined the stairs continuing endlessly, leading her to a black, subterranean realm. She reached the bottom and hurried toward the door. The sunshine made her blink; she covered her eyes.

She went to Mikhail in the evening. He was alone in his house, seated by the pool. One hand dangled, rippling the water.

Nola said, "Come with me."

"You should have knocked."

"Come with me."

Mikhail was silent.

"I thought you cared about Teno. How can you stay here after what happened to your friend? Teno will have to leave now. Only people with souls can stay."

He looked up. "I can't go."

"You must."

"You saw what happened, Nola."

"Yes, I did. It doesn't matter. Your visions are illusions; this proves it. They may be nature's way of easing death, of making it less painful." Something in her recoiled at the words.

"That's not what it proves."

She wanted to strike him. "You can't stay, Mikhail. If Giancarlo goes on, he'll have to try to stop anything the biologists attempt to do. Maybe he'll start with speeches and spreading the word, but it won't stop there. When that doesn't work, there'll be stronger measures. You saw Hilde. She meant it. You ought to be able to figure out what she might want to do."

"I must stay, Nola." His blue eyes searched her face, as if he wanted to say more.

She raised a hand, let it fall, and hurried from him.

As she strode toward Yasmin's house, she noticed that Leif's tent and cart were gone. He would try to warn others. She stared at the spot where his tent had been, hoping he would succeed. She had almost been fooled herself. She could no longer recall how she had felt when, for a brief moment, she had believed Giancarlo.

Yasmin was standing next to the hovercraft. Nola had already packed her things. "I'm sorry you're leaving," Yasmin said.

"I'm not sorry," Nola replied.

"I wish you'd stay. If you would endure the little death, you'd understand."

"Would I? Maybe I'd be like Teno. Maybe I wouldn't see the correct vision."

Yasmin shook her head. "Oh, no. You're human."

"Am I? Are you sure? Where do you draw the line? How many genes have to be altered before you lose a soul? Is there a gene for that, too? Maybe somatic changes would do the trick. If the soul's not made of matter, then how can altering the body change it? You'd better start asking questions, Yasmin."

Nola got into her hovercraft and pulled away. As she turned toward the gate, she saw a shadow in the road. A hand was raised. Nola stopped.

Teno came to the side of the craft. "May I go with you?"

"Where to?"

"There's a town one hundred kilometers south. I have friends there."

"Get in."

Teno walked around the vehicle and got in on the other side. Nola drove through the open gate and did not look back.

They moved toward a hill. "Didn't you bring your things?" she asked.

"There's nothing there that I need."

She glanced at her passenger, thinking she detected bitterness in the words. But Teno seemed composed. "Did it bother you, Teno?" she said carefully. "Going through that, I mean."

"Why should it bother me? I had no expectations, and my curiosity was satisfied."

She signaled her implant and set the vehicle's course, then leaned back. "Maybe you lied. Maybe you lied to them about your vision."

"Why would I lie?"

"I don't know. Maybe you wanted to see what would happen. Maybe you were doing a little experiment of your own. Maybe you wanted to find out whether Giancarlo would abandon his ideas, or find another way to explain what happened to you."

"Is that what you want to think, Nola? Would it make it easier for you to accept his ideas then?"

"I don't care about that."

"Perhaps you do. I saw what I said I saw."

The sky was growing dark. She would see the stars soon, and the familiar black heavens she knew. She would travel through a comforting darkness. She would leave; Earth would once again be a distant globe on the horizon. In the caverns and enclosures below Luna's surface, she would no longer have to look at it at all.

She thought of her work. She would return to it, watching the clouds and gathering the storms, her implant murmuring to her all the while, guiding her again. She might turn her attention from the earth to the stars. The dynamics of a galaxy, awesome and stately, dwarfed human lives; but were they more interesting, more meaningful, than the jagged orbits and splintered attractions of human existence?

She needed her humanity, with all its narrowness, to feel dwarfed, to be awed, to think the galaxy stately. She needed the smallness of self-conscious intelligence. She would fall around Earth, weightless and alone; yet not alone. She needed the peopled earth to be there; but she also didn't need it.

The Summer's Dust

I

ANDREW WAS HIDING. HE SAT ON THE ROOF, HIS BACK TO THE gabled windows. He had been there for only a few minutes and knew he would be found; that was the point.

He heard a door open below. "Andrew?" The door snapped shut. His mother was on the porch; her feet thumped against the wood. "Andrew?" She would go back inside and find that he was still near the house; tracing the signal, she would locate him. He glanced at his left wrist. The small blue stone of his Bond winked at him.

He looked down at the gutter edging the roof. The porch's front steps creaked, and his mother's blond head emerged. A warm breeze feathered her hair as she glided along the path leading down the hill. From the roof, Andrew could see the nearby houses. At the foot of the hill, two kobolds tended the rose garden that nestled near a low stone house. The owner of the house had lived in the south for years, but her small servants still clipped the hedges and trimmed the lawn. Each kobold was one meter tall, and human in appearance. On pleasant evenings, he had seen the little people lay a linen tablecloth over the table in the garden and set out the silverware, taking their positions behind the chairs. They would wait silently, small hands crossed over their chests, until it was night; then they would clear the table once more. A troll stood by the hedge; this creature was half a meter taller than the kobolds. The troll's misshapen body was bent forward slightly; its long arms hung to the ground, fingertips touching grass. At night, the troll would guard the house. The being's ugly, bearded face and scowl were a warning to anyone who approached; the small silver patch on its forehead revealed the cybernetic link that enabled it to summon aid.

Farther down the road, the facets of a glassy dome caught the sun, and tiny beings of light danced. Andrew's friend Silas lived there with his father Ben and several Siamese cats. Andrew frowned as he thought of Silas and of what his friend wanted to do.

Andrew's own house was old. His mother had told him it had been built before the Transition. Even with extensive repairs and additions to the house, the homeostat could not run it properly. The rooms were usually a bit warm, or too cold; the doors made noises, the windows were spotted with dirt.

He watched his mother wander aimlessly along the path. Joan had forgotten him, as she often did. They could be in the same room and she would become silent, then suddenly glance at him, her eyes widening, as if she were surprised to find him still there. His father was different; Dao was completely attentive whenever Andrew was around, but content to ignore him the rest of the time. He wondered if Dao would ever speak to him at all if Andrew didn't speak first.

He moved a little. His right foot shot out and brushed against a loose shingle. Andrew slid; he grabbed for the windowsill and held on. The shingle fell, slapping against the cement of the path.

Joan looked up. She raised her hands slowly. "Andrew." Her voice was loud, but steady. He pulled himself up; he would not fall now. Joan moved closer to the house. "What are you doing up there?"

"I'm all right."

She held her arms up. "Don't move."

"I've got my lifesuit on."

"I don't care. Don't move, stay where you are." Her feet pounded on the steps and over the porch. The front door slammed. In a few moments, he heard her enter his room. Her arms reached through the open window and pulled him inside.

Andrew sighed as she closed the window, feeling vaguely disappointed. "Don't ever do that again."

"I'm wearing my lifesuit." He opened his shirt to show her the protective garment underneath.

"I don't care. It's supposed to protect you, not make you reckless. You still could have been hurt."

"Not at that distance. Bruises, that's all."

"Why did you do it?"

Andrew shrugged. He went over to his bed and sat down. The bed undulated; Joan seemed to rise and fall.

"Why did you do it?"

"I don't know."

"Do I have to have a kobold follow you around? I thought you were too old for that."

"I'm all right." I wouldn't have died or anything, he thought.

Joan watched him silently for a few moments. She was drifting again; he knew the signs. Her blue eyes stared through him, as if she were seeing something else. She shook her head. "I keep forgetting how old you are." She paused. "Don't go out there again."

"I won't."

She left the room. He rose and crossed to the windows, staring out at the houses below and the forested hills beyond. His room suddenly seemed cramped and small; his hands tapped restlessly against the sill.

Andrew was sitting on the porch with Dao and Joan when Silas arrived. The other boy got off his bicycle and wheeled it up the hill to the porch. He parked it and waved at Andrew's parents. Joan's thin lips were tight as she smiled. Dao showed his teeth; his tilted brown eyes became slits.

Andrew sat on the steps next to Silas. His friend was thirteen, a year older than Andrew. He was the only child Andrew had met in the flesh; the others were only holo images. Silas was big and muscular, taller than Joan and Dao; he made Andrew feel even smaller and slighter than he was. Andrew moved up a step and looked down at the other boy.

Silas rose abruptly. Brown hair fell across his forehead, masking his eyes. He motioned to Andrew, then began to walk down the hill. Andrew followed. They halted by the hedge in front of the empty stone house. The troll waved them away, shaking its head; its long tangled hair swayed against its green tunic.

"How about it?" Silas said as they backed away from the hedge.

"What?"

"You know. Our journey, our adventure. You coming with me? Or are you just going to stay here?"

Andrew held out his arm, looking at his Bond. "We can't go. They'll find us."

"I said I'd figure out a way. I have a plan."

"How?"

"You'll see," Silas said. He shook his head. "Aren't you sick of it here? Don't you get tired of it?"

Andrew shrugged. "I guess."

Silas began to kick a stone along the road. Andrew glanced up the hill; Joan and Dao were still on the porch. They had lived in that house even before bringing him home, making one journey to the center to conceive him and another when he was removed from the wombart. They had gone to some trouble to have him; they were always telling him so. "More people should have children," Dao would say. "It keeps us from getting too set in our ways." Joan would nod. "You're very precious to us," Joan would murmur, and Dao would smile. Yet most of the time, his parents would be with their books, or speaking to friends on the holo, or lost in their own thoughts.

Joan could remember the beginnings of things. Dao was even older; he could remember the Transition. Dao was filled with stories of those days, and always spoke of them as if they had been the prelude to great adventure and achievement. Gradually, Andrew had realized that those times had been the adventure, that nothing important was likely to happen to Joan and Dao again. Dao was almost four hundred years old; Joan was only slightly younger. Once, Andrew had asked his mother what she had been like when she was his age. She had laughed, seeming more alive for a moment. "Afraid," she had answered, laughing again.

Silas kicked the stone toward the hill. "Listen," he said as they climbed. "I'm ready. I've got two knapsacks and a route worked out. We'd better leave this week before my father gets suspicious."

"I don't know."

The taller boy turned and took Andrew by the shoulder. "If you don't go, I'll go by myself. Then I'll come back and tell you all about it, and you'll be sorry you didn't come along."

Andrew pulled away. Silas's face was indistinct in the dusk. Andrew felt anxious. He knew that he should be concerned about how his parents would feel if he ran away, but he wasn't; he was thinking only of how unfair it had been for them to assume that he would want to hide in this isolated spot, shunning the outside world. They had told him enough about death cults and accidents to make him frightened of anything beyond this narrow road. He knew what Silas was thinking: that Andrew was a coward.

Why should I care what he thinks? Andrew thought, but there was no one else against whom he could measure himself. He wondered if he would have liked Silas at all if there had been other friends. He pushed the thought away; he could not afford to lose his one friend.

As they came toward the house, Andrew saw his parents go inside. A kobold was on the porch, preparing for its nightly surveillance; behind it, a troll was clothed in shadows. Silas got on his bicycle.

"See you," he mumbled, and coasted down the hill recklessly, slowing as he reached the bottom, speeding up as he rode toward his home.

The kobold danced over to Andrew as he went up the steps. It smiled; the golden curls around its pretty face bobbed. A tiny hand touched his arm. "Good night, Andrew," it sang.

"Good night, Ala."

"Good night, good night, good night," the tiny voice trilled. "Sleep well, sweet dreams, sweet dreams." The troll growled affectionately. The kobold pranced away, its gauzy blue skirt lifting around its perfect legs.

Andrew went inside. The door snapped shut behind him, locking itself. He walked toward the curving staircase, then paused, lingering in the darkened hallway. He would have to say good night.

He found his parents in the living room. He knocked on the door, interrupting the sound of conversation, then opened it. Dao had stripped to his briefs; Joan was unbuttoning her shirt. On the holo, Andrew saw the nude images of a blond man and a red-haired woman; a dark-haired kobold giggled as it peered around the woman's bare shoulder. The flat wall-sized screen had become the doorway into a bright, sunny bedroom.

"Five minutes," Dao said to the images. "We'll call you back." The people and the room disappeared. "What is it, son?"

Joan smiled. Andrew looked down at the floor, pushing his toe against a small wrinkle in the Persian rug. "Nothing. I came to say good night."

"Good night, son."

He left, feeling their impatience. As he climbed the stairs, he heard the door below slide open.

"Andrew," Joan said. She swayed, holding the ends of her open shirt. "I'll come up later and tuck you in. All right?"

I'm too old for that, he wanted to say. "I'll be asleep," he said as he looked down at her.

"I'll check on you anyway. Maybe I'll tell you a story."

He was sure that she would forget.

In the end, he went with Silas, as he had known he would. They left two days later, in the morning, stopping at Silas's house to pick up the knapsacks. Silas's father was out in the back, digging in his garden with the aid of a troll; he did not see them leave.

They avoided the road, keeping near the trees. When they were out of sight of Andrew's house, they returned to the road. Andrew was not frightened now. He wondered what his parents would say when he returned to tell them of his journey.

Silas stopped and turned around, gazing over Andrew's head. "A kobold's following us." Andrew looked back. A little figure in blue was walking toward them; it lifted one hand in greeting.

"What'll we do?"

"Nothing, for the moment." Silas resumed walking.

"But it's following us." Andrew walked more quickly, trying to keep up with his friend's strides. "We could outrun it, couldn't we? It won't be able to keep up."

"That's just what we can't do. If we do that, it'll tell the others, and we'll have your parents and my father on our trail."

They came to a bend in the road. Silas darted to one side and hurried through the brush. Andrew ran after him, thrashing through the green growth. It had rained the night before; the ground was soft and muddy, and leaves stuck to his boots. Silas reached for his arm and pulled him behind a tree.

"Wait," Silas said. He glanced at Andrew, then peered at him more closely. Andrew stepped back. Silas was looking at his chest. Andrew looked down. One of his shirt buttons was undone, revealing the silver fabric underneath.

"You're wearing a lifesuit."

"Aren't you?"

"Of course not. You're stupid, Andrew. Don't you know you can be tracked with that on?"

"Not as easily as with a Bond." He wondered again what Silas was going to do about their Bonds.

"Take it off right now."

"You can't hurt me, not while I'm wearing it."

"I'll leave you here, then."

"I don't care." But he did. He took off his knapsack and unbuttoned his shirt. Twigs cracked in the distance; the kobold had tracked them. Andrew removed his lifesuit and handed it to Silas.

As he dressed, Andrew felt exposed and vulnerable. His clothing seemed too light, too fragile. He watched as Silas dug in the mud, burying the lifesuit with his hands. He looked up at Andrew and grinned; his hands were caked with wet earth.

"Get behind that tree," Silas said as he picked up a rock. Andrew obeyed, flattening himself against the bark. A bush shook. He could see the kobold now. For a moment, the android looked like a man; then it moved closer to another bush and was small again. Its dark beard twitched.

"Silas," the kobold called. "Silas." It shaded its eyes with one hand. "Silas, where are you bound? You should not come so far without protection." The creature had a man's voice, a tenor, but it had no resonance, no power; it was a man's voice calling from far away. The kobold came closer until it was only a meter from Andrew, its back to him as it surveyed the area.

Silas moved quickly, brushing against Andrew as he rushed toward the kobold. He raised the rock and Andrew saw him strike the android's head. The little creature toppled forward, hands out. Andrew walked toward it slowly. Silas dropped the red-smeared rock. The small skull was dented; bits of bone and slender silver threads gleamed in the wound. The silver patch on its forehead was loose.

"You killed it."

"I didn't mean to hit it so hard. I just wanted to knock it out." Silas brushed back his hair with one dirty hand. "It's only a kobold. Come on, we have to go now. Now that its link is out, another one'll come looking for it."

Andrew stared at the body.

"Come on." He turned and followed his friend. They came to a muddy clearing and went around it. Silas led him to a nearby grove of trees.

Two cages rested against a tree trunk. Two cats, trapped inside, scratched at the screening. "I told you I had a plan," Silas said. "Now we take care of our Bonds."

"I don't understand."

The other boy exhaled loudly. "Messing up the signal's too complicated, and we can't take them off and leave them, because the alarm would go out after a minute or so. So there's only one thing left. We put them on somebody else. Or something else. The system can't tell if it's us or not, it only knows that the Bonds are on some living thing. And it'll assume it's still us, because these Bonds are ours. Everyone'll look for us around here. By the time anyone figures it out, we'll be far away."

Andrew stared at his friend. It seemed obvious and simple, now that he had explained. "They might just wander back to your house," he murmured as he shifted his gaze to the cages.

"Not these cats. They're kind of wild. They'll stay out here for at least a day or two." He opened one cage and removed a Siamese. The cat meowed and tried to scratch. Silas stroked it tenderly. "Hold him." Andrew held the animal as Silas removed his Bond and put it around the cat's neck, adjusting it. The cat jumped from Andrew's arms and scampered away. "Now yours."

Andrew backed away. "I can't," he said. "I can't do it." His mouth was dry. He would be cut off from the world without his Bond; he had never removed it except when it was being readjusted.

"Coward. I know what's going to happen to you. You're going to run home, aren't you, and your mother and father'll make sure their little precious doesn't run away again. And you'll stay there forever. You'll be a hundred years old, and you'll still be there, and you'll never do anything. And you'll always be afraid, just like them."

Andrew swallowed. He took off the Bond while Silas held the other cat. He fumbled with the bracelet and dropped it. "Here, hold the cat," Silas said, sighing. He picked up the Bond and attached it himself, then put the cat on the ground. The creature began to lick a paw.

Andrew was numb. He blinked. Silas pushed him, and he almost fell. "We have to go, Andrew. Another kobold'll be here soon."

Later that afternoon, they reached a deserted town. Weeds had grown through the cracks in the road. The wooden structures were wrecks. A few had become only piles of lumber; others still stood, brown boards showing through the worn-away paint. Broken windows revealed empty rooms.

They walked slowly through the town. A sudden gust of wind swayed a weeping willow, and Andrew thought he heard a sigh. He shivered, and walked more quickly.

A stone house stood at the edge of the town. A low wall surrounded it; the metal gate was open. Silas lingered at the gate, then went through it. The broken pavement leading to the front door was a narrow trail through weeds and tall grass. Andrew followed his friend up the steps. Silas tried the door-knob, pushing at the dark wood with his other hand until the door creaked open.

The hallway was empty; dust covered the floor. Andrew sneezed. The floorboards creaked under their feet. Cobwebs shimmered in the corners. They turned to the right and crept into the next room.

Andrew sniffed. "Are we going to stay here? We'll choke." His voice was small and hollow.

Silas glanced around the empty room, then walked over to a tall window facing the front yard. "We can sleep here. If we open the window, we'll have air."

"Maybe we'd better leave it closed." Andrew wondered whether he would prefer a closed window and a dusty room to an open window in the dark. Silas did not seem to hear him; he stared at the filthy windowpane for a moment, then pushed at the window, straining against it until it squeaked open.

"Come here," he said to Andrew. He wandered to the window and peered out over Silas's shoulder. "Look."

"At what?"

Silas pushed his arm. "Don't you see anything, Andrew? Look at the town. It's like it's still alive."

He saw it. The tall grass hid the piles of lumber; only the standing houses were visible, colored by the orange glow of the setting sun. He could walk back to the town and find people preparing supper or gathering in the street. He sighed and backed away, making tracks in the dust as he slid his feet along the floor.

Silas took a shirt out of his knapsack and swept a spot clean. When he was finished, Andrew sat down. Now that he was safe, Andrew felt a little better, even though he was exhausted. He had seen none of the terrible things his parents had warned him against, only old roads, forest, and a deserted town. He said, "I thought it would be worse."

"What?" Silas removed food and water from his knapsack.

"I thought it would be more—I don't know—more dangerous." He shrugged out of his knapsack and stretched.

Silas shook his head. "You listen to your parents too much. Besides, there aren't that many people around here. It's too far north."

"What's that got to do with it?"

"You know. Well, maybe you don't, because you never went anywhere. They don't like seasons, most of them. They like places where it's always the same. Here, the fall comes, and plants die." Silas said the word "die" harshly, gazing defiantly at Andrew. "They don't like to see that, seasons and winter and all."

Andrew accepted food from his friend, opening his package of stew and letting it heat up for a few moments. Silas smacked his lips as he ate. "Sometimes I hate them," he went on. "They don't do anything. I don't want to be like that." He paused. "Once, my father had this party when we were living in Antigua, and this guy came. I forget his name. Everybody was just sitting around, showing off what languages they knew or flirting. And some of them were making fun of this man in a real quiet way, but he knew they were doing it—he wasn't that dumb."

"Why were they making fun of him?"

"Because he couldn't play their stupid little word games. This one woman started saying that there were people who just weren't very smart, and you could tell who they were because they couldn't learn very much even with a long life and plenty of time, that they just couldn't keep up. She was saying it to this other man, but she knew that other guy heard her. She said it right in front of him."

"What did he do?" Andrew asked.

"Nothing." Silas shrugged. "He looked sad. He left a little later, and I had to go to bed, anyway. Know what happened?" He leaned forward. "He went up in this little plane a couple of days later, and he went into a dive, and smacked into this house down the road. You should have seen it blow up."

Andrew was too shocked to speak.

"Luckily, nobody was home. The man died, though. Some people said it was an accident, but I don't think most of them believed it. That man knew how to fly. He went diving right in there." Silas slapped his right hand against his left palm.

Andrew shook his head. "That's awful." He looked enviously at his friend, wishing that he, too, had witnessed such an event.

"At least he did something."

Andrew lifted his head. "But that's terrible." He thought guiltily about his own foray onto the roof outside his window.

"So what? It's terrible. Everybody said so, but it was almost all they talked about afterward. I know for a fact that a lot of them watched the whole thing on their screens later on. A woman was out with her holo equipment just by luck, and she got the whole thing and put it in the system. That's the point, Andrew. He did something, and everybody knew it, and for a while he was the most important guy around."

"And he was so important you forgot his name."

"I was little. Anyway, that's why my father came here. He decided he didn't want to be around a lot of people after that. He kept saying it could have been our house." Silas threw his empty container into the corner and leaned back against the wall, smiling. "That would have been something, if it had been our house. Old Ben wouldn't have ever gotten over it. I'll bet he would have moved us underground."

Andrew pulled up his legs and wrapped his arms around them, imagining a plane streaking through the sky. The room seemed cozy now; the thought of danger beyond made it seem even cozier. Antigua, of course, was safely distant. He looked admiringly at his friend. Silas had seen danger, and nothing had happened to him; Andrew would be safe with his friend.

Andrew was awake in the darkness. The knapsack under his head was bumpy, the floor hard. His muscles ached. He thought of his bed at home.

He supposed he must have slept a little. It had still been light outside when he had gone to sleep. He listened; Silas was breathing unevenly. He felt a movement near him and realized his friend was awake. He was about to speak when he heard a click.

The front door was opening. He stiffened and held his breath. The door creaked. He heard footsteps in the hall, and his ears began to pound.

He wanted to make for the window and get outside, but he could not move. Silas had stopped breathing. The footsteps were coming toward them. He tried to press his back against the floor, as if he could sink between the boards and hide.

A beam of light shot through the darkness, sweeping toward them in an arc. Andrew sat up. The light struck him, and he threw up an arm. He tried to cry out, but let out only a sigh. Silas shouted.

Someone laughed. Andrew blinked, blinded by the light. The footsteps came closer, and the light dimmed. The shadowy figure holding it leaned over, set the slender pocket light on the floor, and sat down.

The intruder's face was now illuminated by the light. It was a girl with curly, shoulder-length hair. She said, "Who are you?"

Andrew glanced at Silas. "I'm Silas, this is Andrew. We aren't doing anything."

"I can see that. Hold out your arms."

Andrew hesitated.

"Hold them out." Her voice was hard. The boys extended their arms. "You're not wearing Bonds. Good. I don't want a signal going out." She had one hand at her waist; Andrew wondered if she were hurt. Then she withdrew it, and he saw a metal wand. She was armed. He lowered his arms slowly and clutched his elbows.

"We're exploring," Silas said.

"You mean you're running away. I'm running away, too. My name's Thérèse. Who are you running away from?"

"Our parents."

"Why?"

"I told you, we just want to look around."

"Then they're looking for you."

Silas shook his head. "We threw them off the track. If they're looking, they won't look here." Andrew was hoping that his friend was wrong. "Do your parents live around here?"

"I'm not running away from parents." The girl brushed a few curls from her forehead. "Where are you from?"

"Oh, a long way from here," Silas answered. "It took us all day to get here. There's only three houses where we're from. There's just Andrew's parents and my father and one woman who's practically never there, so you don't have to worry."

"I'm not worried." Thérèse reached for the light, then stood up. "I'm going to sleep in the hall. I'll talk to you tomorrow."

The boards groaned under her feet as she left; Andrew heard her close the door. He moved closer to Silas. "We can still go out the window," he whispered.

"What if she comes after us?"

"We can wait until she's asleep."

Silas was silent for a few moments. "Why bother? She's running away, too. We might be safer with her, anyway. She has a weapon."

"She might be dangerous."

"I don't know. She's just another kid. If she was really dangerous, she could have lased us right here."

Andrew shuddered. "Maybe we should go home."

"That's all you can think about, isn't it, running home to Joan and Dao." Silas paused. "Something interesting's going on, and you want to hide. Look, if we have to, we can always get away later. All we have to do is go to the nearest house and send out a message, and somebody'll come. Let's go to sleep."

Andrew stretched out on the floor. Silas might be scared, but he would never admit it. He considered escaping by himself, but the thought of traveling alone in the night kept him at Silas's side.

II

They shared some dried fruit and water with Thérèse in the morning. Andrew realized that they would run out of food sooner if they divided it three ways. They would have to go home then. That notion cheered him a bit as they set out from the town.

In the early morning light, Thérèse did not seem as frightening. He guessed that she was about twelve. She was taller than he was, but her long legs and thin arms were gangly and her chest was flat. Her cheeks were round and pink; strands of reddish-brown hair kept drifting across her face, causing her to shake her head periodically. She carried nothing except her weapon and her light, both tucked in her belt. Her shirt and slacks were dirty, and there were holes in the knees of her pants.

Andrew was on the girl's left; Silas walked at her right. Silas also seemed more at ease. He had joked with Thérèse as they ate, finally eliciting a smile. Thérèse was reserved; Andrew wondered if all girls were like that, or only this one. He remembered the girls he had spoken with over the holo, and the way a couple of them often looked at him scornfully, as if he were still a little child.

"Why did you run away?" she asked abruptly.

"I told you," Silas answered.

"I mean the real reason. Are your parents cruel, or is it just that they don't seem to care?"

"My father's all right."

"What about your mother?"

"I don't have one. They used stored ova for me."

"What about you?" she said to Andrew.

"I don't know," he replied. "Silas was going, so I went with him."

"That's not a good reason. Don't you like your home?"

"I like it fine."

"You shouldn't have left it, then."

Andrew wanted to ask Thérèse why she had run away.

"Maybe you ought to go back," she said after a moment.

"We'll stick with you," Silas said. "You don't mind, do you?"

"If I minded, I wouldn't be walking with you, now, would I?" The girl slowed, peering down the cracked and potholed asphalt. "We shouldn't stay on this road." She turned her head, surveying the area. A bridge was ahead. She pointed. "Maybe we should follow the river."

"Fine with me," Silas said. They left the road, scampering down the hill to the bank. The river flowed west; they climbed over rocks and strolled along the grassy bank.

"How long have you been traveling?" Silas asked.

"Long enough," Thérèse replied. "Since spring. A couple of months."

Silas whistled. The girl stumbled, waving her arms in an attempt to regain her balance. Pebbles rolled down the bank. Andrew reached for her, grabbing her arm. She jerked away violently, almost falling.

The slap stung his cheek. He stepped back. "Don't touch me," Thérèse shouted. "Keep away from me." Her arm was up, as if she were about to hit him again.

"I was trying to help." He crouched, holding out a hand. Thérèse was breathing heavily; her cheeks were flushed. Silas moved away from her and came closer to Andrew. The girl lowered her hands.

"I'm sorry," she said at last. "Don't touch me. Don't get too close to me. I can't stand it. All right?"

Andrew nodded. She turned and marched ahead, not looking back. Silas raised his eyebrows, then followed her. Andrew trailed behind. The look in Thérèse's brown eyes had chilled him; he had not seen the heat of anger or the wide eyes of fear, only a cold look of malice and hatred. He stuffed his hands into his pockets as he walked and kept back, afraid to get too close to Thérèse.

By noon they had left the river and found a dirt road that wound through wooded hills. Thérèse had remained silent, but she had also managed to smile at a couple of Silas's remarks. Andrew began to whistle a tune, then turned it into the *1812 Overture*. Silas added sound effects, shouting "Boom!" at the appropriate moments. Thérèse laughed, but her mouth twisted, as if she found the whole thing silly as well.

Then she stopped and pointed. Below them, the road dipped. A woman was walking along the road, her back to them, a kobold behind her. Apparently she had not heard them. She was moving toward a clearing; a small house, surrounded by a trimmed lawn, stood back from the road. A maple tree was in front of the house; near it, several flat stones formed a circle on the ground.

Andrew went as close to Thérèse as he dared. "What now?" he said softly.

She frowned. "We can catch up with her."

"But she'll—"

"Come on." She moved ahead quickly, and both boys followed. The woman stopped walking, lifted a slender white cylinder to her lips, and lit it; she was smoking a cigarette. Then she turned, and saw them.

Her dark eyes were wide. She dropped the cigarette quickly, as if ashamed that they had seen it, grinding it out with her foot. The kobold drew near her protectively. Its white hair was short and its eyebrows bushy; it scowled.

Thérèse, approaching, lifted a hand. "Hello."

"Hello?" the woman answered. Her greeting seemed tentative. She plucked nervously at her long black hair.

The girl moved closer, glancing at the kobold. It drew itself up, adjusting its red cape. Andrew and Silas kept behind Thérèse. Andrew was not afraid of the woman, only of the android, which might move quickly if it thought its mistress was being threatened. He kept his hands at his sides, palms open, in sight of the small creature.

"What do you want?" the woman asked.

Thérèse said, "We need food and a place to rest. Please help us. We won't bother you or anything." The girl's voice was higher, gentler than the tone Andrew had heard on the road. The woman gazed at Thérèse's outstretched hands, and her eyelids fluttered; Andrew was sure she had noticed the weapon at the girl's waist.

The woman straightened. She lifted her head and stuck out her chin, as if ready for a confrontation, but her hands trembled. "What are you doing out here?" Her voice was high and weak.

"We're running away," Thérèse said. "We're experiments." Andrew tried not to look surprised; Silas was keeping a straight face. "These biologists were testing us. I know they didn't think they were doing anything mean, but you know how they are. This one man said he'd help us if we got away, so we're on our way to his place."

The woman frowned. "I never heard of such a thing."

"They do a lot they don't talk about. They can do anything they want, because everybody depends on them. Please don't give us away." Thérèse blinked her eyes, as if about to cry.

The woman pressed her hands together. "You poor things. You'd better follow me."

She led them toward her house. Andrew noticed that she was keeping near her kobold.

The woman's name was Josepha. The inside of her home smelled musty, as if she had been away and only recently returned. She had questioned them, and Thérèse had mumbled vaguely, avoiding answering.

Now the woman sat under her maple tree with a pad, sketching, while the children sat near the house, finishing the food she had given them. Josepha, although seemingly sympathetic, still kept her kobold at her side. The android faced them, hands at its waist.

"Was that true?" Andrew asked Thérèse.

"Was what true?"

"That story about the biologists."

"Of course not." With Josepha in the distance, the girl's voice was once again low and clipped. "It could be true. They made those things, didn't they?" She gestured at the kobold; it lifted its head.

"That isn't the same as experiments with people."

"What would you know about it?" Thérèse replied. "They made them, they made us, they used the same genetic material. They just make different modifications. What's the difference?"

"There's a lot of difference," Andrew protested, thinking of the dead kobold in the woods near his home. "They're limited. They can't do much without direction."

"I had to tell her something," Thérèse murmured. "It doesn't matter whether she believes it or not."

"Why not?"

"Because she won't do anything. First of all, we're kids, so she feels protective. Second, she's afraid. She won't do anything that might put her in danger, and that's why she won't alert anyone. The older people get, the fewer risks they take. Why do you think she's hiding away here? She's afraid. She'll do what we want. By the time she gets around to checking and finds out we lied, we'll be long gone. It takes them ages to make up their minds to do something anyway."

Silas finished his roll and leaned back. "Why take the chance?" he asked.

"I just finished telling you, it isn't a chance. She doesn't want to be threatened. I could wing her with this laser before that kobold stopped me, all it's got is a tranquilizer gun. They'd rather have their life than anything, those people. They beg for mercy; they do anything to avoid death."

Andrew felt sick. Thérèse's words were coarse and disgusting.

"Anyway, she's one of the scared ones," Thérèse continued. "I saw that right away. I've been running longer than you have. I need real food and a good night's sleep. Don't worry, I've done this before, and no one's caught me yet." Her voice was calmer.

"Why'd you run away, Thérèse?" Andrew asked.

She was staring past him, curling her lip. She was very quiet; he could not even hear her breathe. "I had my reasons," she said at last. She pressed her lips together and was silent.

They slept in Josepha's living room. That was where the woman had her holo screen and computer. The girl shook them awake at dawn. She had slept on a mat spread out on the carpet, leaving the large sofa to the boys. Andrew picked up his knapsack and hoisted it to his back while Silas yawned and stretched.

"We'd better get going," Thérèse whispered. She propped Josepha's drawing pad against the back of the sofa. She had written a message on it:

Dear Josepha,

   Thank you for the food, and especially for the bath. We really are grateful. We're going to head west now to find our friend. Maybe he'll call and thank you himself when we're settled. We'll be thinking of you.

                                        Terry, Simon, and Drew

Andrew had thought they'd been clever with their aliases; now, seeing them written out, they seemed a poor disguise. The words had been scrawled in a large, childish hand. Thérèse had transformed herself for Josepha, becoming a victimized and gentle child; she had played the role so well that even he had almost believed it. He and Silas had been merely the supporting players in the performance.

Thérèse signaled to them. They crept from the house, passing the kobold at the front door. The android looked up. "May I help you?" it asked.

The girl stopped. She seemed sad as she looked at the kobold. She raised one hand slowly and patted the kobold on the head. It smiled. "Is she good to you?" Thérèse asked. "Are you treated well?"

"May I help you? I can guide you to the road."

The girl drew back. "No, we're all right. Goodbye."

"Goodbye. It was nice to see you." It waved with one small hand.

The three headed across the lawn to the road. "Are we really going west?" Andrew asked.

"Of course not," the girl answered. "We're going north. Fewer people." She paused. "Maybe you two ought to go back. Josepha could get you home." She said the words stiffly, as if she did not mean them.

Silas said, "We'll stick with you."

She seemed relieved. They hiked along the road silently. The morning air was damp and cool; Andrew shivered. He wondered if his parents were looking for him now, if they had found out about the cats. Then he realized that they would probably search south first, because Silas had always talked about how things were better there.

Silas had fallen under Thérèse's spell. His friend followed her contentedly, as if happy to have found a leader. The ease of his surrender had surprised Andrew. He had thought of Silas as decisive; now he wondered if his friend had ever decided much of anything. His past actions now seemed to be only a surrender to his feelings.

He glanced at the girl as they walked. What would she do if they were found? She seemed desperate. He thought of how she had pulled away and slapped him, of how she had talked about death. She knew about him and Silas, but they knew nothing about her. Would she have hurt Josepha if the woman had tried to summon others? The girl had sounded as if she would, yet she had treated Josepha's android with kindness.

They left the road and began to climb a hill. It was dark under the trees; leaves rustled as they climbed. Thérèse's pockets bulged with cheese and dried fruit which she had taken from Josepha; she swayed as she moved. Andrew ached, though not as much as the day before.

Silas moved closer to him. "I keep thinking about my father," he said between breaths. "He must be worried. I think about it now, and it seems awful. I keep wondering why I didn't think of it before. I mean, I thought about it, but in a way I didn't."

"Does it bother you?" Andrew asked. Thérèse had moved farther ahead of them, setting her feet down heavily and awkwardly as if trying to flatten the earth. Her knees were thrust out; the upper part of her body was bent forward.

"I don't know," Silas said. "As long as I don't have to see it, it's like it isn't there. It's hard to explain. If I went home, I'd see how upset Ben is, and then I'd feel rotten, but here I don't see it. I know the sooner I go back, the better it'll be for him, but I'm afraid to go back, because then I'll have to see him getting mad and upset, and I don't want to."

"We have to go back sooner or later," Andrew murmured.

"I know." Silas sighed. "I didn't think of that, either. All I thought about was getting away and wandering around." He glanced up at Thérèse. Then he looked at Andrew for a moment. His eyes pleaded silently.

Andrew thought: He wants me to decide. Thérèse stopped and turned around, folding her arms across her chest as she waited for them to reach her. For a moment, she looked older, eyes aged and knowing, face set in a bitter smile. The wind stirred the tree limbs above, and shadows dappled her face, forming a mask over her eyes.

In the evening, it began to rain. They found shelter under an outcropping of rock. The rain applauded them as it hit the ground.

Andrew and Silas relieved themselves, pointing their penises at the rain beyond, then sat down. The ground was hard and stony, but dry. They ate their cheese and fruit in silence, then curled up to sleep.

Andrew dozed fitfully. His legs were cramped; if he stretched them, his feet would be in the rain. He stirred, trying to get comfortable. Something pressed against him in the dark.

"It's me," Thérèse whispered. He stiffened, afraid. Silas

was asleep; he could hear his slight snort as he inhaled. "Just don't grab at me, that's all. All right?"

"Sure," he whispered back.

She pressed her chest against his spine, draping an arm over him. Her body shook slightly and she sniffed. He heard her swallow.

"Thérèse, are you all right?"

"I'm fine."

"You're crying."

"No, I'm not." Her body was still. He turned over on his back, raising his knees, careful not to touch her with his hands, and settled his head against the knapsack. He was growing hard; he covered his groin with one hand, confused, afraid she would notice.

"Listen," he said softly, "maybe you should go home." Her hand tightened on his abdomen; he froze, and then went limp. "You could stay at my house first, if you want, or with Silas. They wouldn't mind."

"I can't go home." He felt her breath on his ear. "Do you understand? Not ever. This isn't some adventure for me. I'll always have to hide."

"But you can't stay out here."

"I can. It's better than what I had. They'll stop looking when I'm . . ."

Andrew waited for her to finish. He heard her sigh. She removed her arm. "I won't give you away," he whispered. "I promise."

She was silent. The rain was not as heavy now; the stream of water rushing down the outcropping had become a trickle. I'm your friend, Thérèse. He mouthed the words silently in the dark.

III

They stood at the top of a hill, facing north. The pine trees were thick around them; Andrew could catch only glimpses of the rolling land below.

Thérèse said, "Give me a boost." Silas cupped his hands; she raised a foot, and he boosted her to a tree limb. She scrambled up and gazed out at the landscape. Andrew watched her, afraid she might fall, and wondered if he should get out of the way. She crouched, hung by the limb with her hands, and dropped to the ground.

"There's a house down there," she said. "We can stop there, or go around it." She bowed her head.

"What do you want to do?" Andrew asked.

"I'm asking you." She did not look at him. "I'm going to have to move on sooner or later by myself, you know that. I don't want to get too attached to you."

Silas looked at Andrew. Andrew did not reply. The girl turned and started down the hill, motioning for them to follow. Andrew thought about Thérèse continuing on her lonely journey. She had traveled alone before meeting them. She could handle herself, but the idea still bothered him.

Why did she have to hide, living on the edge of the world? Maybe she hadn't lied about being part of an experiment. Once Dao had told him that some people were afraid of the biologists because they were dependent, all of them, on the scientists' skill. The dependency engendered fear. Thérèse must have made up the story after all.

There were, however, the kobolds and the trolls. He had never thought much about them. He recalled the way Thérèse had looked at Josepha's kobold, as if she were speaking to a person rather than to a being of limited intelligence. Were the androids aware of what had been done to them? Did dim notions cross their minds before being drowned out by their cybernetic links or the commands of their masters?

Andrew went down the hillside cautiously, avoiding the uneven ground and loose stones. He could now see the house. It was a two-story wooden structure, painted white; it stood a few meters from a dirt road overgrown with weeds and wildflowers. The land immediately around the house was dusty and barren, as if plants refused to take root there. A smaller building, its paint peeling, stood in back of the house.

They came to the bottom of the hill and walked up the road.

"I don't think there's anyone there," Andrew said.

The girl glanced at him. "Do you think you could find your way home?" she asked.

"I guess we could. We could always go back to Josepha's house."

"You'd have to tell her we lied. It doesn't matter. I'd have a head start." They walked over the dusty ground toward the house. The lifelessness of the land around the structure was disturbing. Andrew suddenly wanted to flee.

The front door opened. Something fluttered in the darkness beyond the outer screen door. Andrew moved behind Thérèse. The screen door swung open and a kobold emerged, followed by a woman. She wore a long white dress with a high collar; she crossed the porch and stood on the top step, watching them.

Thérèse held her arms out; the boys did the same. "Hello," the girl called out.

"Why, hello." The woman waved. "Come on up here. Let me take a look at you."

Thérèse hesitated. She balanced on the balls of her feet, as if ready to run. She moved a little closer to the steps. "Come on up," the woman said again. "Sit here, on the porch. I haven't had visitors in quite a while."

They went up the steps and seated themselves on the wicker chairs. The woman rested against the railing in front of them. The kobold stood near her protectively; it carried a silver wand. Andrew frowned; he noticed that Thérèse had also seen the weapon. The android's blue shirt and pants were wrinkled; its face was marred by a large nose and wide mouth. The woman beamed, unafraid.

"You poor things," the woman said. "You look as though you've had quite a trip."

"We have," Thérèse said. Now that Andrew was closer to the woman, he could see her face. There was something wrong with it; deep lines were etched around her mouth and eyes, and her jowls shook slightly as she spoke. Her skin was rough and yellowish. Even her hair was strange. She had pulled it back from her face, showing the gray streaks around her forehead and ears.

"Your face," Andrew blurted out before he could stop himself.

The woman glared at him for a moment, then smiled again. "You think it's ugly," she said slowly. "You think it's odd. Not all of us want to look twentyish. I like to look my age." She chuckled, as if she had made a joke. "What are all of you doing way out here?"

Thérèse licked her lips. "We're running away."

"Running away. How sad. I suppose you must have a reason." She held up her hand. "You needn't tell me what it is. People are so thoughtless. I wouldn't let any children of mine run away. You look as though you could use a good meal. Come on inside."

She led them into the house. The front room was small, but clean. Lace doilies covered the arms of the worn blue sofa and chairs; two heavy brass lamps stood on end tables. The desk computer and holo screen were against the wall.

"You just sit down and take it easy. My name's Emily. I'll go get you something from the kitchen." She squinted. "You're not wearing your Bonds."

"Of course not," Thérèse said. "We're running away."

"I'll be right back."

"We'll come with you." They followed the woman to the kitchen and sat at the small wooden table while Emily punched buttons on her console.

"I know what you're thinking," Emily said, turning to face them while the food was materializing. "You thought I might have a communicator here. You thought I'd send for someone. Well, I won't. I didn't move out here so that I could have people dropping in all the time. I don't like people." She grinned. "I like children, though. If you want to go running around the countryside, that's fine with me, but you can stay here as long as you like."

She removed the food, took out bowls, and spooned vegetable soup into them, putting them on the table with glasses of milk and a small loaf of bread. She sat down and watched them as they ate. Andrew forgot his worries, eating the soup rapidly, slurping as he did so.

Emily nodded at them approvingly when they were done. Something in the gesture reminded him of Joan. He tried not to think of his return home. He would get through it somehow, and then it would be over. For now, he was safe.

They slept in the front room. Thérèse had claimed the sofa; Emily had provided two cots.

The girl was awake early. She bumped against Andrew's cot as she rose; he opened his eyes and sat up. He watched as she took food and water from one knapsack and put it into the other.

He said, "You're leaving."

"I left you some stuff in the other sack, enough to get you by."

"You're leaving."

"You knew I was going to sooner or later."

Silas was still sleeping, arm over his eyes. "Listen to me, Andrew," she went on quietly. "I think you should wake him up and get going yourselves."

"Emily'll help us."

"There's something funny about her. I don't think you should stay here. I have to go." She moved toward the door, then looked back at him. "Andrew, if anybody tells you anything about me someday, just remember that it isn't how it seems. I mean, I wouldn't have hurt you two, I really wouldn't have."

"I know that."

"Goodbye. Say goodbye to Silas for me, will you? And get out of here yourselves." She opened the screen door and went out.

He got out of bed and followed. The kobold was outside the door. It let Thérèse pass, trailing her to the steps. A troll sat in front of the house, its long arms folded on the ground. Thérèse bounded down the steps and walked toward the road.

The troll rose and moved rapidly, scampering in front of the girl. She hopped to one side; it blocked her. She stood still for a few seconds, swaying, then hurried to her left. The troll ran, blocking her again.

"Let me pass," he heard her say to the creature. She stepped forward, and it hit her. She backed toward the porch.

Andrew watched, confused and apprehensive. Thérèse turned and faced him. Her chest rose and fell; her pink cheeks were becoming rosier. She squinted and shook her head. She spun around suddenly and danced to her right. The troll blocked her again; it was too fast for her.

Her hand fluttered at her waist. She removed her wand, pointing it at her antagonist. Andrew saw a flash of light; Thérèse cried out. For a moment, he did not know what had happened. The girl swayed helplessly, holding her right arm. The kobold darted past her and swept the rod up from the ground.

Andrew hurried back to Silas and shook him awake. The other boy moaned.

"Silas. Get up."

"What?" He shook his head and stared blankly at Andrew.

"Thérèse. The kobold shot at her."

Silas was awake. He jumped from the cot, following Andrew to the door. Thérèse had retreated to the porch, still holding her hand.

"Are you hurt?" Andrew asked as he opened the door.

"No, just my fingers. I'm all right."

"Listen, there's three of us. If we can distract the androids, maybe you can get away."

She shook her head. "I can't do that. I don't have my weapon now. This is my fault—I got careless. We should have left as soon as I saw she wasn't afraid."

"We'll be all right," Andrew said. "She probably just told them to guard us. As soon as she wakes up—"

"How do you know that?" Thérèse interrupted. "How do you know she isn't trying to keep us here?"

He didn't know. He went back inside and crossed the room to the console. He pressed a button.

"Code, please," the computer responded.

The machine was locked. Andrew shivered, backing away. Thérèse and Silas had come back inside.

"It won't work," he muttered. Thérèse was staring past him.

"How are my young visitors this morning?"

Andrew turned. Emily stood at the entrance to the room. She wore a gingham gown; her graying hair was loose around her shoulders. Another small kobold stood at her side; it, too, was armed.

Thérèse drew herself up, eyeing the woman belligerently. "We appreciate your hospitality," she said slowly. "We'd like to be on our way."

"Not so soon. I haven't had visitors in ever so long. Do take off that knapsack, and I'll get breakfast ready."

"We'd like to leave now," Thérèse said.

"But you can't."

"Why not?" Silas said loudly. His voice was high, breaking on the second word.

"Because I'm not ready to let you go." Emily smiled as she spoke. "Now, sit down. What would you like? Let's have pancakes. That would be tasty now, wouldn't it?"

Thérèse moved toward the woman, stopping when the kobold extended an arm, pointing at her with its weapon. Its black eyes narrowed. "You'd better be careful," Emily went on. "They're very protective of me, and I wouldn't want you hurt because of a silly mistake. Now, sit down, and stop being naughty. I'll get breakfast."

They spent the day in the living room, guarded by the kobolds. Andrew had been unable to eat breakfast or lunch; Silas had lapsed into a sullen silence. Thérèse kept wandering over to the window, as if searching for a way to escape. Occasionally, Emily would come to the door, smiling in at them solicitously. In the afternoon, she brought them a Chain of Life puzzle. Silas applied himself to it, assembling the pieces until he had part of the helix put together, then abandoned the puzzle to Andrew.

Andrew worked silently, trying to lose himself in concentration. The kobolds, standing nearby, watched without speaking. Once in a while, he looked up. The black-eyed android held its weapon with one hand while stroking its dark beard with the other. The blond one near the screen door was still. They were both ugly, the ugliest kobolds he had ever seen; it was as if Emily, with her own lack of beauty, wanted nothing beautiful around her. He wondered if she had made the creatures mute as well.

Andrew broke down at suppertime. Food had been laid out on the coffee table next to the helix. He stuffed himself, not tasting anything. Silas picked at his chicken while Emily hovered, beaming at them. Then she settled herself in a chair and sipped wine. She wore her white dress, but the setting sun in the window made the dress seem pink.

Thérèse was not eating. She scowled at the woman and drummed her fingers on the arm of the sofa. A finger caught in the doily. Thérèse tore at the lace, and it fluttered to the floor.

Thérèse said, "Give me some wine."

"Aren't you a little young for that, dear?"

"Give me some wine, *please*."

Emily poured more of the pale liquid into her glass and handed it to the girl. Thérèse downed it in two gulps and held out the glass. The woman poured more wine. Thérèse leaned back. Her face was drawn.

Andrew's stomach felt heavy and too full. Silas, seated crosslegged on the floor, had stopped eating. Emily said, "Would you like to hear a story?"

"No," Andrew replied.

"I'll tell you one, and then maybe you can tell me one."

Thérèse raised her glass, peering over it at the woman. She said, "Go ahead, tell it. It better be good."

"Oh, it is." Emily sat up. "It's very good. It's about a lovely young woman, like a princess in a fairy tale."

The young people were silent. Emily stared at the helix for a moment. "Once, there was a lovely young woman," she began. "She lived in a beautiful house on the edge of a great city, but she was very sad, because the world beyond was cruel and hard. Even in her citadel, the evil of the world outside could reach her. It was as if everyone was under an evil spell; a dark spirit would come upon them, and they would go to war. Do you know what a war is?"

No one replied.

"That's when people take all their talent and organize themselves to kill other people. Well, one day, something wonderful happened. The wars stopped. They stopped because some people had found a way to keep from dying. Now, before that, they had already found a way to stop people from aging as rapidly; they had a substance that cleared out all the protein cross-linkages."

"We know about that," Andrew said impatiently.

Emily shot him a glance. "Hush, child. Let me finish. These people had found a way to make everyone younger. You see, they were trying to find out about cancer, and they learned a lot about cells, and they found that they could stimulate the body to rejuvenate itself and become younger. No longer did our genetic structure condemn us. When people realized that they could live forever, the world changed. It was made beautiful by those who knew that now they would have to remain in it forever. We call that time the Transition."

Andrew fidgeted. Thérèse sipped her wine. Emily's long fingers stroked the arms of her chair; her pale hands had small brown spots around the blue veins.

"The young woman was happy. She opened her house to others, and they all spoke of the new age, their escape from death. But then the young woman began to grow weak. Soon she discovered that evil was still in her body. A malignancy was growing within her; her cells were out of control." Emily paused. "It didn't matter. The growth was soon inhibited by another substance, which enabled her immune system to control the disease. But later, when she received her rejuvenation treatments once more, the cancer returned. Her body was a battleground; her own cells were at war."

Emily's voice was trembling. Andrew moved a bit closer to Thérèse.

"Do you understand?" The woman's voice was firm again. "It was as if the woman had been cursed. When she received the treatment that would allow her to live, the disease returned, because the same process that caused her body to renew itself allowed those cells to grow. When she took interferon—that is what controlled the disease—she would be well, but growing older. Do you understand now? Each time, she grew a bit older physically than she had been; she was aging—very slowly, to be sure, but aging nonetheless. There were others who had the same problem, but she did not care about them."

The woman tilted her head. "She became a project," she

went on. "Biologists studied her. They discovered that she had a defective gene. The substance that enabled her body to rejuvenate itself triggered a response, and cancerous cells would multiply along with those that made her younger. Now, these scientists were able to keep this gene from being passed on to others, but they could do little for the woman. They tried, but nothing worked."

Andrew sat very still, afraid almost to breathe. Thérèse threw her head back and finished her second glass of wine. Silas cleared his throat uneasily.

"The young woman left the world," Emily said. "She didn't want to be where she could see the youthful bodies and cheerful spirits of others. When she had clung to hope, she had drifted into depression and deep sorrow. Now she released her hopes and accepted her situation, and found a freedom in so doing. Denied life—denied, at least, a full life—she would accept death, and find peace in the acceptance. So, you see, the story has a happy ending after all."

Emily's green eyes glittered. For a moment, her face seemed younger in the evening light.

Thérèse spoke. "The woman can still stay alive. She can still be helped. It's her own fault if she gives up. More is known now, isn't it?"

Emily smiled. "You don't understand. Hope was too painful. Even healthy ones sometimes seek death, even now; you know that. The evil hasn't disappeared, but it, too, has its consolations, even its own beauty. Flowers are beautiful because they die, aren't they? And isn't there a special poignancy in thinking of something you've lost? It's a mercy. That's what people used to say about death sometimes—it's a mercy. It was a good death. He didn't linger, he isn't suffering now, he's gone to meet his Maker, he's cashed in his chips, he didn't overstay his welcome, he's gone to his reward. Many of the old expressions were quite cheerful." She lowered her chin. "There is little new knowledge now, only tinkering, little workshops where they play with genes and make things like those." She waved a hand at one of the kobolds. "Something else died when we decided to live, and that was the possibility of great change. There is no hope for the woman, but it doesn't matter. There is a happy ending, you see. There, I've told you a story. Now you can tell me one."

Silas looked up at Andrew apprehensively. Andrew lifted his head, unable to gaze directly at Emily. "We don't have a story," he mumbled.

"Come, now. Of course you do, all alone in the middle of nowhere without your Bonds."

"No, we don't."

"Maybe your girl friend has one, then. Don't you, Terry? Why don't you tell it?"

Thérèse held out her glass. "Give me a drink first."

"You've had quite enough," Emily said, but she poured more wine anyway. Thérèse rose and walked over to the window; the dark-haired kobold moved closer to the woman. Thérèse turned around.

"All right. I'll tell you a story." She took a breath. "A girl was living with a man. She'd lived with him all her life. He wasn't her biological father, but he was the only parent she had ever known. He'd brought her home and cared for her ever since she'd been born." Her voice shook a bit as she spoke.

"A rather abrupt preface," Emily said. "But do go on."

"At first, he was kind. Then he changed. He began to come to her room at night. He'd make her do things, and sometimes he hurt her. It got to where she sometimes even liked the pain, because he'd be sorry for a while afterward, and he'd be nicer when he was sorry, and do what she wanted. But then it would start again. She tried to run away, but he hurt her badly, and she was afraid to try again. It was all her fault. That's what he made her think. Everything he did was her fault, because something in her led him to do it."

Thérèse's voice did not tremble now; it was flat and toneless. She perched on the windowsill; her face was shadowed.

"She was still growing. She began to change. The man didn't like that, because he didn't like women, only girls. So he began to give her the same thing that kept him young. It was tricky, but he managed. No one found out. They lived alone, and not many people saw her. He was only doing what the biologists do, wasn't he? He was shaping a body to be what he wanted, that's all; that's how he looked at it. The years went by, and the girl grew older, while still remaining a child. The man began to forget that she wasn't what she seemed."

Thérèse gulped the rest of her wine and set the glass on the sill. "The girl was careful. She watched the man and bided her time. One day, she was able to escape, and she did. My story has a happy ending, too."

Andrew realized that he was digging his fingers into his thighs. He tried to relax. Emily was watching the girl out of the sides of her eyes.

"You didn't tell the whole story," the woman said at last.

Thérèse shook her head. "Tell the rest. The girl didn't just run, did she? She killed the man while making her escape, didn't she?"

Thérèse did not reply.

"They're looking for her. She's still missing. She killed someone. You know what they'll do when she's found? They'll send her up." Emily pointed at the sky. "They'll exile her. They'll send her to a prison asteroid, with all the other murderers. She'll have to stay there. After a year of low gravity, she'll need an exoskeleton to live on Earth again. There won't be a happy ending if she's caught."

Thérèse moved her arm, hitting the glass. It fell to the floor, shattering. Andrew started. Emily rose. "Enough stories for tonight, don't you think? It's time to rest now."

She left. The bearded kobold remained; the blond one went out on the porch and stood in front of the screen door. Andrew got up and went to Thérèse. "It isn't true."

She said nothing.

"It isn't true, Thérèse. They won't send you away. They can't."

She pushed him aside and threw herself across one of the cots. He hovered at her side, wanting to touch her, but afraid to do so. She hid her face. Her body was very still.

The kobold made a sound. "Others," it said, and Andrew started. "Others, before. Other visitors. Gone now. Go to sleep."

The raspy voice made Andrew shiver. Silas stood. He picked up a plate and smashed it on the floor. Thérèse turned her head. Silas broke another plate. "Stop," the kobold said.

Andrew went to his friend. "Silas." He reached for the shadowy shape and held the other boy by the shoulders.

Silas shook his head and pushed Andrew away. "I'm all right now." He sat down on the sofa. Thérèse was lying on her side, her hip a dark hyperbola obscuring part of the window.

Silas lifted his chin. "Did you really do it?"

"Do what?" Her voice was flat.

"What she said."

"I didn't mean to. I was trying to get away. He tried to stop me. He should have let me go. When it was over, I was glad. I'm glad he's dead." The cot squeaked as she settled herself. "Go to sleep."

"Go to sleep," the kobold echoed.

Silas said, "We have to get out of here."

Thérèse did not answer. Andrew stretched out on the other

cot. The girl seemed resigned. He realized that Thérèse had only exile to anticipate, more wandering or a prison world. He heard footsteps in the hall; they faded, and the back door slammed. The house was quiet. There was light just beyond the window; the moon had risen.

Silas got up and went around the cots to the window. He put his elbows on the sill. The small shape outside the screen door disappeared; a small head appeared near Silas, making him look, for a moment, like a two-headed creature.

"Come out," the blond kobold on the porch said. It was a black shadow with a silver nimbus around its head. "Come outside."

Silas backed away. The bearded kobold crossed to the screen door. "Go on," it whispered, as if conspiring with them.

Silas came closer to Andrew. "They want to help us."

Andrew shook his head. "No, they don't. They don't want to do anything. Emily tells them what to do. Don't listen to them."

"If I could get away, I could get help. It's worth a try, isn't it?"

"Don't go outside, Silas." He looked toward Thérèse. "You tell him. Tell him not to go."

"Andrew's right," Thérèse said from the cot.

"They said there were others," Silas replied. "Maybe they helped them get away."

"You're wrong. Kobolds can only do what they're told; they have to be directed. They don't have minds." But Andrew heard the doubt in the girl's voice.

"It's worth a chance, isn't it?" Silas said. "Maybe you don't want to go because you know what's going to happen to you when you're caught. You don't want help to come. You don't care what happens to us."

"Don't go," Andrew said.

Silas leaned over him; Andrew could feel his breath. "It's your fault, too." Andrew shrank back, puzzled. "You should have stopped me before. If you hadn't come along, I wouldn't be on this trip. And it's her fault for having us stop here. I'm not going to stay because of what you say." He walked to the door; the bearded kobold let him pass. The screen door slammed behind Silas.

Thérèse slid off her cot and stood up. The kobold made a circle with its wand. She moved closer to the creature and it pointed the wand at her. Andrew rolled off his cot toward the sofa, trying to decide what to do. Thérèse backed to the window. The android's head turned.

Andrew's hand was reaching for the brass lamp near him. He pulled out the cord. He felt that he was moving very slowly. Thérèse lifted a hand to her face. He picked up the lamp. The kobold was pivoting on one foot. He saw its face as he leaped, bringing the base of the lamp down on its head.

It squeaked. The wand flew from its hand, clattering across the floor. Andrew hit it again, and it was still as it fell, its limbs stiff. He dropped the lamp and began to shake.

Thérèse was breathing heavily. "You took a chance," she said. "You really took a chance." She knelt and began to crawl over the floor. "I have to find that weapon."

"Use your light."

"I lost my light."

Andrew remembered Silas. He went to the door. Thérèse was slapping the floor. He breathed the night air and smelled dirt and pollen. Opening the door cautiously, he went out on the porch; his skin prickled as a cool breeze touched him.

The blond kobold was below, in front of the porch. Silas was running across the barren yard, kicking up dust. The troll was blocking him, leaping from side to side and waving its long arms as if playing with the boy. Silas darted to the left, but the creature was too quick for him. It herded him, driving him back toward the house. The boy hopped and danced, coming closer to Andrew.

Andrew came down the steps, pausing on the bottom one. The kobold saw him. He could hear Silas panting; there were shiny streaks on his friend's face. The troll put its hands on the ground and swung between them on its arms, lifting its knees to its chest. It grinned, showing its crooked teeth. Then Andrew saw Emily.

The woman had come around the side of the house and now stood to Andrew's left, watching the pursuit. Her white dress shone in the moonlight and fluttered in the breeze. She raised her hands as if casting a spell, and Andrew saw that she was holding a wand.

He opened his mouth to cry out. His throat locked; he rasped as breath left him. The woman pointed her wand. The beam struck Silas in the chest. He fell. Andrew heard a scream.

He stared numbly at his friend. A black spot was covering Silas, flowing over his chest; his eyes gazed heavenward. "Silas?" Andrew murmured. He swayed on the steps.

"Silas?" The troll stood up; the kobold stood near Silas's head. Dust had settled in the boy's thick hair.

Emily was walking toward him, still holding the wand. She was smiling; the blue stone of her Bond seemed to wink. Andrew faced her, unable to move. His limbs were heavy; invisible hands pressed against him. He saw one white arm rise.

A beam brightened the night. Andrew gasped. Emily was falling. Andrew clutched at his abdomen and spun around, almost falling from the step. Thérèse was climbing through the window; her feet hit the porch. She came to the railing and leaned over it, firing at Emily with her weapon. The white dress was stained. The kobold raised its wand. Andrew dove for it as it fired, and heard a cry. He wrested the weapon from it and knocked the creature aside.

Thérèse was screaming. She continued to fire at Emily. One beam struck the woman in the leg; another burned through her head. One arm jerked. The stone on Emily's Bond was black. Thérèse kept shooting, striking the ground near the body.

His vision blurred for a moment. He found himself next to the girl. "Thérèse, stop." She cried out as he reached for her, and held out her left arm. Her hand was a burned, bloody claw; he gasped, and touched her right shoulder. She tore herself from him and went down the steps to Silas. She knelt in the dirt, patting his face with her right hand.

"I was too late," she said, crying. The kobold sat up, rubbing its head. Andrew gripped his wand, aimed it at the android, then let his arm drop. The troll scampered to the side of its dead mistress. It lifted her in its arms and held her. A sudden gust whipped Andrew's hair; he caught the metallic smell of blood in the summer's dust.

IV

Joan tried to stop Andrew at the door.

"Where are you going?"

"I want to say goodbye to Thérèse."

Joan frowned. "I don't think you should."

"She's my friend."

"She killed two people." Joan's voice tripped over the word *kill*. "She's very ill."

"She's not. She did what she had to. She had to kill Emily."

Joan stepped back. "That woman was very disturbed, Andrew. She needed help, reconditioning. She was ill."

"She wasn't ill. She was going to die, so she wanted other people to die, too, that's all." He thought of Emily's body in the dirt, and his throat tightened; Thérèse had cursed their rescuers when they destroyed Emily's kobold and troll. The troll had looked at Andrew before it died, and he had thought he saw awareness in its eyes.

Joan took him by the shoulders. Her eyes were narrowed; her lips were pulled back over her teeth. "You'll forget all this. The psychologist will be here tomorrow, and that will be that. You'll think differently about this incident."

He twisted away and went out the door. Dao was outside. He let Andrew pass.

A tent had been put up at the bottom of the hill, a temporary shelter for Thérèse and the two psychologists who were now with her. They had questioned the girl and interrogated him; they had set up a tent because Joan had been afraid to have the girl in her house. Now they would take Thérèse away. The evil in his world would be smoothed over, explained and rationalized. Thérèse would not be sent to an asteroid; only people who were hopelessly death-loving were sent to one, and even they could change, given enough time. That was what the female psychologist had told him. They had high hopes for Thérèse; she was young enough to heal. They would help her construct a new personality. The mental scars would disappear; the cruelty would be forgotten. Andrew thought of it, and it seemed like death; the Thérèse he knew would no longer exist.

Thérèse came out of the tent as he approached. The brown-skinned woman followed her; the red-haired man was near their hovercraft, putting things away. Thérèse reached for Andrew's hand and held it for a moment before releasing it. The psychologist lingered near them.

"I want to talk to him alone," Thérèse said. "Don't worry, you'll find out all my secrets soon enough." The woman withdrew. Thérèse led Andrew inside the tent.

They sat down on an air mattress. The girl looked down at the Bond on her right wrist. "Can't get this one off so easily," she muttered. Her mouth twisted. She gestured with her bandaged left hand. "They're going to fix my hand first," she went on. "It'll be just the way it was—no scars."

He said, "I don't want you to go."

"It won't be so bad. They told me I'd be happier. It's probably true. They're nice people."

Andrew glanced at her. "Ben might clone Silas. That's what he told Dao. He's thinking about it. He's going to go away."

"It won't be Silas."

"I know."

Thérèse shook back her hair. "I guess I won't remember much of this. It'll be like a dream."

"I don't want you to forget. I won't. I promise. I don't want to forget you, Thérèse. I don't care. You're the only friend I have now."

She frowned. "Make some new friends. Don't just wait around for someone else to tell you what to do." She paused. "I could have just aimed at her arm, you know. Then she would have still been alive."

"She was dying anyway."

"They could have helped her eventually. She was dying very slowly. I didn't have to kill Rani, either." Her eyes were wide; she stared past him. "I didn't. He was down; he begged me to stop. I kept hitting him with the poker until his skull caved in. I wanted to be sure he wouldn't come after me. I was glad, too. I was glad he was dead and I was still alive."

"No," Andrew said.

"Stop it." She dug her fingers into his shoulder. "You said you didn't want to forget me. If you don't see me the way I am, you've forgotten me already. Do you understand?"

He nodded, and she released him. His eyes stung; he blinked. "Listen, Andrew. We'll be all right. We'll grow up, and we'll be alive forever. When everyone lives forever, then sooner or later they have to meet everyone else, don't they? If we live long enough, we're bound to see each other again. It'll be like starting all over."

He did not reply.

"It's true, you know it's true. Stop looking like that." She jabbed him with her elbow. "Say goodbye, Andrew. I don't want you hanging around when we leave. I won't be able to stand it."

"Goodbye, Thérèse."

"Goodbye." She touched his arm. He got up and lifted the tent flap. He wanted to look back at her; instead, he let the flap drop behind him.

He climbed the hill, trying to imagine endless life. Joan and Dao were on the porch, waiting for him. He thought of Silas. You'll always be afraid, just like them; that was what his friend had said. No, Andrew told himself; not any more. His friend's face was suddenly before him, vivid; Joan and Dao were only distant, ghostly shapes, trying to face up to forever.

The Loop of Creation

I

MERRIPEN STOOD ON THE WALL. A COLD WIND BIT AT HIS FACE, and he bowed his head, pulling his coat more tightly around himself. The wind shrieked. As it died, he leaned against the ledge and his hand touched an invisible shield. He drew back.

Outside the Citadel, snowflakes swirled as they fell, making white patches on the brown earth below, riming the trees of the forest. He felt the wind again; flakes bathed his face and sprinkled his arms with white specks. The shield was down again. He waited. The snow continued to fall, but he no longer felt it; the wall had corrected the shield's malfunction.

Merripen sighed. Were such problems becoming more common, or did it only seem that way? He could count on the shield's failure at least once a season. It had failed during the summer. The temperate weather of the Citadel had been replaced by hot, humid air and thundershowers, forcing him to stay inside until the wall had repaired itself; the repairs had taken two days. He wondered if the shield would eventually fail completely, and told himself it would not matter if it did; the wall would remain.

The wall was high; the ground was over fifty meters below him. Four towers stood at each corner of the wall, guarding the buildings inside the square. The wall could not be climbed;

there were no handholds or niches in its smooth metal sides,
and the entrances were guarded. But someone could fly in if
the shield failed. Merripen shivered, even though he was protected from the wind, and found himself looking up at the gray
sky.

Something moved below. He stepped closer to the ledge and
saw a shadowy figure running through the forest; obscured by
a snowy veil, it was barely visible under the bare tree limbs.

The figure stopped at the edge of the forest, waved its arms
aimlessly, then hurried toward the wall. It staggered, leaving
an uneven trail of footprints behind it on the patches of snow.
It was dressed in a long brown coat; a hood hid its face. Merripen watched the runner calmly, knowing it would be stopped
at the entrance. Then the hood fell back, and he saw the thick
blond hair.

Merripen turned and ran toward the nearest drop. He
jumped into the circular tunnel and floated down through the
wall past lighted entrances until he reached the bottom. He
hurried through the lighted hall.

Two giants stood at the entrance. The dark-haired giant
pulled at the heavy brass door, opening it a little. Merripen
heard a shout from outside. A gust of wind scattered snowflakes across the gleaming floor, and he felt the cold. The giant
picked up the blond man and carried him inside.

The second giant pushed the door shut, then stood with its
back to the entrance. Its small eyes, almost hidden under a
mop of brown hair, stared expressionlessly at the other giant,
who was setting the man gently on the floor.

Merripen waved the dark-haired giant away. "Leif," he
said, taking the man by the arms. Leif swayed, leaning against
Merripen for a moment. He was breathing heavily; Merripen
struggled to support him.

The blond man suddenly crumpled to the floor, almost pulling Merripen with him. "Let me get help," Merripen murmured.

Leif shook his head. "Give me a minute—I'll be all right."
He sprawled on the floor; his cheeks were chapped and red. "I
ran. I was running for a while. I had to stay out there last
night. I had to leave my lifesuit behind. Without my heater, I
would have been frozen."

He drew back his lips, as if trying to smile.

"Where's your hovercraft?"

"Gone. I had to leave it."

"Why didn't your Bond signal for help?"

Leif held out his arms. His hands trembled; he took off his gloves and began to rub his hands together. "Because I don't have it on." Merripen's right hand darted reflexively to his left wrist and touched his own Bond. "I took it off."

"But why?"

"They were tracking me. I had to get rid of it. I stamped on it and buried it. Then I started running."

"Who was tracking you?"

Leif grabbed Merripen's hand and pulled himself up. Then he fell back again; Merripen caught him just before he passed out.

"Get help," he called to the giants.

Nulla fugae ratio, nulla spes: omnia muta,
omnia sunt deserta, ostentant omnia letum.
Non tamen ante mihi languescent lumina morte,
nec prius a fesso secedent corpore sensus . . .

No hope, no signs . . . all doomed; yet death would not dim his eyes nor would his senses leave him. These were the lines of Catullus Merripen now called to mind; the lusty verses had been forgotten.

He sat alone in Peony's garden, waiting for her to join him. Her flowers were orange; vines of giant trumpet creepers wound around the trellis near Merripen, the blooms as large as his arm. Flame azaleas bordered the garden, and miniature orioles, tame and timid, pecked at the seeds Peony had scattered while watching Merripen warily with their beady eyes.

A small, flat screen rested on his lap. Idly, he searched his records, and words appeared on the screen.

Any viable modification must preserve human versa-
tility, human flexibility, the capacity to adapt both
physically and mentally to changes in environment. Ex-
cessive specialization through biological experimenta-
tion on the human form will always be a dead end.

Merripen frowned. Had he actually written those words? Then he had betrayed them, many times over. He thought of the giants who guarded the Citadel, beings with feeble minds and rudimentary emotions, controlled by implants. Yet the

genetic material used in their creation had been human. At
least the giants had been created with an end in mind, however
limited; the same could not be said for other projects.

Merripen searched through more writings, glancing at the
words as they fluttered across the screen. The paper on which
he had written them had long since crumbled away, yet the
words lived on. It seemed to him that the man who had written
them was also gone, and that only his ghost remained.

> Why do so many seek death? Too many of us still
> wish to die, and even the most unoriginal death cult can
> still find adherents. It is as if the mechanisms for death
> were inherent. But why do some seek death while others
> are content to live? Natural selection—

Some words had been crossed out. He went to another page.

> What traits do long-lived human beings need? What
> qualities would enable us to best lead our lives? Perhaps
> by creating beings who do not share certain traits with or
> who have other characteristics, we can discover what it
> is we need. From these different kinds of beings, new
> values can emerge, ones which we might share if we
> altered ourselves somatically.

In a margin, scrawled by hand, he saw another comment:
"Naturalistic fallacy?"

He turned off his screen and set it under his chair. His words
lived on in the cybernetic mind of the Citadel, still able to
haunt him. The cybermind kept what it wanted, as if sensing
that it would one day be the only guardian of the past left. Leif
had been chased back here by those who hated the Citadel and
all it stood for. Many biologists lived outside the centers now,
and had turned against their own work. With that betrayal, the
biologists had lost what power they had. Now the world was
fragmented. In isolated enclaves, unchanging immortals lived,
and waited for the Citadels to die. Most of the houses near
Merripen's had been abandoned. There would be more defec-
tions.

Peony Willis swept into the garden, greeted Merripen, and
motioned with one hand. A kobold with golden hair carried a
glass of wine to him, then withdrew.

Merripen sipped his wine while Peony seated herself. Two

young men appeared, dressed only in orange loincloths. They leaped over the grass, performing backflips and handsprings while Merripen tried not to look bored. One of the men danced near him and smiled, but Merripen ignored him. The pair had been bred by Peony for gymnastics and dance and flirting; Merripen, in his sexual encounters, still preferred at least the illusion of free will.

Peony waved the young men away; they bowed and left. She adjusted her orange robe and frowned at Merripen, who was wearing a red shirt. She lifted her chin and lowered her eyelids, making slender crescents of her black eyes.

"I spoke to Leif Arnesson," she said. "You asked him to go outside for you, and he went, and he found nothing, and the people he saw turned on him and chased him back here. Are you satisfied?"

He did not answer.

"You won't find your children, Merripen. That's what you call them, isn't it?"

"But I spoke to Teno. I was told that they were coming back here, that they . . ." He paused.

"And how long ago was that? Before the wall was built. Even the cyberminds can't find them, because they speak only to the minds of other Citadels."

"I have to find them."

"Why?"

"I don't know if I can explain it to you. We talk about the Transition as if it's something that happened in the past. But it isn't over, Peony. It's still going on. I'm convinced that my children are planning something important."

"And maybe they're not," she said. "And what will you do then?"

"I must find them."

"You're becoming obsessed. You can't go out there."

"I can't go out there," he said slowly, "because of what we've done."

"Is that what you think?" She gripped the arms of her chair. "What would you have had us do? It's the hostility of others that keeps us here. Life must find its niche. Would you have had us destroy the creatures we made? Don't they have a right to live?"

"We went too far." He twirled his empty glass, not knowing what to do with it. The kobold reappeared at his side and took the glass away. "We didn't think, we didn't consider."

The scent of the orange flowers was too sweet, the trilling of the tiny birds was becoming odious. In his mind, he was wrestling with Peony on her tidy lawn, pulling at her long black braids, scattering the birds as he pulled her robe from her body and nuzzled her breasts. He thought of plucking the flowers and dropping them on her smooth olive skin.

Peony lifted one slender arm and extended a finger, as if about to scold him. "Am I listening to Merripen Allen? Are you sure you're not an imposter? I thought you were the one who started it all. Now you don't believe in what you've done, and you're looking for some sort of justification. Well, I won't help you. I won't have you confusing me or anyone else with your doubts. You'll have to look for them all by yourself." She smiled. "And I don't think you have the courage to do that. You're safe here, doubts and all. Think about that."

Leif and Merripen were walking near the north wall. The hills of the Citadel, protected by the shield above them, were still green. Beyond the hills, Merripen could see the glassy pyramid that housed the wombs and the nursery. The nursery garden was empty; briars were growing among the untrimmed shrubs. Near it, the research center, a sprawling rectangle with glittering golden facets, seemed tarnished.

Leif lifted his foot, peering at his healing ankle. "There's something I should tell you," the blond man murmured. "I didn't mention it before because I didn't want to raise your hopes, and I didn't tell Peony because—well, you can guess."

Merripen took his arm. Leif shook his hand away. "I met a woman named Seda in that town, before I had to make my abrupt departure. She said a visitor had come through there a long time ago. She remembered the visitor because he seemed so young, and because he was so unemotional. A cold fish—that's how she put it. Androgynous appearance. Very reserved."

Merripen tensed. "It sounded like one of them to me, too," Leif went on. "She asked where he was going, and he said something about joining friends, then left soon after. She felt that there was something not quite right about him, but obviously he wouldn't have wanted anyone there to find out if there were."

Leif stopped and sat down on a stone bench, stretching out his legs. Merripen sat next to him. "When did she see this person?"

"She didn't know; the memory was vague. Keeping track of time isn't our strong point. I doubt that she would have remembered him at all if I hadn't been asking questions which just happened to jog her memory. I worried about whether I should tell you this or not." Leif's voice sounded sharper. "If I'd mentioned it to Peony, I'm sure she would have told me to keep it from you."

Merripen was silent.

"Try to understand her. She's trying to hold it together here, what little is left. Too many people are gone. She doesn't want you to leave, and if you do, she might not let you come back."

"She can't do that."

"Why not? She's still the Director. A useless title in some ways, but it does give her certain powers. She could keep you out if she feels it's in our best interests. You could go to another Citadel, of course, but even they might not welcome you once the word gets around. You have to understand your place. You were the prisoner; you've given our Citadel a certain legitimacy. If you start questioning what we've done and go wandering off, then anyone might." Leif sighed. "When I was younger, a lot younger, I stuck my nose into everything. I was a zealot. It took me a long time, but I finally learned patience. Let them fight it out beyond our walls, let the Rescuers hunt souls and the others form their isolated little groups. Some will live, and others won't, and we can wait it out. I owed you a favor, so I went outside for you. Wait it out, Merripen."

"You're not going to help me search, are you."

Leif shook his head. "Not any more. I discovered something useful out there, namely that I no longer have my old adventurous spirit. I'd rather be safe."

"And you know I haven't got the courage to go out there alone. And so does Peony. You might as well not have gone at all."

Leif stretched out a hand, but Merripen refused to take it. "I didn't have to tell you anything. I could have lied and told you that they'd left Earth altogether. If you're that determined, I can give you some advice. I think there's someone here who might go with you. At least you could ask."

"Who?"

"Andrew Aguilar."

Merripen frowned. "I don't think I know him. You'd think I'd know everyone. We aren't exactly overpopulated."

"You must have seen him anyway. He came here about fifty years ago. He's not a biologist, which is why Peony won't be concerned with whether he leaves or not."

"What's he doing here, then?"

"He followed Terry. She used to say that wherever she was, he'd turn up sooner or later. Don't you remember?"

An image appeared in Merripen's mind; a small man, dark brown hair, features with an Asian cast to them. Somehow the memory felt unpleasant. He tried to get a fix on it; he must have seen the man at Terry's house. He tried to recall when he had last seen her; she was usually distracted by some project in the aviary, a place he never went. "I don't know," he said. "I guess he didn't leave much of an impression."

"Andy might go with him. He wants to get away for a while —he just needs an excuse. Ask him."

"I will."

"But before you do, think about it some more." Leif got up and looked down at him. "I think if you leave, you'll never come back."

Merripen rose. He hadn't considered that. The world outside seemed formless, the society inside the Citadel secure and safe. He wondered if he should give up that safety on a whim, for a discontent he did not really understand. It was not just the Citadel he might lose; he could lose his life. He shuddered. He clung to this life, as everyone did, however valueless it was.

"I'll come back," Merripen said.

Terry Lamballe lived in a small cottage near the nursery. Merripen had passed it several times and had been inside infrequently; the dwelling always seemed abandoned, closed up and shuttered. He had thought of calling first, then decided to take a chance and walk over. If Terry were busy, she wouldn't be there to answer or would ignore his signal, and he did not want to make his proposal to Andrew Aguilar over the holo.

The cottage was, as usual, shuttered. The pine trees next to the house cast shadows over the roof and made the place seem hidden away, a place of secrets. He approached the door, knocked, and waited. He knocked again.

"There's no one home."

He turned. A man stood in the shadows under the trees. He came closer to Merripen and stopped at the bottom of the front steps. Merripen recognized him now. Andrew Aguilar was short but muscular; his legs were knotted by muscles. He wore a short-sleeved yellow shirt and shorts.

The unpleasant memory was at last jarred loose. Andrew and another man had fought. Merripen could not remember what the fight had been about, and doubted he had ever known, but it had disrupted Terry's party and sent her guests home hastily.

"I wasn't looking for Terry," Merripen replied. "I was looking for you. You're Andrew Aguilar, aren't you?"

Andrew did not answer. Merripen retreated from the door and came down the steps. Andrew backed away a bit, circled, then stood on a flat piece of rock near the path; his brown eyes were now almost level with Merripen's.

"You are Andrew Aguilar," Merripen said again. "I believe we met some time ago. I'm Merripen Allen."

"And you say you're looking for me?"

Merripen nodded.

"Whatever for?"

Merripen was wary. The smaller man was intimidating; he stood on the rock watching him as though waiting for a confrontation. Merripen's shoulders ached; he found himself longing for his usual aimless, placid discussions with others. "I need some help on a project I'm planning."

"A project? Help from me? How novel. I'm not a biologist: I can't help you."

"It's not that sort of project."

"I'm surprised any of you would ask my help on anything."

Merripen was irritated. "Why do you say that? You've been here long enough to find something to do. You're free to become a biologist or researcher any time you choose. I'm sure Terry told you that." He was no longer sure he wanted to travel anywhere with this resentful, hostile man.

Andrew sighed. His shoulders sagged and he smiled faintly. "You're right, of course. I have been helping Terry train some of her birds, the falcons. They're hard to train, and she doesn't have the stomach for it." Merripen frowned; he hadn't known that Terry raised falcons. "They always fly away, though. I release them outside the wall when they're ready. They have to fend for themselves sooner or later." He paused. "I've been thinking of following them myself. So I might not be able to help you."

"But you can. I'm looking for someone to travel outside the Citadel with me."

Andrew widened his eyes slightly and raised an eyebrow. "Travel?" he said softly. "When were you last outside this place?"

"I can't remember."

"Are you planning to leave for good?"

"No." Merripen was beginning to fidget. He pulled at his mustache, then put his hands into his pockets, trying to keep them still. "I might as well be honest with you. I'm a little worried about traveling alone, and you've been outside more recently than I have. There aren't many others here I could ask."

"I see. You need a bodyguard of sorts. Why not take one or two giants? You'd be protected that way."

"You must know why. There are too many places where a man traveling with their kind wouldn't be welcome. I need to find some information. I don't know my destination yet. If you don't want to go, that's fine. Just tell me, and I won't bother you again."

Andrew waved a hand. "I haven't said I wouldn't go." He walked over to the steps and sat down, motioning to Merripen to join him. Merripen sat, noticing that Andrew had not asked him inside. "Tell me why you want to leave this sanctuary."

Merripen folded his hands, trying not to move them as he spoke; he often got carried away, waving them wildly as he gestured, forcing others to back away. "I'm looking for someone. For a group, actually. A long time ago, centuries past, in fact, I had a project. I got together a group of people who wanted to be parents. The children they had were their own—I used their genetic material—but they were different. They were to be more rational, without certain of our instincts, and hermaphroditic. My hope was that they could adapt to extended life more successfully than many of us have."

Andrew nodded. Merripen glanced at him; the brown eyes were expressionless.

"Eventually, the children grew up and went their own ways. They separated and lived among others. Occasionally, one or another would contact me, perhaps out of duty—I was never able to tell whether they had any special feeling for me, or for anyone." He was gesturing with his hands again; he forced himself to keep them still. "A while back, I heard that they were gathering here somewhere, and since then I've heard nothing. I want to find them, see how they're doing. Leif Arnesson went out to see what he could discover, but he's given me little to go on. He suggested I ask you."

"In other words, you want to travel around looking for a group without knowing where they are, or even if they're anywhere around here."

"Yes."

"Why don't you just wait until they contact you again?"

"It's hard to explain." Merripen felt it again, the apprehension tinged with anticipation; his stomach fluttered and his muscles grew tight, while his face began to perspire. He was impatient. He wasn't used to impatience. He was surprised that he could still feel it. "I don't want to wait. I want to find them now. I can't help thinking that it's important for me to do so."

Andrew draped an arm over his knee. "It sounds like a dubious adventure. I don't know." Merripen opened his mouth, and Andrew raised a hand quickly, silencing him. "I haven't decided yet; I'm just thinking out loud. The only safe way to travel is with a lot of planning, and the willingness to feel your way as you go. You can fly, but I think a hovercraft is safer, even if it's slower and exposes you more. You have to make your plans and still be willing to change them quickly if you need to. We could get information from other Citadels, but I doubt we would learn much more than we already know about what's out there, so essentially we'd be traveling into unknown territory." He frowned. "That was the first project, wasn't it? Yours, I mean."

Merripen nodded.

"Terry told me. Terry won't work with human genes."

"I know that."

"She'll only work with birds, and even there she's conservative. She doesn't approve of most of the things you've done. She only stays here because it's easier to do her work here, and because . . ." Andrew looked away. "She's safe. Safe from others and from herself." He smiled. "I've known Terry since I was a child."

"Really?"

"I always come back to her." He stood up. "I'll probably go with you. I suppose we'll need time to prepare. We should wait until spring; it'll be easier then." He turned, went up the steps, and disappeared inside the cottage.

Merripen rose. As he walked under the pines, he wondered again about Andrew. But he had to travel with someone; Andrew was his only hope.

He should wait. The Citadel would protect him. If he couldn't find his children, and if Peony refused to let him return, where would he go? He shook his head. He was scaring himself for no reason. There were other Citadels, and Peony would soften in time, forgetting her disagreement with him.

He would be able to return. He had grown too fearful, he who
had once wanted change. Now he was afraid to alter his life
even for a moment; there was too much time in which he
would have to live with the results of his decisions.

Merripen had fallen into the habit of meeting with Andrew
to discuss their journey. He had hoped that they would not
only plan, but would also use the discussions as a way to grow
accustomed to each other's presence. But Andrew remained
opaque. Merripen could not figure out why he had decided to
leave, or why he had remained in the Citadel for so long with
so little to do. He never spoke of Terry and never even made
the conversational digressions so common among others. He
spoke of equipment or routes, then went his way.

Merripen's Bond signaled; someone was calling. He put
down his glass and turned on his holo, expecting to see
Andrew's image, or possibly Leif's. Instead, Terry appeared.

"Merripen?" She rushed on, heedless of ceremony. "I want
to talk to you."

He sat up on his couch. "Talk away."

"Not like this. I'll come over. I'll be there right away; I'm
nearby. Is that all right with you?"

"Certainly," he said, and her image was gone before he
could say more. He leaned back. He did not know Terry well
and had always considered her an anomaly here, with her birds
and her barely disguised disdain for almost everyone. He supposed that she wanted to talk to him about Andrew. Maybe
she did not want him to leave.

Terry arrived a few hours later, more punctual than he had
expected. She strode past him at the door and sat down by his
front window without a greeting. She brushed a hand through
her reddish-brown hair and crossed her legs, swinging one leg
nervously. He sat in a chair across from her.

"May I offer you something?"

She said, "You're going to leave the Citadel with Andrew."

"So it seems."

"I don't think you should."

"You're not the only one. If you don't want Andrew to go,
then talk to him about it. I don't want to interfere." He
thought of all his plans, but his regret was tinged with relief.

"It's not that," she replied. Her abrupt tone and belligerent
stare were making him uneasy. "You don't know anything
about him. I'm saying that if you go, you should take someone

else." She extended one leg, then crossed her legs again, jiggling her foot. "I know Andrew. I'm the only one who does. You could call it a fixation. He always finds me, wherever I go, or I find him. There are things we can't really share with anyone else, even though we never talk about them. That's how it is." She heaved a sigh. "I don't care if he goes; we can't be together all the time. I've always looked out for him, though. I protect him."

Merripen was bewildered by this contradictory speech. "What is it, Terry? I still don't know what you want."

She uncrossed her legs and was still. "Andrew's afraid. He's always been afraid. He has his reasons, but I won't talk about them. The point is that he keeps trying to show that he isn't. He tests himself against his fears. He'll do something to prove he isn't a coward rather than deciding calmly that it's not worth the bother. I don't even think he would go on this trip of yours if you hadn't asked him to—he would have gone somewhere else he knows, where he'd be safe. But you gave him a challenge. He could do something reckless. It might mean trouble for you."

"What should I do, then? Call him and tell him I've changed my mind? I won't go at all, then. I don't mind admitting that I am afraid. I won't go out there alone."

"Don't be stupid." He started at her rudeness. "It's not that dangerous. I don't care what anyone says. Really murderous people must have died out a long time ago. But Andrew might cause you trouble. He's drawn to danger, in a way."

Merripen stood up. "If you don't want Andrew to go, then work it out between yourselves. I've made my plans." He spoke with a confidence he did not feel. She would talk Andrew out of going, or he would travel with a companion he would have to worry about. He continued to stand, but Terry showed no sign of getting up to leave. At last he sat down again.

Terry bowed her head. "If you insist on going, then be careful. If you get into trouble, just look out for yourself. Don't let Andrew get you into something you can't handle."

"Maybe you've known him too long. He might have changed." He looked at her hopefully for a sign of confirmation. "You might be seeing him the way he was."

She shrugged. "Don't tell him I talked to you. He probably suspects I have, but I'd rather his suspicions weren't confirmed."

Merripen grimaced. Now she wanted deception from him. He hardly knew the woman, and with one short visit she had disoriented him and threatened his plans.

She got up and moved slowly toward the door. "Tell me something," he said quickly. "If it's not that dangerous out there, then why are you here? You don't seem to like it, but you stay."

Terry looked away from him. "I'm dangerous," she said in a low voice. "I'm dangerous to them. I'm all right here." She stared at her hands, as if wanting to thrust them from her. Then she left.

II

Merripen and Andrew stepped outside. The massive door closed behind them with a clang. The light of false dawn, reflected by the vast, flat surface of the wall, lighted their way to the hovercraft. They would go north for a bit, then approach the settlement Leif had visited from another direction. No one would know they were from the Citadel. They had made up a story to offer if they were two visitors from the south, bored with long, idle days.

The night air was cold. Merripen shivered; he had not slept. The sprouting grass glittered after the frosty night; spring would be delayed. Merripen got inside and waited for Andrew, then put in their route. The craft lifted and floated forward silently. Merripen leaned back and gazed at the stars.

He had seen Peony only yesterday. She had asked him again not to go, hinting that she might not let him return, but he had not relented. Then she had given in, apologizing, looking defeated and unhappy.

Merripen still wore his Bond, but he would soon be too far from the Citadel for help to arrive in time. The craft would be their only protection; its motion soothed him.

Andrew was silent. At first Merripen thought he was sleeping, but the other man stirred in his seat and cleared his throat. The hills in the east, outlined by gray light, were black; Andrew's face was hidden in shadow. He said, "It's an odd name."

"What is?" Merripen asked.

"Your name. Merripen."

"It's a Gypsy name. It means life. It also means death."

"I suppose that's appropriate." Merripen heard Andrew move in his seat again. "You should enjoy traveling, then."

"Wanderlust isn't a genetic trait." The hovercraft floated up a hill. If he looked back, he might be able to catch one last glimpse of the Citadel. He did not turn around. He could not go back now. Somehow, the thought eased him; he had been more nervous while planning the trip, while thinking that he could still change his mind.

He rubbed his forehead. His eyes burned, and his eyelids felt gritty. "Terry didn't want me to go," Andrew said.

"I know."

"She talked to you about it, didn't she?"

"Yes, she did." Merripen was sure there was no harm in admitting it now.

"She thinks I'll cause problems, I suppose. We've known each other a long time."

"She told me that." Merripen glanced into the darkness where Andrew sat. "What happened with you two?"

"It's nothing. We've separated before. She told me that if I didn't come back, she'd find me sooner or later. But she's wrong. I don't think she'll leave the Citadel. I'll have to find her." Andrew paused. "We lost a friend long ago—I mean truly lost him. He died, right in front of us. Terry blamed herself in part. I guess I blamed myself, too. We were helped afterward, of course; we could have had the experience completely erased. In fact, I think Terry did, a couple of times, but I always brought it all back when she saw me. After a while, we didn't want to forget. If we had forgotten, our friend would truly be dead. His memory brings us together."

Merripen shivered. It all sounded morbid to him; it was unhealthy to dwell on such things. Did it make Terry and Andrew savor life more to ponder their dead friend? It seemed a perversion. He imagined Terry and Andrew behind the shutters of her house, making love in a room dark as a grave. Whatever gratification it gave them, he could see that it imparted little joy.

"We're not lovers, you know," Andrew continued. Merripen looked at him in surprise. He could now see Andrew's face in the dawn light; his eyes were the black hollows of a mask. "We never were. But that sort of thing doesn't hold people together for long."

Andrew was trying to unburden himself. Merripen did not want to listen. He did not want to know that much about the

man; it would only make him worry throughout their journey
and distract him from his purpose. He waited, but Andrew
was silent.

The sun was high when Merripen awoke. He looked through
the grayish surface of the dome at a deep blue sky and a bright,
round star. The hovercraft was floating over a field of stubby
brown grass toward a forested ridge.

Merripen raised his seat and sat up. Andrew was awake, finishing a piece of fruit. He climbed into the back with the pit,
dropped it into the top of the materializer, opened the dispenser door in its side, and offered a peach to Merripen. "The
town's up there," he said.

"I know." Merripen ate his fruit. "They've probably seen
us already." They had been careful not to bring anything from
the Citadel that might give them away. The craft drew closer to
the ridge; the slope was steep. A dirt road led into the trees.

They floated up the ridge, over the road. The sun was hidden by the trees; something small and furry darted away from
the path. The road was leading them deeper into the woods.
As Merripen began to wonder where the town was, he suddenly saw it. Houses of brown unpainted wood with sharply
angled roofs were ahead, lining the road. The town seemed
deserted. Merripen took over the hovercraft and brought it to
a stop; it bumped the ground lightly.

Nothing stirred among the houses. Merripen thought he saw
a face in a nearby window. Andrew was back in his seat; he
had folded his hands so tightly that his knuckles were white. A
light flashed on the panel in front of Merripen; he heard a soft
chime. He turned on the small screen next to it and saw a dark
face.

"Who are you," a deep voice asked, "and why are you
here?"

"My name's Allen," Merripen replied. "My friend is
Andrew. We're sightseers from the south."

"Would you please give me your personal codes and the
code to your system, so that we can check?"

Merripen gave him the information, and the screen went
blank. They had arranged with a Citadel farther south to have
codes for their false identities placed in the system of a
southern town which, although not friendly to the Citadel
there, was not overtly hostile either. The man would discover
that he and Andrew were two aimless fellows who considered

themselves students of geography. Even so, he was nervous. He tried to steady himself. The worst that could happen was that they would be told to go away; in the absence of any reason for hostility, no one would risk a confrontation. But this town was his only lead.

The man's face reappeared. "Please get out of your vehicle and walk up the street. You'll get your things back when we've searched them. Keep your hands at your sides."

They got out. The sun's warmth was blocked by the trees around the houses and road. Merripen hugged himself while Andrew stamped his feet. They had worn light clothes, as if unaware of how cold it could get in the north. Merripen lowered his hands, remembering the man's warning.

They walked up the street, stopping when they reached an island of grass and benches in the middle of the road. Merripen looked back, regretting that he had left his lifesuit in the vehicle. Three people had appeared and were now climbing into the hovercraft.

A tall man was walking toward them; as he came closer, Merripen recognized the face of the man who had spoken to them. He wore a parka and baggy brown pants; his frizzy black hair was clipped close to his head. He stopped near Merripen and smiled, showing large white teeth, then thrust out a hand.

"Welcome to Pine Point," the man said. Merripen shook his hand and he offered it to Andrew. "My name is Karim. I hope you enjoy your visit. Will you be staying long?"

"We're not sure," Andrew replied. He slapped his sides with his hands and danced a little on his feet.

"You'll be comfortable," Karim said. "We may seem somewhat rustic, but we don't shy away from convenience." He waved one long arm at a house across the street. "You are free to stay there. The house is empty now. One of our residents left us for warmer climes. I suppose it's fitting that men from the south should stay there now."

"That's very kind of you," Andrew said. Karim's glance had fallen to Andrew's pocket, which bulged slightly.

"Excuse me." Karim extended a hand, palm up. "May I see what you have in your pocket?"

Andrew reached in slowly and drew out a knife in a leather sheath. Merripen tried to hide his surprise; he hadn't known Andrew was carrying it. "I like to whittle and carve," Andrew explained.

"May I have it, please?"

Andrew gave the knife to Karim, who drew it out, then sheathed it again. "It doesn't look much like a carving knife." Andrew was silent. "I'm afraid I'll have to keep it. We put all weapons there." He pointed to a low one-story cabin. "If you want it back, you must go there and tell the computer how long you need it for. You may of course have it back when you leave. The only weapons we keep in our homes are trank rods; there is too great a chance of accidents otherwise. You do understand. If there are other weapons in your craft, we'll have to take them, too."

Merripen tried not to show his apprehension. He was not disturbed by the confiscation, but by the realization that the town had weapons other than tranquilizing rods. He silently cursed Leif; he had not even mentioned this. Perhaps he hadn't known.

"It's a carving knife, not a weapon," Andrew was saying. Karim smiled, but kept the knife. Andrew leaned forward as if about to object.

"Don't let me keep you," Karim said. "As soon as we're finished with your craft, we'll bring it to your door." He turned and walked down the road toward the vehicle.

Merripen and Andrew hurried toward the house. As they reached the door, Merripen said, "That was stupid."

"Bringing the knife? We might need it."

"For what? Carving? You shouldn't have brought it."

Andrew ignored him and went inside; Merripen followed. The front of the house was one large room. The paneled walls were bare; there was a fireplace in the wall to the left. A wooden stairway led to a balcony overlooking the room. There was little furniture; a table and chairs at one end by the windows, an old brown couch and two overstuffed chairs near the fireplace. But there was also a computer, and a holo with a large screen, and, by the table, a dispenser.

Andrew prowled the room restlessly, turning his head from side to side. He strode back to Merripen. "I hope we don't have to stay here long."

"Leif told us we'd be all right," Merripen said, trying to believe it. "We just have to be careful."

"Leif might have been wrong. He didn't know about the weapons."

"I'll start worrying when I see a line in front of that cabin." He tried to smile. He heard voices outside and went to the door.

The hovercraft was there. A woman standing near it glanced at Merripen as he came outdoors, then turned away. Karim stood with two other men, gazing up the road that rose before them and disappeared into the forest. A woman dressed in a red parka emerged from the woods; she carried a rifle. Two men behind her struggled under their burden, a deer carcass which was tied to a long pole.

Merripen lifted a hand to his mouth and felt sick. He pressed his lips together. The deer's hide was caked with blood. Karim was staring at him. Merripen's legs shook; he leaned against the door frame. The taller man came over to him. Merripen could not speak.

"We have to trim the herds," Karim said. "Otherwise, they would starve. That would be a more painful death. We don't waste anything. The meat is good and the hides can be made into clothing. The tracking and hunting keep us alert as well."

Alert for what? Merripen thought, keeping his eyes from the deer.

"You believe we live in the world without being part of it," Karim went on. "It isn't true. Go out there while you're here. You'll see the little white rabbits and tiny elephants and even a few little elves. Human beings made them, thinking they were harmless toys. But they live, and they breed, and they eat, and the deer have less because of them. We honor the deer, in our way. But when we see one of those laboratory creations, we use it for target practice. That is their only useful purpose."

Merripen did not reply, and at last Karim left him.

Andrew had met Seda, the woman who had spoken to Leif. He had been paying her visits for three days. Merripen had worried at first that Andrew might push things too quickly and rouse the woman's suspicions, but instead Andrew had been cautious, and Merripen was now repressing his impatience.

Seda had invited them both to her house. Merripen walked with Andrew down the road, passing the spot where the deer had been butchered and its haunches carried away. He fancied he still saw blood on the road. Andrew stopped before one house. It looked like all the others, simple and plain.

Seda met them at the door. "Hello," she said in a husky voice almost as deep as a man's. Merripen studied Seda while Andrew introduced them. She was very small and thin, with birdlike bones; her large black eyes were her most prominent feature. Her smooth, unlined face was like a mask. He could lose himself in her eyes. They were ancient eyes; he saw her age in them and suddenly felt that she knew everything about him. He had kept one fear to himself, mentioning it to no one: that he might meet a person old enough to remember Merripen Allen.

"Please come in," Seda said. She drew them inside, gliding into the room, her long blue dress trailing across the floor. The large room inside her house was cluttered with velvet chairs; a love seat with embroidered flowers and gold arms stood near the fireplace. A chandelier studded with prisms of colored glass hung from the ceiling, and the windows were hidden by heavy red velvet curtains. It all seemed out of place in this setting. Merripen tried to imagine Seda in a parka, tramping through the woods with other hardy residents of Pine Point.

The chandelier tinkled and swayed. Seda waved at it. "Boadicea," she said, and Merripen saw the heavy coils of the snake resting among the prisms. He stepped back hastily. "She's a boa constrictor, of course. Don't worry, she's harmless and very lazy. A friend gave her one of those awful little rabbits a few days ago, so she's quite well fed."

She led them to the chairs near her fireplace. Merripen sat down carefully, afraid the delicate chair might break beneath him. Andrew sat down while Seda draped herself across the love seat, curling her legs. "You didn't pick the best time to come here," she went on. "It gets so muddy during spring. Summer's nicer. Autumn is quite beautiful. From the top of the hill, one gets such a fine view of the foliage."

"Do you have many visitors then?" Merripen asked carefully.

"Oh, no. No one travels often now. It's so much simpler just to wire up, don't you think? Perhaps you don't, since you're here. I've journeyed all over the world wired up to my lovely holo. It's exactly like being there, but without all the problems. I suppose many places have changed since they were recorded, but I can visit them as they were, when everything was so much more pleasant. There are terrible things in the world now, terrible things."

Merripen nodded, trying to think of how to bring the conversation back to visitors.

"You must have met Karim," Seda said. "Such a lovely man, so cultivated. He hasn't spent his life in banal pursuits, unlike others. He's well suited to long life—he nourishes his mind and intellect while exploring our older instincts. If our systems broke down, he would survive, which is more than you can say for some people, who think our cozy cocoons will protect us forever. Karim was a biologist, you know."

Merripen looked up. "I didn't know."

"Oh, yes. He was a microbiologist in one of the off-world research centers. He did important work in cell biology, and also in genetic transplantation using viruses. You can thank people like him for the fact that your body can produce its own ascorbic acid. Don't look so disapproving, Allen." Merripen had started, then settled back in his chair. His memory had been jostled. "Karim still does some work, but it's only pure research now, not the kind of thing others have done. He came back here when he saw what was happening out there."

Merripen tried not to fidget. Andrew seemed calm, his arm draped casually over the chair arm, but his fingers twitched and his face looked tense.

"Oh, Karim still likes to dabble," she continued. "He even has gravitic generators in his laboratory so that he can produce the weightlessness he needs for his cells to remain suspended in their culture medium. But he's not really interested in applications, only the work. We draw the line." Seda raised one thin eyebrow. "I see you still seem disturbed."

Merripen tried to adjust his expression.

"A long time ago, a man wrote: 'Beware of the pursuit of the Superhuman: it leads to an indiscriminate contempt for the Human.'"

Seda lifted her eyes toward the ceiling. "That is our guiding principle here. We do not try to be something we're not. Some of the things human beings are or have become are not pleasant, but we acknowledge them and control them—we don't pretend they're not present and we don't seek to eliminate them, as some biologists have thought they could."

Merripen thought of the dead deer and looked away from Seda's dark, glassy eyes. He was uneasy; he didn't want her to dwell on this topic, afraid she might make a connection and figure out what he was. Perhaps she already had. He gripped the slender arms of his chair tightly, then forced himself to relax.

"It's too bad more people don't travel," Andrew said. "I don't think one could really get the flavor of this place without actually coming here. The pace of the town, the atmosphere—you couldn't get that wired up."

"Oh, I think you could." Seda leaned back and ran a hand through her feathery black hair. "Oh, yes. Anyway, one always has one's imagination." She pursed her lips for a moment. "And it would certainly be better if some people didn't travel at all. We had a Rescuer show up here recently. We realized what he was immediately, because he gave himself away in his conversation with Karim. Of course, we didn't let him in, and he finally went away, but we were all very careful for some time afterward. Karim is no fool."

"I'm sure he isn't," Merripen murmured.

"He's also not all-knowing. We had a most disagreeable fellow here lately. I wish I could remember whether he came before the Rescuer did, or later. Perhaps it was at about the same time. Let me think—it was snowing then. This man was from the Citadel near here, so you can be sure that he was up to no good."

Merripen widened his eyes and smiled blandly. "I hope all your visitors aren't so unpleasant."

"Well, you two are here, aren't you?" Seda sat up, tilted her head, and transfixed him with her eyes. He was trapped by her gaze. "You should have Karim take you out on a trail," she went on, and her husky voice caressed him. "Perhaps I'll go along, too. You needn't take rifles if you're squeamish. I could bring something back for Boadicea."

"I don't know how long we'll stay," Andrew said, breaking the spell. "We may go west, to the lakes. Perhaps we could do some sailing there."

"I wouldn't advise that."

"And why not?"

She frowned. "We never go in that direction. Something very strange is going on there. I've heard rumors. Some of us think that unchanged people live there, living and dying as human beings did long ago. Others say that some sort of experiment is going on. We are not about to provoke them, needless to say."

"Well, then, we won't go there," Merripen said, worrying that he might have to go there, if only to find a clue. One of his children might have gone there.

Seda rose. "I've been neglecting your comfort." As she spoke, she arched her back slightly; the velvet fabric of her dress tightened across her small breasts. "Let me get you some brandy."

They left Seda's house at midnight. She had spoken of her snake, which she praised for its placid, reptilian temperament, and of her skill at archery, and of people she had known, and it was not until they were leaving that Merripen realized she had not told him what he wanted to know. He was oblivious of her words, recalling only the low voice, the large dark eyes, the slender hand that had rested lightly on his arm as they walked to the door. She had told them in parting that she wanted to hear all about them next time, but he suspected that she only wanted listeners who had not already heard everything she had to say. Yet she drew him; her old eyes promised a long flirtation and a skillful seduction.

The town was very quiet as they walked. The moon silvered the road. Merripen stepped on a twig and its crack filled the silence, making him start. Andrew walked with him, head down; he had been unmoved by Seda's glances, perhaps even irritated. An owl hooted in the forest. The cool air bore the astringent scent of pine.

As they came to their borrowed house, he noticed a light through the half-open curtains. He felt relieved that he had left it on; the thought of entering a dark house disturbed him. Andrew opened the door, and they walked into the welcoming light.

Karim was sitting by the fireplace. "What a pleasant surprise," Andrew said, an edge to his voice.

Karim regarded them coldly. In the shadows around the chair, his skin was almost black. His full lips were drawn back, as if he were about to snarl. He said, "You lied to me."

Merripen moved closer to Andrew. The smaller man scowled at Karim. He was suddenly afraid that Andrew would do something rash. "Whatever do you mean?" Merripen asked.

"You lied to me."

There seemed no point in denying it. Merripen tried to decide what to do; he disliked such direct confrontations. He put a restraining hand on Andrew's shoulder. Andrew tried to twist away, but Merripen held on until the other man was still.

He released him, then walked slowly toward Karim. He sat down on the sofa across from him and motioned to Andrew. Andrew sat next to Merripen, perching on the sofa's edge. "You're right," Merripen said. "We lied. You wouldn't have let us in otherwise. We'll get our things and go."

"Please. Not so quickly. I want to know why you came here. You're from the Citadel, aren't you? Don't tell me you aren't. You haven't the manner of Rescuers, and you're not from the south." Karim's hands gripped the arms of the chair. "You must think I'm unobservant. There was something about you which jarred my memory, and then there was that man who visited here last winter. I thought: He was from the Citadel, so maybe they've sent someone else. I knew I'd seen you somewhere. It took me quite a while to locate the memory. I had to put on the Band and relive half my life, even digging through things I'd forgotten altogether. But I finally found it. Merripen Allen." Karim smiled in satisfaction. "People here are so rarely alter their appearance. We cling to the outward signs of an identity which seems stable, but isn't. You should have thought of that before you came here. I'm quite an activist, you know. I have several lectures of yours from centuries back. That was how I verified that it was you."

Merripen's head hurt. I can't show him I'm afraid, he thought. "We're ready to leave," he said. "We don't want to disturb anyone here. I'm not here on the Citadel's business anyway, only my own. They disapprove of what I'm doing. Andrew was the only one who would come with me, and he's not a biologist, only a visitor who was staying there with a friend. The man who was here before came only as a favor to me."

"I want to know what you hoped to find here."

"I came because I had heard that someone here had seen a person I'm trying to find. Seda had said something to my friend that led me to think she'd seen that person a long time ago." Merripen took a breath, leaned forward, and began to tell Karim of his old project and his doubts.

As he spoke, the faces of his rational and strange children rose before him, all with the same steady, calm gaze. He had been gratified when they had turned to him, seeming to place more importance on his guidance than on that of their parents. He had been with them only long enough to see that even he could not know everything about them, that the minds he had thought would be clear as a stream had their eddies and currents. Even their sexuality had surprised him. He had assumed that they would lack interest in that irrational expression of desire; instead, they seemed to think of it as a rational pleasure. It was more than he had been able to accomplish, even after all this time. He had envied and hated them for it; he had wanted angels. In the end, they had left their parents and him, and had done little except lead the same sort of lives they might have led if they had been ordinary human beings. They had taught him nothing; they had not shown humankind the way to a new sort of life.

As Merripen talked, giving as many details as he could, Karim nodded and said nothing beyond an occasional murmur. By the time he was finished, the other man's face had lost its ferocity.

"I see," Karim said, staring past Merripen. "Your friend should have come to me. By the time I had found out who he was, several of the others here were searching for him. They only wanted to send him back with a warning, but he eluded them."

"I think you can understand why he didn't go to you."

"Oh, yes. Our feelings sometimes run high. Can you blame us? So you thought you'd learn something from Seda. That woman has been through so many transformations I wonder that she can remember the day before yesterday. She's had erasures a dozen times at least. Occasionally something floats up from the sea of her unconscious, but it isn't always reliable —sometimes it's an incident someone else related to her. Eventually, she'll have another erasing and be young and lively for a while until she begins to do the same things over again. In the end, she doesn't change at all. It's the same life, endlessly repeated, except that each time her mind ages more quickly and becomes more encrusted. What did she tell your friend?"

Merripen told him.

"You see," Karim responded, "your friend should have come to me. I remember that visitor. I suspected something, but the creature was gone before I could verify my suspicions." Merripen bowed his head. "But not before the visitor spoke of going west to meet friends."

Merripen sat up. "When? When did this happen?"

"Over two hundred years ago; almost three. They might still be there, they might not."

"I've got to find them."

Karim grinned. "You are an odd fellow, Merripen Allen. You are expending a great deal of effort looking for people who might not even be on the planet, and with only the vaguest of reasons. Aren't you making the same mistake over again?"

"What mistake?"

"You made them thinking that they would offer you insights into human life. But of course they can't. Their lives are their own, with their own values. Now you're looking for answers from them again."

"You misunderstand," Merripen objected, not so sure that Karim did. "Pigs can't fly, and birds can't learn calculus.

Perhaps we're simply not suited to extended life the way we are. That's what I thought then. And then I wondered if we could learn something about it."

"If we're unsuited as we are," Karim said, "then why not change ourselves? That seems to follow from what you've said." He was silent for a bit, as if considering the possibility. "But we were very adaptable in the pre-Transition past. Not all of us, of course, only the survivors. Maybe we should simply stick to only minor improvements in the design."

Merripen had no answer to that. "Maybe I won't find anything. But I have to try. It was enough to bring me outside the Citadel when I could have stayed inside, safe." He sighed. "I guess there's nothing more I can learn here. We'll be off in the morning, if that's all right with you."

"Heading west?"

Merripen nodded.

"There is something you can do for me."

"And what is that?"

"Allow me to accompany you."

"And why do you want to do that?" Merripen asked.

"I've been here a long time. Perhaps I need a change."

Merripen did not believe him. He had barely begun his search, and he was losing control of it. "You have no reason to go," he said slowly. "You already know what you think."

"Do I? Am I not allowed to have my own questions? I've done enough here, and I can always come back later. Besides, you should consider one thing. You might have need of me. I know how to hunt, and I can handle weapons. I'm also not afraid to use them. You'd be safer with me. I've lived out here, and you haven't."

"If you had wanted to leave," Andrew said, "you could have left before now."

"I would have, had you not arrived. But I think it's safer to travel in a group." He rose. "Think it over. You may give me your answer tomorrow. I'm prepared to go at any time."

He left them. Merripan got up and began to walk toward the stairs.

"No," Andrew said. Merripen turned. "We can't travel with him. There's something he's not telling."

Merripen turned around. "Do we really have a choice? I suspect that if we don't go with him, he'll follow us anyway. It might be safer to bring him along. And he's right about one thing—he's used to living out here."

"I can take care of myself."

"Maybe so. But even you might do better with someone to back you up. I'm not sure I can trust myself." He thought: I'm not sure I can trust you, either.

He went up the stairs, lingered by his bed for a moment, then peered over the balcony. Andrew was still sitting by the fireplace. "You'd better get some sleep," Merripen called to him.

"I could go back to the Citadel by myself. You'd still have a companion."

"I thought you wanted to get away."

"There are other places I can go."

Merripen turned away and began to undress. He thought of the Citadel and his house, safe behind the wall and shield. He could have been in Peony's bed now. It was not too late to go back; Karim had given him an excuse.

He heard Andrew's footsteps on the stairs. The other man had turned out the light below; Merripen waved a hand, turning on the light between their beds. Andrew passed him silently and shed his clothes, leaving them on the floor. He dimmed the light. The other bed squeaked. Then Andrew said in the darkness, "He can come along, I suppose. You're right, we have to go with him."

Merripen stretched out on his own bed, tired but overwrought. He turned over on his side, then got up again and moved toward Andrew. He reached out, tracing the muscles on the other man's arms.

Andrew drew his hands down to his ribs. "Don't we owe ourselves more of a flirtation, Merripen?" His back arched as Merripen held him by the waist. "It's too sudden. We'll miss half the fun."

"Maybe we will. But it'll be too distracting to conduct one on the trip. And I'm tense now; I need to relax."

"Is that the only reason, your needing to relax?" Andrew's hands were on his hips.

"No."

He got in next to Andrew. He felt his breath on his ear. "First yours," Andrew whispered, "then mine." Fingers brushed the insides of his thighs. He seemed to feel them at a distance; his mind drifted away, thinking first of the children and then of Seda's eyes.

"Andrew," he said as the other man's mouth surrounded him, and he thought only of the tongue tickling his shaft. His body arched and trembled and he heard a moan. For an instant, timelessness held him; then he was sinking, trapped by the earth, caught again in time. An image of the dead deer filled his mind; he wondered why he was thinking of that now. When Andrew turned him on his side and pressed against his buttocks, he did not resist.

III

Karim had closed up his house and exchanged words with a tall, red-haired woman before leaving. No one else saw him off. As Merripen got into his hovercraft with Andrew, he began to wish he had postponed their departure; he would have liked to see Karim's laboratory and talk about his work. And then there was Seda. He sighed. It never died away in him; his rejuvenated body kept it alive. He thought of letting himself age, letting it wither, so his mind would have clarity and peace.

Karim led them; his hovercraft preceded them down the hill. Merripen glanced at Andrew. The other man was staring at him blankly. Andrew lifted one eyebrow and one corner of his mouth curved up. The sexual tension was gone; whatever happened between them now would be only repetition. The experience would be stored in Merripen's mind, eventually to fade and become confused with others like it.

As they emerged from the trees, the dome brightened. The sky was blue and cloudless. Karim was opening his dome. Merripen looked up nervously, then opened his own. He smelled dewy grass and wet ground and, beneath that, the stink of rotting wood. The ridge to their left sloped, becoming a small, treeless hill. They circled around the hill and moved west, the sun at their backs. Karim had talked about danger in the west; perhaps he knew a route around it.

Merripen thought of his lifesuit. He had not put it on because Andrew refused to wear his, and he had not wanted to suit up under the other man's mocking gaze. Karim scorned the suits, saying that they made one careless. It was probably true. They might guard people from injuries, but not from weapons. He tried to tell himself that he would be safe enough inside the craft, while longing for the extra protection.

They floated over a wide field, the grass swishing as they passed. Andrew was wiping his knife, which Karim had returned to him; then he attached it to his belt.

"Do you really need that, Andrew?"

"Of course."

"I haven't seen you doing any carving."

"I haven't found the right kind of wood."

A black cloud rose in the south. Merripen watched as it grew larger, and heard a high, musical note; the cloud separated into small, winged shapes. Andrew began to close the dome; Karim was closing his as well.

"Should we stop?" Merripen asked.

"I don't think we'd better." The birds were flying toward them. They swooped down, and Karim's dome disappeared under the small, feathered creatures. Their dome darkened. Merripen looked up and saw tiny clawed feet and flapping wings. The birds sang sweetly, fluttering their purple feathers.

"They're Terry's," Andrew said, "and harmless. At least they were meant to be, but they've multiplied." The trilling was so loud that Andrew had to shout. "They were tame once. Terry used to wander around with a few on her shoulders and arms." Had they been in the open, Merripen thought, outside their craft, the birds would have landed on them, caroling their songs while they struggled to brush them away.

He saw patches of light above; the birds were leaving. They lifted, a few at a time, and flew away, soaring to the north.

"Terry should be more careful," Merripen said. He could see Karim's craft again; he decided to keep his dome closed.

"They won't survive out here," Andrew replied.

"They seem to be doing well enough."

"They're gentle things. Other creatures will prey on them."

"They'll adapt." Ahead, under the grass, Merripen sighted jagged pieces of asphalt. They floated over the shards, following the old road.

They stopped at noon. Karim got out and stamped his feet. "What now?" Merripen said as Karim came up to him.

"I need to stretch." They stood on a crag overlooking a river. "I think we'd better go south, detour. There are some mysterious settlements straight ahead."

"What do you know about them?"

Karim frowned. "I've never seen them myself. I had a friend who did. He came back to Pine Point with stories about unchanged primitives. He decided to go back for another look, and that was the last I ever saw of him. It's unlikely anyone there could help you anyway."

Merripen walked to the edge of the crag and gazed at the

muddy waters below. "There's a small town south of here I know," Karim went on, "because I've talked to the people there over the holo. I tried to contact them before we left, but I got static, so they might be making repairs. You know how easy it is to procrastinate on maintenance, we don't check as often as we should." He stretched his arms. "Those people might know something, and we have to go that way anyway."

Merripen nodded. Andrew wandered toward them, waving one arm. "Someone's out there," he called. "Look."

Merripen saw only grass, trees, and small hills. "There it is," Karim murmured. Merripen saw a flash of silver behind some maples. "I suggest that we get into our vehicles and press on."

"We could be followed."

"We can worry about that if it happens." Karim lifted his head. Merripen heard the chime. He looked down. All of their Bonds were lighted; someone was calling.

"Let me speak," Karim said, spinning around and striding toward his hovercraft. He climbed inside and pressed the front panel, peering at the screen.

"Hello," a woman's voice said. Merripen leaned over Karim's shoulder and caught a glimpse of a face framed by short blond hair before Karim waved him away. "I didn't expect to see anyone out here. Where are you going?"

Merripen stood up and stared at the distant craft. It was still moving slowly toward them through the trees on this side of the river. "South," Karim said.

"Really? How nice. Have a good trip." Merripen peeked inside again. The face had disappeared from the screen. Karim was scowling.

"We'd better go," Karim murmured.

"Want some company?"

"If you like."

Merripen turned toward Andrew. "You ride in our craft. I think I'll travel with Karim for a bit." Andrew nodded and went to the other vehicle while Merripen climbed in next to Karim.

They moved south, passing the other craft on the way. The woman smiled and waved at them; her dome was down. Karim lifted a hand.

"I guess she's just another traveler," Merripen said.

"She's alone."

"She must be brave. Or very young."

"I don't like her manner."

Karim was silent after that. Merripen stared through the dome at the river for a while, watching the sunlight dance on the water as its gleam followed them. At last Merripen said, "I should have liked to see your lab."

"I don't have anything your Citadel doesn't have."

"I meant your own work. What have you been doing? Seda said you'd been in space for a while."

"That was a long time ago." Karim paused. "We think we've changed things here, but it's nothing to what happened there. Those born on Luna already had bodies adapted to that world, and the same was true of those living in orbit. Their skeletal bodies seemed normal enough to them; the environment had already altered them, so what difference did more changes make? They no longer lived on Earth, and they could build their own ecologies, so why worry about changes in themselves? They were already living in the most unnatural of environments, and they were free to be whatever they liked. So they believed. They did not realize what limits they had placed on themselves until much later. Each group became a prisoner of its own artificial world, and it was too difficult to adapt to another. There they are." He gestured at the sky. "I think they built their own tombs."

Merripen shook his head. "That didn't have to happen."

"Of course it didn't have to happen. They had the universe before them, but instead they turned inward rather than looking out. Only the people on the moon saw what was happening in time. They exult in their humanness and, strange as those bodies might seem to you, those skinny, pale, elongated forms, they are at least human. I'm surprised you didn't live in space. Your ideas certainly have been tested there."

Karim's talk had only made Merripen doubt the purpose of his journey. He leaned back in his seat. "What sort of work have you been doing since you returned?"

"Not very much." He turned toward Merripen. "Don't get me wrong. I've had my doubts, but I don't object to the idea of change. I simply believe that it's very important to understand your goal, your purpose."

"You can't always know that ahead of time."

Karim looked away. It was obvious that he did not want to discuss his work; perhaps he felt that it was too trivial. Merripen watched the river, then said, "What brought you to Pine Point?"

Karim folded his arms. "Originally, it was the solitude. Of course, there hasn't been any solitude there for a while. People joined me by ones and twos. Soon, I was rarely alone. Not that I minded—being alone can become disturbing, especially in such an isolated spot. But the presence of others doesn't always mitigate one's loneliness."

"I know," Merripen responded, thinking of the Citadel.

"The sameness of it was reassuring, though, after what I'd seen off-Earth. We developed our own rituals and customs. I would have been happy simply to live in the forest itself, unencumbered." He was silent for a moment. "That would have been impossible, I suppose. We do need our support systems."

Merripen nodded, thinking of the hovercraft that shielded them from the world outside.

"I went home once. I mean my real home, the place where I was born and raised. I could only get a shuttle to the coast, and then I had to make my way home by glider, because the jungle was impassable by then. My home had been just outside Kampala. I searched. For a while, I thought I had made a mistake, had forgotten where it was. But I hadn't. It was gone, as though it had never been. Don't ever go home, Merripen." He leaned forward and studied the board, then pressed a panel. Merripen heard a metallic whine. "We're being followed, tracked."

"By whom?"

"By that woman, I suspect."

Merripen looked around, but saw only Andrew's craft. "But why?"

"I told you I didn't like her manner. She wasn't cautious enough. I think she's a Rescuer."

Merripen tensed. "What do you think she'll do?"

"She may do nothing. She may get bored and go away, or she may contact us again."

Merripen leaned back. Rescuers were probably the only truly fearless people left, because they did not fear losing their lives. There was no defense against such a person. The Rescuers looked beyond this life, to the afterlife they believed would be theirs. He thought of the distant craft and shuddered. He wondered how many Rescuers there were now; perhaps not many. Their ways were not conducive to long life. He tried not to be afraid. There was one Rescuer, if that was what she was, and three of them. Even so, she had the advantage. Her life was one of her weapons.

Karim said, "It must have been hard for you to leave the Citadel."

"It was. I had to bring Andrew. I couldn't have traveled alone."

"Few people can. I wouldn't have relished traveling alone myself, even though I wanted to leave. I *had* to leave." Merripen again wanted to ask him why, but something in the other's tone discouraged him from doing so.

At dusk, they stopped on the top of a hill. Below them, a dirt road wound through underbrush and came to a dead end at the bottom of the slope. Karim got out and stretched. Andrew was pacing. He stopped, shading his eyes with one hand. As Merripen approached him, Andrew said, "She's out there."

"Can you see her?" Merripen peered at the long shadows.

"No. But she's there."

Karim walked over to them. "I have a suggestion. I think we should keep going and sleep on the way. I don't care for the idea of traveling at night, but—" He waved a hand at the land below. "We'd reach Harsville sometime tomorrow, and we can set the crafts to follow old roads and clearings, so we shouldn't run into obstructions. We'll be safer once we reach other people."

"And what happens," Andrew asked, "if we should get stuck somewhere? At least here we have a view of everything below."

Karim smiled. "You won't be able to see much by night. We'd be safer on the move. Up here we're exposed. We'd have to sleep in the vehicles anyway. We might as well keep moving."

Andrew stared sullenly at the ground, then lifted his head. "Very well." He frowned at Karim's back as the other man returned to his craft.

Merripen rejoined Andrew. Their hovercraft floated down the hill after Karim's. Merripen adjusted his seat, lowering the back. Andrew was already stretched out on his side. Merripen closed his eyes.

He stood on the wall and lifted his face to the warm sun. He turned and gazed at the houses below. The research center and the nursery had disappeared; instead, a stone castle stood in the center of the town. He saw young people walking toward the castle and recognized his children. They had come back to him at last. He flew, soaring over the people below. Their faces were turned up to him. He was falling.

He jerked, and raised his head. The sky was black and starless. He sat up slowly. Andrew mumbled something sleepily and turned over on his back.

Merripen reached out cautiously and touched a panel. The craft was silent; the woman was no longer tracking them. He stretched out again, trying not to think of her.

Shadows danced across his eyelids; he saw a red glow. He opened his eyes. The sky in the east was scarlet.

Andrew was already awake; he was in the back, hovering over the dispenser. He handed Merripen a cup of tea, a muffin, and jam. Merripen ate his breakfast silently and handed his cup and plate back to Andrew, who dropped them into the cleaner and then crept toward the toilet, closing the door of the booth behind him.

The road ran past a forest. Merripen stared out at the abandoned apple trees, barren of fruit. He tried to imagine being without the craft out here, without their dispenser. He would not have known how to survive. Karim, at least, knew how to hunt and could find edible plants. The thought of eating dead animals and dirty leaves made him feel sick. He glanced at the materializer as he raised the back of his seat. Once people had thought it would be possible to travel using a variation of such a device; this long, dangerous journey would have been unnecessary. He could have stepped into a booth and, in an instant, stepped out at his destination. A safe way to travel; everyone had wanted it. But the man who would have stepped out would not have been him, only his duplicate; the safe way to travel would have killed everyone who used it. Would he have known? Probably not. He would simply have vanished, and another Merripen would have led his life.

"I wonder how close we are," Andrew murmured as he climbed back into his seat. "I hope Karim knows what he's doing."

"He's more experienced than we are."

"So he says."

The sky was growing cloudy; Merripen wondered if it would rain. Karim's hovercraft floated into an opening in the trees, and they followed. The darkness seemed reassuring. The sun gleamed on the dome of Karim's craft as it floated back into the open, came to a stop, and settled to the ground. Merripen took over his own craft and pulled up to Karim's side.

In the distance, near the horizon, another hovercraft stood on an old bridge leading over a small river. A blond woman stood beside it.

Karim got out of his craft; Merripen and Andrew hurried to him. "She must have guessed where we were going." Karim sighed. "There's only one thing to do. We can't show her that we're afraid. We could just go over the water and avoid the bridge, but she would only follow us anyway. If she says anything, act friendly and sympathetic." He turned toward them. "You realize, of course, that we can say nothing to her about our work, or what we're trying to find out."

Merripen nodded.

"It's unlikely she'll do anything, unless we provoke her."

"What if she follows us to that town?"

Karim frowned. "They'll keep her out."

"There must be something else we can do," Andrew said angrily.

"What would you suggest?" Karim narrowed his eyes. "Ride up and shoot her? I haven't become a murderer yet."

"That isn't murder," Andrew said. "It's self-defense."

"It's nothing of the kind."

"We could shoot her with a rod and sabotage her craft. We'd be far away by the time she came to her senses."

Karim seemed to be considering this; his dark face was taut. "We might miss," he said at last. "And even if we don't, her craft or her Bond might call Rescuers. I suggest that we continue on our way." He turned toward his vehicle, then paused. "One more thing," Karim said. "Don't use your screen to talk to me. She might tune in."

She was waiting on the bridge, leaning against the side of her craft. She held no weapon; she had left them room to pass. She was a small woman. The hands at the edges of the sleeves of her baggy white jacket were slim. She wore boots and brown pants. She smiled as they drew near; her mouth was broad, her cheekbones high, her pale eyes large. Her strong features did not seem to match her small body.

Karim's craft slowed to a stop; Andrew pulled up behind it. Karim opened his dome, and Andrew did the same, glancing apprehensively at Merripen as the dome slid back.

"Hello," the woman said.

Karim growled a greeting.

"I thought I'd see you again. Please do get out. You must want to stretch a bit."

Merripen waited until he saw Karim moving around the front of his craft, then climbed out himself. "Go ahead," Andrew muttered. "I'll wait." He rummaged at his side and picked up a silver wand. Merripen shot him a warning look, then joined Karim. The taller man wore a bland, placid expression.

"You're going to Harsville, aren't you?" She did not wait for an answer. "I thought so. I took a shortcut. Do you know anyone there?"

Karim mumbled something which could have been yes or no.

"I don't. I've never been there. In fact, I don't know this area at all well. What's the matter with your friend?"

"He's not feeling well," Merripen replied.

"That's too bad. I can help him."

"He'll be all right. He's just tired."

"My name's Eline. Who are you?"

"I'm Merripen. This is Karim. The fellow over there is Andrew."

"What are you doing out here alone?" Karim asked.

Eline poked at the asphalt with her toe. "Oh, just moving around." She narrowed her eyes. "I'm a Rescuer." Merripen tried not to betray his surprise that she had said it outright.

"We are truly fortunate, then," Karim said smoothly. "Had we run into any difficulties, you would have been nearby."

Eline stood up straight, looking relieved. "Right. I'm glad you understand. Some people don't at all. We're here to help. I've even got my equipment."

"Oh, I understand," Karim said. "I sympathize, in fact. People like you are always disparaged by those who are concerned only with passing matters."

"I know." She sighed. She seemed young; she had none of the hesitancy or weariness Merripen was used to seeing. She had probably grown up with Rescuers, knowing nothing else. "They think we should just tend to their bodies. But the soul is more important, surely."

"Too many of us simply can't look beyond our own world," Karim said, sounding sincere. "That is to be expected, I suppose." He bowed slightly. "But we must be on our way."

"I'll follow you."

"As you wish."

As Merripen returned to his craft, he could feel Eline watching him. He got in and Andrew leaned toward him.

"So she's going to follow." He closed the dome as Merripen settled in his seat. "Wonderful. I wonder where Karim learned how to sound so convincing." They followed the other man across the bridge, while Eline tailed them. "I've heard they torture people into accepting their truth."

"I've never heard that."

"How could you?" Andrew stretched out his legs. "Maybe we should go back."

"We can't. She'd only follow. If she saw where we were going, I don't think we'd get there."

"We're having bad luck." He glared at the back of Karim's craft.

The road curved over a hill. The morning rain had stopped, but the sky was still pewter. Karim's craft hovered at the crest, then settled to the ground. Andrew drove up beside him.

Below lay what had been Harsville. The ruins of four houses lay scattered over blackened earth; two others, partly burned, had broken windows. Only one cottage was untouched, but the yard in front of it was strewn with furniture and clothing.

Merripen was unable to speak. Eline had pulled up. She had opened her dome and now stood on her seat, staring out at the ruin. Her mouth was open.

Merripen turned toward Andrew, but the other man had left the craft and was moving around the front toward Eline. He grabbed her arm and pulled her from her craft, dragging her over the door and onto the ground. His knife was out. He twisted one arm behind her back while holding the knife to her throat.

Merripen's legs shook as he got out. Eline's eyes were wide. She struggled and her face contorted. Andrew twisted her arm more tightly.

"You knew," Andrew said.

"I didn't." Her eyes pleaded with Merripen silently.

"What happened?"

"I don't know."

Andrew pricked her throat with the point of his knife, and Merripen saw a drop of red. He felt dizzy. Karim had crept up to his side and was watching Andrew warily. "I don't know anything," Eline said again. "I haven't been here before."

"I see," Andrew said. "You're not afraid of me. You have

your other life to look forward to. I hope you like it, because I may be sending you there soon.''

Eline's face was pale. Merripen thought he heard her whimper. Karim said, ''Let her go.'' Andrew glared at him. ''Let her go.''

Andrew lowered the knife and pushed the woman from him; she fell, sprawling on the ground. Karim helped her up. She clutched at his arms with trembling hands.

''I thought you people weren't afraid to die,'' Andrew said harshly.

''I am,'' she said. Her voice was high. ''I've fought against it. I've tried to have more faith.'' She clung to Karim, who stood stiffly, as if unable to decide what to do with her. ''I was sent out alone, to test myself. But I'm still afraid anyway.'' She let go of Karim and sat down hard on the ground, covering her face with both hands.

''That was stupid,'' Karim said to Andrew. Andrew put his knife away, then began to walk down the hill toward the town.

Eline looked up as Merripen went to her. ''I didn't know about this,'' she said.

''I know.''

She stood up, wiping her face with a soiled sleeve. Karim went back to his craft and leaned inside; he stepped away and the craft moved down the hill slowly. After sending the other two after it, he returned to Merripen's side. ''Let's walk down.''

Merripen hesitated. Eline's face was frozen; she lifted her chin. ''What could have happened?'' Merripen asked.

''We knew that there were strange things going on north of here. We'd better try to find out what happened.''

Merripen followed Karim down the hill, Eline at his side. Andrew had already reached the bottom; his back was stiff as he strode into Harsville. ''Are you all right now?'' Merripen asked the woman.

''I'm fine. I'll get over it.'' Her face had a hard look now, as if she had decided to be brave.

The three vehicles floated into the town's main street and set down in a row. Andrew leaned against one, head down. Karim approached the unburned cottage, threading his way through the debris on the lawn. He went to the door and looked inside, then came over to Merripen. ''It's been stripped clean. The people must have left a while ago, and then raiders came and took what they could.'' Andrew had moved to the edge of the lawn; he was watching Eline.

Merripen wandered toward another structure, peering at the burned building. He stopped, raised a hand to his mouth, and moaned softly. Under blackened timbers, the bones of a human hand gripped the ground; the wrist still wore a tarnished Bond. He stood there silently until he felt a hand on his back. Karim steered him toward the cluttered yard.

Merripen sat on a torn-up chair which wobbled under him. He said, "They didn't leave. They were killed."

Karim was silent as he seated himself on a rotting leather ottoman and rested his arms on his legs. Then he murmured, "We can't stay here."

"I know."

"Where are you going to go, Merripen?"

Merripen glanced at Eline, who had wandered into the middle of the road, out of earshot. "I don't know. Back to the Citadel, I suppose."

"You're going to give up?"

"Why shouldn't I? I've seen all I need to see. I see what we are, what we always were."

"I could go on with Eline. That would give you and Andrew a chance to go back."

Merripen heard a cry, and turned. Eline was staring down the road; Andrew stood next to her. Eline's hands fluttered.

A band of men had emerged from the trees and was walking toward the road. They were unshaven, dressed in dirty pants and tops made of hides and fur. But they also carried silver wands. The slender weapons were pointed at them.

Merripen was afraid to move. The other man plucked at his sleeve, helped him up, and guided him toward the road. "Don't try for a craft," Karim whispered. "They'll shoot before you reach it." They stood with the others as the men walked toward them. He peered at Andrew, relieved to see that the man had not reached for his knife.

Merripen thought: We should have stayed in our craft; we would have been safe. His face grew hot; he felt his legs tremble. He wasn't ready to die, even after all this time. He suddenly envied Eline. If she could hold on to her peculiar faith, she would meet her death calmly. Merripen was afraid not only that he would die, but also that he would die badly, begging to be spared, pleading with the strange men who were now approaching them. He hoped that he would die quickly, and just as strongly hoped that he would not die at all.

The men stopped a few feet away. Merripen did not move.

Karim was still; then, slowly, he lifted his arms and held out
his hands, palms up.

A brown-bearded man stepped forward; the others lowered
their wands. Merripen held out his own hands, as did Eline.
Andrew frowned, but extended his arms after a few moments.

The men before them seemed to relax. Their eyes gazed at
them placidly. Merripen drew a breath. He suddenly had the
impression that the men were being controlled by some outside
force; they seemed to be waiting for someone to tell them what
to do. Perhaps implants were directing them.

Brown-Beard, who seemed to be the leader, said a few
words, but Merripen did not understand them. He glanced at
Karim. Abruptly, the band was around them, pawing their
bodies and searching their pockets. One man seized Andrew's
knife and held it up. A man jostled Merripen; he heard a
laugh. Then he was being pushed. He stumbled, but kept on
his feet.

The men spoke again, babbling. Karim frowned. "I think
they want us to go with them," he murmured. They were being
herded up the road; as they left the town behind, Merripen
tried not to think of their abandoned vehicles and the burned
buildings. They had been spared, though he did not know
why.

IV

The singing of the men was harsh and unmelodious; Merripen found himself walking in time to their rhythm. Eline
wobbled a bit as she walked. One of the men walked near her,
holding her arm when she seemed most tired. Once, when they
stopped for a moment, the man reached out and touched her
hair gently. She stiffened, but did not pull away.

In the afternoon, a light rain began to fall, and the air became misty. They came to plowed fields ready for planting;
ahead, through the mist, Merripen saw the ghostly shapes of
buildings. As they came closer, his surprise grew. The fields
surrounded a village of straight roads meeting at right angles
and square, tidy houses built of wood and stone. The center of
the town was dominated by a windowless white marble building; stone steps led to its flat roof. Did these unkempt men live
here? It was hard to believe.

As they left the fields, people came out of the nearest
houses. Unlike the men, these people wore clean white

garments, the women in long robes, the men in short kilts and shirts. Children babbled at the men and ogled the newcomers; Merripen had never seen so many children. Soon they were surrounded by a sea of bodies and noise. One young woman made signs at Merripen with her hands; not knowing what to do, he smiled, and she laughed.

Brown-Beard stopped in front of one house and greeted the woman in the doorway, who held a baby, then waved his arms at Merripen, who finally understood that they were to follow him inside. The crowd drifted away as they entered.

Merripen surveyed the room. In the center stood a long wooden table and benches; mats covered the floor. One corner near a window seemed to be a shrine of some sort; a little table held a small clay figure of a bearded man. The beard had been painted a bright yellow. With a shock, he saw that a small holo screen had been hung on the wall behind the table.

He had no time to wonder at it. A young man pushed him; Brown-Beard and another man led them up wooden stairs to the second floor. They opened a door and pushed their prisoners into an empty room. The door closed behind them. Merripen tried the door; it was bolted.

Eline sat down on the floor. Karim went over to the window and looked outside while Andrew fidgeted. There was another door near the window. Merripen went over to it and pushed it open. He saw a porcelain toilet and a sink with chrome faucets.

He started to laugh. Then he began to shake, and had to sit down. "A bathroom," he said. "A holo screen downstairs. It makes no sense."

"Yes, it does," Karim said as he sat down. "Someone's helping them, or controlling them." He paused. "Or else they've regressed, gone backward."

Merripen shivered; his clothes were damp from the rain. "I wonder why they brought us here."

"I don't know. I think we were lucky. They looked ready to kill us. I saw them change when I held out my hands. Such an obvious gesture."

A man opened the door and threw in four bundles of cloth before closing it again. Eline got up and unwrapped one of the bundles, holding up a shirt. "I suppose we'd better bathe and put them on," she said.

"Are we just supposed to do whatever they want?" Andrew said from the corner where he was sitting.

"We have no choice." Karim rose, picked up one bundle

of garments, and went into the bathroom, closing the door.

"Nice little place," Andrew said harshly. "Nice, friendly people when they're not burning down houses."

"You don't know that they did that," Merripen said.

"Don't I? Who else could it have been? I'll bet they were returning for more loot." He scowled. "Did you notice? They have a lot of children here, and I saw a few graybeards in the crowd. You know what that means. They live and die." He turned to Eline. "This is a good place for a Rescuer, don't you think? All these unchanged people—maybe you can recruit a few."

"You don't understand," Eline replied.

"But I do."

"No, you don't. We don't object to minor genetic engineering, as long as we don't become something else. And we accept long life because it gives us a chance to prepare ourselves for the higher state, the life beyond. We mustn't die before we're prepared, but we know there's nothing to fear in death, because our souls don't die." Her voice shook slightly.

"You must believe it," Andrew said. "You've shown such fortitude yourself."

Eline bowed her head, but not before Merripen saw her tight mouth and icy eyes.

Bowls had been pushed through the door. Eline rolled up her long white sleeves and began to pick at her food. The shirts and pants she and Andrew now wore were too large; the two looked like children hiding in the darkening room, puzzled about why they had been shut away.

Merripen inspected the meat and vegetables in his bowl, thought of where the food might have come from, and set the bowl down. Karim took it and ate heartily, while Merripen and Andrew shared a loaf of bread, washing it down with water.

Karim finished eating, wiped his hand on his tight white shirt, rose, and wandered over to the window. Merripen followed and stood next to him. The sky had cleared; lavender clouds edged with orange hung near the distant hills. The sun was low. Below them, a procession moved through the street; other groups of people were converging on the marble building in the town's center. The marble was pink in the evening light. Five women in blue robes were climbing the steps to the top of the building; on the other side, ten men, also in blue robes, had reached the roof. One of the men in blue looked familiar; Merripen peered at him and recognized Brown-Beard.

"It looks like some sort of ritual," Merripen said to Karim. Eline now stood near him, hands on the sill. Andrew suddenly elbowed his way in between Merripen and the woman.

"Look," Andrew said. "There's no one below us now. They're all going over there. We could get away." He pointed. "It isn't that far. We could hang from the window and drop."

Karim turned. "We'd have to travel by night, on foot. And we wouldn't get far if they came after us."

"We can try."

"It won't work."

The crowd was still. Merripen could no longer hear their murmurs. They were waiting for something. The people on the roof raised their arms.

A dark object appeared in the west, a ship flying out of the sun. The people on the roof cried out and prostrated themselves. The dark shape grew larger. It was a bullet-shaped gravitic ship; it gleamed, its silver surface catching the last light of the sun. It swept down over the town and hovered above the roof; then, slowly, it dropped to the surface.

The side of the ship opened. A bearded blond man emerged; he wore a long red robe. The people on the roof groveled; the crowd below hid their faces in the dust of the street. The man touched a silver necklace at his throat and then spoke. Merripen did not understand the words, but the voice was clear and resonant, probably amplified. A few of the blue-robed people were crawling toward him, heads down. Brown-Beard held out his hands; he seemed to be speaking. The red-robed man nodded.

Brown-Beard, still kneeling, waved his arm. Two other men crawled to the edge of the roof and called to the people below. Several men at the edge of the crowd rose and moved in Merripen's direction.

Andrew leaned out the window, as if ready to jump. The men were running through the street below; Merripen heard footsteps on the stairs. "They're coming for us," Andrew cried.

The door swung open; howls filled the room. Merripen was dragged away from the window; he saw Andrew struggle and Eline try to pull away. He was forced down the stairs and into the street; fingers dug into his arms. They made their way past houses with open doors and through the crowd of kneeling people; heads rose, and eyes watched them pass. They were pushed toward the steps and borne upward to the roof; the blue-robed men reached out and hauled them up the last step.

Merripen's knees were about to give way. He reached for the person nearest him, and clutched Karim's arm. The blue-robed men backed away from them; the blond man stared at them impassively. The women on the roof knelt. The men stretched out their arms; they were holding silver wands, pointing them at Merripen and his companions.

Merripen knew he was going to die. He was past being frightened; his body was stiff and his heart thumped slowly. He raised his head; the blond man's face would be the last thing he would ever see. The cold gray eyes stared back at him and then, incongruously, the man winked.

Before Merripen could react, he heard the amplified voice once more. The robed men lowered their wands. The voice said a few more words and the crowd below shouted out a response. The blue-robed people backed away, arms out, heads down.

The blond man motioned to them. Merripen approached him cautiously, Karim close behind him. Part of the roof slid open, revealing steps leading down into darkness. The man pointed at the steps, then led them below.

As the roof slid shut above them, light flooded the room. The stairs faced a large holo screen; two walls were decorated with friezes. One wall showed a giant blond man with tiny figures at his feet; the other was of a disklike sun, its rays touching a painted village. Merripen descended the stairs and stood with his companions, looking uneasily at his savior. The man removed his silver necklace and spoke in normal tones; Merripen shook his head, not grasping his words.

"Do you understand this?" the man said, and Merripen nodded. "Good. Let's leave this sacred spot. You look a little shaky."

A door slid open near the painted village and the man led them into a smaller room. Long white couches without backs lined the pale walls. "You are truly blessed," the man went on. "You're also lucky. Sit down." He waved at the couches.

Merripen sat. Andrew sprawled near him. Karim sat with Eline, who reached for his hand. The blond man stretched out on a couch near one corner. "My name is Domingo," he said. "Just another name to you, perhaps, but for these people it holds quite awesome connotations." He smiled and fingered his golden beard. "Don't worry, you're safe here. You're greatly honored, in fact."

Karim scowled. Andrew said, "What's going on?"

"Haven't you guessed? I am their god. They were going to sacrifice you to my greater glory. But I'm showing you even greater favor by allowing you to dwell here in my temple." He laughed. "Don't look so woebegone. You were very lucky to be caught on my day; they were expecting my visit. They must have believed you were sent here for me. I see you didn't resist, or they might have killed you where you stood. Their voices must have told them you were sent as a gift."

"Their voices?" Merripen said.

"You'll be all right now," Domingo said, ignoring the question. "You may even spawn a cult of your own. Anyone so favored by me must be sacred, after all. I'm glad you're here. Any god can get lonely. We'll talk." He sat up. "But now you should rest." He rose and left the room.

Andrew sighed as the light dimmed, leaving only a soft glow near the floor. "He must be mad," he murmured.

Merripen got up and stretched out on another couch. He supposed that they were all still prisoners, but he was too tired to worry about it now. His muscles were sore, and his legs twitched as he tried to relax. Karim had reclined on the couch perpendicular to his; he tossed and turned, and Merripen heard him rasp. "Karim?"

"I'm all right." His voice sounded weak. Merripen reached out and touched the other man's forehead; it felt hot.

"You're not well."

"It'll pass. I just need rest. My body can repair itself."

Merripen withdrew and curled up, too exhausted to argue.

He opened his eyes, not knowing where he was. It was still dark. He waited for his eyes to adjust to the dim light, then leaned over Karim, feeling his brow again. The fever was gone, but the skin felt dry and leathery. Merripen frowned.

Karim opened his eyes suddenly. "Are you feeling better?" Merripen asked.

"I'm all right now. Perhaps the rain gave me a chill." Karim sat up slowly. "Is it morning yet?"

"I suppose it must be."

"It feels like morning. It might even be later. I think we slept very deeply." He stood up. Andrew and Eline were still, their faces toward the wall. Merripen followed Karim to the door.

They peered into the next room. The ceiling opened and Domingo walked down the steps, carrying two bowls of fruit.

A bolt of bright red cloth hung from one of his shoulders; a dead rabbit was draped over one of his arms.

Merripen swallowed. "I hope that's not our breakfast," he said.

"Oh, no. They're only small offerings." Domingo passed them and they followed him into a small side room. A round glass-topped table and six metal chairs with black-cushioned seats stood in the center of the room. Domingo dropped the rabbit and fruit on the floor next to his materializer. "We'll give you something more appetizing." He kept the cloth, adjusting it around his neck. "Please sit down." He removed pastries and omelets from the dispenser, setting them on the table.

Merripen was hungry. He sat down and began to eat while Domingo poured coffee. He ate quickly, barely tasting the omelet. Karim picked at his food. Domingo sprawled in one chair, sipping his coffee, glancing from Karim to Merripen.

"I'm glad nothing happened to you," Domingo murmured. "You might have been killed, or, at best, been brought here as slaves, and then it would have been harder for me to help you." Merripen narrowed his eyes. "This society has a rigid hierarchy. Strangers are either enemies or slaves. They would not have been able to place you in any other position—unless, of course, you could have convinced them you were gods."

Karim wiped his lips with a napkin. "Are they unchanged people?"

"In a sense, they are. They're what we might have been long ago. I made them." The blond man chuckled. "Then, of course, they bred themselves. Now there are many of them. There are other villages besides this one." He paused. "I am their god. I have a temple like this one in every village. I also speak with them over the holo when I'm away. The priests enter the temple at certain times to hear my words directly, and each home has a shrine provided with my messages—prerecorded, of course. But they hear me at other times as well. When one part of their minds speaks to the other, it is often my voice they hear."

"An implant," Merripen said.

"Not at all. Their minds are divided; each side of the brain is separate. You see, they're not conscious of themselves. When their right side directs their left side, they hear it as a voice directing them—my voice, or that of someone with authority over them. They do not know self-doubt, self-consciousness, depression, and other such advances our minds have made." He shifted in his seat. "Do you know the feeling when you're working, say, or concentrating on a particular task, and you lose yourself in it, coming to yourself only later?" He leaned forward. "They are that way all the time, lost in what they do. A voice directs them, and they act. They do not question or doubt. They live out their lives and die, but they do not really know death, because they continue to hear the voices and see the images of those who are gone. They do not know time except as a cycle; they may mark it, but they live in the present."

Karim put down his cup. "Why?"

Domingo was silent for a few moments, then stood up. "Come with me."

He led them to the steps, and they climbed to the ceiling. It slid open above them; Merripen squinted at the blue sky and billowing clouds. They walked out onto the roof. The sun was up. Out in the fields, Merripen saw the brown backs of workers. In the streets below, women stood in groups or nursed babies, while others worked on cloth or pounded grain with pestles. One old man nearby was shaping clay into bowls; another spoke to a group of children. When their eyes moved toward the men on the roof, they lowered them quickly and bowed.

"I've favored them," Domingo said. "Once again, I'll live among them for a while. Perhaps I will leave them a child." Merripen glanced at him, and Domingo smiled. "That man who brought you here—he's one. That's why he holds the rank he does. I brought his mother to the temple here and lay with her. Of course, I had to put her in suspension afterward while I made adjustments in the zygote, but she carried the child to term and I blessed it."

Karim's eyes were narrowed with anger. "Why?" he said hoarsely.

"Can't you see?" Domingo waved his arm at the village. "There is no evil here. There is no sin, only innocence. It is a paradise, in a way. We ourselves might have risen from that state, or fallen from it."

Merripen looked down. Everything in him recoiled from the man and what he had done. "You did it for power," he said. "Whether or not it's right has no meaning for you."

Domingo seized his arm. "Look below. Are they unhappy? They are what they are. I'm not the first biologist who ever made a new sort of being. If it hadn't been for me, they wouldn't exist."

Merripen could not speak. Karim opened his mouth, then closed it again. Domingo let go of his arm. "It didn't begin this way," he went on. "At first, it was only a small experiment. I made a few and raised them. I had a question to ask. Were we once this way, bicameral people with divided minds? Did our self-consciousness arise when the complexity of the mind made it know itself, when the connections between the two hemispheres grew stronger and the cerebral cortex developed further? I wanted to test the theory, but then I realized I couldn't do that with only a few individuals. I wanted to see what a community could do, to know how such people would live from day to day, how much they could manage, whether it was indeed possible for such people to build, and farm, and make pottery, and make a community, and plot the courses of the stars, and do all the things our ancestors did, without knowing themselves. So I made more, and gave them tools, and sent them out."

A breeze fluttered Domingo's hair; the sunlight gilded it. A cloud drifted in front of the sun, and Domingo's face was shadowed. The lips under the blond beard were drawn back; the gray eyes were bluer. Karim was a dark specter in white, arms folded, a silent judge.

"It was painful to observe them," Domingo said. "Many died. But they learned quickly, perhaps because I couldn't heartlessly leave them to themselves. Even now, I help them. I give them food if there's a danger of famine. I try to make their lives a bit easier."

"Did you prove anything, then?" Karim asked.

"It's difficult to say. I suppose they could go on without me, though it would be more unpleasant without the things I've given them. But it's hard to think of leaving. I've been with them so long." He stroked his beard. "I have to keep to a rather rigid schedule, visiting the villages at specific times for seasonal festivals, accepting offerings, speaking over the holo, sometimes staying in one place for a while."

"We stopped at a town called Harsville," Karim said, and his voice was strained. "It had been burned. Some of the people there were murdered. Was that an offering to you? That's where we were when we were found. Was that their doing, these innocent folk of yours?"

Domingo stepped back. "I didn't know about it until too

late. I would have stopped it otherwise. Believe me, the ones who did it were punished." He held out his hands. "You have to understand. The people there tried to defend themselves, but you can't do a good job of that when your enemy has more men to send against you, and no fear." He lowered his hands. "They're breeding. They have many children. They'll need a new village soon. Eventually, I may lose control—I don't know."

"What are you going to do about them?" Karim asked.

"What would you suggest I do?" Domingo said harshly. "Kill them? Terminate the project?"

"You could begin to change them," Karim responded. "You could introduce normal children into the population and change it within two or three generations."

"Oh, no. I would only have other godlings contending with me for control, and they would have an unfair advantage over the others. It would change the society at the cost of great suffering. Is that what you want? Imagine these people having to live through that, with no way to fight it or even to know what is happening to them."

"You could make them sterile. Call them to the temple and make the adjustments—you can do that." Karim tilted his head. "The ones alive now could lead out their lives, but there would be no children."

Domingo lifted his head. "You're talking about genocide."

"I'm talking about ending this project."

"It would be genocide. They're here now—they've living beings. They have a right to their existence, and to their children's as well."

"You made them."

"It doesn't matter who made them now."

Karim turned and paced to the edge of the roof and stood at the top of the marble steps. A woman below looked up, then bowed. Merripen thought: What makes us do things like this? What perversity makes it seem reasonable? He shivered; the air was turning cool.

Karim walked back to them. "You talk about their right to exist," Karim said, "but you let them die. You could have made them immortal—you have the means."

Domingo had no answer to that. Karim walked toward the opening in the roof and disappeared down the steps.

"There will be more of them, then," Merripen said.

"Probably. They have many children."

"And that means that the rest of us will either have to confront them eventually or keep retreating. Didn't you consider that?"

"I have. It's no concern of mine. Our world is dying anyway. We'll either choke in its decay or abandon it. These may be our heirs." Domingo gestured at the people below.

Merripen was silent, thinking of his own project. His children were to have been the inheritors if humankind did not adapt. He felt as though Domingo had stolen their heritage.

"Think of it," Domingo went on. His broad chest rose and fell under the red robe. "Their society will grow in complexity. Sometime in the distant future, if my hypothesis is correct, they will know themselves. And I will have made them. They'll worship me even then, even when I no longer live among them. They'll be a new human civilization, and everything they do will be because of me. There's beauty in it. Can't you see that?"

Merripen backed away. Domingo was mad. Perhaps the isolation from others like himself had made him mad, or maybe he had always been that way. He thought: We're all like him. We don't know ourselves. The old brain rules, and reason makes up stories after the fact.

Domingo held out a hand. "Follow me," he said. Merripen was unable to refuse. He followed the golden-haired man down the steps. People bowed as they passed them in the streets. They came to a house; a woman with silver in her hair and a baby in her arms met them at the door. Domingo said something to her, growling the words; she bowed and left them. They walked inside.

A young woman, hardly more than a girl, stood before them. Her long dark hair hung to her waist; her cheeks were pink. She glanced fleetingly at Merripen with her brown eyes, then knelt, one arm out.

"She's yours," Domingo said. "Do you understand? She won't question it, and you'll do her family an honor. They'll pray that she has your child. Go on."

Merripen stared at the slender form, realizing with horror that he wanted the young woman, that her passivity had stirred an old instinct within him. His legs carried him toward her. She raised her eyes to his face. There was a malignancy in her gaze for a moment, an evil, calculating look, as though she had suddenly linked the disparate thoughts in her mind. Then it was gone. Her lips curved and her eyes pleaded, slaves of instinct's force.

Merripen turned away and fled. He stumbled through the street, stopping near another house. He leaned against the cool stones. Clothes rustled and voices murmured as people gathered near him. A little child grabbed his leg. A woman tried to pull the child away, but Merripen picked him up and held him, pressing his cheek against the curly hair. "You can choose," he said to the child. "You can choose."

Domingo came up to him, took the child away, and led Merripen back to the temple.

Domingo told his story to Andrew and Eline that afternoon. Andrew had said nothing to Merripen about his reaction; Eline had remained silent and sullen. Domingo had disappeared into a room near the holo, closing the door behind him; Andrew had muttered something about finding a way out and had gone up to the roof with Karim.

Merripen found Eline by the glass-topped table, helping herself to wine from the dispenser. She poured out a glass for him and put it on the table with the wine bottle and her own glass. She threw herself into a seat and gulped the pink liquid.

Merripen sipped. "This must be disturbing for you," he said awkwardly, "feeling the way you do about biological experimentation."

She shrugged, drained her glass, and poured another. Merripen lowered his eyes. All of them seemed to have arrived at an unspoken agreement; they had not told Domingo that she was a Rescuer, and she had not volunteered the information. Neither had they told the blond man that Karim and he were biologists. If they were to stick together, they couldn't let Eline know that, and they had to stick together if they were to find a way out. Domingo might eventually let them go, or he might, if he sensed divisions among them, toy with them instead; he was used to manipulating people. Merripen wanted to ask the man certain technical questions about his original experiment, but could not without revealing what he was.

Guilt stung him again. For a moment, he had been thinking of Domingo only as another scientist. Had he done anything Merripen had not done himself? Merripen had created humankind's possible successors, while Domingo had made their ancestors live. Domingo's children had made him a god, while Merripen's had abandoned him.

"Cheer up," Eline said. She was pouring another glass of wine. He watched her warily. She was drinking too much; he did not want her confronting Domingo in an alcoholic rage. "We're safe enough for now."

"As long as Domingo's happy with us."

"Oh, I think he is, so far."

Merripen narrowed his eyes. "Were you planning to flirt with him?"

"Is that a suggestion?" she said harshly. "Don't be ridiculous. You heard what he said. He's used to stupid cow-eyed women who submit to the god. He wouldn't be interested in me. He's been eyeing Andrew, though. That would be a nice contrast for our host, a virile, forceful fellow after all those servile females."

Her cheeks were flushed; her lips glistened. Merripen reached for the bottle, not because he wanted more wine, but because he did not want Eline to drink any more.

"It might not be such a bad idea," she went on. "Maybe Andrew could force him to take us back to Harsville."

"No. I'll tell him to be patient. He'll listen. He may not like it, but he'll listen."

She toyed with her glass, twirling it by the stem. "Maybe Domingo didn't have such a bad idea. I ought to get him to take me into the town. I might have a nice, agreeable man who'd enjoy making love to the god's friend."

"You wouldn't like it," he responded, too forcefully. Her eyes widened. "You don't seem that disturbed by what he's done. I thought you would be."

"You think I'm simpleminded." She drank; he saw her throat move as she swallowed. "He said that he had created human beings without self-consciousness. We don't object to anyone making something that once existed—an extinct species, for instance. That's what these people are."

"That's only his theory. He hasn't proved it. He never can. He can only show that it's possible."

"He must have had evidence for the assumption." She paused. "I'm not saying others like me would accept it," she continued in a low tone, "but then they've never confronted this sort of situation. I must hope for some guidance." Her eyes stared past him, as if she were no longer conscious of his presence.

Merripen heard Eline pacing during the night. He listened, afraid to open his eyes. In the morning, she seemed calm; she even smiled at him.

She took to following Domingo around. She peered from behind the door when Domingo welcomed his priests and sat on the steps near the roof whenever he held a ceremony there. She even began to learn the language of the community. It had once been an old, dead language, chosen by Domingo; now it lived and had been changed.

At least Eline had found something to do. Karim rested and slept, as if he were still ill, while Andrew divided his time between spying on Eline and looking for a way to escape.

Merripen sat at the table with his breakfast. He had fallen into passivity and depression; the temple seemed the only place on Earth. He was unable to concentrate. He had been watching Domingo for a sign that he was tired of their company and would let them go, but the man, while ignoring them most of the time, seemed to want them around.

He stared at his coffee cup, as if slowly becoming conscious of the china. He had always eaten this sort of breakfast at the Citadel—cereal, fruit, two cups of coffee, no more, no less. He had, unknowingly, been armoring himself in old habits, as if the familiar routines would turn the temple into his home instead of his prison. In two hours, he would exercise; at night, he would wash before going to sleep. If he kept at it, the habits would become chains.

He got up quickly and went into the next room. Eline was sitting on the floor next to the holo; she wore a Band around her head. He did not get too close to her; lately Eline would draw back if one of the men came near. He waited until she took off the wide, round circlet and set it on the floor.

"Why are you learning their language?" he asked.

"Why shouldn't I learn it? I need something to do. I'll learn what I can." She ran a hand through her pale hair. "It helps me to understand these people a little. Their minds aren't the only division in them—they even speak of their bodies as if an arm or a leg is somehow a separate thing, connected to but not really a part of the person. And feelings—rage, or joy, or whatever—are seen as entities that come upon them from outside."

"We speak that way, too, at times."

"Yes, but not with the same emphasis. And perhaps that in itself is more evidence for Domingo's theory. I don't know. He gave them the language. If he'd used a different one, maybe they would be different." She leaned back and rubbed her forehead. "They're so much like us, and yet there's that wall between their minds and ours that I can't quite penetrate. That's more disturbing and intriguing than if they had looked and acted unlike us."

He nodded, thinking of his own project. "I would have thought," he said, "that you would have been very unhappy here. Yet you've already adapted to it."

She smiled. "I'm being realistic. We might be here for a while. You and those friends of yours haven't been doing much. Karim's tired all the time and Andrew starts drinking pretty early in the day."

"You, of all people, shouldn't be critical of him for that."

"I start early myself. That's how I know. But Andrew drinks out of impatience and restlessness. I drink to celebrate."

He was about to ask her what she celebrated when Domingo's door opened. Merripen wondered how long he had been standing behind it. The blond man raised one hand in greeting, then walked toward the dining room. His shoulders sagged; his head was bowed. Merripen hesitated, then went after him.

"Domingo."

He kept his back to Merripen for a few moments, then turned. His pale eyebrows were drawn together; his hand rested on his chest, as though he were in pain. He straightened.

"When will you let us leave?"

Domingo did not answer.

"You'll have to leave yourself; you've said you have obligations in other villages."

"Obligations." Domingo brushed back a lock of hair which had fallen over his forehead. "It's true. You may think I can do what I like here, but I'm bound, too. I've thought of leaving them altogether. They could get along without me. My image would be here; the shrines and my recordings could guide them. But what if they needed me later? I'm afraid to go."

"Maybe you're just afraid to be among people like yourself, people who can judge you. Or do you actually have scruples?"

"I don't know."

"When can we leave?"

"When I choose to let you go." Domingo passed his hand over his forehead. "Don't be so impatient. You may be leaving sooner than you think. I've been lonely." He seemed to be trying to reach out to Merripen; his gray eyes were rimmed with red.

Merripen spun around and left the room, crossing the alcove. He found Andrew and Karim sitting on a couch, backs against the wall. Karim's hands were still; Andrew's danced nervously on his thighs. "We have to do something," Andrew said.

"What would you suggest?"

"Walking out through the village. We're sacred now, aren't we? No one would stop us."

"Domingo could."

"It's better than waiting."

"He could order them to stop us. He could tell them to kill us on the spot."

He heard Domingo's heavy footsteps on the stairs; he was climbing to the roof. Andrew rose quickly and went out; Merripen, apprehensive, hurried after him and followed him up the steps.

The sky was hazy; the air felt damp as he stepped out onto the roof. He blinked, feeling disoriented after having been inside for so long. The village below was quiet, the streets empty; even the craftspeople had gone inside with their wares. Domingo stood at the edge of the roof.

Andrew glanced at Merripen, then walked over to Domingo. The blond man turned to face him. "I know you won't let us go until you're ready," Andrew said softly. Merripen moved closer to the two men in order to hear Andrew more clearly. "Maybe you'll be ready if I tell you that Eline is plotting something."

Domingo raised an eyebrow. "And what is she plotting?"

"I don't know. I haven't spoken to her. But I've been watching her, and she's making plans. I know it. In your own interest, you ought to let us go." He took a breath. "Do you know what she is?"

Merripen stepped forward, holding up his hand. "She's a Rescuer," Andrew went on. Merripen lowered his hand. "You must know what that is, even hiding away here. It's a cult. They rescue souls. Sometimes their idea of rescuing them is to kill the people in whom the souls reside. She may try to rescue some people here."

Merripen's anger at Andrew faded. Domingo would have to act now. But the blond man seemed unconcerned. He gazed calmly at Andrew, then at Merripen.

"She's learning," Andrew continued. "She's learning fast. You'd better get her out of here."

Domingo turned away. Andrew, chewing his lip in frustration, retreated, disappearing below the roof. Domingo said, "Come with me." Merripen hesitated, wondering if he should go after Andrew. "Don't worry, it's just for a walk. No young maidens, no temptations." He descended the steps to the street.

Merripen followed, looking uneasily from side to side. They passed open doors. Domingo stopped in front of one house and put his hand on the wall for a moment; the people inside murmured to one another. He led Merripen through narrow alleyways and past smaller houses until they came to the edge of a field.

A group of young men and boys had gathered in the fallow field; they carried javelins. Two men saw Domingo and bowed. Domingo waved at them to go on. One boy ran with a javelin and hurled it; the weapon arched against the sky and struck the ground, quivering.

"Some day, I won't be able to walk through the streets like this," Domingo said. "Do you know what is happening? Soon they'll build another village, and another, and another. My authority will weaken. Already there are those who travel from one village to another, to trade. I think they may begin to hear other voices more clearly than mine. The villages are beginning to diverge. You might not notice the differences, but I do. The ceremonies vary slightly, the language is accented differently, the pottery and jewelry and clothing are changing. One group wears white, another yellow—some embroider their shirts with designs, while others paint the insides of their tombs. It's all a sign. Even I can't stop it; I can only postpone it. I'll become too distant a figure to hold them. Their world will become chaotic, even without intervention from outside. And one group will begin to grow conscious of itself, and when that happens, they'll sweep over the other settlements in a wave of terror and murder. Those who are cruelest will inherit everything."

"You can stop it," Merripen said. "You can keep the population small, you can—"

"And why should I stop it? Should I deny them self-consciousness, and abstract reasoning, and the chance, one day, to look beyond their simple lives? They deserve their time." He frowned. "I was hoping you would understand. Perhaps I made a mistake."

He led Merripen back through the village. People were watching from their doorways; they bowed as Domingo passed and peered through their fingers at Merripen. He saw their eyes and wondered what they perceived; did they see a continuous procession, or a series of discrete moments with no connection? Did he pass through the street, or appear and reappear? He caught the eyes of one man; the hazel eyes were cold as he watched Merripen from under cupped hands. He remembered the young woman. As he moved toward the temple, he felt the man's gaze on his back.

They climbed to the roof. Domingo stopped and put a hand on Merripen's shoulder. "You know old myths, don't you? Some have common elements. A god, or set of gods, rules—the first gods. But their days are numbered. They are replaced by new gods. Often they know who will topple them." He went to his ship and rested against it, head down. "I'm so weary," he said as Merripen came up to him. "I'm so tired. I see what's coming, and I'm caught in it. I have to see it through."

Merripen's neck was stiff; his muscles were taut. His back prickled. There was despair on Domingo's face; the gray eyes stared past him into a void. Merripen had seen that look before. It was the look of a dying man, a potential suicide, a signal that something had gone wrong, that cells were beginning to die and biological systems were breaking down.

"I can help you," Merripen said rapidly. "You haven't been taking care of yourself, you need treatment. Come away with us."

"Don't you think I know what's happening inside my own body?" Domingo waved away the hand that Merripen was offering. "I can repair it. But my mind goes on. A mind is a strong thing. It can create its own illness, and harm the body all over again, and make you want it to happen even as you struggle against it. It's a feedback loop. It's also part of you, and you can't kill it. We've never been masters of ourselves. We're still too young, not much past my people here."

"You need to come away."

Domingo sagged against the ship. "I want you to go," he said softly. "Do you hear? I want you to leave. Get your friends and bring them up here."

Merripen waited, wondering if Domingo was somehow testing him.

"Go on," Domingo whispered.

Merripen hurried below. He found Andrew drinking with Eline at the glass-topped table; Karim had just removed a bowl of soup from the materializer. Andrew scowled as he looked up; Eline glared at Andrew over her glass. Her cheeks were pink, her lips drawn back. Merripen said, "Domingo wants us on the roof. He says he's going to let us go."

Andrew looked at Eline and smiled, showing most of his teeth. Karim put down his bowl and came toward Merripen. Andrew rose, and Merripen ushered the two men out of the room. They were halfway up the stairs before Eline came out and followed them. She walked stiffly, keeping her left arm straight at her side, as though she had hurt it.

They went out onto the roof. Thick clouds hung low in the sky, pressing against the distant hills. Domingo had opened the side of his ship. A large transparent bubble floated out and rested on the roof; Domingo came out after it.

"It'll be crowded," Domingo said. "But I think you can all fit." He motioned at Karim. "You'll have to stoop. I've set it for Harsville. I can't leave you to wander the roads, and you should make an impressive departure."

Andrew looked at the bubble suspiciously. The streets were filling with people. Karim took Andrew's arm. "We'd better get in," he said.

Eline said, "I don't want to go. I'd rather stay here."

"Would you?" Domingo lifted an eyebrow. "Of course. I knew it would be you. You can stay. I can see you've been planning for it." He turned his eyes from her to Merripen. His gaze was steady, his face composed. He reached inside his robe and took out his silver necklace, putting it around his neck.

Domingo called out in his amplified voice. This brought more people into the streets below the temple; the javelin throwers were rushing from the field. Eline backed away from the men and stood to one side; her right hand was on the wrist of her stiff left arm. The priests were climbing the steps, smoothing their robes, as if they had just pulled them on. The side of the bubble slid open. Andrew got in, then Karim, who had to stoop. Merripen looked from Eline to Domingo, then followed his friends into the bubble.

The bubble closed and lifted slowly. Domingo spoke in his strange language; Eline moved to his side. The bubble hovered over the roof; Merripen pressed his hands against the curved surface and looked down. They drifted away; Domingo's voice seemed to follow them. He was chanting; the priests knelt. The globe floated over the bowed backs of the people below.

Andrew pressed against him; Karim peered over his shoulder. Merripen watched the roof recede. The small figure of Eline stepped away from the blond man. Her right hand darted toward her left wrist. Merripen saw the beam of light before he knew what it was. Domingo fell, arms out, sprawling on the roof. Eline bent over him, pulling at his neck with one hand, holding her weapon with the other. Merripen thought he heard a cry from the crowd. Eline was putting something around her neck. She stood up. Her amplified voice pierced the bubble. The people on the roof had pressed their heads to the marble surface; those in the street were on their knees.

The bubble fled from the village, flew over the fields, lifted above the treetops, and carried them over the road leading to Harsville.

Their vehicles were undamaged. They had all changed their clothes for warmer ones. The bubble sat among the debris in front of the unburned house. Light glowed from the dome of Eline's craft; Andrew was inside it. Karim drove his own vehicle across the road, past a mound of burned rubble and up a hill, coming to rest among the trees. Andrew turned off his light and followed; Merripen trailed after him.

The sun was setting; the ruins below were being transformed into shadows that masked the destruction. Andrew got out of Eline's craft and went to Merripen; he leaned against him as he sat down. He rested his hand on Merripen's shoulder for a moment, then withdrew. "I hated being so far off the ground in that bubble." Andrew paused. "What are we going to do?"

"I don't know."

"I think we should keep going. We have Eline's craft now, we could send it ahead as a scout."

"But we don't know where to look," Merripen said.

"We can still go west. We have plenty of time to look." Andrew chuckled in the dark. "You knew this wouldn't be easy. Did you expect someone to draw you a map?"

"I think you're just trying to prove you're not a coward."

"I think you're afraid to test your ideas. You can console yourself with stories about your project's destiny. You just went on this trip so you could tell yourself you tried."

"Why is it so important to you to keep on going?"

"Maybe I have my own questions. And maybe I'm doing it for Terry. Maybe I'd like to bring her something besides old memories."

"I see. It's your quest."

"Maybe it is."

The screen in front of them chimed; a light flashed. Merripen started, then waited, expecting to hear the Citadel's signal; Leif might have found something out. The screen chimed again. Someone else was calling. He reached out and pressed the panel.

Eline's face appeared on the small screen. Her eyes were cold. Karim's image peered out from one corner; he, too, had answered the call.

Merripen did not wait for a greeting. "What do you want?" he said harshly, suddenly afraid that she would come after them.

"To say goodbye," she answered. "To explain."

"You killed Domingo."

She twisted her mouth into a half-smile. "Of course I didn't kill him. He was stunned. He's in suspension here in his temple. That makes you feel better, doesn't it? From my point of view, he might be happier if he were dead—his soul would be at peace—but you obviously don't agree, and he might not have been ready for the higher state. Think of it. He has a great privilege. He might awaken someday to see what his people have become."

"Why did you do it?" Karim's voice asked.

"It came to me the second night we were here. I suddenly knew what my purpose was, whom I had to rescue. These people are as we once were. If I stayed with them, I could help guide them to the truth. But I couldn't leave Domingo in control. He would have gone on doing things in his own way, and I would have had little influence. The only way left was to usurp him. I found one of his wands and kept it with me, under my shirt. My chance came sooner than I had expected; I had to act before he figured out what I might do. Now I can begin to change things—a little at first, more as time goes on. Gradually, they will begin to glimpse the truth, and their souls will be saved." She paused. "It came to me in a vision. I know now I did the right thing."

Merripen leaned back. Visions, glimpses of eternal truth— Domingo would have said that they were only remnants of their once divided minds, their former longing for authority. Once, the voices had spoken to them; they had lost them as they became conscious of themselves. Prayer was only a way of calling to such voices, which would never again answer them so clearly; Eline's conviction that there was a life after death was another remnant of the past. He sighed. She was closer to Domingo's people than she realized.

"I wanted you to know," she went on. "Domingo didn't try to stop me. He must not have known what would happen. His reason was failing."

"He knew," Merripen said. "He was waiting for it." He could see that she was skeptical. He thought of telling her what Domingo had told him, but he doubted it would sway her. "They're changing, they're developing on their own now. They won't forget Domingo so easily, and now that they know one god can fall, they may begin to think of toppling the new one themselves."

"They'll follow me." She laughed softly. "They might be our future. Think of that. Everything we've done just brings us back to the beginning again."

"No," Merripen said. "You're wrong." Karim's image winked out. Eline said her farewell and her face disappeared. The trees above him stirred and a strong wind gusted through the dark town below, scattering pale streamers of cloth.

V

They sent out Eline's hovercraft at dawn. It floated south over the meadow below Harsville and on toward the low hills beyond before bearing west.

They waited until it was out of sight, then began to track it. Andrew rode with Merripen. He jerked his head toward Karim's craft, which was following close behind. "Something's wrong with Karim. Did you notice?"

"I've been noticing for a while," Merripen replied.

"He looked sick this morning. I watched him take a turn around Harsville while you were eating breakfast. He looked dizzy; he staggered a bit. He's hiding something."

"I know."

"We'd better keep our immune systems working. It might be contagious."

The empty craft was traveling farther from them; Merripen turned on the screen and gazed through the vehicle's eyes. It passed an empty wooden shack, still standing in a field.

The spirit of the journey seemed to return to him; the calming lassitude, the anticipation of reaching his goal. He lost his impatience. The journey itself could be pleasurable, viewing the landscape, breaking up the trip with stops along the way. Then he thought of Domingo, and Harsville, and the hunters of Pine Point. The illusion vanished. He was traveling through a dead world; it was their graveyard. Were there others like Domingo? He was sure that there were. His impatience returned. He had waited too long.

"Do you miss Terry?" he said to Andrew.

"No. I always return to her, but I don't miss her. Haven't you noticed that you don't really miss anyone unless it's someone you think you might never see again?"

"No, I haven't noticed that. I can miss plenty of people I think I'll see in a few hours if they're close to me."

"But you don't miss them. You feel their absence, you remember them, but you don't miss them. The pain isn't there."

By noon, patches of blue were appearing in the sky; the sun nestled between two clouds. Merripen had dozed, and then eaten; his muscles were stiff. They were traveling through a river valley, floating near one bank. On each side, the trees were thick; the land would soon be nothing but forest. He looked at the trees, at the dark shadows under their boughs. It wasn't his world. They had somehow been carried through space without realizing it and were now somewhere else, not on Earth. He looked up at their familiar star and shook off the fantasy.

If he traveled long enough, he might see the world. He could come to an ocean, cross it in a small airship, alight on an island, drift on after a rest. Once, he could have asked a satellite to transmit pictures of the land, the settlements and towns, before setting out, but the satellites were silent now. It did not matter; they would have shown him buildings, even people, but not Domingo's dream.

Ahead, the river curved, then widened. Gnarled and twisted trees clung to the edge of one bank, their snaky limbs almost touching the water. He looked at the screen. The empty hovercraft was crossing a field. Still tracking it, they moved away from the riverbank and toward the thinning trees. There had once been a road here; now it was overgrown with grass and green shoots which would one day be more trees. They followed the grassy road.

A bright flash of light flickered on the screen; Merripen

squinted and leaned forward. The light moved, becoming the metal of another craft which was now approaching the empty one. "Someone's out there. Look."

Andrew leaned over and looked at the screen. The panel hummed; someone was trying to call the empty craft.

"Should we answer?" Merripen asked.

"I don't see why not. We're still far enough away to run for it." Andrew smiled sourly. "We could always lead them toward Eline."

Merripen hesitated. The strange hovercraft was still approaching. At last he opened a channel.

A round-faced, red-haired woman stared out of the screen at him. *"Bonjour,"* she said. *"Salaam, do-briy d'en, konnichi wa,* hello."

"Hello will do," Merripen replied.

"Hello, then. Isn't there anyone in that thing?"

"No, it's our scout."

"Clever. My name's Jorah. May I ask you why you're traveling?"

"We're trying to find some friends."

"Trying to find? Don't you know where they are?"

"If we knew, we wouldn't be wandering around here looking for them." He felt irritated by her manner, even though he realized that she was probably just as suspicious of him as he was of her. "We didn't know there was anyone out here. We have no intention of disturbing you."

"You won't disturb us," she answered. "We won't let you. Just a warning. I'm not out here alone. Tell your empty craft to stop a kilometer from here."

"We weren't planning to stop."

"You have nothing to fear as long as you're not Rescuers. You don't look the type. They're usually sneaky or blatant. We're ready to protect ourselves."

"You made that clear."

"If you want to stop, you may. I'll give you lunch. If you don't, then I'll stop wasting my time."

Merripen glanced at Andrew, who nodded a little. "All right," Merripen answered. "We'll accept your offer."

The empty craft sat outside a large, faceted dome. Through the dome's clear sides, Merripen saw a pit and several tents. Jorah stood at the dome's entrance; two men were with her.

He waited inside the craft; Karim pulled up to his side. Jorah and the two men did not move; he noticed that they all carried wands. Karim got out of his craft. Merripen, surprised, motioned to him. Karim tapped on his door; Merripen opened it.

"It's all right," Karim said. "I've seen one of the men before. He stayed in Pine Point some time ago."

Merripen and Andrew got out and followed Karim to the dome's entrance. Merripen walked slowly, his body tensed for flight; he was still wary of strangers. Karim spoke to the smaller of the two men and introduced his companions; then Jorah led them inside.

Here the air was not as humid. They walked near the edge of the pit. The pillared, stony façade of an old building jutted out from one side of the pit; tables piled with shards, trays, and papers stood in front of the building. "We're archeologists," Jorah said. "We just started digging here." She led them to a tent; the two men left them and scampered down into the pit. Merripen and his friends sat outside the tent while Jorah went inside, coming out in a few moments with a tray of tea and bowls of rice and vegetables.

She sat down while they ate. "Where are you from?"

"I'm from a town in the north," Karim said. "My friends are from a Citadel near it."

Merripen peered over his cup and met Jorah's amber eyes. "I suppose we'll be excavating it one of these days," she said. "Your Citadel, I mean."

"You'll have to wait a long time."

"Not so long. Not so long as you think."

They finished their food in silence. Jorah watched them solemnly. "What are you excavating?" Merripen said at last.

"A small pre-Transition town." She waved a hand. "We're working on the town hall, trying to dig out the records. We have to do most of the work ourselves. On my first dig, we got some kobolds from a Citadel, but they didn't work out. They were too careless—it was too hard to train them to take care of the artifacts they found. We were so busy trying to make them do it right that we finally had to do it ourselves." She paused. "There's so much to do, and not enough people to do it. We were so confident when we started. I thought: We have all this time, we can recover the past—all of it. We can find every important site, build up nearly a complete record of the human past, record it all, analyze it." She shook her head. "I was naive."

"Were you?" Merripen said.

"People were very destructive during the Transition. It was as if everyone wanted to forget the dead past—dead in every sense of the word. Cities were torn up and rebuilt, some favorite sites were restored at the cost of others nearby, towns and farmhouses were cleared to make room for gardens and campsites and parks. Even before that, a lot of old sites had been destroyed by carelessness or greed, and then the materializers added to the problem, because many people duplicated artifacts from different times—I've found necklaces of Eighteenth-Dynasty Egypt all over the world." She shrugged. "Few people thought it mattered. The discontinuity between our world and the past was too great. The past was gone, and we had an endless future. Certainly we had nothing in common with those short-lived people."

"You should have an easier time of it now," Andrew said.

"Not really. Now nature is the enemy. As we dig here, other sites are crumbling away, or being flooded or buried. We're just trying to save what we can."

"Maybe it doesn't matter," Andrew said. "The past, I mean. It doesn't have the same meaning; it's something that happened to another species, in a way."

"Perhaps. But I think if we could understand what happened then, we'd know more about ourselves, too. Maybe we'd understand what's happening to us now. I want to know as much as I can about which societies died out, and why, and which ones could change and why. I don't know—maybe I'm bringing too much of myself to this, maybe I'm not seeing what's there. I look at these scraps and make up stories about them." She sighed. "Enough. What about you? Who are you looking for?"

Merripen explained as briefly as he could; Jorah nodded and did not interrupt. She frowned when he finished and looked uneasily toward the pit.

"This may have nothing to do with the ones you're trying to find," Jorah said softly. "But about ten years ago, six or seven hundred kilometers from here, I did see something strange. We'd been digging at a site that had seemed promising but didn't pan out. I was tired and discouraged, so I went out alone in a hovercraft. The land's flat there. I would have seen anyone coming for a long way, so I wasn't really being reckless. My craft was driving and I wasn't paying too much attention to where it was going, but after a while, I noticed that it was going in the wrong direction."

She glanced at the pit again, as if afraid someone would overhear her. "I checked it. There was nothing wrong. I reset it—I was going north—but it kept bearing east. So I got out and stretched out my arm. I felt a field, an invisible field. I couldn't penetrate it, and my craft couldn't go through it."

"A shield," Merripen said.

"Like the ones around Citadels? But this one was huge. Whatever generated it was a lot more powerful than anything I know about." A tall woman hurried past, toward the pit; Jorah stopped talking and toyed with the teapot until the woman disappeared into the pit.

"I got a little nervous," Jorah continued. "I took out my binoculars. All I could see was flat ground reaching toward the horizon. Finally I thought I saw something move, but it might have been my eyes playing tricks. I was scared, but still curious. I decided to measure the diameter of the shield. I rode around it. It was at least fifty kilometers wide, maybe more. I've forgotten. Something had to be in there, but I didn't see it."

Merripen clutched his cup. Karim raised his eyebrows; Andrew put down his bowl. "Maybe I should have stayed there," Jorah said. "Maybe I should have brought my friends to check it. I left. I went back to our site and I didn't say a word. I had bad dreams about it. Once I thought that there might have been people inside it from out there." She waved at the sky. "I dreamed that they'd come here to make the earth over, to tear it apart. We left our site soon after that. I never went back, and I didn't report it. It was obvious that whoever left the shield there didn't want intruders, and I was afraid of what it might mean."

"Tell us how to get there." After he spoke, Merripen felt surprised. He could be heading toward something even more dangerous than Domingo's village. Andrew was nodding; Karim seemed oddly indifferent.

Jorah said, "So you're going to go."

"We might as well. We have no other leads."

"I don't think you should."

"Then you shouldn't have told us about it."

She grimaced. "I'm just resentful, I suppose. You're going to go there, and I was too frightened to stay. I guess I'm not used to dealing with anything that's still alive. I sometimes feel like a grave robber." She gazed toward the pit. "And sometimes I don't know whether I'm digging here or burrowing through my mind." She lifted her head. "When will you leave?"

"Right away," Merripen said.

"I'd better give you directions, then."

By the next day, the hills had given way to flat land. A sea of grass rippled before them to the horizon; darker bands flowed over the grass as it swayed. Under the wide sky, Merripen felt small and exposed; the small fluffy clouds overhead were so low it seemed he could touch them, while those in the distance appeared to be thousands of kilometers away.

He was riding with Andrew, Karim's craft at their side. Far ahead, the empty craft was a fat insect swimming in a green and brown sea. Merripen thought about Karim. The man no longer seemed ill, but he had been keeping to himself ever since their departure from Jorah's site.

Merripen had awakened in the night, while they were resting near the side of an old road, and had noticed that Karim was not in his craft, though his light was on. Peering into the darkness, he had at last spied Karim standing in the road, arms out, face turned toward the stars. Merripen had pretended he was still asleep when Karim returned. He had said nothing to Andrew.

Karim's craft floated ahead, then settled on the ground. The high grass bowed under it. Merripen stopped behind it and signaled to the other man. There was no answer.

Merripen was out of his craft and walking toward Karim's when the other man emerged, a wand at his waist and a pack on his back. His dark eyes were clear; he smiled. "It's done," Karim said, and his voice was deep and full again. "I'm going to leave you here."

Merripen shook his head. Andrew had come to his side. "What are you talking about?" Merripen said.

"Surely you can guess. It must have occurred to you earlier. I'd done my work with viruses, using them to transmit certain traits, to change genes, to transplant new ones. I became my own subject. I considered this for a long time; I knew what I was doing. That's why I had to leave Pine Point. I'm not as I was."

Merripen stepped back. Karim looked as he had, yet his eyes

seemed lost in the contemplation of a vision Merripen could not see. "What have you done to yourself?"

Karim opened his hands, flexing his fingers. "All my senses are sharper. The air itself can nourish me; I'll need little food. I can live in the world. I no longer have to hide from it." He lifted his head. "I carry a symbiote—its cells are replacing my own even as I speak. I taste the wind, I see its sound. It blows from the south now—I smell the ferns and the traces of moss, the swamp air. I'm stronger. I can heal myself almost instantly."

"But why did you do it?"

"Because I want to live in the world, out here. I thought about it so many times as I went out hunting or hiking—it's time for us to return to that. But we can't as long as we cling to our devices, the things we need to stay alive, the things that separate us from the world. You think I'm mad." Karim shook his head. "But I can be fed by sunlight, I can pluck that weed"—he waved at a leafy green plant—"and be nourished by it, because my body will change it to food. I can live as we were meant to live. We made a mistake when we set ourselves up as Earth's rulers—we are only part of it, and perhaps not the most important part, either."

Karim looked down at the Bond on his wrist. "I no longer need this." He removed it and dropped it on the ground, crushing it under his foot. "This is where I'll leave you. Take my hovercraft—I left a record of my work in its computer, in case anyone wishes to join me. Perhaps you will if you don't find your friends."

"No," Merripen said. "You don't know what you're doing."

"I know exactly what I'm doing. I feel my mind shedding its doubts and intellections as a snake sheds its skin. Farewell." Karim turned and walked away.

Andrew moved quickly. He darted toward Karim and seized his arms; the taller man shook him off. Andrew grabbed him again. Karim turned, lifted him gently, and flung him to the ground. Andrew got up, dazed but apparently unhurt. Karim began to run, his head and shoulders bobbing above the grass.

"Come on," Andrew said. "We've got to stop him. We'll go after him in our craft and put him in suspension until we can get him to a Citadel." Merripen did not move. "Come on."

"Let him go."

"But he could die out there."

"Let him go. It's what he wants. Death is part of it. In that world he loves so much, creatures die all the time." He remembered the look on Karim's face as he had turned away; he had seemed lost in joy. He envied the other man suddenly. Karim would roam the deserted land, at peace. Earth would sing to him. He might live a long time. He wondered if Karim could live forever that way.

Andrew said, "It's affected his mind."

"Perhaps it has. But he chose it." Merripen gazed over the plain at the retreating figure, which grew smaller until it was hidden by the grass.

Merripen, riding in Karim's hovercraft, had finished scanning the man's records. He felt depressed rather than illuminated. His journey seemed an exercise in futility. Everything he had seen convinced him that he should never have left the Citadel; if he went back now, he would want to tear it down, little by little, leaving only the walls as a warning. He thought of Karim roaming the plains, of Jorah digging through bones and ruins, of Eline and Domingo, of the burned husk of Harsville. All of it was, at least in part, his legacy; his actions long ago had helped bring it about.

The sun was low in the violet sky. Eline's craft, far ahead, suddenly veered and turned north. Merripen sat up. It had reached the shield. He took over his craft and drove more quickly, catching up with Andrew, and tried to signal to him. The screen stayed blank; something was interfering with it. Andrew looked toward him and motioned at his own screen.

They rode on until their vehicles met the shield, bumped against it, trembled, and then veered north.

By nightfall, they had circled the barrier completely, but had seen nothing inside it except scrubby land, dotted by shrubs and small trees. The vehicles now sat silently in the dark, noses against the invisible shield..

Andrew punched out supper. The two men ate in their seats, keeping their lights low even in the darkness. Merripen finished eating, then poured more wine.

"How long do you think we'll have to wait?" Andrew asked.

"I don't know. We don't even know what we're waiting for. We can hope that they'll notice someone's out here and come out to check. Maybe we should hope they don't see us at all."

Andrew waved a hand at the bottle of wine that sat on a

ledge behind their seats. "Don't drink too much of that. One of us should stay awake while the other sleeps."

Merripen nodded. Andrew brooded for a few moments, then said, "Do you think you can sleep now?"

"Yes. I'm very tired."

"Good. I'll stay awake, then. I know I can't sleep."

Merripen put down his seat, trying to get comfortable. The inside of the craft darkened. Andrew stirred in his seat, touched Merripen's arm gently, then withdrew.

Someone hidden by the darkness came to stand at Merripen's side, watching him silently. He was afraid to move. A warm wave rippled over him. He threw up a hand and cried out. He broke into wakefulness; Andrew was holding him.

"You felt it," Andrew said. "I felt it, too."

"I think they know we're here."

"Lie down. Try to get some sleep."

A hand touched Merripen. He opened his eyes; it was light outside. He sat up and looked at Andrew. "You didn't wake me."

"I couldn't have slept." Andrew was sipping tea. "I thought for a moment that there was something on the other side, but I couldn't see, and I was afraid to get out and look. There's nothing now." He put down his cup. "I think I can rest now. Give me a couple of hours." He lay down on his seat and closed his eyes.

Merripen leaned against his door, then forced himself to open it and get out. He undid his pants and pissed; the stream arched over the grass and bent as it met the barrier. He walked toward the shield and stood there silently, wondering how long he would have to wait. He could live here for a long time, waiting. It might be a good way to live, waiting, never meeting his goal. He pressed his hands against the shield and pushed; his palms tickled. "Come out of there," he said to the air. His voice was hollow. "Damn you." He was slipping. He would lose himself and Andrew would have to take him back to the Citadel. He kicked the shield and his toes tingled.

He looked up. There was a bulge on the horizon. It grew larger and became another hovercraft, traveling toward him. He stared at it for a time, then whirled around and ran toward his craft. He jumped in. Andrew sat up.

"Someone's coming."

Andrew raised his seat and looked out. The strange craft, its dome opaque, was still moving in their direction. It stopped just behind the shield. Andrew was pale. Merripen leaned forward, ready to back up and hurry away if necessary, trying not to think about whether he could actually escape.

The craft faced him. He began to wonder if there were anyone inside it after all. He thought of hovercrafts and computers and mechanical devices going about their business, with no one left to guide them. Then the craft's door opened. A woman in blue pants and a white blouse stepped out; she shook back her long black hair.

"Josepha," Merripen whispered, and he was outside again, running to the shield. "Josepha." He put out his hands. She came to him and opened her mouth and he thought he saw her lips form his name. She went back to her craft and leaned in, then stood up.

He put out his hand again, and this time the shield was gone. "Merripen," she cried.

They sent all the hovercrafts inside before the shield was raised again. Josepha was laughing and clinging to his hands, then backing away with the familiar worried look on her face, a tense mouth and a line between her eyebrows. He took her arms and rested his head on her shoulder for a moment, then introduced her to Andrew.

He was staring at her, head tilted to one side. "What's the matter?" Merripen asked.

"It's nothing." Andrew turned toward Josepha. "I thought you looked familiar. It's nothing."

Merripen took Josepha's hand again. "Your children—are they here?"

"Everyone's here. All the parents, all the children. We've been here for a long time. This shield is their doing. That, and other things. How far did you travel?" She did not wait for an answer. "It must have been hard. I can see it in your face."

Merripen let go of her and stepped back. "A long time. And in all that time, you didn't ask me to join you."

"I guess we thought you wouldn't want to come. I don't know. Your part was over. No one had seen you for so long."

"I see. What happened later didn't concern me. And maybe you didn't want me here, judging the results."

Josepha was silent. Then she said, somewhat coldly, "Follow me. I'll take you to them."

He and Andrew got into their craft and followed hers. "She's one of the parents," Andrew said.

"Yes."

"I'm sure I've seen her somewhere." Andrew turned slightly in his seat. "You're hurt because they came here without you."

"I guess I am."

"You shouldn't be. I don't think you ever quite understood how others sometimes felt about you biologists."

"I certainly did," Merripen replied. "I hid in the Citadel, didn't I?"

"I wasn't talking about that. I meant before. I don't quite know how to explain it to you, Merripen. You were the artists, we were the paintings. Even people like me, who never had anything more than minor changes, were made by you. You made the lives we had possible. You gave us long life, and then you gave us elves and trolls and giants and other creatures, and we got used to your being offstage, letting us have the illusion that our lives were our own. It's disconcerting to have you reappear onstage after that. Do you understand?"

"No," Merripen said, afraid that he did.

"I don't think anyone here meant to hurt you."

"It doesn't matter whether they did or not. They have. And it doesn't matter what we made. It'll all disappear."

"I don't believe it."

"I went through a long, useless journey that only shows me how pointless this trip was."

"Maybe the struggle was worth it. You don't know yet."

Merripen lowered his eyes. He was afraid to look up, afraid of what he might see. Would eyes accuse him silently as he passed? Would they turn away from him? Would the children have become something he could never comprehend? No, Josepha was here, with the other parents; perhaps that had kept his children at least a little bit human. He covered his brow with his hand.

"Look," Andrew said. Merripen did not move. "Look."

He forced his head up. The flat land dipped here, giving way to a giant crater. Now he knew why he had been unable to see anything from outside the shield. The crater's sides were smooth and grassy, covered with shrubs and trees. The houses below had been built of wood and stone and brick. There seemed to be no order to the settlement; the roads were uneven and twisted, the plots of land unmarked by boundaries. Near the edge of the town, he saw three houses in a cluster; toward the center, one long wooden house was surrounded by a flower garden.

As they drove down the slope, people began to gather in the roads. They did not crowd together, but stood in pairs or small groups along the sides of the paths. As Merripen's craft drew nearer, he began to recognize faces. Gurit Stern was near a trellis, still with crow's-feet around her eyes and lines etched near her mouth. Kelii Morgan's ample form was partly hidden under a long shirt; his chubby brown face glowed. Edwin Joreme seemed impassive; Chen Li Hua, with her gray tunic and clipped hair, was ascetic. He recognized them all, surprised that he could, and yet they had changed in some way. They held back from his vehicle; they did not approach it, they did not wave or shout greetings.

Josepha stopped in front of a gray wooden house with a porch and got out. Merripen drew up behind her, and he and Andrew followed her to the door. Chane Maggio stood there with his child Ramli and a small, dark-skinned child whom Merripen did not know. Merripen looked around quickly. Other young children had entered the street in front of the house; two held up their hands solemnly while the others watched him without moving. In the distance, near a stone house, he saw two men with infants in their arms.

He turned to Josepha, unable to speak. His eyes stung. She came to his side and took his hand. He looked back at the children in the street, who drew their eyebrows together as they stared back.

"Whose are they?" he managed to say. "Yours?"

She shook her head. "Theirs. Teno's, and Ramli's, and Yoshi's, and Aleph's, and all the rest. Theirs."

Merripen tried to smile. They had children. But his satisfaction was tainted; they had brought their replacements into being, just as he had. He gazed at the child with Chane, suddenly conscious of the skull under the thick dark hair and brown skin, and thought of death.

VI

Merripen walked with Josepha through the settlement. From the edge of the bowl-like depression, the place had seemed disorderly, but here, the hidden order emerged. Each building seemed close and accessible while at the same time private; he could walk to each house easily along the roads, but would then meet with stone steps through gardens, tree-lined paths, or lawns covered with mazes of shrubbery, before reaching the doors themselves. A few of the younger children wandered after them as they walked; they were subdued, as their parents had been at that age.

"What's it been like here?" he asked.

"You'd probably find it quiet." He thought of the moribund Citadel, and smiled. "We teach the children, we learn. We put up the shield for protection. We felt that we needed it."

She led him to the end of the curving road. Ahead, set in the grassy slope of the bowl, he saw a large, flat, metallic surface; an entrance slid open, and a figure emerged. "An underground city?"

"No." She drew him to the slope, and they sat on the grass. "You made them, Merripen. They don't live the way we do, they don't think in our way. I've lived here all this time, and maybe in some ways I'm more like them than like the woman I was." Her face seemed to contradict her words; she drew her eyebrows together and frowned. "But even now, I find that they're opaque to me, that I can't quite sense their motivations except intermittently. If they have a passion, it's curiosity—if they have an overriding motivation, it's the use of their reason. They want to seize everything, gobble it up, but with their minds, not with force or guilt or anger. And they don't work or learn as an escape from anything or as some sort of compensation—they do it for itself. Their motivation is pure. With us, something always pulls us back or sullies the accomplishment."

He nodded. "But then why are they hiding here?"

She leaned forward. "They're not really hiding. They're preparing." She waved a hand at the metallic rectangle. "That is our gateway, Merripen. If you walk in there, you'll find yourself inside a large asteroid out beyond Saturn."

"A materializer," he said, thinking of the implications.

"No, a transformer. It takes the matter of our bodies and alters it, then beams it to the asteroid, where it's restored to its original form. It's your atoms that it reconstructs, not a duplicate with your memories and form. The transformer is mostly their work, of course. A few of us assisted them." There was an edge to her voice.

"Are they going to live in the asteroid, then?"

"Eventually, they will. Earth is finite, while their lives are open-ended. Only the universe will satisfy them now."

"I see," he said, and to himself: I was right. The sky above was darkening, growing purple in the dusk; he looked up at the dark blue clouds. "They don't have our limitations."

"No, but we can follow their example. They've been our mentors. Teno sometimes acts like a parent, while I'm a child. If an example is worth following, can't we follow it, however frail and fallible we are?" She sounded as though she were asking the question of herself.

"I suppose we can. Are you going to live with them in their asteroid?"

"Of course." Josepha sounded oddly defensive. "We haven't discussed it, but it's understood. We've changed—we're happier living with them. What we value isn't really that different."

We and they. Us and them. The dichotomy was in her words, even as she sought to minimize it. Below, four youngsters were strolling toward a house. They all had the same androgynous bodies; their loping gait was neither an aggressive stride nor a dainty walk. "When did they start having children?" he asked.

"Very recently. They're biologists, too, along with everything else. They used the lab for some of them, and had others naturally." He started. "They called it testing the equipment, and said it was a rational thing to do. Oh, they did some work on the zygotes, made sure no defects were present before carrying them to term. Teno had two that way, one as father and one as mother. They said they just wanted to be sure that they weren't dependent only on the labs, but maybe there was more to it than that. I was with Teno during the delivery—I saw the look of satisfaction when it was over. Teno nursed the baby, too." She gazed at the houses below, now black shapes with lighted windows. Her face was shadowed, but he could still see the frown and the line between her brows. "I don't know. Maybe I imparted more to it than was actually there. It's hard to tell. They said they would use the labs from now on because it's safer, but Teno said it had been an instructive experience." She brushed back her hair. "You'll be glad to know that they bred true—they didn't have to make *those* alterations."

She had said that she was happy here; she had told him that she and the others wanted to stay with their children. Still, she frowned, and talked of barriers, and wore her anxious look. She had not changed as much as she thought.

"Maybe you shouldn't have come here," she said in a low voice.

"Don't say that," he said. "I went through too much to get here."

"We all did. But that wasn't what I meant."

He drew her to him, and lay with her in the grass. He smoothed her hair and cupped her breast until she reached for him. They were still for a moment.

She said, "You've changed."

"Not really."

"You're warmer."

"I always had to control my feelings."

"I refused you twice, Merripen."

"That was a long time ago."

He felt her gentle hands under his shirt. He thought of the nearby houses and the closeness of the road, and then she sighed in his ear and he thought only of her.

A child was watching them when he awoke. Merripen sat up, rubbing his eyes. The sky was already gray; it was morning. The child stared, saying nothing, and sat down by the road; he thought he saw something of Josepha in its eyes. He rummaged awkwardly for his clothes, pulling them on under that steady gaze.

He was lonely. Being with Josepha had not dissipated the feeling. She had been gentle and then fierce, conveying unspoken demands. He had not known what she wanted, earthy wrestling or erotic spirituality, and he had had the sense of a woman struggling to keep certain things under control. He wondered if living here, going about her life under the calm, unemotional gaze of her child, had done that to her, or if she had always been that way. He remembered his first visit to her —the isolated house, the emotional distance she had kept. He sighed. He had trouble understanding her; what must it be like for her, trying to see into the minds of his children?

Josepha opened her eyes and saw the child. She picked up her shirt and shielded herself with it for a moment, then let it fall. "Laurel," she said, and the child came to her and took her hand. "Teno's child," she said to Merripen. "The younger one. The older lives with Yoshi." She released Laurel's hand, then picked up her clothes and shoes.

She rose and walked toward the road with Laurel. Merripen followed. Her buttocks bounced a bit as she walked. He caught up to her as they approached her house.

Andrew was at the door. He looked at Josepha, then at Laurel, and walked out onto the porch. He stopped Merripen on the steps. Josepha raised her eyebrows.

"I'll be there in a moment," Merripen said. She went inside with the child. Andrew drew Merripen down the steps to the path.

"I need to get away for a while," Andrew said. "I'm going to take a hovercraft out and go for a ride. It'll be safe enough behind their shield. I'll be back by evening."

"You don't like it here."

Andrew shook his head. "I just need some time alone to think. I was talking with that fellow Chane last night. I told him a little about the Citadel, and he told me about life here, and then he started reminiscing about the Transition. He's very old; he remembers it."

"I know."

"It wasn't actually the Transition he wanted to talk about, though; just how he grew up, what his home was like. He'd had some bad times, but he wanted to talk anyway. He made some pretty gruesome jokes. He said that a long time ago, you had to be able to laugh at things or you would just give up in despair. We started drinking. And then those two, the others, Teno and Ramli, came in, and that was that. We spent the rest of the evening talking about mathematics. At least they did, and I listened."

"What's wrong with that?"

"Nothing. Except that I got the feeling Chane goes through his life here wearing a mask. They try so hard to be like Teno and Ramli and the others, and it must gratify them or they wouldn't still be here, but they're not like them and they never really can be."

"Josepha told me that they were going to live with them in space."

"I heard about that, too. I don't know. It's peaceful here. In a way, it's very pleasant. I just need to get away for a while."

Andrew went to his hovercraft. Merripen entered the house. Chane was up, sitting with Ramli, Teno, Laurel, and another child at the table. The large front room was surrounded by doors leading to smaller rooms. Josepha came out of one door and sat down at the table; she was wearing a long blue robe. Merripen joined them. Chane smiled tensely and passed a bowl of fruit. Teno and Ramli were conversing, speaking in a language which sounded familiar; Merripen could grasp only a few words.

Teno finished eating and came over to Merripen, sitting

down next to him. Teno had not changed; the gray eyes stared out at him from a smooth, youthful face. The eyes were clear, hiding nothing; Merripen felt for a moment as though he were looking at himself through Teno's eyes. The barrier between them was still there, but it was his barrier. "Why did you come here, Merripen?"

"I wanted to see you."

"But why?"

"I wanted to see how you were. I thought . . ." He paused, wondering if Teno would understand. "I thought I might have failed. I thought that if I could find you, I'd know if I'd been right or wrong."

"And were you right?" Teno's mouth twitched.

"I don't know. I suppose I was. You have your children and a community, so you must be a viable design."

"A viable design?" Teno's mouth curved. "So it's the design that's responsible."

"I don't know."

"People like you live here, too. Don't you suppose that our society has something to do with what we are? Do you think our values are merely the product of our physiology?"

"I'm sure it has something to do with them."

"Perhaps it does. You valued certain things, certain attributes. Here we are, the embodiment of what you treasured in human beings. You should love us more than anyone."

Merripen thought he heard a low chuckle. He turned and saw Ramli's impassive dark eyes. "But then," Teno went on, "maybe you, too, have come to see us as something unnatural."

"Not at all," Merripen said quickly.

"I think we're in the line of development you might have taken. Consider this—men and women were becoming more like each other all along. You had to be, because your children required attention from both parents if they were to adapt successfully to the social environment that had become more important than the physical one you had subdued. Two people banding together, able to compare their experience and ideas, were likely to be more successful, in the biological sense, than isolated individuals or those whose ideas of their own places in society differed so radically that they were unable to give their young a coherent view of the world. There were always exceptions, of course, but I'm speaking in general terms. You were already selecting not for successful individuals, but for more successful pairs." Teno paused. "Why not go a step further, and conceive of one individual with the features of each member of a pair? It might have happened anyway, in time. Sudden evolutionary leaps have occurred in nature—does it matter that you used a laboratory for yours? It seems natural enough to me. It's the only way your species will change now, because as long as you remain here with your long lives, in some sort of equilibrium, you'll halt the course of evolution —which strikes me as a most unnatural course of action. Those are some of the notions I've played with, in somewhat simplified form."

"I never thought of you as anything except my children."

"That's not quite true, Merripen."

"It was your minds that concerned me. I wanted you to be free of the instincts that can still overpower us. The rest was almost an afterthought."

"Really? How do you know it wasn't an inherent part of the goal you sought, whether you realized it or not? It certainly seems a more reasonable biology to me." Teno rose, lips curving again in a half-smile, and stood at Merripen's side until he got up, then led him to one of the smaller rooms, closing the door behind him. The room, except for a platform and mattress against one wall and a large, wall-sized holo screen, was empty. The room had to be either Teno's or Ramli's; if it had been Josepha's or Chane's, he would have seen a painting, a vase of flowers, a rug, a mirror.

Teno sat on the edge of the bed. "You could have joined us before. Remember when I last spoke to you, long ago? You were building your wall. We didn't know exactly what we would do, but we had decided to live together again. At first, we were by ourselves, and then we thought of asking people to join us. We had lived in their world; it seemed fitting to ask them to live in ours. We thought of our parents. So we contacted them, one by one. We told them the same thing we told you. Every one of them—and they were all still alive, they hadn't in the end become prey to the self-destructive urges that have plagued so many of you, so you must have chosen them well—every one asked to come here immediately. You didn't. I waited for you to ask where we would be and when you could join us, but you didn't."

"I didn't want to interfere."

"You think of it as interference, as if you could not live as just one person among others, but would dominate." Teno frowned. "But that wasn't your only reason. You were having your doubts then—I saw it in you. And we couldn't have those doubts here. You might have communicated them, and we might have lost our courage."

"I didn't think you knew fear."

"We can reason our way to a cautious course of action. We can analyze something to the point where moving from one step to another seems fraught with danger."

Teno rose and went to the screen. The wall became a doorway to another world. Emerald-green grass bordered pale stone steps leading to white sand and a silver lake; slender birch trees stood in the distance. Merripen gazed past Teno, searching for the horizon, but the land beyond curved up like the side of a cup, enclosing the world. Distant hieroglyphs sharpened into curved roads and houses. He looked up; small winged shapes flew in the diffuse, yellow light. Near Teno's foot, a single white flower bloomed.

"Our new home," Teno said. "The inside of our asteroid. We can be artists as well. Earth isn't for us."

Merripen moved to Teno's side. The face near his was flushed, mouth open, eyes wide. "Think," Teno went on. "Endless space, endless time to explore it. There's so much to learn."

Teno seemed to be waiting. Merripen thought: They have one secret they haven't shared. Even in them, the old brain could dominate, confusing reason and will. The gray eyes watching him no longer seemed clear; a promise flickered behind them.

He reached for the slender arms and drew Teno to him, knowing now why he had been brought to this room. It would not be the way it had been with Josepha; nothing would be hidden.

Teno stiffened, then gently removed Merripen's hands. "You misread me."

Merripen backed away, confused. "I thought—"

"I'm sorry. If you wish—"

"No." Merripen said it fiercely. The image on the screen disappeared. He stared at the blank screen until he heard the door close behind him.

He cursed his body, his betrayer.

He sat alone in the room until Josepha came for him. She led him through the quiet, empty house and out to her garden, seating him in a canvas chair. He saw no exotic plants here, no kobolds among the flowers, only lettuce and marigolds and tomato vines.

Josepha sat on the grass next to him and lit a cigarette. A stream of smoke curled up from the tip; she exhaled a small pale cloud. "Teno told me," she said.

"Everything?"

"Don't look so ashamed. We've misunderstood, too. I don't know why they make love. They don't seem to think of it the way we do, looking for someone to fill some lack in us. That's what we do, isn't it—look for someone who will complete us somehow, who's an opposite or who complements one in some way. I don't know whether they do it simply to satisfy some physical urge or whether they see some reasonable purpose in it. They don't flirt or play any of the games. Once, they came to us, but they no longer do."

She bowed her head. "Once," she continued, "Teno came to me. I couldn't accept it. They see nothing wrong with it, as long as they're dealing with another adult and not a child. It makes a kind of sense, I suppose. If you live long enough, it should make no difference. You're two different people."

Teno had spoken to her. So his children did not keep secrets. Merripen had a secret, though, one that he would not share with Josepha. He had wanted to seize Teno, to shake the slender body, to force some passion into those calm gray eyes. It had been only a momentary impulse which had swept from him, leaving shame in its wake. He had wanted to drag Teno down and force submission, and he did not know why.

He thought of the asteroid, and of all of them trapped together inside it for an endless voyage. For Teno, it would be a home; for Merripen, it would be a prison. Yet its beauty drew him; the promise of the endless journey attracted him. He could reach Teno's calm and clarity intermittently; why not always?

He thought of Karim. The man had seen a life he wanted, and he had not shrunk from changing his body to get it. He could do the same. The depth of his self-loathing seemed to block his throat, making him unable to swallow or speak. He had wanted his children to be different from him. Why was he unhappy now because they were different?

He hid in the dark, alone. He was a mind without a body; his thoughts bore him up, lifting him above the house and over the shield to the sky. The trees below were only shrubs; the lakes were puddles. He was a noetic stream carried by the wind.

Merripen's door opened. He stirred on the bed; he was once again bone and flesh and brain. The small lamp next to him glowed; Josepha's long dark hair fell over his chest as she sat down next to him.

She drew up her legs and wrapped her arms around them. He touched her sleeve; she was still. "You want to talk," he said.

"I guess so. I can't sleep."

"You need to relax."

"No, I don't need to relax. I relax enough at other times." She ran the words together. She was tense; she rubbed her legs with her hands. "Chane's asleep; I didn't want to wake him. He's heard it all before, anyway."

"Once you turned me away because of Chane. Do you remember?"

"Oh, yes. Was that me? It seems as though it was someone else." She turned toward him, bouncing a bit on the bed. "Endless, eternal love. It's possible, isn't it? Except that it isn't that way; it ebbs and flows, it changes. The unspoken promises change. Sometimes it's everything to you, it's in everything you do. Sometimes it's in the background, always present but not conscious. Sometimes it's an obsession, and sometimes it's a long, quiet friendship. Sometimes it's two different things for the two people. Right now, Chane and I are at the friendship stage." She stretched out her arm and stared at it for a moment. "Think of the Josepha you first met. There isn't a single molecule of her left—if there is, it's something else now."

"Josepha."

"I'm so old. Sometimes I think about how old I am, and I can't believe it."

"Everyone feels that way sometimes."

"Do you, Merripen?"

"Occasionally. But my body keeps fooling me into thinking I'm not."

She laughed. "I wanted to die. Before the Transition. I tried to kill myself. I thought I wanted to die, but maybe I didn't, really. I wanted to escape, I know that—sometimes my despair was so strong I couldn't fight it, couldn't resist it."

He took her hand. Her fingers drummed against his

knuckles. "I'd sit for hours, staring at nothing. I'd be unable to speak. I couldn't eat, couldn't dress myself. I'd wait for it to pass, and often it seemed it never would." She drew her hand away. "The slightest thing would make me cry—a measure of music, a bird in the tree outside, the way my coat would sag when I hung it up. Sometimes I wouldn't leave my home for days because I was afraid I'd start crying in a public place."

She leaned back against one of his pillows. "I failed people close to me," she went on. "There was always that dark part of me they couldn't reach. They would say, 'What can I do?' and I'd have to say, 'Nothing, there's nothing you can do, just leave me alone.' That's one of the most horrible things you can do to someone who cares about you, because they have to watch it and there's nothing they can do—they're helpless."

"Josepha," Merripen said, afraid.

"They called it an illness, the despair I felt. I wasn't functioning well; I needed therapy. I know why people had to believe that, and why some still believe it—because then they could act. They didn't have to stand by; they could do something. They could give it a name—no matter if the name stigmatized you or turned your reality into a sick illusion. They didn't have to believe that there are things we can't control, that there are parts of us we can't understand, that you might be showing them a truth they can't accept, that only an insensitive person would never feel the despair. It was bad because it often led to suicide—a mortal sin, the sin that can never be forgiven—and a social wrong, because others would be left to clean up your mess. It didn't matter that it ended your pain, that you might think it better to die as you were and escape the pain, rather than living on as someone other than yourself, having to dampen or kill that part of you. It was better to take your autonomy away, to deny you that choice. And when the world changed and we could have everything, and yet people still wanted to die, that proved it was an illness, didn't it?"

"You can't mean what you're saying," Merripen said.

Her face grew taut. Then she smiled. "I've heard that, too. 'You can't mean it.'" She spoke more gently. "Did I really want to die? I don't know. I could never think of myself as not existing, so maybe I didn't. But I wanted to escape. I hated my body; I struggled against limits, and finitude, and the despair that showed me all too clearly what the limits were. Sometimes I had a mania—I could do anything, I saw things so clearly, I could work until I dropped, and then the despair would return and immobilize me. They called it an illness. Was it? Didn't it simply mirror life? We struggle, and then it's over."

"You're here," Merripen said. "You won that battle, didn't you?"

"Did I? I don't think so. We're always fighting ourselves, all of us. We have a divided nature. You know that's true—it's why you made Teno and the others. Isn't that so?" She did not wait for him to answer. "I wanted things to be other than what they were, and so do you. The longer we live, the more apparent our limits are."

He put his arm around her and she rested against him. "You shouldn't have come here," she murmured. "I'd forgotten most of this. I could pretend it wasn't so, and somehow you brought it all back."

She was calmer now. He thought of pulling off her robe, drawing her to him, losing himself in lovemaking, but sensed that she did not want that now. So he held her, while subduing himself.

Merripen remained in Josepha's house, but withdrew from the life around him. He ate his meals alone, or with Andrew, in his room. He read old novels, telling himself he was only brushing up on languages while knowing dimly that it was imaginary worlds of sensation and highly charged emotions that he sought. He lingered at the edges of small groups, catching scattered words. Andrew spent time with some of the young children, once taking a few on a bird-watching trip, but Andrew, too, had withdrawn, and did not speak often to Merripen.

He watched his children while feeling that he was learning little about them. He missed the signals of rivalries, grudges, passions, hidden and overt aggression. Even those like him were able to act as though they had escaped their irrationality, but he saw the looks of doubt, the worried frowns, the up-turned eyes searching for approval. They trailed after the androgynes as though they were pets trailing their masters.

He had failed.

His children would go on, and raise their children, and travel to the asteroid, and he and the others, in thrall, would follow. But their despair would grow deeper; they would continue to fall short, and their sorrow would finally destroy them. He wondered how they had lived with it for so long.

He knew what he had to do. He would begin another project, but this time, he and Josepha and Chane and all the other parents would be the subjects. He would not keep fearing what he might be after the change. He would dig through the muck to his old brain, and root it out.

Merripen heard a knock. He looked up from his lap screen. "We're having supper now," Teno said from the open door.

"I'll have mine here."

"Please join us this time. We'd like your company."

Merripen was about to refuse, but Teno's eyes seemed to plead with him. "All right."

He followed Teno to the table. He sat at one end; at the other, Andrew was feeding a piece of fruit to Ramli's child, Albah. Josepha smiled at him tensely, and Chane nodded. Teno sat with Laurel. Merripen poured some wine, nibbled at his mushrooms, then cleared his throat.

"I've made a decision," he said.

The others turned their heads toward him.

"I'm going to begin some research. I am going to try to find a way to alter our bodies so that we can be like you." He gestured at Teno, then at Ramli.

Andrew raised his eyebrows. "But why?" Chane said.

"Can't you see? It's the only way. I've seen what's happened here. It'll be better for all of us."

Josepha looked down, as though Merripen had raised a forbidden topic. Teno gazed at Ramli, and something passed between them. Ramli's head turned toward Merripen again.

"You're making a mistake," Ramli said.

"No, I'm not." He faced Teno. "You theorized that our descendants might have been like you in time. Is it reasonable to wait? Why not now?"

Teno raised a hand. "No, Merripen. You haven't thought it through. You're not looking at what you can be, or what you are; you're trying to find a niche. So many of you do that, as if there is some golden space that can enclose you and guarantee you happiness. But there are no golden spaces, not for us, not for any of you."

The others were silent for a while, then began to talk. Merripen picked at his food, then pushed the plate away. Josepha was looking at him. Merripen glared at her. *You know I'm right—speak out.* She lowered her eyes.

Teno and Ramli got up abruptly, reaching out for their chil-

dren. Ramli went to Chane, held Albah out, then whispered
something to him. Chane started, then smiled. Teno went to
Josepha's side. She kissed Laurel, then looked up at her child.

Teno said, "I love you, Josepha."

She held Laurel more tightly, then handed the child back to
Teno. "Thank you for saying it," she said softly. "You don't
have to."

"I wanted to say it now—it's important." Teno crossed to
Merripen's side and stood there with Ramli and the children.
"Thank you, Merripen, for giving us our lives."

Merripen stared at them, puzzled. They left and went to
their rooms.

He was soaring with Josepha over the settlement. When he
looked toward her again, Teno stared back at him. They flew
toward the hill and were suddenly over a silver lake; he looked
down through the clear water at the white pebbles below it.
They flew into the black night and the distant stars danced; he
could see them through Teno's transparent body. Teno spoke,
but the words were lost in the wind.

"Merripen."

He opened his eyes. Josepha was standing over him, her red
silk robe tied carelessly at her waist; the tip of her cigarette was
a bright red eye. "Merripen!" There was desperation in her
voice.

He sat up. "What is it?"

"Something's wrong. I woke up a little while ago. I saw a
group go by outside, Yoshi and some others. They were going
toward the transport." She sat down on the edge of the bed.
"I didn't think anything of it at first. I sat down and had some
tea, and then I suddenly had the feeling that the house was
almost empty. You get used to people being around; you feel it
when they're gone. I went to Teno's room, and then to
Ramli's. They aren't here. Laurel and Albah are gone, too."

"Is Chane awake?"

She shook her head. "No. Please come with me. I'm
afraid."

He got up and pulled on his robe, following her out of the
house. She dropped her cigarette and ground it into the path
with her slippered foot. The street was quiet; he saw Gurit at
the door of her brick house. Josepha pulled at his arm, leading
him down the road toward the grassy slope.

They climbed toward the transport. Merripen was apprehensive; was Josepha going to take him to the asteroid? He thought of his body turning into tachyons, streaking through space; he feared that transformation.

As they approached the entrance, part of the silver wall slid open, showing him a dark cavern. They entered, and the cavern grew lighter. Twenty transparent cylinders, each large enough to hold a few people, stood to one side.

Josepha went to one and pressed her hand against it, then turned to Merripen. "It won't open."

A figure was taking shape in the center of the cavern. Its edges grew sharper, and Merripen recognized Teno. Josepha ran to the image, as though she could embrace it; her arms passed through it. "Teno," she cried. Teno gave no sign of having heard her.

"I don't know how many of you are here," Teno said, "but this message will be repeated each time one of you enters this room. We have shut down the transports and will soon be leaving this system. We are saying farewell."

Josepha stepped back. Her hands fluttered before her face.

"I know you had assumed that we would travel together," Teno went on, "but it's better this way. Our paths are different, our needs are not the same. We knew we would have to leave you behind, and you are probably now thinking that it was cruel of us not to have told you before. Nothing any of you said precipitated this action; we had planned it long ago. Please believe that. When your shock and surprise wear off, you'll be happy that you didn't come with us."

The gray eyes gazed toward Merripen, then turned in Josepha's direction. The gesture seemed awkward, as though Teno was pretending this was a real conversation. "We have much to learn, about ourselves as well as other things. We must find out who and what we really are, and especially what we should become. You would have tried to hold us back, seeing in us only what you wanted to see, while we would have been trying to make you more like us. Perhaps our evolutionary paths are not the same. We may become something which you will become in time, or we may turn into something you never can be. We needed you for a while, but no more. We had exacerbated the divisions inside each of you; you were struggling to escape yourselves instead of confronting yourselves. You have time now to find out who and what you are, to create your own purpose. You may not find one—you may have reached a dead end. I don't say that to be cruel. You've tried to destroy yourselves in the past, and perhaps that part of you that seeks death will never wither away.''

Josepha leaned against Merripen; he reached for her hand. Her pulse beat with his own. "Stay with one another, if you can,'' Teno continued. "We've left you the only legacy we could leave—our journals, our observations, all of our research—it's all here. And, of course, you have your memories. Perhaps you'll choose to follow us, or to change the world you have. We may meet again, though I don't think any of us will be the same then. Please understand. I don't ask you to forgive, though you will in time. We loved you, in our way. Farewell.''

The image dissolved, shimmering as it disappeared. Josepha was biting her lower lip; her dark eyes shone. She bowed her head, and her long hair hid her face. Merripen stared at the spot where Teno's image had been.

What had they been told? Had Teno said that they could not follow as they were, that they had to change? Or were they caught by their past and unable to escape it? He had come here too late, in time only to catch a glimpse of what was now gone forever. Better if he had never come at all.

"Teno's wrong,'' Josepha said. "I think they're going to find that they're divided inside themselves, too. It was so easy for us not to see it when they were here, it was so easy for them not to see it—they could ascribe it to our influence. Now they'll have to confront themselves.'' Her voice broke.

"Josepha?'' he murmured.

"It's all right. I think I must have known it would happen all along. We tried so hard. We should have realized we couldn't have stayed with them. Isn't it odd? Only Teno speaks, so I get to see my child one last time. You'd think they all would have left messages. I suppose it didn't occur to them. The message is the same, so it doesn't matter who delivers it, but you'd think they'd understand by now that it would matter to us.'' Her mouth became a narrow line; her hand trembled slightly.

He turned. Chane and Gurit had entered the cave. Gurit hurried to Josepha and put an arm around her while Chane looked uncertainly toward the cylinders. The image began to form once more. "I don't know how many of you are here,'' Teno began.

Merripen went outside.

Merripen sat on the slope. Below, he could see Edwin Joreme digging in his garden. Josepha ambled through the streets with Chen Li Hua; Alf Heldstrom sat on his porch reading; Chane was visiting Dawud al-Ahmad. They had all been ghosts living in bodies for days; now they were returning to themselves.

Teno and the others had not, after all, lacked compassion. Each had left a personal message, locked inside the system until after their departure; they had apparently recorded them some time ago. So it had not been his arrival that had caused their leavetaking. That would have to console him. They had left him no message.

Andrew was climbing toward him. He looked back for a moment, stood over Merripen, then sat down. "I'm ready to leave," he said. "You'll still be here when I get back, won't you?"

"Yes."

"Good."

"How soon will you return?"

Andrew shrugged. "I don't know. Maybe by next year. It depends on Terry. She'll be afraid to leave." He raised his head. "I can tell you now. I don't know if she would want me to, but I'll say it anyway. It isn't just the death of our friend that bound us. Terry killed two people a long time ago."

Merripen held his breath for a moment.

"It wasn't what you think. One of them was tormenting her, and the other would have killed her, and me as well." Andrew lowered his eyes. "It was self-defense. If she hadn't done it, he would have died, and I would have, too. Our friend did. But it marked her. For a long time, she didn't feel anything about it, but when she did, the guilt almost destroyed her. She couldn't forgive herself. She was afraid it might happen again. You can't imagine the guilt she felt. Two people might have lived, might be alive now, could have changed and repented, maybe even been forgiven, and that was denied to them. I had to keep coming back to her so that she would remember that he'd given me my life. It's my debt to her. She kept me sane." Andrew shook his head. "She's lived with death too long. I want her to come here."

"We may not have much to offer her," Merripen said. "I don't know what will happen."

"Yes, you do. You'll do what they asked you to do. Go down there and talk to people. They're relieved. They feel they've been given another chance, even though they won't admit it outright. They're reconciled. They're starting to accept themselves, and then they'll be ready for your new project, and theirs.''

Merripen raised his eyebrows. "What new project?"

"Yours. The one that you'll all begin when you're ready. The next transformation, the next Transition. Don't tell me you haven't been thinking about it—I know you have. But you have to build a society first. We haven't had one for a while, only isolated people running after their own lonely dreams.''

"What about Leif, and Peony, and the others? Do you think they'll come here?"

"I don't know," Andrew replied. "They'll have to decide that when I tell them. If they don't leave, they'll die there, you know, one way or another." He paused. "Is there anything you want me to say to them?"

"Just tell them I found my children."

Andrew rose and went down the hill toward his hovercraft. Merripen watched him get in and float away down the road and up the far slope until his craft disappeared over the top.

The wind touched him, whipping his hair; clouds sailed across the sky. Dust danced in the streets below, and trees swayed. The wind caressed him and lifted his spirit; his mind soared above the slope, then dipped, returning to him again.

Children were only one way of facing the future. It's that uncertainty, he thought, or taking what is to come into our own hands by becoming our own posterity.

The shield was down. Everything was before him again, he realized with surprise.

The Golden Space

HE WAS AWAKE. HE MOVED HIS TOES SLOWLY AND PRESSED HIS fingers against his palms until he could feel warmth returning to his hands. He opened his eyes and stared blindly. Lifting his arms, he pushed against the flat surface above him until it shifted and fell with a clatter. He smelled dirt. He blinked and saw a patch of dark gray in the blackness overhead.

Sitting up, he removed the bands and wires from his arms, legs, and chest, then took off the circlet binding his head. Above him, a wind whistled, then died. He took a breath, tasted dust, and began to cough.

Soon he felt able to stand. He got up and stamped his feet, raising dust; he coughed some more. He folded his arms over his bare chest; he would have to find something to wear.

As he stumbled through the dark, he stretched out his arms and felt a wall. He ran his hands along it, feeling grit and bumps and then an empty space. He moved toward the space cautiously. He could see nothing; he shuffled forward and bumped his knee against an edge, touching something smooth and hard—a tabletop. As he ran his fingers along the surface, he felt another object. He lifted it, feeling the rounded bumps at one end, and then recognized it.

A cry escaped him. He dropped the bone and staggered backward, lost his balance, and fell. Choking and gasping for air, he drew up his legs, then forced himself to stand. He was holding a piece of torn fabric in his hand; he must have fallen on it. He wrapped it around his waist and crept back to the outer room.

Why was he here? He reached up to rub his chin and felt his thick, matted beard. How long had he been suspended? He walked forward until his toes met a step. Crouching, he began to climb the stairs, feeling his way with his hands as he went. His knees scraped against shards; his palms pressed against pebbles.

The opening in the roof had not widened when he reached the top step. He squatted and pushed at it, then pulled himself through the narrow space. He wriggled out and sat in the dirt, head bowed.

It was warmer outside; he was no longer shivering. The hazy sky was glowing faintly. He turned his head and glanced over his shoulder.

A grassy, leaf-strewn mound was behind him, covering part of the roof. He stared at the spot where his ship should have been, and trembled; he would be helpless. The roof was almost level with the ground; to his left, masses of earth sloped, forming a hill.

The village was gone. He covered his eyes; his shoulders shook. He heard whistling and chirping nearby; birds were singing their morning songs. A low moan accompanied them, the deep, strangled voice almost drowning out the delicate melodies, and Domingo realized that he was weeping.

The dawn came swiftly, appearing as a gray light over the misty blue hills in the east. It became a pale glow and was followed by a swollen red eye. Fog lay over the hills in long streamers.

His beard was wet; beads dampened his chest. His stomach rumbled. He would have to decide what to do. He could wait here, but the weedy ground, the clumps of trees and bushes, and the buried temple all showed that this place had been forgotten and abandoned. He had no food and no water. No one was likely to find him if he stayed. No one. He shivered. Was there anyone left to find him?

Domingo cleared his throat. The hollow, rasping sound startled him, echoing in his ears. He struggled to compose himself. He would go back inside and find what he could and then decide what to do. He would not think any further ahead than that.

He had been crawling in the dust, feeling for objects, before he thought of searching the platform which had held his suspended body. There, sealed in a drawer hidden in the side, he found clothes and a small pocket light. The light was dim, but bright enough to show him that every room except one was blocked by rubble.

He put on the clothes, noting that the shoes were too tight, and went into the next room, trying not to look at the bones. The skull on the table grinned at him in the faint light. Mounds of debris had settled in the corners of the room; pieces of metal were in the dirt. He gritted his teeth in dismay; his materializer had been destroyed.

He left the room and climbed back to the roof. The day had grown warmer. Domingo sighed; at least he had not awakened in winter. He had no weapon. He would have to find water. That would keep him alive for a while, and then . . . and then . . .

He had told himself that he would not think any further ahead than that. He gazed at the wooded land, trying to orient himself, struggling to remember where he might find a creek or a river. The trees near him were tall and leafy, with thick trunks; he wondered how long they had been growing here. He would have to look at the stars tonight and see what they told him. Had the Big Dipper lengthened, or become a wedge? Would he even be able to see it? He did not know whether it was early or late summer, or how far the equinoxes had precessed. He hoped the sky would be clear, and was suddenly afraid of what the heavens might show him.

He thought: I'm going to die. He would have no way now of extending his life; the forgotten village showed him that. Even if he found a stream and learned how to fish and hunt, he would die; he would age. It would never come to that; a disease would kill him first, or a wild beast. Blood rushed in his ears and his head throbbed while his heart beat a protest.

He saw the small hand holding the wand, raising it toward him. He had known it would happen and had not fought it; he had chosen his fate, expecting death. Eline had rendered justice, in her way, leaving him to see his legacy. Perhaps she, too, had eventually been judged. He left the roof and walked toward the forest.

The forest had grown dark; when Domingo looked up through the boughs, he saw heavy, gray clouds. He heard a distant trickle and hurried toward it, cracking twigs under his feet and stirring the leaves. The end of his shirt caught on a tree limb; he tore it away. Burrs stuck to his pants. He stumbled on until he reached the brook.

The water sang as it rushed over a pebbled bed and lapped against rocks. He scrambled down the mossy bank, crouched, and drank, lapping at the water.

He sat up when he was done, wondering now if he had been careless. But the water had tasted clean and fresh. He would have to find something to eat. The water had quieted his stomach, but he felt faint. Mushrooms grew under the trees nearby, but some might be poisonous. He thought of making a pole and line and trying to fish, and almost laughed out loud; he had no skill at that. Perhaps hunger would sharpen his wits and give him the skill.

The thought sobered him. He stood up and decided to follow the creek. He would have to make a weapon; perhaps he could find a sharp stone.

He heard thunder as he reached a bend in the creek. The rain dotted the silvery water and pattered against the rocks.

He tried to sleep under a tree. Its boughs sheltered him from the intermittent rain, but his hair and clothes were damp, and the air had grown colder. Leaves rustled; two bright eyes were watching him. He started up, and they vanished.

He dozed uncomfortably, hearing the pinging of the rain in the brook. A voice sang in the forest; a clap of thunder silenced it. A sheet of rain came down, wetting him as he clung to the tree. The rain subsided, and Domingo heard the high-pitched voice once more.

He could not see in the dark. He called out, but the voice did not answer. Bowing his head, he tried again to sleep. A dream came to him: A friend guarded him; he tried to see who it was, but the dark shape remained indistinct. He was safe. He slept.

By morning, Domingo was shaking; his teeth chattered. The rain had swelled the brook, which now covered much of the bank near him. Aching, he hung on to the tree as he stood; his knees wobbled.

He staggered as he began to walk, his shoes pinching his blistered feet. His legs carried him along, making him lurch. He shivered and stumbled on until his knees gave way and the ground rushed into his face.

He lay very still for a long time. His cheeks were burning; his face was hot under his beard and a weight seemed to press against his chest. Slowly he realized that it was growing dark. Someone was with him; he felt a presence. He cried out and thought he heard an answering sigh. The ground was soft and wet; its coolness soothed him. Then he began to shiver once more. He was ill; he could feel the fever drawing on his flesh, consuming him. The fever ebbed and flowed, coursing over him in waves.

Domingo heard the voices. The villagers were here in the forest. He listened to their whispers and the chatter of their voices, unable to make out the words. They were hiding in the shadows, waiting for him to die.

Someone touched his hand. He drew in his breath; his lungs burned. Strands of light fluttered near him as he heard a musical whine. *Come with me.* The voice was inside him. The shining streamers became a loop, then a helix. *Come.* The fire in his lungs subsided, and his head cleared. He got to his feet, feeling as though someone were lifting him. He was having delusions; the illness was affecting his mind. He tried to resist, but the invisible hands steadied him.

He walked among the trees, letting himself be guided by his unseen companion. He was traveling away from the brook and would soon be lost in the forest, yet the darkness calmed him and he felt no fear. The sounds of night were muffled; owls hooted and crickets chirped distantly. A dark shape rose before him, growled, and melted away.

The trees parted before him. He was at the edge of the forest, gazing over a black plain. The night hid the plain's features; the starless sky was a void. *Stay,* the voice whispered.

Domingo sank to the ground. His fever returned. A light rain fell, sprinkling droplets on his upturned face. He would die in the open. He thought of the voices his villagers had heard inside themselves. Some part of himself had led him here.

He reached out and touched slender stems; he smelled the scent of wildflowers. He clutched at the blossoms, pressing them to his face, and then dropped into the fragrant bed.

The sun awoke him, its warmth penetrating his throbbing head. He brushed blue petals from his beard. His neck was stiff and his lungs were filled with fluid. He rasped as he breathed. He coughed, bringing up phlegm, and nearly choked.

He felt too weak to rise. He could no longer smell the flowers, and his pain had settled in his chest. Calmly he wondered how long he would live. He turned his head and gazed through slim stalks at the grassy green meadow. In the distance, a large white sail fluttered in the breeze.

Domingo forced his head up. The sail became a white pavilion supported by golden poles. He extended a hand. A

robed figure left the pavilion and walked toward him slowly;
he thought he saw two smaller figures behind it. The vision
swam before him. Was it part of a last delusion? Was his mind
only easing his death, or did others still live? He clung to the
hope as his lungs flooded. The white-robed figure seemed to be
running now. He fought for air, clawed at the flowers; a red
mist covered his eyes, then turned black.

The stranger lay inside the transparent carapace, arms
folded over his unmoving chest. The woman stood before him,
then turned back to the pavilion. The girl and the boy had
come back outside; their bare brown bodies gleamed with
sweat as they raced around the carapace, then ran toward the
woman. The boy threw himself on the ground; the girl settled
slowly next to him, brushing a streak of dirt from her tiny
breasts. The woman sat down, smoothing the folds of her
white robe.

"Tell us another story," the boy said.

The woman rested one hand on his black hair. "Which story?"

"About the dead worlds."

"We've heard about them before," the girl said. Her blond
curls bounced as she shook her head.

"I want to hear about them again."

"You can see them for yourselves," the woman said.
"Those worlds tell their own story. I saw it written on the faces
of the dead and in their records. Those worlds will always
circle ours, because we keep them in space as a warning. And
what do they tell us?"

The boy shrugged. "Not to do what they did."

"That isn't it," the girl answered. "Some of the worlds left,
didn't they? They wander through space and I'm sure they
know everything there is to know. They'll never come back
here. Only the dead ones stayed."

The woman smiled. The girl glanced at the stranger, then
looked down. "Tell us about the labyrinth," she said.

The boy frowned. "We know about that, too," he protested.
He raised his head. "Why's it up there, anyway?" he asked.

"The labyrinth? We don't really know. It was there when we
first went to the moon. I suppose it was once only the hollowed-
out caves and corridors made by the people who long ago lived
there, but when you're actually walking through it, you wonder if
they meant it to be part of an elaborate game as well."

"Where did they go?" the girl asked.

"I don't know. They left nothing behind to tell us. No one did, except the dead worlds."

"And the Guardians," the boy said. The girl tilted her head and looked at him from the sides of her eyes.

"The Guardians didn't leave anything behind, either," the woman said softly.

"They might have stayed themselves," the boy said. "They might still be here." He leaned forward. "I think one was here last night. I felt it. I woke up and felt someone near me, and heard a voice. It sounded like a song."

The girl tossed her head. "There are no Guardians," she replied. "You were dreaming." The boy lowered his eyes. "It's just a story, isn't it?"

"It might be just a story," the woman said gently. "But it's a very persistent one, so it could hold a bit of truth. There's so much we don't know, you see. We know about the dead worlds, and we know from their records that there were others who lived on Earth and in space who left and never returned. We've found the walls and the bones of giants, but nothing telling us who they were. And we know nothing about the Guardians, only stories and myths and occasional feelings that they're present, like yours."

"You don't believe me," the boy said.

"I believe you."

"I think you had a dream," the girl murmured.

"But I was awake when I felt it. And then we found him." He pointed at the stranger.

"I'll tell you what I think," the woman said. "But it's only speculation, so it may be just a story, too. Some think that the old stories about the Guardians were just a way of explaining certain events, and a way of consoling ourselves as well. Life was once very hard, and people needed to believe in something. Invisible beings, existing in our world but not really part of it, were supposedly guiding us and protecting us, but actually all we were perceiving was something inside our minds. It was part of ourselves that spoke to us, and we personified it—we thought of it as something outside our minds. Do you understand?"

The children nodded.

"But I think it's possible that the Guardians might have been real. We know that others, a very long time ago, changed themselves and lived in what we call the dead worlds. Why couldn't others have chosen to shed their bodies and transform themselves into something immaterial—Guardians, for example?"

The girl shook her head. "How? And if you could see or hear them, they'd have to be made of something, and we could prove they're real. And why don't they come out and tell us about themselves if they're real? Why would they hide?"

"I don't know," the woman answered. "Perhaps they revealed themselves only for as long as they thought they were needed. They might have tried to turn us from our crueler impulses. We don't need them now. We have everything; we live as long as we wish. Maybe now they only watch us, knowing that we must make our own choices, or maybe they, too, have left Earth. Perhaps they were the ones who created us so long ago, if in fact we were made by those ancient people instead of being a group they somehow forgot."

The girl sighed. The boy looked toward the man under the carapace. "I wonder who he is," he murmured. "He looked so sick, so lost."

"He must have had an accident," the woman said. "It's fortunate we were out here. We'll take him with us and heal him. He'll be well." The man was still, suspended, at peace. "He'll live, and maybe he'll tell us his story."

About the Author

Pamela Sargent holds a B.A. and an M.A. in philosophy from the State University of New York at Binghamton. Her first novel, *Cloned Lives,* was called "solidly realistic, humane and well proportioned" by Ursula K. Le Guin. Michael Bishop said of her second novel: *"The Sudden Star* demonstrates a command of multiple points of view to rival that of the master, Philip K. Dick." About her third novel, *Watchstar*, Sonya Dorman wrote: "It's good to read a story in which the heroine has a spiritual life as well as an emotional one, and is a person of intellectual courage." Ms. Sargent has also published a collection of short stories, *Starshadows*, and has edited the anthologies *Bio-Futures, Women of Wonder, More Women of Wonder,* and *The New Women of Wonder. The Golden Space* is her fourth novel. She lives in upstate New York.